A Billionaire WOLF FOR Christmas

TERRY SPEAR

sourcebooks
casablanca

Published by Sourcebooks Casablanca, an imprint of Sourcebooks, Inc.
P.O. Box 4410, Naperville, Illinois 60567-4410
(630) 961-3900
Fax: (630) 961-2168
sourcebooks.com

Printed and bound in the United States of America.
OPM 10 9 8 7 6 5 4 3 2 1

Thanks so much to Mindy Seal, who gave me the kernel of a great idea for Dreaming of a White Wolf Christmas*! She loves the wolves, and I'm thrilled to be able to dedicate this Christmas book to her.*

Chapter 1

GRAY WOLF PHYSICIAN AIDAN DENALI STARED AT THE blood sample under the microscope and the notes scribbled on paper nearby. He wasn't going to get anywhere with this. Not without new wolves to test. As much as it killed him to do so, he was delaying his search for a cure for the *lupus garous*'s reduced longevity until after the Christmas holiday. Maybe his twin brother, Rafe, was right, though Aidan hated to admit it. Perhaps joining Rafe and his family early would give Aidan the break he needed, and he might gain new insight into what was happening with their kind. He could even bounce ideas off his brother and Rafe's mate, Jade. Normally, Aidan wouldn't have considered leaving his research behind for that long. Not until Jade and her son, Toby, had come into their lives. They had given him and his brother even more of a family, and Aidan enjoyed the change in dynamics.

Still, he couldn't help but worry he was going to fail in his mission when so many people were counting on him. The concern among the wolf shifters was that if something in their environment or genetics had caused them to live shorter lives, their longevity might continue to shorten and they would eventually age even more quickly than humans. He just wished all the time he'd spent on his work had resulted in some headway.

As to the matter of his brother having found the

perfect she-wolf… Well, Aidan had to get out of his lab to pursue female interests if he was ever going to be successful at having a family of his own. And when he did go out with a she-wolf? His date invariably would ask about his work and if he was getting anywhere with it. He'd say no and explain the reasons, and then he'd be back to thinking about the issue and forget all about the she-wolf!

Frustrated with his lack of progress, Aidan put away his notes and locked up the lab. When he made his way to the living room of his home in the Klamath Mountains of northwestern California, he saw Ted Gallagher, one of his bodyguards, raising his brows in question. Ted was an even-tempered, muscular redhead who could take down the meanest of wolves.

Yeah, Aidan normally never left his lab at this hour. He was known to be a bit obsessed and a workaholic. "I'm going to the chalet earlier than planned."

"Hell, Doc, that's good news. I mean, I guess if you're not bursting at the seams with news of a cure."

Aidan understood what Ted meant. "I can work on it at the chalet, if I'm not too busy playing with Toby and visiting with my brother and Jade."

As soon as Aidan spoke the words, Ted got a call. "Uh, yeah, this is Ted Gallagher, Dr. Denali's personal assistant." Ted eyed Aidan, waiting to see if he wanted to take the call.

Aidan had told both of his bodyguards to call themselves personal assistants if they had to explain who they were. They took his calls while he was in the lab and wouldn't interrupt him unless it was important.

His other bodyguard, Mike Stallings, joined them.

"Yeah, just a minute." Ted covered the phone's mouthpiece. "Everett Johnston is calling from the gray wolf pack in Bigfork, Montana. He was originally with the Seattle pack led by Ronald Grayson."

Aidan perked up at hearing from the wolf. Anything to do with the Seattle pack interested him, since it was the only pack he'd located that hadn't allowed him to test members' blood. "Let me speak with him."

Ted handed the phone over, and Aidan said, "This is Aidan Denali. How may I help you?"

"Hey, Doc, this is Everett Johnston. You checked my blood when you came out to Montana. You tested my mom's and sister's too. But Dr. Holly Gray, who is with the Seattle pack, called my sister, Tara, and told her she was worried about a pack member who has been banished. He's currently living in the Glacier Peak Wilderness. Holly and my sister are friends. They were just talking about him and how Holly keeps searching for him when she can, but she hasn't been able to locate him.

"I thought since you have a cabin in the Wilderness, if you could find him, maybe he'd give you a sample of his blood." Everett cleared his throat. "What I'm really hoping is that if you can find him, you'll bring him here to live with the Montana pack. I've talked with our pack leaders, and they said they'd be willing to take him in. He's a good guy, and he needs a home with a pack."

Aidan opened his mouth to say he'd be glad to, but Everett continued to talk, sounding worried he might not be able to convince Aidan to look for the lone wolf.

"We know the Seattle pack has refused to allow you to sample their blood. Who knows? Nick Cornwall's blood might give you the break you need, if you haven't had any success yet. I suspect that all you'd have to do is tell him the Seattle pack refuses to allow you to gather samples of their blood and he'd be agreeable."

Thrilled with the prospect, Aidan had only needed the call to action: offer Nick the opportunity to find a home among the wolf packs Aidan knew and take him there, and possibly get a blood sample from him too.

"Why did the pack leader banish him?" Making sure the wolf was in good health would be Aidan's first priority. Getting a sample of his blood could be a boon. But if Nick was a problem wolf, foisting him off on a pack could prove troublesome. Aidan wasn't about to do that. He'd take him in and deal with him the best he could instead.

"He wasn't banished for any good reason! It really was a shame Ronald kicked him out. Poor guy lost his mate and was having a difficult time coping. Ronald said Nick was causing trouble for the pack. I can't imagine anything being further from the truth. If you search for Nick, just be careful. Holly Gray said several members of the Seattle pack are staying at a group of cabins south of the peak and running in the area this week. She'll be looking for him again. *Alone*. There are grizzlies and wild wolves out there. She shouldn't be by herself. Then again, maybe it would be best to avoid running into their pack and, if possible, go to Glacier Peak Wilderness after they're gone. At one time, Ronald had declared the Wilderness a free zone for other wolves to visit, but he could have changed his mind. He's like that."

"Thanks. I'm free at the moment, but I have a family gathering in a couple of weeks. I need to get this done now if I'm going to do it before the holidays. I'll try to locate Nick." Aidan couldn't believe what a rotten ass Ronald was.

"Good luck, Doc. I sure hope you find him. If you do, tell him he's more than welcome to join our pack in Montana. Also, we have several widows that we took into the pack."

"Okay, sounds good. One other thing. Why is he living in the wilderness? Why not just move out of Seattle and find a home someplace else?"

"He had to sell his home and sold off everything else. At least he's retired and has an income, but he's been so distraught over everything that he just left and is living out there for now. He probably doesn't know where other packs are located. Even if he does, he might feel that with the stigma of being banished, no one would take him in anyway. Not to mention he's lived all his life in the Seattle area. He's older and more set in his ways. Oh, I asked Holly if there was a chance you could get the pack leader to change his mind and agree for the pack to give blood, but she said no."

That would have been the best Christmas present ever. "Okay, thanks. I'll let you know if I locate Nick and can convince him to allow me to fly him out to Montana." They ended the call, and Aidan felt he had some direction in his research again. And hope.

Ted was frowning. "Must be a combination of good and bad news."

Mike folded his arms across his chest. "Yeah, his intermittent frowns and an elusive smile say so."

"Scratch my last comment about going to the chalet. We're packing for a cold-weather camping trip. We're going to the cabin near the Glacier Peak Wilderness. A lot of equipment is always there: snowshoes, climbing gear, cross-country skis, and snow bikes, and I have a lab there. Though I suspect we'll be running as wolves. The Seattle pack is staying at cabins south of there, but we need to locate a wolf they banished from the pack. And possibly convince him to fly with us to meet the Montana pack."

"I'll arrange for transportation." Ted pulled out his phone.

"Actually, you don't have to go with me," Aidan said, heading for his bedroom to pack and thinking maybe if he ran into Dr. Holly Gray, her pack wouldn't object as much to a lone wolf.

"Like hell we don't." Mike pulled out his phone. "You might just need us this time... Hey, Chet, we need a car dropped off at the private airport near Glacier Peak Wilderness... Just be on standby. If Doc says we need you for additional guard detail, we'll let you know. Thanks." Mike turned to Aidan. "You sure we don't need Holloway on this mission?"

"No, Hugh's sister is due to have triplets anytime, and he told his twin he'd be there for her. We don't need three bodyguards." He didn't need even one.

The Wilderness area was vast, and locating the wolf probably would take much longer than the two weeks they had to search for him—unless Nick wanted them to find him. Aidan couldn't envision why Ronald had kicked the widowed wolf out of the pack. He couldn't imagine anything worse than losing the comfort of other wolves during a time of deep sorrow.

If Nick didn't want to join the Montana pack, Aidan was certain one of the others would be eager to take him in. Though the one in Montana could be a good start for him. Like Everett had said, they had taken in several females who had lost their mates. Who knew where that could lead? In any case, Aidan would fly Nick to every pack location he knew until he found the pack Nick felt comfortable with.

This might be just the break Aidan needed to find a solution for his research and a way to reach out to an emotionally wounded wolf.

As soon as the men all had their bags packed and had joined one another in the living room, Ted asked, "Do you think the guy will even want to talk with you?" He began hauling the bags out to the SUV.

"If we're lucky and can even locate him." Aidan gathered anything else he might need from the lab. Every getaway place Rafe and Aidan had purchased for their use had a room dedicated to Aidan's research. Aidan loved his brother for knowing how important this was to him.

"What about shopping for your nephew for Christmas presents? You said you were going to do that before you left, and there might not be much in the line of shopping out there," Ted said as they loaded into the vehicle.

"Yeah. Right." Aidan got on his cell phone and looked for the shopping mall closest to where they'd be staying. "We can drop by the mall, pick up what we need, buy groceries at a store nearby, and then drive to the cabin and settle in. Once we've done that, we can start doing a grid search of the area surrounding the volcanic mountain and learn if Nick's still there."

"What about the Seattle pack?" Mike asked.

"Everett said his former pack considered the area a

free zone for wolves. We've never had any issues when we've stayed at the cabin before."

"Were they in the vicinity at the time?" Ted asked, because he and Mike had never been to the cabin.

"Maybe not."

Mike snorted. "That pack hates outsider wolves. I bet you if we run into them in the Wilderness, there will be trouble."

"Don't give Doc any ideas. He's liable to scrap with them just to get them to bleed on him so he can test it," Ted joked.

Mike and Aidan laughed.

"Why haven't I thought of that?" Aidan smiled, but he was serious. It could work.

They drove to the private airport nearby and loaded the plane with their gear. As soon as they arrived at the private airport in Washington, a car was waiting for them. Because of Rafe's and Aidan's wealth, all they had to do was call ahead to make arrangements for anything they needed and it was done. Rafe's billions had been made in real estate deals. Aidan's billions had mostly come from the pharmaceutical research he did for years before he became so caught up in the longevity issue.

At the mall, the trees in the parking lot were decorated with white Christmas lights, and every parking spot was filled. They drove around and around and around, looking for a free parking spot, while other cars were doing the same. Then Aidan saw a sign for valet parking. "There. Valet parking. Go for it."

Christmas lights sparkled all around the mall too. Aidan had never bothered to decorate his place. There was no need, since he never planned to be there for the holiday. Rafe had always gone all out because he held a charity ball at his place every year right after Thanksgiving weekend. That was all the Christmas decorating Aidan ever needed. A quiet gift-giving on Christmas morning and the brothers and their bachelor friends doing whatever they wanted made for the perfect Christmas: flying off to another location, running in the woods as wolves, fishing, hiking, exercising in Rafe's gym, partying—whatever they were in the mood for.

This was the first year Rafe had a mate and son. It wouldn't be quite the same. And Aidan was looking forward to that. He could envision the tyke's wide-eyed expression when he saw all the wrapped packages under the tree. Many years ago, Christmases had been homespun affairs for him and his brother, with every-one making something special for everyone else. He'd always thought fondly of his mother for making such a big deal of loving a tea towel he'd created for her after her favorite one caught fire. She'd used that towel until she died. Rafe had made her a bread box, teasing Aidan that sewing was for girls.

But when Aidan had to stitch him up after a wolf fight, Rafe didn't tease him anymore.

When they entered the store, Aidan remembered how much he disliked shopping in stores, instead purchasing what he needed online. He and his bodyguards made their way shoulder to shoulder through the crowds. He hadn't expected to see so many people at the mall, but he reminded himself it was Saturday and getting close to Christmas. Normally, he wouldn't go shopping at a mall for *anything* this time of year.

The trio made their way through the noise and confusion, noticing all the shops adorned with Christmas decor. Aidan had ordered everything else for the family for Christmas, but he'd wanted to pick up some special things for his nephew and had waited too long to do it online.

The mall in Lynnwood was only seventeen miles from Seattle. It was entirely possible they might run into some of the Seattle pack members.

"Hope we don't have any trouble." Ted was eyeing everyone in the mall as if they could be potentially dangerous gray wolves.

Aidan was ready to deal with them if he and his bodyguards had to. He suspected the Seattle wolves wouldn't make much of a scene at the mall though—too many shoppers, too many witnesses. And none of them would want to be hauled off to jail.

"You're sure the info about the banished wolf living up here is still valid?" Mike asked, poking around at some Christmas sweaters on a table. "I guess I should have asked this earlier. Everett Johnston left the Seattle pack a while ago."

"The pack's doctor told Everett's sister that she's looking for him, but she hadn't found him. We can't know for certain, not until we investigate a bit, but I have to check on any leads I get."

When it came to solving puzzles, Aidan quickly became obsessed.

If humans had known about it, they might have thought it was a boon for the wolf shifters to age so slowly, one human year for every thirty, and although that had changed to one year for every five, the wolves were still just as fortunate. But the wolves' lengthy longevity had been their normal life span. How would humans see it if they suddenly aged more rapidly to such a degree? They'd feel the same pressure to do something about it.

Mike ran his hand over a suede jacket on a rack. "Are you still getting tons of emails and phone calls from pack leaders, asking what you've learned because older family members are dying much *younger*?"

"Yeah, more of late."

"You know, even if we find Nick, he might not want to give a blood sample or care anything about our longevity issues," Mike warned as they headed into one of the larger department stores. "Especially since he's lost his mate."

"Yes, I agree, Mike. There's no guarantee that we'll find him or that he'll want to help. But if I can offer him help, I'm going to. If he wants to help us, I'm all for it."

As wolves, their sense of smell was better than humans'. Everything was bombarding Aidan all at once, from the smell of humans—colognes, perfumes, body odor—to the stacks of Christmas spice candles sitting on a tall shelf nearby. Their wolf hearing was better too, and the Christmas music playing overhead and the constant chatter all around Aidan made him long for the quiet of the Wilderness.

Looking around for the toy section, he saw Santa and a long line of kids waiting to give him their Christmas lists. Aidan paused for a moment and watched as a boy about the age of his three-year-old nephew, Toby, sat on Santa's lap, looking up at the white-bearded man. Aidan wondered if Rafe and Jade would take Toby to see a Santa too. His brother's life had changed so much recently—going from billionaire bachelor to mated wolf with a kid—but in a good way.

Aidan glanced around and saw the toy department nearby. "I'm going over there to look for gifts," he told his bodyguards.

Mike was eyeing the cute Santa's helpers in their green-and-white-striped tights, red tutus, and striped elf hats.

"Yeah, we'll be right here." Ted turned to watch the elves too, especially a cute redhead.

Aidan chuckled under his breath.

He and his brother didn't have a pack, per se, but since Jade and his brother had mated and were raising Toby, all of them—Rafe's bodyguards, his administrative assistant, and Aidan—had started seeing themselves as a pack. Rafe and Jade had become their de facto leaders.

Everyone watched out for the boy, who, unlike the rest of the wolves, was newly turned, though he had some wolf roots. That meant Toby kept them on their toes, especially when the full moon was out. With other young wolves, the mother's shifting compelled the child to shift, but it didn't work like that with Toby. He didn't have a lot of control over his shifting.

Aidan looked through the toys, wanting to get Toby a kid's microscope or other scientific equipment. That's what he would have liked as a kid that age, though they didn't even have toy stores where he and Rafe grew up. And nothing like science toys for kids either. A large stuffed wolf caught his eye. He didn't think Toby would have space in his bed to sleep if Aidan bought him any more stuffed animals.

He reached for a hundredth-anniversary tin of Lincoln Logs and spied a kit for preschoolers that claimed to be a first science kit. He also saw a junior microscope, a 3-D solar system, and a puzzle of the phases of the moon. Wishing department stores like this one had shopping carts, he was grabbing the tin of Lincoln Logs when he heard a woman and teenage girl frantically yelling, "Joey! Joey!"

From the sound of panic in the women's voices, Aidan was certain the boy had gotten away from them, and they couldn't locate him in the crush of shoppers. Instantly, his thoughts were transported to a much earlier time when he'd become separated from his parents and brother on a visit to the Gold Rush town of Placerville when they went in for supplies. Fortunately, one of the grizzled old miners had taken him in hand, bought him a root beer, and helped him look for his family. Because of that, Aidan knew how it felt to be separated from loved ones in a crowd of unfamiliar people.

Worse, fearing someone might take off with the boy and disappear for good, Aidan began looking for one who appeared lost, wishing he knew how old the boy was. Then he spied a woman hurrying a boy about Toby's age out of the store. He was pulling at her to let him go, his head riveted toward the sound of the two women calling out Joey's name.

Although suspecting the boy *was* Joey, Aidan hoped he didn't accost the wrong woman, a mother leaving the store with her own kid. On the other hand, he didn't want them to disappear into the mall if she wasn't the boy's mother and was attempting to abscond with him.

"Joey!" Aidan called out, his voice much deeper,

more commanding, more easily heard above the din of conversations and Christmas music than the women's, figuring the boy would respond to his name being called, if he was indeed the right boy.

The boy turned and looked straight at him. Aidan was running toward him, but of course the preschooler didn't recognize him. He did seem to recognize the name. Aidan quickly reached the woman and the boy, catching his bodyguards' attention, and they both raced to help Aidan.

With the tin of Lincoln Logs still in one hand, Aidan grabbed the woman's arm with his other hand and stopped her from leaving the store. He quickly asked the boy, "Do you know this woman?"

Eyes wide, the boy shook his head. At the same time, Aidan could smell the boy's scent—a gray wolf. The woman was human. The boy took a deep breath, his lips parting, and he seemed to realize Aidan was a gray wolf too.

"Are you Joey?" Aidan asked the boy.

He nodded.

Struggling to free herself from Aidan, the woman kept trying to yank her arm out of his firm grasp. She suddenly released the boy and, at the same time, swung her purse at Aidan, striking him on the side of the head. The purse had to be filled with something hard and heavy because the impact knocked him to the side. He lost the tin of Lincoln Logs but continued to hold tight to the woman's arm, wrenching the purse from her grasp and dropping it on the floor.

Aidan's head was throbbing where the woman had struck him, his vision blurring a bit. *Damn it.*

Ted and Mike reached him, and Mike quickly grabbed the woman's arm. Aidan took the boy in hand. Ted had his phone out, ready to call 911. The dark-haired woman's tan face turned pasty white, and her dark-brown eyes narrowed. "His mother told me to take him to see Santa Claus."

"Santa Claus is back that way." Aidan didn't believe the woman for a second, but he had to be sure. He took Joey by the waist and settled him on his hip, holding him close and in a reassuring manner. "What's his mother's name?" he asked the woman, hoping the boy wouldn't blurt it out, but the boy remained quiet.

"Beth," the thirtyish woman said.

Aidan asked Joey, "Is that your mother's name?"

Joey shook his head. Then the boy saw someone coming and smiled. Aidan turned to see two blonds, both blue-eyed and wearing jeans and sweaters, frowning at him, most likely because he was holding on to Joey. Were they wolves too? He suspected they had to be.

The woman appeared to be around thirty, the other an older teen around seventeen or eighteen. Both had the same oval-shaped face, the same full pink lips and narrowed eyes. As much as they looked alike, Aidan assumed they were related. But not to the dark-haired, brown-eyed boy.

Both looked at Aidan's sweatshirt and frowned even more. *Real Men Howl* was embroidered across the front of it.

Only another wolf would get the humor.

Chapter 2

"OHMIGOD, JOEY. I'M SO GLAD YOU'RE SAFE," THE WOMAN said, drawing close to Aidan, her eyes filled with concern. She was maybe five four or five five, her snow boots adding another inch to her height.

Aidan smelled her feminine floral scent and that she was a gray wolf too, both of which had him pulling in a deeper breath and taking a closer look. She was wearing a blue parka and a glittery white sweater. Her cheeks were a little flushed from trying to chase down the boy. Her blond hair was pulled into a bun, and soft straggles of blond curls framed her pretty face. Her clear blue eyes sparkled under the bright store lights, captivating him.

For a minute, he just stared at her, and then he snapped out of his uncharacteristic fascination with a woman. He was glad she was a wolf, which helped convince him the boy belonged to her or her pack.

She reached for Joey, and though the boy raised his hands out to her, Aidan still didn't hand him over right away. He had just rescued the boy and wasn't about to give him to anyone else until he was assured Joey would be safe. "Are you his mother?"

"His mother's friend." The woman gave him an annoyed look when he didn't release Joey to her right away. "My sister was babysitting him, but he got away from us." Then her eyes widened. She must have smelled that he was also a wolf.

She reached for the boy again.

Aidan still didn't hand him over. Now it was more a case of learning where these three were from. The Seattle pack? Or another?

Ted was already calling the police about the woman who had tried to leave the store with the little wolf boy. Thank God, she hadn't managed to leave before Aidan found her and stopped her.

"I'm Dr. Aidan—"

"Denali," the older blond practically whispered, her eyes wide.

His mouth gaped a little. He would have remembered her if he'd met her before. The way she reacted to knowing who he was… Did that mean it was good news, or bad? "Uh, right."

"I'm Holly Gray. And this is Marianne, my seventeen-year-old sister." Now Holly seemed eager to meet him, and Aidan was relieved.

"*Dr*. Holly Gray," Marianne said as if she didn't want Aidan to think her older sister was any less important than him.

She was the doctor Everett had told him about, and a friend of Everett's sister. "Dr. Holly Gray." Aidan smiled at both ladies. He handed Joey over to Holly, but Marianne wanted to hold him.

"Everett Johnston mentioned you to me." Aidan frowned at Holly. "Have we met?"

"You *would* have remembered my sister if you had met her, you know," Marianne said, a brow raised, her lips unsmiling as she rested Joey on her hip.

Aidan curbed the urge to laugh at Marianne's words, though he smiled. "I'm sure I would have."

Mike was still holding on to the attempted kidnapper. The store security officer was with them now, asking them and the woman questions.

"Have I met you before?" Aidan directed the question to Marianne this time. He was certain he hadn't met the girl either. He was eager to speak to them further in private, and maybe he could have the doctor's blood tested if she approved, and—

Marianne shook her head. "We're from Seattle, you know. Ronald didn't want us to meet you."

Aidan's enthusiasm faltered. He'd hoped they might be more agreeable after he'd saved one of their own.

Holly kept looking at the side of Aidan's head, and he finally felt blood dribbling down it. The attempted kidnapper must have broken the skin when she bashed him in the head with her purse. The wound was just beginning to throb.

"You…look like you could use a couple of stitches." Holly pulled some tissues out of her purse and applied pressure to the wound. "Head wounds bleed a lot though."

Mike and Ted were smiling at him. Yeah, way to get the girl, except she was with the Seattle pack, and that pack had nothing to do with any wolf outsiders. Still, she was taking care of him, maybe because he'd rescued the boy and taken a beating for it. She was so gentle that he really liked her bedside manner.

"Do you live near here?" Holly asked, frowning.

"Not here. In the Klamath Mountains region of California, but we're visiting here for a couple of weeks." If it took that long to find Nick. "This is the closest mall we could find to do some Christmas shopping. We have a cabin near Glacier Peak." Realizing she was still holding the tissues against his wound when she didn't have to, Aidan reached for them. "I can do that."

She shook her head. "I've got it."

Doctor to the rescue? Aidan was amused, impressed, and even...attracted to her.

"We're staying at cabins near there too. Just hold still so I can stop the bleeding. It's the least I can do after you rescued Joey. I"—she glanced down at his sweatshirt—"like your...sweatshirt, by the way." She paused. "Are you still doing your research?"

She acted interested, and Aidan thought maybe the pack members *had* changed their minds. Or maybe, as a doctor, she was a little more curious about the situation than the rest of the pack.

"Yeah, I'm looking for someone who was with your—"

"Holly!" some guy yelled.

Aidan turned to see the man who sounded so hostile.

A dark-haired guy strode toward them, looking from Aidan to her as if he could kill them both for being too physically close to each other. The boyfriend? Her mate?

That's also how Aidan would expect someone from the Seattle pack to act.

Then again, the situation did look rather intimate as she continued to press the tissues against Aidan's head and stood resting her body close to his. He couldn't help but breathe in her fascinating scent and enjoy her sweet Ivory soap, wolf, and womanly fragrance. Embarrassingly, his own body was beginning to react to her closeness. Despite the approaching male and his obvious anger, she didn't budge from where she stood. He admired her for standing her ground.

The guy who had yelled was still trying to get through the crowd of shoppers, and Aidan asked her, "Your mate?" He'd be disappointed if the guy was, because from the looks of it, he wouldn't want her to have anything to do with Aidan and his research, while he'd begun to hope she might help him out.

"No. He wanted to be, but we've had some major issues of late." She didn't seem to regret that.

Aidan was glad, though he told himself that was only because the guy was being such a jerk. Getting involved with a woman who was with that pack could be a problem, since the pack leader wasn't allowing anyone in.

As soon as the guy moved into their space and started acting like he was going to pull Holly away, Aidan stiffened, but Holly quickly said, "Cool it, Jared. This nice man rescued Joey from an attempted kidnapper, and the woman gave him a head wound."

Jared cast a dark smile in Aidan's direction, as if he was amused the human woman had gotten the best of the wolf who wasn't in their pack. Jared turned his attention to Holly. "Let's go."

"We have to speak with the police. You can go, and I'll see you later," Holly said, dismissing him.

Now it was Aidan's turn to cast Jared a dark smile. He liked a woman who had a mind of her own. He noticed she didn't offer introductions, and he didn't bother with them either.

"Like hell you will." Jared folded his arms, and Aidan figured that was the end of getting to know Holly, even though she didn't release her hold on the tissues she was still pressing against his head. "Why don't you let him hold on to that, or is he about to faint?" Jared asked with a snarl.

"He needs to be stitched up," she said.

Aidan wondered if it was all that bad or she was just making excuses to tick off Jared.

"He can go to the emergency room. He won't have to worry about it in a couple of days anyway."

Just then, several police officers burst into the store, while all kinds of shoppers were watching the spectacle.

Aidan explained to the police how he'd heard the women calling for Joey and had seen this dark-haired woman hurrying for the exit, dragging the little boy with her.

Holly had tried to pull the tissues away from his head when he was speaking to the cops, but the blood gushed forth as soon as she did, and she'd quickly mopped it up with a tender touch. Aidan really could get used to her touching him.

"Call the EMTs," one of the cops said. "How did this happen?" he asked, frowning at Aidan.

"The attempted kidnapper struck me with her purse. It felt like it had a ton of bricks in it."

One of the cops lifted the purse, and before he looked inside, he said, "It feels like she has a gun in here. Do you have a gun in the purse?"

"No," she said defiantly.

He searched the purse, and sure enough, she had a 9 mm and several pieces of jewelry: necklaces, earrings, bracelets, all still attached to their merchandising cards. "Where'd you get these?"

"I bought them."

"No sack for them? Have you got a receipt?" the officer asked, his dark brow raised.

"I didn't want one. I told the clerk I didn't need a sack or receipt."

"Which clerk?"

She waved her hand at the jewelry counter, but she looked like she wanted to run. They took her over to the counter, where they had to ask customers to move aside while they questioned the two clerks. The two women nodded when they saw the jewelry but then shook their heads. The police officers brought the woman back to where Aidan and Holly were standing and took everyone's statements, eyewitness accounts, and even the boy's testimony. Then they handcuffed the woman for attempted kidnapping, carrying a concealed weapon without a permit, and retail theft.

The police officer told the EMTs who Aidan was and how he'd been injured when they arrived. Aidan felt foolish in front of Holly and everyone else who was standing around gawking as the medical techs took care of his forehead. "You'll need stitches, Dr. Denali," one of them said.

Apparently, Holly hadn't been exaggerating.

"Thanks, I'll have it taken care of," Aidan said.

"You really should have your head looked at. It's bruising, and you could have a slight skull fracture," the EMT said, appearing as though he thought Aidan wouldn't go to the hospital.

"All right, I'll have it looked at," Aidan repeated, trying not to sound annoyed. It was bad enough he had to admit the woman had gotten the better of him in front of Holly and her sister and that irritating wolf Jared.

Smiling, Holly explained to the EMT, "He's a doctor. They make the worst patients."

The EMT chuckled.

"Like you too, Sis," Marianne said, smiling at her.

Aidan was amused at the family dynamics between the two sisters.

"Ally White has had felony convictions for two other attempted child abductions," one of the police officers said to another as he got off his radio. "She's on probation, and it's illegal for her to possess a firearm."

Then the officers led her out of the store, the EMTs left, and Aidan and the rest of them were free to leave. But Aidan sure wanted to speak further to Holly.

"I have a medical kit at my cabin," she said. "I always carry one when we take trips, so I can sew up the gash."

"I've got a kit in my car," Aidan said, in case her pack wouldn't like him showing up at their cabins.

"She's not going to your car," Jared said to Aidan, then switched his attention to Holly. "And if Ronald were here, he'd tell him to go to the nearest hospital. The EMT says he needs to learn if he has a fracture. You can't take care of that at the cabin."

Holly looked disappointed but finally agreed. "He's probably right. About the EMT, I mean. I would feel awful if something happened to you because you didn't get checked out thoroughly at a hospital."

"We'll take it from here," Mike said and moved in to help Aidan out of the store—as if Aidan needed the aid.

"I still need something for Toby." Aidan wasn't about to allow his men, or anyone else, to treat him like an invalid.

"We can come back later to shop for your nephew,"

Ted said, and Aidan swore he'd mentioned the relationship so Holly would know he wasn't a mated wolf with
a child.

"It'll only take a minute. I know just what I want."
With customers swarming all over the merchandise,
grabbing armfuls, and heading for the checkout counter,
Aidan was afraid the items he'd picked out would be
gone by the time they got back.

Mike picked up the tin of Lincoln Logs Aidan had
dropped, and Aidan pulled a business card from his
pocket and handed it to Holly. "If you ever need my
help, just let me know." The way Jared was glaring
daggers at Aidan, he was sure the guy would take the
card from her and tear it up as soon as Aidan and his
bodyguards were out of sight.

She smiled at Aidan and took the card, glanced at it,
and said "Nice wolf" before tucking it down her shirt.
"Thank you."

Jared's face reddened, and he looked like he was
ready to blow his top.

Aidan smiled at her, even though his head now felt
like it was splitting in two.

"Thank you for saving Joey," she said ultra-seriously.
To his surprise, she gave him a warm hug—her breasts
pressed against his chest, her body against his groin—
and smiled a little.

He was sure the smile he gave her in return was on
the wolfish side.

Before he could hug her back, she quickly moved
away. Then she, her sister, the boy, and the brute of a
gray wolf headed toward the entrance to the mall. She
was telling the guy off the whole time.

"You are such a jerk, Jared. Why can't you be civil with others who aren't in our...group for two seconds? He rescued Joey, more than I can say for you! He's a *real* hero."

Aidan smiled, and damn if he didn't want to get to know the doctor better, blood sample or no. His blood was coursing like fire through his veins just from her intimate embrace. It hadn't just been a thank-you hug, as far as he was concerned. Then again, maybe she'd only meant it in a way that told Jared he couldn't tell her what to do.

Ted paused to see Aidan still watching Holly leave the store. "Hell, I swear the Denali brothers have all the luck in rescuing women with kids and befriending them, even if the kid isn't the woman's this time."

"Do you think that jackass is going to let her keep your business card?" Mike asked. "If I had to guess, I'd say no."

"I agree with you. Though she seems to be sticking up for herself well enough. She might hang on to it. That pack has serious issues, but it was nice seeing someone who wasn't as antagonistic toward others of our kind as the leaders are. Which makes me wonder if more of the people in their pack would be receptive to speaking with me and giving blood if they could do it without the leaders knowing. Not that I'd want to get any of their people into trouble." Aidan reached the table where he'd seen the science kit, the microscope, and the other toys he wanted to get, but Ted and Mike hurried to grab the items. With hands full, they went to the checkout counter and waited in the long line until Aidan could pay.

"Hey, Doc, you really don't look well," Ted said, frowning.

"I just need to get something for the headache, put some ice on the bruising, and lie down for a while."

"Rafe is going to fire us," Mike said to Ted.

"Yeah, I was thinking the same thing."

"He's not going to fire you. After we leave here, just take me to the nearest hospital. I'll get checked out, and they'll say everything's fine. We'll get our groceries and continue on our way to the cabin."

The guys shared looks, and Aidan added, "There's nothing we have to report home about."

Both Ted and Mike were by the book when it came to reporting issues to Rafe. He insisted on it, and Aidan had given up trying to convince them they worked for him when Rafe paid their salaries, which Rafe had also insisted on. Despite Aidan having his own wealth.

After they bought the presents, they went to the nearest hospital to have tests run. To Aidan's annoyance, the doctor had him admitted overnight. Aidan suspected the way his head pounded, his nausea, and his earlier blurry vision meant a mild concussion. Not enough to require more than an overnight stay for observation though. Not when *lupus garous* healed more quickly than humans.

After the staff admitted Aidan to a room and he was settled into bed, Ted said, "Don't worry, Doc. We'll run out and get you your favorite ice cream or anything else you want to eat."

Aidan closed his eyes at the suggestion. He was still nauseated, and if either of the two of them mentioned food again, he was going to throw up.

He was about to fall asleep from the pain medication

when he heard Ted talking on his phone. "Hey, tell Rafe that Aidan got into a confrontation with a woman who was stealing a boy at a store and she clobbered him... Yeah, he'll live, but he's at the local hospital for observation... He's sleeping right now."

Aidan sighed. He'd really wanted to keep this a secret from his brother. He knew Rafe would be annoyed with Ted and Mike for not protecting him better from a purse-wielding kidnapper, and he didn't want his brother giving them grief.

He smiled a little. Not when he'd had a chance to meet a pretty she-wolf from the Seattle pack, save the boy she and her sister had been watching over, and maybe, just maybe, have gotten an in with her.

He was glad that Ted hadn't mentioned that the boy was a wolf or where the Seattle pack was staying currently. Better Rafe didn't know the boy was with that pack or that Aidan had already riled one of its members.

Chapter 3

AFTER SPENDING ALL AFTERNOON SHOPPING AT THE mall—hoping Jared would get lost, but he didn't—Holly refused to ride with him back to the cabins where the pack was staying. She'd driven to the mall with Marianne and Joey, but she suspected Jared wanted to air his grievances with her in private. She couldn't quit thinking of tall, dark, and wolfish Dr. Aidan Denali. Dark-brown hair and eyes that penetrated her very soul—and gave her delicious shivers. She loved his *Real Men Howl* sweatshirt, indicating he had a sense of humor. And how their pheromones had come into play when she was touching him. How he had reacted to her closeness. How she had wanted to prolong that closeness. She'd never met another male wolf she was instantly attracted to. Maybe because he wasn't with her pack and she needed to meet some new male wolves.

But she didn't think so. Every womanly urge she had zeroed in on him, not the other men with him. Maybe because he'd saved Joey? She didn't think that was the only reason.

"Give me Dr. Denali's business card," Jared demanded.

"No. I'm calling Dr. Denali in the morning to learn if he's okay." Holly would call him a little later today, once a doctor had time to check him out. She stalked toward her car, Marianne hurrying to keep up while carrying a worn-out Joey.

"You know what my brother will say if he learns you've had any contact with Denali," Jared said, stalking behind them.

"*He. Saved. Joey.* What's Ronald going to say to that? Give it a rest, Jared." She unlocked the car doors and waited for her sister to buckle Joey in the back seat.

Jared glowered at Holly, hands on his hips. She brushed past him—bumping into him because he wouldn't get out of her way, which only made her angrier—and climbed into the car. As soon as Marianne was buckled in, Holly started the engine, knowing Jared would tell his brother what had happened, and she was certain she'd get a lecture. She'd been getting a lot of them lately, and she was sick of it.

She drove off, and Jared headed for his truck in another area of the parking lot.

"Uh, so... Dr. Aidan is nice," Marianne said.

"He is. And he *did* save Joey."

"Like the time that wolf saved you when you were little, right?" Marianne asked.

"Yes. Just like that. And that man was my hero. He wasn't part of our pack. Not all wolves from other packs are bad, despite what Ronald and his brother say."

"Um, so...Jared said the reason they have such issues with other packs is that, several different times, packs from other areas have wanted our territory and fought us to take over."

"That was a long time ago, and I feel it's just an excuse to keep us isolated from other wolves. Ronald and his brother have control issues. His enforcers are borderline bullies."

Marianne was twirling some of her hair around

her fingers. "Yeah, but they did make a ruling not to befriend any outside wolves, because that's how it happened. The wolves from the other packs got friendly, learning the strengths and weaknesses of our pack, and then tried to take us over, you know."

"Right, but not all wolves are like that," Holly reminded her sister.

"I heard a rumor that before Jared and his brother were born, their mom mated an outsider wolf." Marianne rolled her eyes. "Like, you know, that would ever happen. I figured it was just a made-up story."

"No, it's true, but no one who lived during that time talks about it."

Marianne's mouth dropped open. "For real?"

"Yeah. Fred, the wolf their mother mated, was the leader of the last pack that tried to take over ours. He killed his own pack leader and took over. Nick was still our pack leader at the time. The other pack had only males, and Fred thought if he mated Jared and Ronald's mother, he'd have an in. Oh, I'm sure he cared about her, but he also wanted to lead a pack that was established in the area and that had females."

"Because there was a shortage of them."

"Right. Except Nick fought and killed him. Nick didn't blame Gwendolyn for mating the wolf. She was truly smitten with him, and she hadn't known of his devious plan. It nearly destroyed her when Nick had to fight and ultimately kill Fred. But she cared about her pack too and was friends with everyone. If her mate had had his way, all the fighting-age wolves in our pack would have been slaughtered, unless they were beta enough that Fred could have controlled them. Gwendolyn felt he'd used her to learn the strengths and weaknesses of the pack."

"That's who Jared and Ronald's dad was? Fred? Really for real?"

"Yeah. It's *not* one of those stories that the pack likes to share. I only know about it because Nick and I had a heart-to-heart talk about what was going on with Jared and Ronald's issue with other packs. Nick knew I wanted to be in touch with other packs. He finally told me the background. Both Jared and Ronald felt their father had betrayed their mother and her family. They felt they bore the stigma, even though those who had lived during that time didn't share who their father was with the younger generations. But when they were older, their mother told them who their father was and what had happened. She died years ago, unable to cope with the betrayal. She felt others believed she was responsible for the deaths of the men who defended the pack from her mate and his men."

"Oh. Well, great. That means Ronald and Jared will never change their minds about opening the pack up to others. I'd like to meet some people my age who aren't just in our pack." Marianne folded her arms in a huff.

"Boys?"

Marianne blushed. "And girls."

"He has to accept change. We need fresh blood in the pack. Or we're going to have to go outside our pack to find mates, which means leaving the pack altogether."

"Like finding Dr. Aidan Denali?" Marianne smiled. "Jared couldn't have gotten any redder than he did when you hugged the doctor. *Literally*."

"Good."

"We need a new pack leader," Marianne said.

"Yeah, we do, but don't let anyone else know you said so."

"Hey, are you going to give up Aidan's business card?"

Holly smiled.

"Cool. You memorized his phone number, or you put his number in your cell. You know Ronald will want to check your cell."

"Which is why your first assumption is correct."

"You memorized it. I wish I had your memory, you know." Marianne was really quiet for a while, and then she suddenly wiped away the tears trailing down her cheeks.

Holly realized how much Marianne had been trying to keep her emotions in check before this. She'd felt just as horrified, scared, and relieved when they'd caught up with Joey, but since Marianne had been responsible for him, she felt really bad.

"Like, I was so scared when Joey ran off and so mad at myself for not holding his hand when he didn't want me to. I could have lost him for good." Marianne sniffled. "Not that it's as important as losing him, but I think I lost my babysitting job, *for real*."

Holly reached over the console and patted her sister's shoulder. "Joey needs a leash. Everyone says how precocious he is. Why do you think his mother wanted you to take him to see Santa? She couldn't handle trying to keep track of him and his three siblings all at once. Not with the crowds at the shopping center this time of year."

"So I wasn't the only one he's run away from?"

"Heavens no. His mother just doesn't want to use a

leash on him. It makes her think of confining a dog. But I think if anyone else takes him anywhere, he should be on one."

They both glanced at Joey in the back seat, but he was fast asleep.

"Sounds good to me. I hope she doesn't fire me. I like taking care of him and the other kids in the pack." Marianne eyed Holly thoughtfully. "You like him, don't you?"

"Aidan? Dr. Denali?" Holly quickly corrected herself.

"Yeah, Aidan. Dr. Denali." Marianne laughed. "He's cute. So were the men with him." She frowned. "Do you think they were his bodyguards? They didn't seem to be just friends. Not as protective as they were. And you should have seen the way they were both glowering at Jared. *Literally*. I swear, if he'd attempted to peel you off Aidan, or he'd tried to take Aidan's business card away from you, they would have pounded on him. I was actually kinda hoping they would to knock some sense into him."

Holly agreed. "Aidan was getting ready for a fight if Jared didn't back off. I think the two men might have been Aidan's bodyguards."

"I wonder if he's had trouble."

"Sure. If the cure for wolves aging faster could be sold, someone might make lots of money off it. Maybe even Aidan, though from what he told Ronald when he met with him and I was out of town, he planned to give the cure away for free, if he could identify the issue and resolve it."

"I bet you'd love to work with him. I know you wanted to be able to share our blood samples with him, but I mean *really* work with him. *Up close*." Marianne glanced at her sister. "You didn't answer me. Do you think he's cute? Aidan?"

Sexy, hot, appealing, yes. And protective and heroic. When Jared got in her space, Holly knew Aidan was about to take the wolf down. She'd been annoyed with Aidan for holding on to Joey when she'd reached out to take him, but she'd realized he was just making sure the boy belonged with her and Marianne.

Holly just smiled at her sister. Who wouldn't have thought the doctor was cute? She wouldn't have hugged him so close or for so long if she hadn't thought that, and she'd gotten rather a…surprise. He'd been hot and aroused.

When they finally reached their cabin and pulled into the parking area, she saw Ronald on his cell, staring hard at her, his mouth turned down. Jared must have told him all that had happened. Even though the boy's rescue had been a godsend, she figured Ronald was more concerned Holly had been friendly toward Aidan Denali. She had every intention of speaking with Aidan again, first to see how he was faring and then to thank him again. This time without Jared's interference.

"You're in trouble now," Marianne warned.

Holly climbed out of the car, and Marianne lifted a sleeping Joey out of the back seat. "I'll take him home and give his mom the news. Unless you want me to stand by you while you talk to Ronald."

"I'll be fine. Let me know what Joey's mom says concerning what happened."

"That I'm fired, I'm sure!" Marianne gave Holly a hug, then carried Joey to his mom and dad's cabin.

Ronald ended his call and approached Holly. "You weren't there when Dr. Denali visited our pack in Seattle, but we told you before that you're not to speak with him. His issues are his issues, not ours."

"And like I've said, his issues could very well become ours too. Not to mention that he saved Joey! Aidan was bashed in the head, bleeding profusely, and most likely suffered a concussion, just because he was protecting the boy. He had no idea we were even wolves to begin with." At least Holly assumed he wouldn't have known. "And he didn't know we were with the wolf pack out of Seattle."

"But you told him."

"Of course. Why wouldn't I?"

Ronald spit on the ground. She frowned at him for being so vulgar.

"You don't speak to him again."

She raised her brows defiantly. "Just so you know, I *will* be calling him to see what the doctor said about his head wound."

If it weren't for her family—they wanted to remain with the pack—she would tell Ronald off and leave the pack. But she knew if she did, Ronald would make it virtually impossible to see her family or have any other contact with them, or he'd banish them too.

Ronald continued to glower at her. He only bit his tongue because she was their pack doctor and well respected. Finding another among the wolves would be a real challenge.

Why couldn't she leave well enough alone? Because she kept feeling she could help Aidan, and now that she'd met him and seen how much he was like the wolf

who had saved her when she was little, she really wanted
to meet with him and talk about what he'd learned. She
wanted to make a difference too. They hadn't even
known what was happening to other wolf packs before
Aidan came to them. Was her pack immune to the
changes? She'd tested everyone in the pack and learned
none of them was aging any faster than before. But
she'd only been testing them once every quarter, and
only those who had reached puberty and older, since
that's when the aging slowed down for them.

"Is that all you have to say to me?" she asked Ronald.

"When you talk to him, you speak about his head
wound and nothing more."

As their doctor, she took care of her pack members'
injuries, which was an important role for her, but she
also wanted to determine what had changed for other
wolves. Because her pack's longevity hadn't altered, her
pack leaders didn't want her to get involved. At least
according to Ronald. He thought everyone would bleed
them dry, trying to come up with a cure, if they knew
their pack's DNA hadn't transmuted.

"Have you heard anything from Neil Booker?" Holly
asked, changing the subject, though she was trying to
make a point. If Ronald kept pushing, he was going to
lose more disgruntled pack members.

"Barry said Neil joined some pack in Nevada."

"Is Barry keeping in touch with him?" Holly couldn't
believe Ronald would allow it.

"Hell no, or he'll be out of the pack in a flash."

She was about to say something more to Ronald when
she saw her sister coming her way. Marianne smiled at
her. "Joey's mom was thrilled he was safe. She wanted

to have Dr. Denali's business card to give him a call and thank him. She also said she's getting a leash for Joey, for real."

Holly was glad the boy's mother wasn't angry with Marianne. She pulled the business card from her bra and handed it to Marianne. "She's still going to have you babysit for her?"

"Yes. But Joey's on notice, literally."

Holly smiled. "Good. He might be precocious, but he needs some rules."

Ronald snickered. "Just like you."

Holly shook her head and walked off to her cabin.

"No talking to Denali, beyond seeing about his health." Then Ronald followed Marianne.

Holly wondered if he planned to take the business card from Joey's mom after she called Aidan. His phone wasn't listed, and he only gave his number out to pack leaders to learn about their longevity concerns. Though she imagined if someone needed to talk to him about his research, the wolf could have Aidan's number to get in touch with him.

When she entered the cabin, her mom asked her all about what had happened at the mall, her dad listening in, her brother shaking his head. News sure traveled fast in a pack.

Marianne joined them while Holly was telling her family what had happened.

"You probably guessed Ronald took Dr. Denali's business card and tore it up," Marianne said to Holly.

"No surprise." Holly had Aidan's number memorized, and if anyone else needed it, she'd give it to them.

"After he saved Joey?" their mom said, her expression one of disbelief.

"Yeah, see, that's some of what's wrong with this pack. Or, I should say, its leadership." Holly thought her family might finally agree with her, yet no one made any comment.

—⁓—

At the hospital, Aidan got a call from a woman who told him she was Joey's mother. He appreciated hearing from her, again thinking this might affect how the Seattle pack members viewed him and his work. "I can't thank you enough for saving Joey," she said.

"I am glad to have been there and in a position to intervene."

"Well, thank you. We're grateful to you. If there's anything we can ever do for you, just ask."

"Thanks, Mrs.—"

"Just call me Trudy."

"Thank you, Trudy." Aidan, of course, thought of asking for a sample of her blood, but that wouldn't be appropriate. Though he couldn't help but think about it. She again thanked him, and they ended the call.

He finally fell asleep in his private room, but later that night, someone barged into the room, banging the door against the wall. His heart gave a jolt. His eyes popped open, and he was more than surprised to see Rafe crossing the floor to his bed, looking worried and annoyed at the same time. Two of Rafe's bodyguards stepped inside the room in front of the door. Aidan groaned, glad he had a private room, or his twin brother and his men would have given a roommate a heart attack. He'd nearly given Aidan one!

"What are you doing here?" Aidan growled. "I'm

fine. I'll be out of here by tomorrow morning, after-noon at the latest." He hadn't wanted anyone to make a big deal out of this, treating it as if it was more seri-ous than it was. He cast Ted and Mike an annoyed look. He'd never expected his brother to come to see him. The two brothers were close, but this was really uncalled for.

Looking serious, his bodyguards shrugged. They knew Rafe would have been madder at them if they hadn't told him what had happened and the story came out later.

"If they hadn't called me about what had happened, I would have fired them." Frowning, Rafe folded his arms as he peered down at Aidan. "I spoke with your doctor."

"Rafe…" Aidan was certain his brother had insisted on speaking with the doctor no matter what he had been doing at the time.

"Hey, you want to know the hot water we'll all be in if you're not at the chalet to see Toby for Christmas? All he asks about is when you're going to be there." Rafe sounded like he was trying to lighten the mood, maybe figuring he'd acted a bit rashly in coming here. He could have talked to the doctor over the phone!

Aidan smiled. He adored his nephew too. He hadn't thought he would be that into kids before Toby came along, but he was a cute kid and reminded Aidan of Rafe and himself when they were that age.

Frowning, Rafe peered down at Aidan. "I have half a mind to fly you there right this instant."

"I have business to take care of here."

"It's Christmas. You need a break, a longer break than you intended to have. Hell, you have a lab there.

You can work to your heart's content and still visit with us. Then Mike and Ted can go home early."

"Rafe, I might have a chance to make some headway with the Seattle pack. Some of them are here right now." Aidan hadn't wanted to mention that part—about the Seattle pack staying at the cabins nearby—but it was the only way to explain why he'd want to stay. Besides, his men had probably told Rafe by now that the boy he rescued and the two females with him were from the Seattle pack.

"That's the woman I was telling you about," Ted said. "She's a doctor too. Maybe she's more open-minded than the rest of the pack. She definitely took a shine to Doc."

"Yeah, she couldn't keep her hands off him," Mike added with a smirk.

Rafe stared at Aidan, as if he couldn't believe a she-wolf with the Seattle pack would be interested in him.

"She was keeping pressure on my head wound. I bled a lot. You know how head wounds are. And she's a doctor. I gave her my business card and hoped she'd get in touch with me before I leave to spend Christmas with you and the family."

"Speaking with the woman when her pack is disagreeable and in the same vicinity as our cabin isn't a good idea," Rafe said.

Aidan suspected mentioning his other urgent mission wouldn't make Rafe feel any less apprehensive about him being here. Not that Aidan was going to listen to Rafe and go right to the chalet.

When Rafe looked like the issue of the woman helping Aidan didn't sway him, Aidan finally let out his breath and told him the rest of it. "I have a lead on a man who lives in the mountains that I want to get in touch with."

Rafe looked at Ted and Mike as if to confirm that Aidan wasn't hallucinating.

"Yeah, boss, that's what Everett said. He used to be a Seattle pack member but now lives with the Montana pack," Mike offered.

Rafe scowled at them. "Where were the two of you when Aidan got his head bashed?"

"Chasing after him. One minute, he was looking at toys for Toby; the next, he was on the run, trying to get around the crowds just like we were," Ted said. "We promise we'll keep a better eye on him next time."

"You'd better." Rafe pulled up a chair and sat next to the bed.

Aidan groaned. "You can't do anything for me. Go home and be with your family."

"You're family too. Do I need to have Chet and some others stay with you?"

"No. Ted and Mike are fine."

"If you have any trouble, you let me know at once." Rafe let out his breath in an exasperated way. "I'm going to wait until you're released tomorrow and then go with you to the cabin. Tell me what's going on concerning this mountain man. Then you need to sleep."

"Nick Cornwall is known to live in the area." Aidan explained everything else about him to his brother. "Since Glacier Peak is the remotest of the five active volcanoes of Washington State, we shouldn't run into humans while we're searching for him around there."

"You think you can traipse all over the Wilderness in your condition looking for him?" Rafe looked stern.

Aidan knew his brother was just worried about him.
It all had to do with the *lupus garous* who'd tried to
take him hostage to find the cure for their longevity
issues. Which was why Aidan now had bodyguards. He
couldn't believe how protective his brother had become.
"I'll be fine tomorrow. You know I will."

"You're taking Ted and Mike with you though,
correct?"

"To search for Nick, yeah." Aidan closed his eyes.
He couldn't believe Rafe had flown out to check on him.
On the other hand…he could.

Aidan was already thinking of ways to reconnect with
Dr. Holly Gray. Nick was his focus because he was concerned about the older wolf being out in the Wilderness
by himself through the winter months. Holly might
know something about where he was, even though she'd
told Everett she couldn't locate him.

The way Holly had looked at Aidan with such adora-
tion for saving Joey…

Aidan wanted to see her again. Seattle pack or no.

Chapter 4

AFTER AIDAN WAS RELEASED FROM THE HOSPITAL THE next day, he convinced Rafe that he didn't need to escort them to the cabin. Finally agreeing, Rafe and his bodyguards left, to Aidan's relief. Rafe was only the older twin by five minutes, but when Aidan's life had been threatened over his research, everything had changed between them. Even though Aidan had saved Rafe's life a couple of times when he'd been in wolf fights by giving him blood transfusions, setting broken bones, and stitching up wounds! Rafe was being an overly, *overly* protective brother.

After Aidan and his men finished their grocery shopping, they piled into the car.

"You're supposed to take it easy," Ted reminded Aidan as he took the wheel and began the drive to the cabin.

"You're beginning to sound like Rafe, and one of him is enough."

The guys laughed.

"I'm resting all day, and we'll take a run tonight," Aidan told them. After sleeping so well last night, he was feeling much better. He'd wanted to start their search for Nick as soon as they could, though he suspected Ted and Mike would try to talk him out of it. He wished they hadn't already been delayed so much.

"I'm fine. If my head begins to pain me, I'll let you

know, and we can return to the cabin." Aidan sighed
and rubbed his temples. A headache was pooling there,
although the bruising from the bashing he'd received
was starting to fade. He opened his laptop and considered a map of the mountain and surrounding wilderness.
He probably should start out on the easier trail today,
since his head didn't feel a hundred percent.

After closing his laptop, he set it aside and shut his
eyes to rest on the way to the cabin. It seemed as soon as
he closed his eyes, Ted was slamming a car door shut.
Aidan quickly sat up, thinking they'd stopped for gas, but
they'd parked at the cabin already. He couldn't believe
he'd actually fallen asleep. The guys started unpacking
the bags while frowning at him and looking concerned.

"I'm fine." Aidan climbed out of the car and grabbed
his laptop and another couple of bags.

"Rafe called, checking up on you when you didn't
answer your phone," Mike warned.

Hell.

"We told him you were just resting your eyes, but
he said you would have heard your phone. Sorry, Doc."
Mike grabbed a couple sacks of groceries.

Aidan's phone rang and he was hoping it was Holly,
but it was his brother. "Yeah, Rafe? I just saw you a
couple hours ago."

"Mike said you were out for the count."

"He told you I was resting my eyes."

"Yeah, but when you're resting your eyes, you hear
your phone go off. Are you okay?"

"Yes. Now who's being the doctor?"

"Someone has to be where you're concerned. He told
me you were going on a run tonight. I don't think you

should. You need to rest up further. Wait until tomorrow morning."

"I'll be fine. Give Jade and Toby a hug for me, will you?"

"If you run into any trouble, you call me."

"Thanks, Rafe, I will." But Aidan didn't expect to have any real trouble.

"Okay, well, we're still on the way home. I'll call you later. Or you call me."

"All right. I will."

After they ended the call, Aidan received another, this time from Rafe's mate, Jade.

"Rafe told me you'd been injured by the attempted kidnapper of a little wolf boy. Are you sure you don't want to come here earlier?"

"I'll be there as soon as I can. I promise. I'm fine, really. I just talked to Rafe."

"He said he couldn't get hold of you because you were out cold."

"A mere exaggeration. I'm okay."

"All right. Toby's bouncing on his toes wanting to talk to his uncle Aidan. Here you go."

"Uncle Aidan? Can you come home, and no more bad guys can hurt you?"

Aidan smiled. "I won't let any more hurt me. But I had to save a little boy from someone who tried to take him from his family."

"Like me, Uncle Aidan. Mommy says you are a hero."

Aidan laughed. "You be good for Santa. Give your mommy a hug, and I'll see you as soon as I can. Protect your mommy until Rafe gets home."

"Okay. Here, Mommy. Uncle Aidan said I gotta give you a hug."

"Hey, Aidan, you be careful. Rafe said you're playing with fire around that Seattle pack."

"I'll be careful. Love you and Toby. I'll see you soon."

When they ended the call, Aidan winced as he felt another ripple of pain across his skull.

He had told Ted and Mike not to let on that he was hoping to still connect with the Seattle pack. He regretted telling his brother at the hospital last night. The Glacier Peak Wilderness wasn't the Seattle pack's territory as they'd claimed. The city was nearly seventy miles southwest of the peak. Still, running into the pack up here might cause trouble. Aidan couldn't understand why they were so reluctant to have their blood tested. Their reluctance made him more than curious.

"Are you both going home for Christmas?" Aidan had hoped the men would. Ted and Mike needed to be with their families.

"Yeah, Doc. Since you're spending Christmas with Rafe and he's got his own guards, there's no need for me to watch your back. You know if you need me, I'll stick around," Ted said. "But Rafe felt they'd have it covered."

"Same with me. Going home to the folks," Mike said. "Toby will have fun seeing snow, won't he?"

"Yeah, first time to take Toby skiing. And he'll love running through the snow."

"He'll love making snowmen too." Ted carried another load of groceries into the kitchen.

They finished unloading the groceries and the bags, though Ted and Mike kept telling Aidan they had this, afraid he'd tire out and wouldn't be able to run later. He'd carried his bags to his room, then returned to the kitchen to make coffee for everyone while they put away the groceries.

"Where are we running exactly? You want both of us to come, right? You don't want Mike to stay home and guard the place, do you?" Ted asked.

"Mike? What do you mean *I* should stay home and guard the cabin? What about *you* guarding the cabin?" Mike asked.

Aidan smiled at the two men. They had become the best of friends, and he felt lucky to have them for his protection. He pulled out his laptop and showed them the map of the Wilderness area. He ran his finger along the path he thought they could take. "We could start up the south side on the trail to White Pass."

Ted looked worried all over again. Normally, a wolf would take the more difficult trails to avoid running into humans. But Aidan figured it was a good idea to take it easy, just a bit. That way, he'd be able to travel farther. If they smelled any sign of Nick, they might be able to locate him early.

"From what Everett told you, that trail runs close to the Seattle pack's cabins," Mike mentioned. "You sure you want to run in that direction?"

"It's his head I'm worried about," Ted said.

"It's the rest of him I'm worried about," Mike said.

Aidan chuckled. "All right. You're probably correct, and we should avoid getting too close to those cabins." Though he had hoped to catch a glimpse of Holly and talk to her again. But as a wolf, that would be difficult. "We can take the more northern route. If my head bothers me, we'll return to the cabin sooner." Though he had no intention of doing so. Once he was on a mission, that was all that mattered. He'd deal with a headache later.

"Most humans travel through here in the summer, if they venture this far into the Wilderness at all, since it's remote. The chance of us seeing anyone is unlikely. At least that's what it says here." Mike showed them a hiker's trip report.

"Right." Aidan noticed he had missed a call from last night, probably from when he was sleeping deeply from the pain medication. The name looked familiar: Ronald Grayson, the leader of the Seattle wolf pack. Which made Aidan suspect Jared had told him what had happened at the mall. Aidan was certain Ronald hadn't changed his mind about allowing him to draw blood from their pack members for his research, despite saving one of their boys.

Aidan called the pack leader back while Ted poured a cup of hot coffee filled with cream for him. One nice thing about his bodyguards was that they loved to cook. Before they'd shown up, Aidan was always skipping meals when he was in the middle of his research, too focused on what he was doing. Now that they were around and didn't have other duties, Ted and Mike wouldn't let him miss a meal. Of course, they wanted to eat too.

"Thanks, Ted." Aidan took the cup of coffee from him and moved into the living room. "Hi, this is Dr. Aidan Denali," he said to Ronald. "You called?"

"Some of my pack members said you were running in our territory."

"Seattle? Nope. Haven't been there since the first time I spoke with you there."

Ronald growled a little over the phone. "We claim the area surrounding Seattle as our own. The mall in Lynnwood too."

"We're not there now, and we're not setting up business in your territory. As to the mall, well, hell, who knows what might have happened to Joey if I hadn't stopped the woman from taking him out of the store."

Ted and Mike had left the kitchen and were watching Aidan as if they thought a fight could break out right there and their services would be needed. They both gave him smiles and thumbs-up. They were ready for some action.

"Just because you and your brother have a lot of money doesn't mean you can go anywhere you please and do whatever you please. You leave my people alone and stay the hell away."

"You're welcome for saving your kid," Aidan said. The guy really needed an attitude adjustment. Or to be replaced.

The phone clicked dead in Aidan's ear.

He pocketed his phone and took a sip of his coffee. "That was Ronald, leader of the Seattle pack, and he told us to stay away from his pack members. I suspect Jared told on us."

"I doubt either Holly or her sister did," Ted said.

"I swear Holly would have talked to me further, if it hadn't been for Jared butting in." Aidan finished the rest of his coffee.

"After the way she hugged you, I'd say so." Ted headed back into the kitchen.

"Yeah, he's got that hero thing going with saving little kids."

Ted started looking in the cupboards. "I think even if you or I saved the boy, she'd still have been interested solely in the doc. Did you see the way she looked at him when she learned who he was?"

Mike joined him in the kitchen. "Awestruck."

"In love."

"Intrigued," Mike added.

Aidan laughed. His bodyguards could sure be entertaining sometimes. They were just having fun at his expense because they'd never seen him around a she-wolf that he was as interested in.

"Ready to make a meal?" Ted asked.

"Yeah, what sounds good?" Mike replied.

Aidan was looking out the window at the mountain, the accumulated snow on the ground, and the mist of snow in the air. He wanted to locate Holly in the worst way—to learn if she had wanted to meet with him. He wanted to let her know they were searching for Nick, since she had also been trying to locate him. Wouldn't that give Aidan even more leverage with her?

"One pretty little she-wolf," Ted said, and Aidan looked back to see both men chuckle as they watched him. "Did you notice she didn't give him a brief thank-you hug that would have been just a...thank-you?"

"Hell, no, that was a lot more than an impersonal embrace," Ted said. "Something I could have gotten into."

"She was trying to show Jared she wasn't going to be told what to do, while annoying him at the same time," Aidan said.

Both men glanced at him and smiled.

"Whatever you say, Doc." Ted pulled a package of hamburger out of the fridge and held it up. "Hamburgers?"

"Sounds good," Aidan said.

"What are you working on now, Doc?" Ted began setting out all the ingredients: hamburger, onions, lettuce, tomatoes, cheese, mushrooms, pickles, buns, and condiments.

That was one thing Aidan hadn't counted on either, that his bodyguards would be interested in his research.

Mike had been an army medic and was interested in the biological aspects of what was going on with their bodies. Ted loved to organize things. Even with cooking, he'd get all the ingredients out, set them all up in order, and work more efficiently than Aidan ever could. Ted had been fascinated with setting up charts to see if any correlation existed between different types of data Aidan had collected.

Both men had wanted to help since they weren't doing much bodyguarding. Aidan was glad to have them on the team.

"You know all he's thinking about is convincing the pretty wolf doctor to go out with him and share her blood." Ted began slicing up the onions and mushrooms.

Mike laughed. "Sounds like Doc's a vampire instead of a wolf. Mushrooms and onions on your hamburger, hold the cheese, right, Doc?"

One mouthwatering, blond she-wolf on the menu was all Aidan could think of. "Yeah, thanks." His cell rang, and when he saw the caller ID, he smiled. *Dr. Holly Gray*. He suspected she was going to thank him again for saving Joey. He'd really go for another one of her body-squeezing, hot-blooded hugs. "This is Aidan."

Both of his bodyguards stopped what they were doing and glanced in his direction. He must not have sounded like his usual professional self.

"Hey, um, it's Holly. Uh, from yesterday. At the mall."

As if Aidan would forget. "Yeah, I'm glad you called. I didn't get your number. Did Jared give you any further grief yesterday? I half expected him to take my business card away from you. I was ready to deal with him."

"I assumed you were ready to tear into him, even though you'd been injured. No worries. I'd already memorized your number."

"So he did take the card from you."

"From Trudy, Joey's mother, after she called to thank you for saving her son. But I called to see how you are. I tried last night, but I was having reception issues."

"I received two stitches, but the cut is healing fast, and I'm good to go." Aidan wasn't about to heed Rafe's warning to stay away from Holly. "I'm running in a bit. Did you want to meet up with me?"

Ted and Mike chuckled.

"You must have a death wish. Yes, I'd love to run with you, but I wouldn't dare. Are...the two men who were with you your bodyguards?"

"They are. And my personal assistants. Great cooks too."

Mike gave him a thumbs-up.

"They won't be enough muscle to protect you," she warned. "Stay to the north side of the peak. We generally run on the south side. It's less dangerous for our families."

"What do you know about Nick Cornwall? I want to locate him and test his blood in case there's anything different about it. I've come to a dead end with finding new wolf packs or loners. When I learned of him through Everett Johnston, he said he was concerned about Nick's health."

"Oh, Nick. He was with our pack forever. One of our first leaders. I swear Ronald didn't want to have him around because he felt he couldn't live up to Nick's leadership skills. Nick was a good leader, charismatic. None of this business with being antisocial with other packs. When his wife died, he withdrew more and more from the pack. He would leave for weeks at a time. I thought it was because everyone was a constant reminder of the mate he'd lost. Ronald banished him because he said Nick was causing trouble for us. He wasn't. He was depressed and more like a lost soul. He couldn't help how he felt, and a lot of us were furious that Ronald made him leave.

"Some of us searched for him, but Nick is extremely wily, and unless he wants to be seen, you won't ever find him. He moves his camp all the time to avoid park people running across him while he's living in the wilderness. Over two hundred lakes are in the area, many of them not even named and extremely treacherous to reach, but I've heard he hangs out around some of them while he fishes. Even though he can shift into a wolf, he would still have to hide all his belongings so no one could find his stuff while he's out hunting or running as a wolf."

"Was he a loner before he became the leader of the pack?" Aidan asked.

"No, he and his mate formed the pack. He was the life of the party. After he stepped down from the role of leader, he served as our Santa for years while his wife was alive. He was friends with everyone. I think that's why it was hard for him to be banished just because he was having such a difficult time coping. And everyone respected him, while a lot of us don't respect Ronald." She let out her breath. "You wanted to see Nick for his blood work?"

"Yeah, but only if he's interested in providing it. At this point, I just want to offer to put him in contact with other packs I know. He can live out his years surrounded by others of our kind. In terms of the longevity issue, he might not care about living a longer life anyway after having lost his mate."

"People are funny like that. You might think he'd want to join his mate in death, yet living out there, despite the harsh living conditions, he still isn't giving up." She paused. "You really want to find him a new home?"

"Yes. If he wants, we'll fly him to where other known packs are and see if he can find one he'd like to stay with. As pack animals, he shouldn't have to live on his own, if that's not the way he likes to live. Silver Town might be a good place. They have a psychologist. And the Montana pack has an inordinate number of widowed female wolves."

"He might not be looking for another mate," Holly warned him.

"No, but he might enjoy all the pampering the women would give him."

Mike chuckled. "He wouldn't know what hit him when the women began fighting over him."

"You just never know," Aidan continued. "But an older wolf shouldn't have to be living in the wilderness on the periphery of a pack."

"Okay, then I want to help you locate him. I've tried before. I can't say that I would be any more successful than you, but if we locate him, he'll recognize me and know I don't wish him any harm. Wild gray wolves, grizzlies, and wolverines live in the area. He needs to know you're not some of the wilder population hunting out there," Holly said.

Aidan couldn't have been more pleased. "How will you get away from your pack so they don't know where you're going and send out a search party?" He suspected that since Ronald had banished Nick, he wouldn't want any of his pack members looking for the older wolf and bringing him back. And Ronald certainly wouldn't want her to be in the company of wolves outside their pack while she looked for Nick.

"I'll let my family know I'm going to look for Nick to see if he's all right. I've come out here on my own half a dozen times since he was banished three months ago. He lost his mate nine months ago."

"You don't think Jared will be keeping more of an eye on you now that I'm in the area?"

She laughed. "Yeah, maybe. That's why you need to stay to the north. We don't go there. We've spied grizzlies up there, and we have too many families with us. We're more careful with them."

"Grizzlies."

"Yeah, but I'm still going with you. Do you know the area at all?"

"I do, but I've never gone in search of a *lupus garou*.

We'll try to cover as much terrain as we can, and not on the regular human trails."

"I agree. I'll meet you at Spider Gap."

There was no maintained trail, and even in summer, the Wilderness was snow-covered. At this time of year, ten to twenty feet of snow covered the whole area. The descent on the north side was a challenge for back-packers, but hopefully the wolves could make it where humans had more difficulty.

"Okay?" she asked.

"Yeah, we'll meet you there. Do you want to do it in an hour to get a head start? We're getting ready to eat hamburgers." He'd decided he wasn't waiting until tonight. It could be more dangerous because of ava-lanches or crevasses.

"You're sure your head can take the steeper trails?"

"If I can't, you can doctor me."

She chuckled. "Okay, see you in about an hour and a half after I grab a bite to eat."

Yes! Aidan couldn't wait to see her again. He ended the call, and Mike shook his head.

Ted turned the hamburger patties on the grill. "That was Holly? And she's going to help us track down Nick?"

"Yeah."

"I told you the brothers make all the right moves and know just what to say to win a girl over," Ted said. "All he had to tell her was that he was going to help poor Nick, and Doc had hooked her."

Mike laughed. "Here we thought he wasn't a real go-getter when it came to she-wolves."

"There haven't been too many around our area—although now Jade has half a dozen women sewing her children's and women's lingerie designs to stock in stores—but Doc's been too busy with his research anyway," Ted said. "Until now."

"I always thought he would scare them off when he brought out his hypodermic needles to draw blood," Mike said.

"Very funny." Aidan hadn't found any of the women appealing—no common interests, no spark. Not like he'd felt with Holly.

"Well, don't ask Holly for her blood right away, 'kay, Doc?" Ted said. "I think the doctor likes you, but you could blow it big time if you start asking her to give some of her blood for your research."

Aidan wanted to get to know the intriguing wolf for a lot more than that. "Don't tell Rafe we're running with her in the Wilderness. He's liable to return and give us all grief."

"I'm not mentioning it to Rafe unless we all get into trouble," Ted said.

"Right, not a word. He will never know...unless it's like Ted said," Mike added. They sat down to eat their hamburgers, then got ready for the run.

Aidan sure hoped they wouldn't have trouble with the Seattle pack over this. On the other hand, he had no intention of taking any guff from Ronald and his minions—if they should run into them. He just hoped Holly wouldn't have issues with them. And he hoped they found Nick healthy and eager to join a new pack.

Chapter 5

HOLLY WAS ENTHUSIASTIC ABOUT LOCATING NICK, AND having male wolves with her for protection was important. But she hadn't been able to ask anyone in her pack to go with her. Fearing that would get them in trouble with Ronald, she'd always gone alone in pursuit of Nick. She suspected others had hunted for him too, in the guise of taking a run on the wild side.

She just hoped she would be more successful searching with the men than she had been on her own.

Ronald had known she was looking for Nick, but he thought that was only because of her concern for the older wolf's health and welfare due to her occupation. He knew she hadn't had any success in finding Nick, so he didn't care if she searched. As long as she didn't bring him back to the pack, and as long as Ronald didn't know she was going with Aidan and his bodyguards, they shouldn't have a problem. They would have to watch out for other wildlife, crevasses, avalanches, and anything else that could be a danger for them though.

Holly quickly prepared tuna-fish sandwiches and chips for her parents and brother and sister, hoping no one would notice how rushed she was or that she was serving lunch earlier than they normally ate.

Her mother frowned at her. "You look like you're in a hurry."

"She's going to look for Nick," Marianne said. "You know she always does."

"I agree with Margaret. You've never been in this much of a hurry," her dad said, looking as concerned as her mother. "Are you planning to travel farther in your search for him this time?"

"Yes. I figure Nick knows when we're here and stays somewhere farther from the cabins to avoid running into us." She sat down and began eating her sandwich. "If I can't find him, I'll probably go again early in the morning. I'm getting way too late a start as it is today."

Everyone joined her at the dining table.

Her brother grabbed a potato chip and pointed it at her. "I want to go with you this time."

He hadn't had any interest in going with her before, and she shook her head. "You'd slow me down."

His jaw dropped a little. "You'd slow *me* down."

"No." She said it with such finality that everyone started watching her. She wished she'd been a little subtler in her response. "I haven't had any luck before. I'd waste your time."

"I'm going." Greg looked so serious that she couldn't believe it.

"I agree." Her dad added a pickle to his plate. "You should have someone go with you in case you run into trouble."

She was glad her whole family didn't offer. Her mother and Marianne were eyeing her with suspicion.

"I'll be fine. I've always been fine. I'll be home before you know it."

"I'm going with you, Sis," Greg said, as stubborn as she could be.

She curbed the urge to say *damn it* and nodded. She didn't know what to do. Pretend that she'd just run into Aidan and the other men? Greg might worry they were wild wolves and try to protect her. She didn't want him to know she was running with them, not when Ronald would forbid it. And then what? Greg would have to tell him the truth. She didn't want her brother getting into trouble over her actions.

Still, she had to tell him. Maybe when she did, he'd be a man and let her go alone but not tell Ronald what she was up to. She could only hope.

She finished her sandwich and headed for her room.

"As wolves, right?" Greg asked, finishing his lunch in a hurry.

"Yes."

He followed her into her bedroom and shut the door. "Tell me what this is really about."

"You can't tell *anyone*."

Greg's eyes widened. "You know where Nick is?"

"No. But Aidan, Dr. Denali, is meeting me, and we're searching for him together. His bodyguards will be accompanying us too."

"Why would he want to look for Nick?"

"He wants to ask him if he can take a sample of his blood."

Greg grunted.

"And to find him a home. Nick shouldn't be living out there as a mountain man. The older he gets, the harder it is on him. And he's not a lone wolf."

"Okay, I agree. I'll go with you. But don't you think we should tell the rest of the family?"

"If they know, they could be in hot water if Ronald

learns about it and they didn't tell him." Holly didn't want them to be banished from the pack too.

"We need to tell them. And then we'll go."

When had her seventeen-year-old brother grown up so fast? "All right. But we have to make this quick."

Holly walked out to speak to her family and saw Jared standing at the front door, her sister still holding on to the doorknob. Holly's heart plummeted. She hoped his sensitive wolf hearing hadn't allowed him to overhear what they'd been discussing in her bedroom. Then again, they'd been keeping their voices low so the rest of her family couldn't hear what she was up to, and Greg had closed the bedroom door.

"I thought we could go on a wolf run together, Holly." Jared didn't look like the prospect thrilled him.

"Thanks, but—"

"We're going to make snowmen." Greg smiled as if he were a kid again and was thrilled to build one. "That's where we were headed. Now."

"Me too," Marianne quickly said, casting a glance at Holly, looking to see if she would go along with it.

"Snowmen." Jared sounded like he didn't believe them.

Holly hoped he didn't offer to make one with them, but she loved her younger brother and sister for playing the game.

"I'll clean up the dishes so you can go play," their mom said, sounding amused.

Holly grabbed her parka, gloves, hat, and scarf and set them on the back of the couch so she could put them on. She hated getting her sister involved in this too.

Marianne grabbed her tasseled hat and pulled it on

her head. Then she seized her jacket and scarf and put them on. "You can make your own, Jared."

No, no, no, he couldn't.

"Thanks, but I'll pass," Jared said, his gaze switching from Marianne to Holly. "I'll run with you later tonight then."

She gave him a nod, then jerked on her parka. Greg was all ready to go and moved toward the door, showing his alpha nature by trying to force Jared out of the way. Jared smiled darkly at Greg.

"Last one to make a snowman is a rotten egg," Greg called out, racing off.

"Best one wins, not the fastest one made," his sister said, still tying her scarf around her neck as she tore off after him.

Now what? They'd take forever making three snowmen. And Holly would miss meeting Aidan and his men. He'd worry, and she wouldn't be able to call him. No doubt he'd already be on his way to the meeting place in his wolf coat.

Jared stepped out of Holly's way, and she hurried outside.

"Later," Jared said to Holly and left.

He wasn't even interested in dating her, so why the change of heart? The business with Aidan at the mall yesterday? Maybe he'd like a hug too? Never!

Holly raced after her sister and brother and found them about a quarter of a mile away, starting to build the bases of their snowmen.

"What is going on with you really?" Marianne asked, shoving another handful of snow onto the base.

"We're on a mission that you shouldn't know about," Greg said, slapping a snowball against his snowman.

"A mission," Marianne said, glancing at Holly.

"To look for Nick," Holly said.

"Well, you said that already." Marianne tilted her chin down. "There's more to it than that. And I want to help."

"No." Greg grabbed another two handfuls of snow. "It's too dangerous."

"If it's too dangerous, the two of you shouldn't be going. You know Jared will check later to see if you built your snowmen or not," Marianne said.

Holly saw her parents headed their way. *Great.*

"Looks like it's about time to tell the family what you're up to," Greg said.

"So, there's more to this business of you looking for... Ohmigod, you're going to meet up with Aidan Denali, aren't you! I want to go too," Marianne said.

Holly thought her sister had a crush on Aidan, or maybe one of his bodyguards. "No. I didn't want any of you to know about it."

"Know about what?" their mother asked. To Holly's surprise, her mom and dad began to build a snowman.

"I'm meeting with Aidan and his bodyguards to search for Nick."

Her parents stopped working on the snowman and straightened.

"I didn't want to tell you because I didn't want you to get into any trouble with the pack."

"I'm going with her. I have to see this guy she's got the hots for." Greg smiled at her and she grabbed a wad of snow, made a snowball, and threw it at him. He dodged it, but it splattered on his shoulder.

"I'm just doing what I always do, except that I'm running with them for protection," Holly said.

"We'll finish your snowmen. Go, take off." Her dad smiled a little.

Her mom worked faster. "Eddie, keep adding snow."

Holly couldn't believe her parents would cover for her like this.

"Me too?" Marianne asked, looking hopeful.

"No, not you," their mother quickly said. "You're supposed to run with Joey's family tonight. And you have to make your own snowman. No telling how long Holly's little adventure will last."

"Whatever." Marianne sighed but hurried over to give Holly a hug. "Give him a kiss for me?"

"We'll be wolves." Holly hugged her back. Then she headed in the direction of where she would meet Aidan and the others.

"Just strip and shift, and we'll take your things with us so no one finds your clothes," her mother said. "We'll use our hats and scarves for the snowmen."

In case anyone happened to be watching them from a distance, Holly and Greg went into the woods, stripped, and shifted.

"Be careful, the both of you," their dad said.

Holly woofed back, and then she and her brother ran off through the woods. Her twin sister and brother were both gray wolves with black saddles and blonder faces, chests, and bellies, unlike her. She was blond. All over. Which made her stand out from the rest of the pack members, but not in a good way. Some thought she was from an Arctic family up north and her parents had adopted her. Her mother and dad had always claimed she was their flesh-and-blood daughter, even though the twins mirrored their parents' coloration while she didn't. But that was as wolves. As humans, she and her sister were both blue-eyed blonds, the same as their brother, and they did look similar.

She trusted that she was just unique in her wolf form and not really adopted, even though others had told her she should do DNA testing to see. But she had no intention of doing so.

She hoped to hell this plan of hers worked, that they ran into Aidan all right and that Jared didn't learn about any of it. But if he came out to see the snowmen and found her mom and dad building them while she and Greg were nowhere in sight, Holly knew they'd all be in trouble.

Chapter 6

AIDAN WAS ANXIOUS FOR HOLLY'S ARRIVAL, AND HE AND HIS men had been waiting for her for some time. He was hoping she hadn't had trouble on the way when he spied a wolverine, light brown in color, foraging in the woods, oblivious to them. The animal looked like a small bear, larger than Aidan had ever seen before, maybe three feet long. Wolverines were omnivores, but they wouldn't mess with a pack of wolves. Not that they wouldn't attack an animal many times their size—a caribou even—but usually only if the caribou was weak. Three wolves would be too much for one wolverine to handle.

The wolverine glanced around, saw the wolves observing him, and quickly retreated into the woods.

Worried about Holly, Aidan started loping in the direction of her resort. Ted and Mike joined him. Then a gangly, teenage male wolf walked out of the woods from about an eighth of a mile away. He spied Aidan and his companions and suddenly stood stock-still.

Aidan expected the younger wolf to be with a pack. Was he a wild wolf or with the Seattle pack? Now they had a new dilemma. If the teen was with Holly's pack, he might tell on her for running with them. Even so, Aidan woofed in greeting to let the teen know he was a friend, not a wild wolf.

The wolf turned his head and woofed, as if telling someone else he'd run into trouble.

Aidan sure as hell hoped it wasn't Ronald. Then he saw a pretty blond wolf. A female, fully grown, but not as big as the males. Aidan barked at her, and then he smiled, showing off all his wicked canines. He did so to tell her they weren't the enemy, hoping it was Holly, but Ted bumped his shoulder with his own, and Aidan lost the smile. Maybe he did look a little like a wolf hungry for female companionship. Ted and Mike lay down on the snow to show they were relaxed and not ready for a battle. Aidan thought about setting his rump down on the ground and waiting for her to join him so she and the teen wouldn't feel threatened.

The female nudged the juvenile, then ran forward. Aidan stood in place, tail up, ears perked, eager to greet her. The wolf had to be Holly. Despite the cold, Aidan was panting, and when he saw Ted grinning at him, he pulled his tongue in.

The younger wolf raced after her, trying to keep up with her fast pace.

Unable to stay put, Aidan loped to greet her. His bodyguards rose to their feet, but they didn't join him. He wondered why the younger male had accompanied her, and then whether he was a younger brother.

The female slowed down as Aidan drew close, but he didn't. He was used to his friends and family being dressed in their wolf coats and easily sharing the wolf camaraderie. The two wolves had no need to be cautious once they saw Aidan and his men. With a new wolf, a she-wolf, Aidan had to mind his p's and q's and be a gentleman. Not to mention, he had to get close enough to smell her scent—since the chilly breeze was carrying theirs away from them—to make sure it was Holly.

As soon as they were within breathing space, she touched her nose to his. He smiled, moved in closer, and nuzzled her face, and she licked his. *Hell yeah!* He licked hers back, and she smiled. He liked how they seemed to have a good rapport, both as humans and as wolves.

Then she turned to the teen wolf, and Aidan inclined his head to him in greeting. He thought the younger wolf looked a little startled. Maybe he was surprised Holly was so affectionate toward Aidan when she didn't know him that well? He hoped that didn't get her into trouble later. He'd forgotten about everything but greeting her in a way that said he was interested in her.

She barked at Aidan, and he figured she wanted to head out to try to find Nick.

Aidan agreed and led the pack through the deep snow to make sure it was safe for the others. Ted or Mike would probably feel that should be their role, but the decision to come here had been his and he knew the area—while Ted and Mike were new to it—and felt responsible for everyone. He had a sneaking suspicion they might have even decided it was best he went first, to prove to Holly and the teen that he was real hero material.

Trekking this way was scenic, affording them a five-star view of Glacier Peak covered in pristine snow and the surrounding jagged mountains. The mountain boasted more glaciers than any other in the continental United States. The first part of the journey was across level, forested land. In the summer with the humidity high, it could feel like a jungle. Today, so close to Christmas, it was snow-covered and cold and dry.

At least Aidan only had a mild headache for now.

They raced through snow packed enough that it rose

only knee high. They leaped over fallen trees, smelling for any signs of wolves, and Aidan was glad Holly was with them. Not only because he liked being with her, enjoying the wilderness together, but because she and the teen would recognize Nick's scent. He hoped she was right when she said the wolves from her pack didn't come in this direction. His group really didn't need the hassle of encountering them.

They loped for about three hours, relishing the cool breeze in their fur and the smell of woodsy scents, of rabbits and birds, and of fresh mountain air. The run worked out the kinks and gave Aidan something else to think about for a while: the beauty of nature. And running with a beautiful she-wolf. Though he could have a one-track mind when he was on a mission, he realized just how much the she-wolf had caught his attention.

Every time she stopped to sniff the air or the ground, standing so regal, the breeze catching her blond fur, he had to observe her. Not only to see if she had caught Nick's scent, but just her. He loved to watch the way she moved. The way she held her tail up and her ears perked. Her serious expression softening when she saw him studying her. And then the wolf smile she cast him that made his heart skip a beat.

Hell, he was totally smitten with the wolf.

Since the area had been declared a wilderness area and not a park, there weren't any rangers, ranger stations, or rescue shacks. And because it was one of the more adventurous hiking areas, not as many people would come this way. Visiting the area in winter was only for the most thrill-seeking of hikers. If they'd been hiking as humans, cold weather gear, snowshoes, and

ice axes would have been necessary. Rafe had that kind
of gear stocked at the cabin for anyone that came to
stay. But when they were in wolf form, their rough pads
helped keep them from slipping on ice.

They headed into the more rugged terrain, away from
areas where humans would likely be, mainly because
Aidan was certain Nick would avoid the human areas.
Aidan was also watching for any depressions in the
snow that could be signs of hidden crevasses. Hikers,
skiers, snowboarders, and snowmobilers could crash
through a snowbridge and into a crack in a glacier in a
heartbeat, falling just a few feet unscathed, if they were
lucky. He remembered seeing kids playing on a glacier
in the summer last year and wondering where their parents were. They obviously didn't have enough sense to
know how dangerous it could be. Luckily, nothing had
happened to the kids, but just the same, they shouldn't
have taken the risk.

His focus on scents again, Aidan wondered, with
more than 570,000 acres of mountainous wilderness, if
could they even find Nick. The Cascades were cloaked
in clouds and fog, typical for this time of year. The
snow-covered mountains, clouds, and fog made the
scenery appear mystical and magical.

Aidan had been here with his brother for every
season: spring for long-distance skiing, late summer and
fall for long hikes as wolves, winter for snow biking
and skiing and to see the beautiful skies and lakes, the
sun shining down on the mountain peaks, and the falling
night that brought with it the pink-and-orange sunsets.

Which made him think about seeing a sunset with
Holly up here. He suspected she'd need to return to her

cabin with the other wolf before nightfall. If it had been just him and his men, he'd have stayed the night, curled up with them, and waited until dawn to begin searching again. But he didn't want Holly and the other wolf to cause their pack alarm.

They'd combed several areas for hours, and it was getting to be time to begin the descent and head home. They were standing high on a craggy rock, looking down at a snowfield, when he saw a wolf moving across the snow below.

Holly saw the wolf too. Her tail straightened, and then it began to wag. Aidan hoped that meant the wolf was Nick.

She lifted her chin and howled, the most hauntingly beautiful sound he'd ever heard. The boy lifted his chin and howled along with her.

The wolf turned to see them standing high above and waited. He didn't howl back. He just watched them. They couldn't reach him from this point, and it would take them a couple of hours or longer to safely make their way down to him. But it would be too late then for Holly and the boy to return to their cabins without worrying their pack.

The wolf had to wonder who the strange wolves were and why Holly and the boy were with them.

Holly turned to Aidan, and her expression told him she wanted in the worst way to go to Nick. He woofed at her, reminding her that she needed to return home, as much as she wanted to meet up with her former pack mate. Aidan howled to let the wolf know what he sounded like, so Nick would recognize him if they saw each other from a distance like this again, in case Holly and the boy couldn't travel with them tomorrow. The wolf would know Aidan was friends with Holly and the boy. Maybe the wolf would even think Aidan was Holly's mate.

That had real appeal. Finding a she-wolf he'd be this fascinated with had been the furthest thing from his mind when Aidan had come on the mission to locate Nick. He hadn't given the notion any space in his brain where other she-wolves were concerned, even back home. But Holly... She tempted every wolfish sense of his.

She licked Aidan's face and smiled, a real indication she was interested in him in a courting way. *Hot damn!* He knew she was feeling the same way he was. Aidan lifted his chin and howled a joyful howl, telling her and the others gathered here that she'd made his night.

Ted and Mike were showing off their teeth in grins, shaking their heads, but they didn't look surprised. The younger wolf did. He'd retracted his panting tongue and was just staring at Aidan as if he couldn't believe what was happening between Holly and him.

When Aidan looked down at the older wolf, he was sitting on the snow, waiting to learn what they were going to do. Maybe he planned to disappear once they made their move, and they wouldn't be able to see which direction he went as they made their way down the ridge to where he was. Or maybe he was showing them that he intended to stay, and they could meet up with him.

Despite wanting to speak with the wolf in the worst way tonight, Aidan was determined to get Holly and the boy back to their meeting place so they could return to their cabin before too much more time passed.

He woofed at her again, and she barked at the wolf

down below, and Aidan began to follow the trail he'd made in the snow. Then he cut a new one to carve more of a straight path to the bottom where they could catch the smoother trail and return to where he'd met her and the boy.

She nipped at him to go in a different direction, one that would take him on more of a path to reach the wolf. If it hadn't been for Holly and the boy, Aidan might have attempted the dangerous path. Though without the wolf being in any kind of distress, it would be better to start out again in the morning.

For now, Holly and the boy were his priority.

Chapter 7

IN THE WORST WAY, HOLLY WANTED AIDAN TO GO TO NICK. He looked so isolated. So all alone. She couldn't stand it. But she knew why Aidan was pushing her to go home. She couldn't allow the wolves in her pack to worry that she and her brother were in serious trouble, as much as she wanted to find a path to reach Nick and tell him how Aidan hoped to help him find a new home. She wasn't sure Nick would appreciate it, but she certainly did.

The fog and clouds were clearing and the sun was setting, coloring the Douglas firs, junipers, and pine trees in a wash of pinks and purples and golden light reflecting off a lake and the snow. For a moment, Aidan stopped to look, as if he also was mesmerized by the beauty. He glanced back at her. Maybe he wanted her to have a chance to enjoy it before they lost sight of the lake.

It was truly beautiful, but she wished Nick was with them, enjoying it with a group of wolves and not all alone.

They continued traveling away from Nick's location. The trek took them forever to reach the base of the mountain and the spot where she and her brother had met Aidan. A full moon lighted their way, though with their wolves' night vision and their enhanced sense of smell, they could find their way home without any trouble. The moon reflected off the white snow, making it appear much earlier in the evening than it was. When they reached the rendezvous spot, she woofed at Aidan to thank him. He smiled and licked her cheek.

To her surprise, Aidan shifted and said to Holly, "I'll call you when I reach the cabin to make sure you got back all right. Both of you. If you want, we can meet up here, and we'll go first thing in the morning to try to find Nick."

She woofed her agreement.

"Take care, and if you have any trouble, any trouble at all, you let me know." Aidan shifted back into his wolf.

Appreciating his concern, she licked his face again. That was so uncharacteristic for her. She was never that friendly with a wolf she didn't know. And even with male wolves she knew, she was careful not to show a lot of affection or they might get the wrong idea. With Aidan, she *wanted* him to know how delighted she was to have met him and how much she appreciated his help with finding Nick.

Then she woofed at the men to let them know she treasured their help too. They inclined their heads, smiling. She and her brother tore off after that, hoping to get home before it was much later, hoping that no one had heard the two of them howling. Or Aidan's howl. As far away as they'd been, she didn't believe anyone would have. Not unless some of the pack had ventured a lot farther from the cabins than they normally did, or in the direction she and Greg had gone.

Thankfully, she saw no sign of anyone looking for them. Snowy clouds drifted in, and snowflakes began to float to the snow-covered ground. How Christmas-like it was here! One of these years, she vowed to spend the holidays here.

They finally reached the place where Marianne and their parents had built the snowmen. All five of them. A family. She smiled, thrilled they'd helped her and Greg out. Then she worried. Had anyone caught them at it?

She looked back at Greg. He was rubbing up against one of the snowmen, the tallest of all of them. He was an inch taller than their dad, so it made sense that he was claiming that one as his own, though his hat and scarf gave away the identity too. The snow was beginning to fall faster now, the clouds filling the sky. She hoped Aidan and his men made it back to their cabin all right, and she wondered where it was.

Then she and her brother raced off to reach the cabin as the snowflakes fell.

She suddenly saw movement in the trees to the west. Her heartbeat quickening and afraid it would be Ronald or Jared, she turned to see Marianne coming to intercept them. Sighing with relief, Holly was glad it was just her sister, but then she worried something was wrong at home.

To her surprise, Marianne tackled her in a fun way. Greg stared at them for a moment in surprise. Marianne turned her attention to Greg and tackled him. He growled back in play.

He was a lanky wolf, an aggressive male, but he was easy on Marianne. When he turned on Holly, she wasn't as easy because she was full grown. She wondered if Marianne was here as a subterfuge to pretend to Ronald, if he was nearby, that they had been together for a while, just playing around.

After a good twenty minutes of wild wolf playing, they were panting and trying to catch their breath. The three of them collapsed in the snow and smiled at each other. That's when Holly realized four unsmiling male wolves were watching them from the woods. She wanted to tell them to lighten up, to find something fun to do. To get lost. She hoped no one from the pack would search for Aidan, learn where he and his men were staying, and threaten them to make them leave. She nipped her brother's ear and ran off. Her brother and sister bounded after her, barking and having fun.

When they reached the cabin, she heard voices inside. Jared's and Ronald's. *Crap!*

She stopped at the front deck of the cabin, and she and her brother and sister paused to get a breath. She thought of going to one of the bedroom windows and getting in that way, but they would be latched. Then she nixed that notion anyway. She wasn't sneaking in and making up some lame story to satisfy Ronald.

Holly nosed at her brother and sister to go around back so she could say she had gone off on her own. But they shook their heads. She loved them, even if they gave her grief sometimes.

She woofed at the front door to let her parents know they had returned. Her dad opened the door, his forehead wrinkled with anxiousness. "We were beginning to worry about the...three of you."

Holly woofed in a happy way. Jared folded his arms and gave her a disagreeable look. Ronald was scowling, and her mother cast her a wry smile. Holly hated seeing Ronald and Jared there, but nothing could be done about it.

She raced inside the cabin and back to her room to shift and change. Greg and Marianne followed her lead. She hoped they would let her do all the explaining. She wondered how long Marianne had been away from the cabin though. That was going to be tough to explain. She had no intention of telling Ronald or Jared they'd seen Nick. Since Ronald had kicked him out of the pack, it was none of his business.

When Holly was dressed in a soft, lavender sweater, jeans, and mukluks, she returned to the living room, staying far away from Ronald and Jared, afraid they'd smell Aidan's scent on her. She should have taken a shower first! It wasn't that she couldn't deal with Ronald and his brother, but she didn't want them to hassle Aidan and his men. "Sorry for worrying everyone. I was out looking for Nick, like I always do when I come out here, and went a little farther than I usually do."

"That was partly my fault," said Greg, dressed in jeans, a sweater, and socks, as he joined her. "I was egging her on to go farther than she wanted to, but she didn't want me to show her up, now that she's getting so old." He smiled at her.

She smiled right back at him. He could be so cute when he wasn't being a teen.

"Really," Ronald said.

"Yeah, I went looking for them because it was getting so late. And gave them heck for it too." Marianne smiled at Holly and Greg.

"That's why you tackled us?" Greg asked. "I should have known."

"A little sibling rivalry is fun. But I'm exhausted." Holly gave her brother a sharp look, faked, of course. "It's *not* because I'm getting old. I'm taking a shower and hitting the sack before anyone else takes dibs on the bathroom." She needed to leave before either Ronald or Jared had a chance to smell Aidan's scent on her. At least Greg hadn't touched Aidan, so if he got too close to Ronald or Jared, it wouldn't make any difference.

There was a little matter of supper, but she wasn't mentioning it, hoping Jared and Ronald would leave before she came out to speak to her parents about what had happened.

"Wait," Jared said. "I told you I wanted to run with you. Why didn't you come get me after you made your snowman?"

"You know I always look for Nick when I come here. Besides, you agree with Ronald about banishing Nick. I didn't think you'd want to go against your brother's order and help me seek the old wolf out. That's always my priority."

Jared ground his teeth but didn't contradict her.

"I had such a late start that I didn't want to stop searching for him once I was out there. As *if* I need to explain myself to you."

"Come on," Ronald said to his brother, but then he suddenly turned to face Holly as if it was an afterthought. "You'd better not be seeing that Dr. Denali."

"I saw him at the mall. That's a long way from here. Why would I be seeing him here?"

"Did you locate Nick?" Ronald asked.

"As many acres as there are out here, I probably won't ever. But I won't give up searching for him every time we visit." She'd also come there on her own, trying to find Nick. Ronald knew that too, because she had to let the pack know she wouldn't be available anytime she left. "I want to make sure he's all right. Night all." Holly turned on her heel and headed for the bathroom, walked inside, and shut the door. She began to strip and turned on the shower, hoping that Greg had gone to his room and wouldn't be interrogated next.

When she heard the front door close, she hoped that meant Ronald and Jared had left. A tapping at the bathroom door had her grabbing a towel. "Yes?"

Her mother said, "They're gone. You can come out and tell us what happened. At least your version. Greg's telling us his."

"Be out in a second." No telling what her brother was saying.

When Holly left the bathroom, everyone was sitting down in the living room smiling at her—all but Greg, who was grandstanding. The rest of the family looked surprised. Surely, he couldn't have already told them all that had happened.

"Uh," Marianne said, "he didn't tell us anything much except that you were wolf kissing all over Dr. Denali."

Holly's face felt hot with embarrassment, and she could have slugged her brother. "I was thanking him for saving Joey and for helping us locate Nick." She gave her brother a scathing look, but he only laughed. "Didn't you tell them about finding Nick?"

"You came out of the bathroom too quickly."

"If you must know," their mother said, "once Greg told us about you kissing the wolf—"

"That you have the hots for," Marianne interjected. "Greg's words, not mine. Though you sure gave the doctor a warm hug at the mall too."

"—Marianne was asking for more details," their mother continued.

"Aidan wants to help Nick find a home with another pack. And he helped Greg and me locate him. We couldn't reach Nick before it got dark, and Aidan insisted he return us home rather than go after Nick. It could have been dangerous trying to make it down the ridge to locate Nick. Aidan wants to ask him for a sample of blood for his research, sure, but he also wants to find him a home."

"Oh, that's wonderful," her mom said, tears of joy in her eyes.

"Yes, it really is. I just hope Nick waits for us to return and accepts Aidan's generous offer. Aidan was concerned enough about Greg and me, not wanting to worry the whole pack, that he let go of his mission and returned us to where we'd met him earlier. I know he wanted to escort us all the way home, but he didn't want to cause trouble for us with Ronald and Jared."

"No one discovered we were the ones who made your snowmen," their dad said, "so you're in the clear."

"They're beautiful," Holly said.

"I helped." Marianne sounded proud to have been instrumental in the deception.

"Thank you."

"Are you going to try to see Nick tomorrow?" their dad asked.

"Yes, with Aidan and his men. He said he wants to go first thing in the morning." Holly looked at Greg. "Do you want to run with me again, or do you think it's too much of a risk for both of us to go this time?" She really was glad he'd gone with them, but she didn't want him to feel obligated, especially if it could get him in trouble with Ronald.

"I have to stick to you," Greg said, propping himself on the arm of a chair. "Who else is going to share *all* the juicy details of the trip otherwise?"

"I guess you don't want me to go," Marianne said, not sounding too unhappy about it.

"You have to wolf-pup sit, don't you?" their mother asked.

"It's Greg's turn."

"Glad I don't get saddled with wolf sitting all the time." Her brother had to wolf sit, like everyone in the pack, and he loved playing with the kids, but he had that macho-male teen stuff going on, so he didn't like to let on he enjoyed it.

"Next time we go shopping, the family wants you to be in charge of Joey, not for the run tonight though. I forgot to mention that to Holly," Marianne said.

"Maybe he'll mind you when he doesn't mind Marianne." Holly knew Greg liked to teach the pups the rules from an older teen's perspective, so he was just giving Marianne a hard time.

"We're going for a wolf run tomorrow evening too," their mom said.

"We'll leave super early in the morning, I imagine," Holly said.

Greg groaned. "Make it a night mission."

"No. Hopefully, if we leave before anyone's up and about, we won't get caught."

"Okay, well, just wake me when it's time."

"I will."

In the past, Marianne and their brother would have been running with the other teens. Since Holly had made it known she was interested in helping wolves from other packs, Greg's girlfriend had ditched him—which upset Holly too. She hadn't wanted her actions to affect her family, but she felt the pack had serious issues they needed to deal with. Maybe the other teens in the pack were also ostracizing her brother. That thought stoked her ire.

Marianne's friends had cooled it off with her too, which was part of the reason she was spending so much time wolf-sitting for the Dewitt family.

Holly suspected Ronald wouldn't want her to leave the pack because they needed a wolf doctor, so he'd made some allowances for her rebellion. Otherwise, she assumed she would have been out of the pack like Nick. They knew she'd still want to see her family too. What if the condition reducing wolf longevity was contagious, and she ended up creating the same issue for her family when she visited them? But pack members had met other wolves, and nothing bad had come of it.

For the moment, Holly felt her relationship had strengthened with her family just like it had been before Aidan Denali had come into their lives, spreading word of gloom and doom. But his news had made her think that before long, they could face the same issue as other wolf packs.

The conversation soon switched from the issue with Nick to Dr. Denali being in the area.

"What's going on with you and Dr. Denali?" her dad asked Holly. He and her mother had headed to the kitchen to fix a supper of mini pepperoni pizzas and spinach salad, with the rest of the family joining them.

Greg grabbed one of the carrots his mother had just peeled and began chomping on it. "She wants to work with him to save the wolf world."

Their parents both looked sharply at Holly, but they'd known how she'd felt about this all along!

"It's a free world," Holly said. It would have been, if they didn't have a pack leader who was so controlling. Some packs needed strict rules—or at least some of their members needed stricter rules. She didn't feel anyone in her family did. "And I want to help him with his research."

"She's interested in him too, not just to work with him." Greg filled glasses with ice and water.

"He's a doctor like her." Marianne set the table, and Holly was grateful her younger sister was sticking up for her. "Not to *again* mention he rescued Joey." She seemed impressed by Aidan's actions, and Holly was glad for it.

"Don't you think you're going to cause issues with Ronald if you persist with this?" her dad asked. "I worry about you." He said it in a way that showed his concern, but he didn't sound like he wanted her to stop what she planned to do. Just that he wanted her to be sure she'd thought over the consequences.

"What if he had another doctor working with him on the problem? Maybe he could find a cure faster." Holly couldn't understand all the unfounded antagonism Ronald felt toward anyone who wasn't in their pack. Yeah, sure, they'd had problems in the past. But not everyone was a problem wolf. She was certain not all packs were trouble either. And the pack's past problems didn't mean they'd have any further issues.

"*We* don't have a problem," her dad reminded her.

"*Now*. Not right this very minute. But what if we begin to experience a faster aging process? What if we could have stopped it before it ever became an issue for us?" Holly didn't believe she could come up with the cure just because she knew what Dr. Denali had already discovered, but maybe if they bounced ideas off each other, he could figure it out. Trying to do this all by himself, he had to feel discouraged sometimes.

On the other hand, Aidan might really be a lone wolf about doing his research, and having anyone else suggest something could rankle him. She only knew that his brother was a billionaire real estate mogul and Aidan was just as wealthy from his pharmaceutical research. She'd heard some of the packs were contributing funds for his research, but he didn't seem to have an assistant working with him. She did wonder if he could review her pack members' blood to determine what had changed for the others and why theirs hadn't changed. She was willing to give him her blood, if Aidan thought it would help.

"You know, we should treat this like *The Walking Dead*." Greg sounded serious.

"Zombies?" Holly didn't have the faintest clue how that would be relevant.

"Yeah. One bite from them, and they could turn us into one of them." Greg took another bite of his carrot.

Marianne rolled her eyes.

"Have you discovered any changes in our cells?" her mother asked.

Holly's mother could be more reasonable than her dad, but Holly felt the way she'd asked was a reminder that Holly *hadn't* found any discrepancies, so they *didn't* have a problem. And to leave well enough alone.

"Yes."

Her mother raised her brows.

Holly shrugged. "For those who worship the sun. Even though we have faster healing genetics, the sun's rays are taking a toll on their skin."

"Idabel," Greg said. "She sits out in the sun all the time. Her wolf genes don't have time to repair the damage."

"Exactly. And for those who don't get enough exercise, that's creating health problems." Holly carried the pizzas to the table. "Most of us get plenty of exercise because we love to run as wolves, but a few couch potatoes in the pack don't, and it shows. Eating fruits and vegetables…" She glanced at her dad and brother to point out who she was talking about. Even though her brother had just eaten a carrot, he would often forgo his veggies for strictly meat and more meat.

"We're wolves." Greg served up the pizzas. "Meat eaters. Carnivores, not omnivores."

"We're human too, and that makes us omnivores." Holly and the rest of their family took their seats at the table. "And one of the women in the pack, who drinks only sodas—no milk, no cheese, or other calcium-rich foods—has lower bone density and higher fracture rates. Her bones appear to be much older than they should. So even though we have faster healing genetics, we can sabotage our health by eating too many foods lacking in significant nutrition."

"That's the issue with prematurely aging as humans as well as wolves, but what about the longevity issue with our kind?" her mother asked.

"That's what I want to know about. If I worked with Dr. Denali, maybe I could learn something that would be important to us." Holly lifted a slice of pizza and took a bite.

"Are you thinking of staying with him?" her dad asked. "That could only lead to more trouble for us."

"I want to work with him online, if he's agreeable."

"What if Holly's right?" Marianne asked. "What if she and Dr. Denali are right in assuming we could all end up aging *faster* than humans if we don't learn what caused the others to change? I mean, we could be in real trouble too."

"Exactly." Holly served some of the spinach salad and poured blue cheese dressing over it. "By then, it could be too late for a lot of us." She looked at her parents this time.

One thing they enjoyed as wolves was the family unit that was so important to them. Their parents would be around for a much longer time. Being there when the grandkids and great-grandkids came was something everyone looked forward to. The generations all helped one another over the years. Holly didn't want to lose that connection.

Her mother reached over and squeezed Holly's dad's hand, giving him a pointed look.

He let out his breath on a heavy sigh.

Her dad and brother had been the staunchest opponents of her meeting with the doctor once she'd learned what was going on with the other packs and what he was doing to help resolve the issue. Holly realized what working with him could mean to her family if Ronald found out. Her parents loved their pack and their antique and craft shop in Seattle, and she didn't want them forced out. In addition to that, her patients in the pack would have a hard time finding another doctor. She hoped that would be enough of a reason for the pack leader to leave her family alone.

No matter what, she felt compelled to do this. To help other wolves, even maybe the one who had rescued her so many years ago, if he was still alive. And she really, really liked Aidan.

"What about this other business with the doctor?" her dad asked.

"There is no other business," Holly said.

"Oh, there's *other* business." Greg laughed.

Not to be baited, Holly finished off her pizza and took her plate into the kitchen. "Off to really take my shower now."

"Don't leave without me in the morning if I'm hard to wake," Greg said.

"I'll wake you." Holly headed for the bathroom, and after she showered, she returned to her bedroom. Wearing a pair of flannel pj's—pink and blue and yellow featuring snowflakes, reindeer, and snowmen, making her feel warm and whimsical—she climbed into bed. She pulled her cell phone off her bedside table and saw she had two messages from Aidan, asking if she'd gotten back all right.

She loved how he followed up on his promises and wished she'd checked her phone earlier. In contrast, Jared would tell her they'd do something together and then forget or decide he didn't want to do whatever it was with her, and he'd never let her know he'd changed his mind and made other plans. Without her. Aidan's actions showed he really cared, and she appreciated that. But what would he think when she told him that her people weren't aging any faster than before?

Chapter 8

HOLLY CALLED AIDAN BACK. "HEY, HOW ARE YOU FEEL-ing?" She'd worried he might have overdone it because of the distance they had traveled today, though he might play it down and not be honest with her. She also wondered how he'd take the news when she told him her pack's blood hadn't changed and she was willing to offer hers to him to study.

"I'm fine. Thanks for asking. I wanted to make sure you were okay. I texted instead of calling, in case it was safer for you."

"Ronald and Jared were here, but they didn't suspect anything."

"Good, though you should be able to do as you want as long as it's legal. Do you make house calls?"

"Don't tempt me." Then she frowned, her medical training coming to the forefront. "Are you really feeling poorly?" She was ready to dress and head over to his place right that minute, if he was feeling bad. Even though he had held his head up as a wolf, his ears perked, his tail high, all alpha posturing as they made their way across the wilderness, she swore she'd seen him wince a few times when they stopped to search for scents.

"Truthfully? I think I'm okay, but having a doctor check me out would verify that."

She laughed. "What time in the morning did you

want to look for Nick? We could meet at the same place we did today."

"I don't want you to get into trouble with your pack. I was thinking we'd go it alone this time."

"Thanks for worrying about me, but whenever I'm here, I look for Nick to see how he's doing, so if I don't accompany you, I'll be going with Greg."

"They may be fine with that, but not with you running with wolves who aren't in your pack."

"True. I'm usually alone so I don't risk getting someone else in trouble."

"Except that Greg was with you tonight."

"He's my seventeen-year-old brother, twin to Marianne. He insisted on accompanying me. He wanted to meet you and protect me. I think mostly he wanted some adventure and to see Nick. Besides, we'll end up together anyway, since I'm sure we'll all be headed in the same direction—to the last place we saw Nick."

"I agree. I just don't want you getting into hot water with your pack leader. You didn't have any problems when you arrived home?"

"Jared and Ronald were interrogating my family at the cabin. They were worried because we'd shown up so late. I told them we had gone for a wolf run, looking for Nick. Which is the truth. Jared was mad I had run without him when he'd asked me earlier to run with him."

"I thought you weren't mating him." Aidan sounded disappointed and a little growly.

"I'm not. I think he's more concerned someone like you might be prowling around and catch my attention."

"Was he right?"

She chuckled. "Yeah. Does bright and early work for you?"

"Hell yeah. Meet you in the morning at six. And thanks for giving me an intro to Nick."

"He probably wondered if you were new to the pack, or if my brother and I had given it up and joined your pack instead."

"You can, you know. We're not a typical pack, but my brother and his mate and I would love it if you joined us. Your family would be welcome too. I don't know how you put up with such a disagreeable pack leader."

She couldn't believe he'd offer for her to join his pack. And her family too. Did that mean he would agree to her working with him? Regardless, offering for them to be part of his pack was an honor. "No one can challenge Ronald, and most don't want to leave their homes and businesses behind in Seattle. Oh, and you haven't asked, but if you're equipped to take blood samples there, I'm willing to give you mine."

"Hot damn. Yes, I am, and I'd be forever grateful."

She wasn't sure how he'd react when she gave him the news, but she really hoped that it would make a difference in his research. "We don't have your longevity issues."

He didn't say anything for a moment.

She could imagine how shocked he was to learn that. She'd been just as shocked to learn other wolves were having issues with it. "Are you still there?"

"You said you're still aging at the same rate as before?"

"Yeah."

"You've tested everyone's blood in the pack?" Aidan sounded serious but excited too. "And they're all the same way? Every one of them?"

"Three months ago, yes, ever since you came to get samples from us, I've been doing so. Ronald was worried his own longevity had been affected, but he was also concerned that if someone else had the affected DNA, he or she might infect us. And you know what that means. They'd be kicked out of the pack. I monitor it once every three months. My next time to check everyone's blood is in January."

"What about Everett Johnston, his mother, and his sister, formerly from your pack? I tested them, and they had the same issues as us."

"They left before we knew about the situation, and I couldn't test them. I didn't realize they have the issue too. The same thing with Nick. I don't know if his blood will show the same as yours or if he'll have the longevity we have."

"Do you mind if I come for your blood now?"

"You're kidding. Okay, I know you're not kidding, and I understand. But no. It's too dangerous for you to come into our resort. I'll come to your place. Just give me directions."

"I'll meet you where I did earlier and bring you here."

"Are you sure your head is okay?"

"Hell, it's never been better."

She chuckled. "Yeah, research first, right?" Not that she blamed him, particularly when he'd learned how unique her people's blood was. "Okay, I'll head out."

"As a wolf?"

"It would be faster, and I'd have better luck avoiding being seen." She was excited to be a part of the research in person, not just online. She truly hoped her blood would give him a chance to make a breakthrough in his research. And she'd love to see the results of his work if he had it available.

"I'll meet you there. Ted and Mike will come with me in case we have any trouble."

"All right. I'll let my family know. Be there in a little bit." If her blood could provide a cure for the other wolves, she would be thrilled. Doing something for their kind on a grander scale would be the highlight of her life.

When she left the bedroom, she found her mother sitting on the sofa reading a Christmas mystery and her dad reading a magazine featuring antique Christmas decorations. Seeing her emerging from her room again, they both raised their brows.

"I'm going to see Aidan and give him some of my blood."

Her dad shook his head and continued to read an article in his magazine. This was such a nice getaway for her parents. Others in the pack were manning the store while they were here.

"You're a big girl," her mother said, "but I hope you know what you're doing. If you have any romantic notions about the good doctor, he may burst your bubble. He's interested in his research and solving the longevity mystery. He wants you to help locate Nick for the same reason. That doesn't mean he has any romantic inclination toward you." But her mother was considering her with an inquisitive look, as if she wanted to know if there truly was more going on, after all that Greg and Marianne had said.

Her involvement with Aidan could cause problems for her and her family. On the other hand, she knew she'd have to find a mate outside the pack sooner than later, because no one in the pack suited her, so no matter where she found a mate, it was going to cause trouble.

"When it comes to helping our kind, you know my feelings on the subject," Holly said.

Her dad didn't look up from his magazine and sighed. "You know that wild look in Holly's eyes means she's going after what she wants."

"*Is* he what you want?" her mom asked.

"Mom, Dad, I'm thirty, for heaven's sake. I don't want to cause trouble for the pack, but you know I'll be looking outside the pack for a mate." When both her parents opened their mouths to say something, she held up her hand to stop them. "It doesn't mean Aidan and I have any common interests, except we're both doctors, we both care about Nick, and we want to help the wolves out in any way that we can. Beyond that? Who knows."

"It's Christmas. Miracles can happen." Her dad flipped to another page in his magazine. His comment was in reference to her losing out on settling down with Jared. Since he was the pack leader's brother, that would have given her better standing in the pack. As if she would have lost out.

"Have you ever felt the compulsion to do something you know is right, despite the obstacles?" Holly asked her dad.

He smiled. "Yeah, I mated your mom."

That wasn't what Holly was thinking of, but it fit. Her mom's parents hadn't thought her dad had enough drive to provide for their daughter. Holly liked that her dad was so laid-back, but for herself, she'd prefer someone who was more of a go-getter. "Okay, right. And that's how I feel."

"Dr. Denali might not want your help beyond giving blood," her dad said.

"Which is fine. I at least want to offer my assistance. By examining my blood, maybe he can see why our longevity hasn't changed, or maybe he can tell if it will. Sticking our heads in the sand won't make the problem go away."

Her dad looked up from his magazine. "I agree."

"But you didn't before."

"Ronald has us believing that if we associated with anyone in other packs, we might become affected. If they discover you've gone to see Denali, they may kick us out of the pack."

"If you want me to stay—"

"No, but we may have to leave the pack."

Holly guessed she should have already talked with her parents about this. Not about Aidan, because he was still an unknown quantity, but about her leaving the pack to find a mate and how it would affect them. "Are you okay with that?"

Her dad nodded. "We've all discussed it, and the way we're being treated now, yes. Besides, your mother and I have talked about the issue of never allowing fresh blood into the pack. It needs new blood before we begin to create brand-new issues."

Which was what Holly had been saying all along. "I agree. All right. I'm leaving now. I'll try to return as soon as I can."

"Are you going as a wolf?"

"Yes. I can move faster, closer to the ground, quieter. I love you and Mom." She hugged her dad.

Her mother shook her head. "Just be careful. If he breaks your heart, I'll send your dad to take care of him."

Holly smiled and hugged her mom, and her dad winked at her.

"I might not return tonight, if it's a long way off and might be better just to stay there overnight. He's got two bodyguards, so it's not like I'll be alone with him. Not that I need a chaperone or anything," Holly quickly said.

"You told Greg he could go with you tomorrow morning to look for Nick," her mom reminded her. "You know he'll be hurt if you don't take him with you."

"He'll go with us. We'll meet up at six, same place that we already agreed on. Instead of the two of us meeting Aidan and his men, I'll be with them already, and Greg can join us. I can call him in the morning to wake him, but he might need a firmer touch. Someone prodding him in person."

"You don't want Greg to go with you tonight?" her mom asked.

"No. You know how much he hates giving blood, and if we go over there, he'll feel like he should too. He'd never wake up in time to go in the morning if I dragged him out of bed now. That's saying Aidan offers for me to stay the night. I'm just winging this as I go. I've got to leave, or Aidan and the others will think something prevented me from going."

"Be safe," her dad said. "And have a good time."

"Be careful," her mom said.

"I will be. Thanks." Holly went to her bedroom, yanked off her pj's, and shifted, then ran out of the bedroom.

Her mother opened the front door for her. It was still snowing. Holly hoped it would settle tomorrow. They might not be able to go in search of Nick if it was too bad.

"Love you," her mom said, and Holly licked her mother's hand.

Then she ran into the woods and headed for the path she'd taken before, hoping no one would catch her out in the whiteout, smelling for the signs that she'd come this way earlier. The snow had half buried their tracks already, though she used the same ones as before, passing the five snowmen and continuing to the rendezvous point. She thought back to her parents' comments. She wasn't going to see Aidan because she thought he was mate material, was she?

Of course, she was. Why go tonight of all times? In the middle of a snowstorm? Sure, Aidan didn't want to lose the opportunity to sample her blood. And neither did she. Still, she wanted to see him again, and not just in her wolf coat. And not just for giving blood.

She heard something coming and hid in the woods until she saw three wolves: Aidan and his men. She barked a joyful bark and hurried out to join them. She nuzzled Aidan, who greeted her in kind, and then Ted ran off, Aidan and Holly in the center running side by side, and Mike bringing up the rear. Trying to convince herself the only reason she was doing this was for the sake of their wolf-kind, she couldn't quite contain the excitement she felt at being with other wolves. Males. Bachelors. Not of her pack. She suspected her wolf's biological need was pushing her for more where Aidan was concerned.

She didn't even know if Aidan would want her to stay the night, she reminded herself. Maybe they didn't have enough room for another body. She'd play it by ear. She wouldn't suggest it. She had her pride, after all.

He gave her a wolfish smile.

Okay, so maybe if he didn't suggest it, she would. To hell with pride.

Chapter 9

WHEN THEY FINALLY REACHED THE CABIN, HOLLY expected it to look similar to their rental cabins: front deck, boxy building, maybe high vaulted ceilings, fireplace, and skylights.

Instead, Aidan's place was a mansion of a log cabin with a covered wrap-around deck on the two-story structure, big windows all across the back of the place with a view of the mountains, three natural stone chimneys, and she suspected enough bedrooms so she could have her very own.

When Ted stopped at a wolf door to let her go in first, she sighed. A wolf door too. Of course. The place was owned by wolves, unlike the rental cabins they were staying in.

She entered the house and was wowed all over again. All the floors, walls, and ceilings were covered in honey-oak paneling, making the cabin warm and inviting. A large stone fireplace was situated on one wall, and comfy beige sofas—enough for about a dozen guests—were placed around it. A large Turkish tapestry rug of navy and beiges covered the center of the living area, and she could see a full-size kitchen and dining room that seated a dozen nearby. The flow of the floor plan was open, making the cabin appear spacious and even larger than it was.

Aidan woofed at her to let her know to stay in the

living room and he'd return in a moment. He ran off
to his bedroom, but she stuck with him. She assumed
he was going to get her something to wear, but being a
doctor and a wolf, she wasn't modest. She just wanted
to get on with business, give him a sample of her blood,
and hopefully find a bedroom to sleep in before they had
to get up so early.

He smiled at her and shifted, then dug around in
a couple of drawers. He was so hot: tight ass, well-
developed leg muscles, arm muscles, whole body muscles. He was a hot, hot specimen of a wolf doctor. Who
would have ever thought?

He tossed a pair of light-gray sweats on the bed and
smiled at her because she was gawking at him while she
licked her lips. She couldn't help it. He was total mate
material. Physically, at least. His abdomen perfectly
sculpted. His legs and arms beautifully muscled. His
package oversized. Yeah, he looked like one hunk of a
mate prospect.

She shifted and grabbed the sweatpants, then pulled
them on. When she was slipping the sweatshirt over her
head, he tossed a pair of socks on the bed.

Then he began getting dressed too, pulling up boxer
briefs that cupped his nice, full package in a formfitting,
ultra-sexy way…like she wanted to.

Mike and Ted had retired to other rooms, and she
heard them opening drawers.

"It's hard to believe your pack's longevity hasn't
changed at all." Aidan pulled on a dark-gray sweatshirt,
hiding his beautiful chest.

She sighed. Here she was, thinking about how sexy he
was, and he was still thinking of her as a blood source.

"I was surprised to learn the other packs were having trouble over this, because we weren't. Our pack leader doesn't want us to be 'infected' with the longevity problem, like the other wolves have been. Which means our pack members keep to themselves. The problem with that notion is that some of the younger wolves will have trouble mating wolves who aren't related to them…in the near future! Idiot pack leader!"

"Hell, if you're not worried about me infecting you, I'm certainly eligible and would be great for the gene pool. Top of my class at Johns Hopkins School of Medicine."

She chuckled. "And you're completely modest." Was he serious about being eligible to court her?

He smiled.

Then she frowned, hating what Ronald was doing to the pack. "It's an intolerable situation. The pack doesn't want to lose my skills, so they keep an eye on me. I want to find a way to protect my family, ignore the dictates of the pack leader, and aid the other wolves at the same time."

She'd always wanted to reach out to other packs, learn about them, and befriend them—and she did whenever she could. Jared, who was supposed to have mated her, had dumped her faster than an eyeblink as soon as he knew her views on helping Aidan. He and his brother's version of Big Brother, Big Wolf, were keeping an eye on her.

"Let's get this done quickly so I can return home and get some sleep, or I'll never make it to the rendezvous point tomorrow."

Aidan studied her for a moment. Yeah, she'd

chickened out about suggesting she should stay here for the night. If all he really wanted was her blood, it was probably best to end this fascination for him right now. Though his eligibility and gene pool comment made her think he was interested in more. And she loved his sense of humor.

"I was hoping you would stay the night," he said as he led her out of the bedroom.

Yes! She wanted to pump her fist in victory.

When she didn't jump at the chance to agree with him, he continued, "You can sleep longer, and we'll have breakfast early and head out." Maybe he was afraid she thought he sounded too eager to get to know her better, and she was backing off in a hurry.

"My brother will still meet us at the rendezvous place." She wanted him to know that right away in case he had any trouble with it.

"Sure, that would work. It would be better if you stayed the night."

She frowned at him. "You're not really feeling bad, are you?" The hospital had kept him overnight for observation, she'd learned. Maybe he was afraid he couldn't handle returning her home and then coming back here after all the running they'd done.

He smiled. "Come on." He escorted her the rest of the way down the hall to another room. "I told you I was fine. If you really prefer returning to your cabin after I take your blood, we could do that, but you'll probably need to rest up a little. You'll also be more tired when we start out so early in the morning."

"Not you though."

He chuckled. "Yeah, me too. And the guys after

escorting you back. I wouldn't think of letting you go alone. Though I haven't given up on convincing you to stay here either."

That was more like it. When he opened the door to the room, her lower jaw dropped. "Holy cow. You have a whole lab set up here?" What a setup. She would love to have one as nice as this at her clinic.

"Yeah, it was the only way Rafe could get me out of my house. We set one of these labs up at each of the places we own, so when I stay at them, I can work on my research and visit with the family too."

"What a wonderful brother." She sat down on a chair and rolled up her sleeve. "But you do other stuff besides work, right? When you're visiting with family, for instance." She couldn't imagine anything duller than a mate who was such a workaholic. She tended to be rather a workaholic too, but she wanted more out of life than that. And if she had a mate, she had plans to do all kinds of fun things with him.

"Sure. All guy things. Until Rafe found his mate. She already had a son who wasn't a wolf."

"How did that happen?" Holly was genuinely surprised and hadn't ever heard of a wolf who had a human son. Unless she'd adopted him. But she'd never heard of a wolf doing that either. Unless she'd been turned and her son hadn't been.

"She had a child by a human, and then the child was turned by another child in the pack."

"Oh, okay. I hadn't heard of any wolf having a child by a human."

"It's rare, but it does happen. The father also had some wolf roots. At three years of age, Toby is a *lupus garou*, but he doesn't have control over his shifting like the rest of us do. We're all royals."

"Wow, he must require a lot of supervision. Everyone in our pack is a royal. In my family, we had hardly any human roots for centuries."

"Okay, good to know. I'm trying to determine any common denominator in the longevity stats. As to Toby, the official paperwork shows he is Rafe's son, so no one knows otherwise."

"That's really good of Rafe. I imagine that was an adjustment, from bachelor wolf to the dad of a newly turned wolf child, especially when you don't have anything but bachelors in your group, right?"

"Right. It's been a life-changer, but Rafe slipped into the role without a hitch, and he adores Toby. We all do."

She really admired Rafe for taking a mate who had a son so newly turned and calling him his own flesh and blood. The boy would need that kind of support system, especially to get him through the early years. "That's who you were shopping for at the mall when you rescued Joey."

"Yeah. Toby's a cute kid, and he's got several more protectors: Rafe's assistant manager, our best friend who's another billionaire, and Rafe's bodyguards. When I'm with them, I spend a lot of my time playing with Toby. I don't even think about working. I'm dedicated to finding the solution to the problem, but not to the exclusion of having some fun," Aidan hastily added.

He was good with kids. Aidan sounded like he was offering his résumé, and at face value, he seemed like he might make the perfect wolf mate. "That's good to know. Sometimes when I'm trying to figure something out, I just have to get out of my usual surroundings, and then it comes to me. Taking a break can be a good thing. I love to do all kinds of outdoor activities—camping, hiking, running as a wolf. That helps to ground me."

"I agree, and I'm into nature too. I don't see how a *lupus garou* couldn't be. I also have an interest in herbs for medicinal purposes, jigsaw puzzles for stress relief, rock climbing, skiing…"

"Snowball fights, snowman building…"

Aidan chuckled. "Snow forts…"

"Snow castles, snowshoeing, ice skating."

"Everything but the ice skates for me. No wolf guy would be caught dead in a pair of skates."

She laughed. And she loved a challenge. "Then I'll have to show you how much fun it can be."

"Snow biking." Aidan took a sample of her blood. He was so gentle that she didn't even felt the prick of the needle, and then he bandaged her arm.

"Snow biking?"

"Yeah, with chains on the tires or fat tires. They even have the Iditarod Trail Invitational, a race in Alaska for snow bikers."

"Do you ride in it?"

"Nah. Most of us don't like to be in human competitions. Besides, we just enjoy the ride."

"Sounds like fun. I didn't notice any Christmas decorations here," she said. Their rental cabins weren't decorated either because they weren't staying for the holidays. She was wondering if he planned to leave before then too. She thought how much fun it would be to spend Christmas here at his cabin.

"We were just here to look for Nick for the next

couple of weeks. I'm going to my brother's and my chalet in Colorado for the holidays. Jade, Rafe's wife, will make sure the place is decorated to the rafters. What about you?"

"I'll be home with the family. We do it every year. Nothing wildly exciting."

"Do you wanna come with me? We could make it wildly exciting."

He looked so eager for her to agree that she wondered what he had in mind. She could imagine quite a bit: skiing, snowman building, snowmobiling, and ice skating on a frozen lake, since he was going somewhere nice and snowy. And that would mean her getting him in a pair of skates to ice skate with her. She could imagine going with him to California, running on the beaches, building sand castles, and running through the surf, and that all appealed to her too.

"Mike and Ted are going home to their families. It would just be Rafe, Jade, Toby, two of Rafe's bodyguards, and me. Jade would love to have another woman there so she doesn't feel all the men will gang up on her."

Jade would love to have her there? What about Aidan? Holly wasn't interested in joining them just so she could give Jade company, though she'd enjoy talking to her, sure. But she wanted to get to know *Aidan* better.

Holly wondered if Aidan had rejection issues and thought that if he mentioned Jade needing her, she'd be more comfortable saying she'd go. She couldn't imagine why, as hot as he was and as considerate as he always seemed to be. At least he had been with her so far.

"I'd have to talk it over with my family." She normally made her own decisions without consulting her family, and she thought they'd be pleased, surprised, and maybe a little envious that she would do something different for the holidays. It would be the first time she hadn't been home with the family for Christmas. She wanted to make sure it would be fine with them and that they wouldn't feel hurt.

At the same time, she didn't want to appear too over-eager to stay with him.

Aidan pulled his phone out of his jeans pocket, and she laughed. She hadn't expected him to be so hopeful she'd go with him. "All right." She never went anywhere or did anything spectacular. This could really be fun and special for her.

She took the phone from him and called her mom. "Hey, Mom, it's me. I'm safe at Aidan's house. I've given him my blood, and I'm staying the night."

He smiled, looking pleased to hear it.

"How many bedrooms does the cabin have? Is one of his guards going to sleep on a pullout couch?" her mom asked.

"Uh, let me ask." Holly figured they'd have enough bedrooms, but maybe other rooms were like this lab and not bedrooms. Not that she felt she should have to ask Aidan about the sleeping arrangements, but that was one of her weaknesses. Pleasing her parents to a fault, sometimes. And this was one of those times when she felt she had to satisfy them, just to make them feel comfortable about her staying with a bunch of men she didn't know that well. They were all wolves, after all, to her mother's way of thinking. And her parents hadn't vetted them.

"Do you have enough bedrooms so I'll have my own? Mom wants to know." She smiled at Aidan, wanting him to know it was just the way her family was but that she didn't have an issue with it, one way or another.

She'd like to sleep in Aidan's bed with *him*! She couldn't help thinking about hugging his sexy body.

"And your dad," her mom said. After all, she was with three *bachelor* wolves.

"And Dad." Her cheeks were feeling way too warm.

Crinkles appeared under Aidan's eyes as he smiled. "We have eight bedrooms, three full bathrooms, and a half bath. You have your choice of *any* of the bedrooms."

Holly closed her gaping mouth. She wanted to ask if her whole family could stay there! But then she wondered: occupied or not? Did he mean she could stay with him? Not that she'd suggest it, or do it…but moving right along. "Did you hear Aidan, Mom? I have a choice of any of the five free bedrooms. They have eight total, plus three full baths." She wasn't going to mention he'd offered *any* of the *eight* bedrooms.

"I was thinking it was a cozy cabin rental," her mother said, sounding just as astonished.

"No, it's one of the Denalis' homes. A log cabin *mansion*. Aidan invited me to spend Christmas with his brother, his mate, and their son. If you think you won't miss me too much…"

"Oh my, Holly. You know what you're saying."

"That I'm going to do something different for Christmas for once in my life." With a hot male bachelor wolf who promised her it would be wildly exciting. The trip didn't mean that she was mating him. But she knew that was what her mom would be thinking.

Her mother burst into tears.

"Mom?" Holly felt bad. "Okay, that's fine. I'll be home for Christmas." She had already begun to dream about the fun time she could have at a chalet with Aidan, but not if she broke her mother's heart. She sighed.

"Oh, no, no, that sounds like so much fun! You go, dear. Don't mind me. If I were young and single, I'd jump at this chance." She paused. "*Yes*, I said if I were single and hadn't met you, Eddie." Another pause. "You'll have a great time, Holly. And I'm so excited for you. Our firstborn is finally leaving the wolf den."

Holly laughed. She had a home of her own, so she wasn't exactly living with her parents. She just needed to find the right mate to love and cherish. "Are you sure, Mom? You won't miss me?"

"Of course we'll miss you, but we'd feel terrible if you missed out on such a wonderful opportunity… Yes, yes, she'll have her own bedroom," her mother said to her dad.

Holly stifled a laugh. "You're sure? I mean, about not being with all of you for Christmas?"

"Yes. I'm thrilled for you. This is a wonderful opportunity, and I've always hoped you'd be able to do something like this. About tonight…that sounds like a better notion than running back here and having to get up so early."

"Okay, I know Greg has to be sound asleep, so can you tell him in the morning that we'll just meet him at the same location where we met Aidan and the other men? Same time we planned on."

"Yes, I'll let him know."

"We're headed for bed now." She rose from the chair. "Night, Mom, and thanks."

"I'm thrilled for you, really. Marianne will be envious. Greg probably will be too. You deserve it. Night, honey."

"Night."

Things were really looking up! Hopefully, they could find Nick tomorrow and convince him to return with them to Aidan's cabin, and he'd agree to find a home with a new pack.

But then she thought of leaving her pack doctorless and how Ronald would treat her family if she left for good. She was torn between doing what she wanted to do and what she felt she needed to do to protect her family.

Chapter 10

HOLLY SMILED AT AIDAN, WHO WAS GLAD SHE WAS STAYING the night and visiting with his family for Christmas. He couldn't have been more pleased.

"Let me show you the rooms." Aidan first took her to a room decorated in pinks and greens because it was closest to his room.

"This is mine." Then she moved toward him and clasped her arms around his neck and kissed him, her mouth pressing against his in a sweet way, her luscious breasts pressed against his chest.

He wrapped his arms around her back and pulled her tighter against his body, having wanted to do this ever since she tended to his head wound. Then he kissed her, wolf to wolf, man to woman, sweetly at first, then building the tempo. God, he'd never kissed another wolf like this, never a woman who charged his pheromones like she did.

Even now, their tongues tangled in a way that was wickedly seductive.

She finally broke free from the kiss, though she was still holding on to him, and he loved the way she molded to him. "Thanks for Joey and Nick. I hope my blood will help you in some way with your research."

"If it doesn't, it was still worth it." Being with her was well worth it. "Are you sure you want to sleep here? Not in another room?" He motioned to his own bedroom. Nothing ventured, nothing gained. He had to offer, even if she said no.

"I suspect we'll both get more sleep on our own. We might talk about research all night otherwise."

He smiled. She was probably worried about more than talking.

"Definitely my loss. I might have learned the secret to the longevity mystery. But there will always be tomorrow." Then he frowned. "I've always wondered why Ronald wanted to avoid other packs. Does he worry we'd learn the truth? That your people haven't changed?"

"Probably. Before he even knew about the problem, he worried another pack would try to take us over. Attempts have been made three times in the past. It made an impression on him—the stories retold over the years about our losses, the rival wolves' defeat, and all."

"Okay. I wondered what the deep, dark truth was where he was concerned. Good night, Holly. Thanks for staying the night."

"Thanks for offering. Night, Aidan." She gave him a brief kiss, then closed the door before they got embroiled in anything further.

He felt like he was standing at the top of Glacier Peak with the whole world at his fingertips. More than anything, he wanted to get together with her. Not just for research.

When she'd come to his room, not shy about seeing his nakedness or him seeing hers, he was glad. He swore she'd been seriously thinking of hopping right into his bed with him. She was one hot and very sexy she-wolf.

———∿∿∿———

Early the next morning, Aidan dressed and headed to his lab, wanting to check Holly's blood sample to see if he could make out anything that would indicate why hers hadn't changed. To his surprise, Holly was already looking at a blood sample under the microscope. "See anything?"

She jumped a little, looking guilty that she was using his lab without him being there. "I would have to compare my blood cells with the blood of someone whose cells are aging faster."

"Mine."

"But not this minute. We need to eat and get on our way. Maybe after we search for Nick?" she asked. "I should have asked permission to use your lab."

"You're free to use it anytime you want."

He was worried about the trouble she could get into with Ronald, if someone in the pack learned she was running with Aidan and his men. Maybe she hadn't planned to search for Nick all that long today and intended to return to her pack for the rest of the time. But he planned on spending all their daylight hours looking for the older wolf. Then again, he would appreciate any time he could be with her.

"You probably have to return to your resort early today."

"I can do what I want. And I will. Let's see how it goes. We might find Nick early on, if he wants us to, and I'm really hoping he does."

"I am too." He took her place at the microscope and studied the cells. "Beautiful."

She laughed. "Inside and out, right?"

He looked up at her. "Yeah." And he wasn't talking about blood cells.

"Breakfast is served," Ted called from the kitchen.

"I'd love to work with you on this. We could do video chats to share information. If you think it won't get you in trouble with your pack leader," Aidan said.

"I've love to work with you also. I've got pictures of the blood samples I've taken of my pack members and the actual refrigerated cells," she said as they headed downstairs to the dining room. "I'm worried we might end up having the same trouble as the other packs. I've wanted to see if we could work together on this, but I've been concerned about how Ronald will react. He could banish my family from the pack, and anyone else who agrees with me giving you the information. Even though it might help my people if I shared their blood samples with you without their knowledge, ethically I can't."

"I understand, and I would feel the same way. You're sure you're okay with coming with us today?" Aidan pulled out a chair for her to take a seat at the dining table.

"I am. Are you sure I can't help with anything?" she asked Ted.

"Just to tell us what you want for breakfast. We've whipped up omelets and pancakes."

"I'll have an omelet, with cheese and bell peppers, if you have them."

"I sure do. Pancakes for you, Doc?" Mike asked.

"Yeah. Thanks."

Mike served the pancakes while Ted added cheese and bell peppers to Holly's omelet.

"In response to your question about going with you, yes. Ronald knows I'm always searching for Nick when I visit here. The part about me running with you? That's his problem. We're working on the same mission, so he can deal with it. My parents are all right with it. They know where this can lead if Ronald goes ballistic. Which is always a possibility."

Ted served her omelet. "Coffee? Tea?"

"Coffee with cream and sugar, thanks," Holly said. "I thought you said they were your bodyguards."

"Yeah, but they like to cook. Good thing for me. I cook, but I was skipping meals all the time. They keep me on more of a schedule."

She shook her head. "You're a doctor. You should know better."

"Agreed." Ted brought over his own breakfast omelet. "That's what we kept telling him. He gave in and started to listen to us."

Mike sat down to eat pancakes. "Only because we're persistent."

Aidan chuckled. "They were hungry too and didn't want to eat without me."

"Maybe we should talk to your pack leader and change his mind about talking to other packs," Ted said.

"No. He's stuck in his ways, and if you hassle him, he'll get ugly really fast."

"If your family has to leave the pack, we'll help them get resettled in California, if they'd like," Aidan offered. He didn't want her family to feel they'd have to abandon all they'd worked for because of their pack leader's issues, but if it happened, he wanted them to know they had the Denalis' help.

"Thank you. I'm sure they'd appreciate knowing that. Change is hard for everyone, which is why most of us just put up with Ronald and his crap."

Aidan got a call on his cell and looked at the caller

ID. "It's your brother." He answered the phone. "Hey, this is Aidan. I'll hand the phone over to your sister."

"Thanks. I wish I'd known she was going to stay with you last night. I could've gone with her and just left from there. Jared's been prowling around the cabin, waiting to see if Holly leaves here, I suspect. I'm headed out through my window, and I'll meet you west of where we met yesterday to throw him off my tracks if he should follow me. I don't expect him to. He wants to check in with my sister, I figure."

"Okay, that sounds good. Here, I'll let you talk to your sister." Aidan handed the phone to her.

"Hey, Greg. What's up?"

While her brother talked to her, they finished eating and cleared away the plates.

"Are we going to have trouble?" Ted asked.

"Maybe. We'll just have to keep an eye out for Jared. I suspect he won't try to fight us, but he may return to the cabins to gather reinforcements if he wants to make an issue of this. Or tell Ronald," Aidan said.

"That would be great if she could send the photographs of the pack members' blood cells." Ted loaded the dishes in the dishwasher. "I overheard the two of you talking when I came down to make breakfast."

"Yeah, it would, but I'm not counting on it." Aidan poured himself another cup of coffee.

Then Holly said to her brother, "Are you sure you want to meet with us? You could just be a decoy, if you feel the need to be adventurous." She took a deep breath. "Okay, so you still want to go with us. We can use another pair of eyes and your nose to help us, so we'll see you in a little bit. If Jared chases after you, go back to the cabin. I'll return home sooner than I planned." She paused. "Yes, I'll be home tonight."

Aidan was disappointed she wouldn't return with him to the cabin. Both Ted and Mike looked at him. He told himself he'd wanted her to stay with him because of her interest in his work, but it was more than that.

"See you soon." She ended the call and found everyone watching her. "You're as bad as my family."

The guys all laughed. After Ted finished putting her plate in the dishwasher, everyone stripped and shifted in their rooms, then joined one another at the wolf door.

Aidan hoped they didn't run into any trouble with Ronald or Jared and that Greg would be all right. They headed out, but when they finally reached the rendez-vous point, they didn't see any sign of Greg. They'd had farther to run, but if he'd tried to run too far west, he might take more time to reach this spot. Still, Aidan could sense everyone's anxiousness.

Aidan woofed at them and headed west. He hoped Greg was going to come directly east to meet up with them. He hoped they didn't miss him. Ted woofed and stayed put. He was going to wait in case Greg took a different route. But Mike stayed with Aidan and Holly as their protection.

About a mile away, they smelled Greg's scent. A trail through the snow led north. They followed it, and Aidan was glad it was just Greg's, with no one following him. When they continued north, Aidan suspected Greg wasn't moving back east to rejoin them. Was he trying to be a decoy, as Holly had suggested? Then again, Aidan hadn't noticed other tracks indicating anyone was tailing Greg.

Aidan was torn. He didn't want to continue in this direction and leave Ted behind, but he didn't want to miss Greg if the teen ended up turning east and heading back south to meet up with them at the original location. He decided to keep moving. If they finally found Greg and he wasn't heading in the rendezvous direction, Aidan could howl for Ted to join them.

Because of the fresh powder from last night's snowfall, the snow in the area created a prime avalanche zone. While looking for the teen wolf, Aidan had been watching for any small slab releases as he ran through the snow. As wolves, their footprint wouldn't be as great as the other forms of locomotion. Still, he was keeping an eye out for any movement that could indicate unstable snow and a potential slide.

A breeze picked up, sweeping the top snowflakes off the base and creating a snow fog, with clouds covering the sun above so that the snow and sky were gray, and then Aidan saw a wolf coming toward him. *Greg.* Relief washed over Aidan and he woofed at him.

Greg woofed back and hurried to join them. Holly nipped her brother, gently scolding him.

They were about three miles from where they'd left Ted. Aidan raised his chin and howled. He didn't want to leave Ted in suspense, even if they were a long way off. From far away, he heard Ted howl back. He was coming.

Greg moved away from them toward the way he had come, indicating he wanted them to follow him. Holly woofed at him to tell him to stay until Ted joined them.

He kept pacing, and Aidan suspected Greg had a lead

on where Nick was. Aidan woofed at Mike to stay there and wait for Ted. They could follow him and the Grays as soon as Ted joined him.

Mike frowned.

Aidan knew Mike wanted to stay with him to protect him. Aidan woofed at him again. This time, Mike inclined his head.

Aidan looked at Holly to see what she wanted to do. She moved toward her brother, who was waiting in anticipation, his tail straight, his ears perked, and Aidan nodded and moved toward Greg. With a grateful wave of his tail, Greg headed back the way he'd come, and Aidan waited for Holly to follow in Greg's footsteps. Aidan brought up the rear to watch their backs.

They had traveled about a mile when Aidan got a whiff of another wolf's scent. Nick's?

Greg suddenly stopped in his tracks. Aidan thought he might have seen Nick, but when he didn't budge, Aidan moved to the right of him to see what he was watching. A grizzly fishing at a stream.

They were way up above and a long distance from him with a beautiful view of the mountains. From this vantage point, Aidan could see the trail Greg had made in the deep snow, and it led all the way to the creek. Aidan made the decision to stay put. They could go way around the bear, but he opted for staying here for a while. Even though Greg looked anxious to keep pushing on, he waited for Aidan to make the decision. Holly was watching Aidan, shaking her head, telling him not to tangle with the grizzly.

Aidan wouldn't risk their lives by following Greg's trail at this point. If the grizzly had been attacking Nick, that would have been a different story. Aidan licked Holly's muzzle in an affectionate way, and her jaw dropped before he gave her a toothy wolf smile, then watched the bear again. He was serious about her joining his pack.

The grizzly finally moved off downstream. Aidan began to lead the way this time. He'd follow his nose and Greg's trail. He wanted to be in the forefront if they ran into trouble.

They had made it down the ridge into the valley when Mike woofed from where they'd been a short while ago on the ridge. Both Ted and Mike were standing at the crest, and then they began to make their way down the ridge. Aidan and his group waited for them, the five of them more of a threat to a grizzly.

When his bodyguards reached Aidan and the others, they greeted them, Ted and Mike wagging their tails, glad to be with them.

Aidan again led the way until they reached the stream, where he looked downstream to see if the bear was anywhere in sight. It wasn't. They moved across the cold stream, and Aidan again followed Greg's trail.

They headed back into the woods. Then Aidan smelled a campfire. Someone was cooking fish.

Nick? Hopefully it was, and he'd stay put while they tried to reach him.

Holly suddenly came around Aidan and moved in front of him on the trail. He figured she wanted to be the first one to greet Nick so as not to alarm him.

She suddenly woofed, letting him know they were coming.

They went through some underbrush, and then

Aidan saw the white-haired, bearded man hunched over a fire.

"Well, hell's bells," the older man said, looking over at them. "What took you so long to get here?"

Chapter 11

HOLLY WAS SO THRILLED TO SEE NICK ALL BUNDLED UP next to his fire that she ran to him and jumped at him like an unruly pup. She woofed in greeting. He ran his hand over her head in a heartfelt caress, his eyes tearing up. God, she knew he'd missed the pack and felt bad to be out here. He couldn't have been satisfied with living like this.

She was glad he was happy to see them and hadn't run off, angry with her for being part of the pack that had banished him.

His response was a small smile, and she swore he looked just like Santa Claus with his white beard and hair, his whiskers partly frozen. "Welcome to my camp. Is he your mate?" He glanced in Aidan's direction as the wolf moved in beside her.

She shook her head.

Greg woofed, wagging his tail.

"I'm glad to see you too, Greg." Nick motioned to the tent. "Change of clothes inside if you want to converse with me human style," Nick told Aidan.

Holly would let Aidan do all the talking. In the meantime, her brother sat by the fire, eyeing the fish in the frying pan, looking ready to forget his manners and eat it. Ted and Mike joined him by the fire, appearing as though they were going to stop him if he even thought of eating Nick's meal. She was glad to see Nick seemed to be doing well, and by the look of it, he was eating and was perfectly healthy, though he'd lost some weight.

Aidan went inside the tent, and within a few minutes, he had shifted, thrown on some warm-weather clothes, and joined them by the campfire. He sat on a log that would probably be used for the fire later, unless they could convince Nick to go with them. Holly settled down next to Aidan, her body resting against his leg, and he reached down and ran his hand over her head.

"I'm Dr. Aidan Denali."

Nick took a seat on a camp chair. "The one who was looking to take blood from all the wolves and figure out what's wrong with us or, I should say, with others of our kind who aren't in the pack. I know. Everett Johnston called me a while back and told me, concerned I might be like everyone else and need to have my blood checked. What difference does it make for an old wolf like me?" He raised a white brow. "You came all the way out here to track me down to take my blood? It's half frozen." He motioned to Holly. "At least she was worried about my health, I 'spect. I know you tried calling me too, but I wasn't in the mood to talk to anyone in the pack."

"That's not the only reason we were trying to track you down," Aidan said. "If you'd allow me to, I'll help you find a pack you would like to join. If you're interested."

Looking surprised at that bit of news, Nick's gray eyes widened a bit. "You're with a pack?"

"We don't have an official pack, but yeah, if you'd like to join us, we'd be glad to offer you a home. I've been testing wolves' blood wherever I can find a pack. I've gotten to know several and keep in touch with all of them. That means a lot of packs you could check out, and I'm sure you'll find one that will suit you. Everett Johnston was the one who called me about you."

"He was banished like me. Did you know that? He was the accused bank robber."

"Wrongly accused, and that was all cleared up, but he had no intention of returning to the Seattle pack. Then I spoke with Holly, and she confirmed you were living in the area. She was trying to check on your well-being, but she hadn't been successful."

"What does Ronald say about it? I can't imagine he would like Holly and Greg out here with you and... your friends?"

"My bodyguards, Ted Gallagher and Mike Stallings. And I'm sure you're right about Ronald, but he has no say in where you go, and Holly and Greg felt compelled to find you. Running around by themselves was too dangerous up in this area," Aidan said. Holly licked Aidan's cheek. He smiled at her and wrapped his arm around her to give her a hug.

"What if I visit another pack and don't like the people or their politics? Or they don't like me?" Nick asked. "I could be trading one bad pack leadership for another."

"I've met the others. They've all taken in other wolves, welcomed them, even if they've been newly turned. Ronald and his men are an exception to the rule. It's completely up to you. My brother has a couple of private planes. He has tons of resources. We'd be willing to fly you all over to visit with each of the packs and to visit with my family too. If you don't like what you see, you can return here, if you'd rather live like this. Though it means Holly risking her neck looking for you, concerned for your welfare. She won't be giving up on you. If you like one of the packs, even the couple we've located in the Scottish Highlands, and they're agreeable, then you can stay with them."

"Scotland? And wear kilts? No, thank you." Nick rubbed his whiskers. "You'd do this for me just because I'll give you some of my blood?"

Aidan smiled. "No. As much as I want to find a cure or solution to this problem, you don't have to give me any of your blood. I still want to offer you a chance to be with a pack again. One that's more agreeable and that you enjoy being with. Unless you like living in the wilderness all on your own."

Holly knew Nick didn't. She just prayed he wouldn't be too proud or stubborn to take Aidan up on his offer.

Tears filled Nick's eyes again, as if he'd never thought anyone would offer to take him to live with another pack and he might find a home again. She wanted to hug him. Instead, she got up and licked his cheek. He laughed and patted her back. "Hey, Doc, it's okay. I know you wanted to see me and make sure I was okay, but I wasn't ready to make any changes in my life after Ronald kicked me out. I was feeling down, depressed, sorry for myself, and angry with the world when I lost Millicent. She and I have had a lot of long talks while I've been out here." He glanced at Aidan.

"I'm not crazy. I just had to do a lot of soul searching. I'm not cut out to be the Santa Claus of the Glacier Peak Wilderness. It's time to have a nice, toasty-warm home to live in again. And real people to talk to." Nick took the frying pan off the fire and motioned to the golden, pan-fried cutthroat trout. "I was going to have this, but...have you got steaks at your place?"

Holly looked back at Aidan, hoping he had steaks, just to convince Nick to go with them. Though she suspected the old wolf would go with them even if all he got to eat was more fish.

"Absolutely, and lots of other good food you might want to eat. My two bodyguards are practically gourmet chefs. You'll have a five-star meal for sure. And a soft bed in your own bedroom and a hot shower. You can warm yourself by the fireplace."

"Steak, seared on both sides, works for me." Then Nick frowned. "Whiskey?"

"Got a fully stocked bar," Aidan said. "And you can visit the other wolf packs via a private plane. Meals on the flight too."

"Well, hell, what are we waiting for?"

"Would you prefer to run as a wolf to the cabin, and we'll carry your gear?" Aidan asked.

"Hell yeah. These old bones aren't meant for this much cold for this long. For a while, it was fine, especially when it was warmer, but I'll sure take you up on a warm bed, a hot shower, and a hot meal."

Greg was eyeing the freshly cooked fish, and Nick dished it up on a tin plate for him. "Here. Knowing you, you could eat this *and* a steak. Have at it. Hate to have swum in a cold lake for the meal only to throw it away."

Wagging his tail, Greg woofed, then gobbled up the fish. Holly wasn't surprised. She swore all four of his wolf legs were hollow.

Ted suddenly walked inside the tent. He called out from inside, "Just shifting and getting dressed." He came out just wearing a sweater, pants, and socks. "Doc, why don't you run as a wolf too? I can carry all of Mr. Cornwall's gear."

"Okay. Just know there's a grizzly bear somewhere near the stream where we were," Aidan warned him but waited for Nick to use his tent to strip and shift before Aidan went in to remove Nick's spare clothes.

"All right," Ted said.

"Yeah, that grizzly has been in the same area as me for a while. Luckily, he's been finding his own food and has left me alone." Nick entered his tent, and a few minutes later, he came out of it as a pure white wolf.

Aidan went inside and removed Nick's clothing, then shifted and came back out as his beautiful gray-wolf self. Holly noticed the men all watching her as she eyed Aidan. They were sure to think she had more of an interest in him than just sharing her blood and helping him in his research.

Ted had taken the parka and boots Nick had been wearing and finished dressing.

Holly was certain Aidan hadn't offered Nick help to find a pack just to prove something to her. He genuinely cared. She hoped Aidan had enough steaks for everyone, because now that Nick had mentioned it, and after the long hike they'd made, she was looking forward to having one too.

She suspected Greg would like to join them. He'd been instrumental in finding Nick. She was sure Aidan would welcome him to eat lunch with them too.

They waited while Ted packed up the tent, put out the campfire, and rigged up the backpack so he was carrying everything and ready to move on.

They made their way across the stream and all the

way to the area they had to climb. Ted was leading the way, carrying Nick's gear. He was setting the pace because as a human carrying all that equipment, he was the slowest of the party members. Nick followed after that, moving slower than the younger wolves, but he would still walk faster than poor Ted. Holly thought maybe Mike would offer to carry some of the burden, but she suspected he felt he needed to be a wolf to help protect everyone if they should run into trouble. Greg followed behind Nick, Holly next, then Aidan, and Mike was bringing up the rear.

It was a long wolf run back to the place where they were supposed to have met up with Greg, but before they got there, Ted paused for a break and drank some of Nick's bottled water. The wolves had paused to drink out of a stream.

"Hey, Doc, I know you would have asked if you had thought of it, but Greg and Holly are welcome to join us for steaks at the cabin, right?" Ted asked.

Aidan woofed. Greg was panting, his tail wagging enthusiastically.

"That is, if there's no problem with Greg and Holly going with us," Ted added.

Greg vigorously shook his head. Holly barked to say it wasn't a problem.

"Okay, it's a deal. Since we don't need to go to the meeting place, I'll take us in a more direct route back home." Ted started off again, and the wolves followed him.

Holly was glad they were taking a more direct route so they'd be farther away from her own cabins. She was afraid Jared might be looking for her at this point. Maybe he'd be searching for Greg now too. At least they hadn't run into Jared so far. And they'd found Nick. She was so glad he was healthy looking, a little thinner than he had been, his cheeks and nose a little windburned, but his step was sure, and he seemed just as strong as before. It was easy for anyone to break a leg out here or sustain a sprained ankle, as rugged as the terrain was. He could have even incurred injuries if he'd had to fight over food and territory with a grizzly or a pack of wild wolves when he was running as a wolf. People who traveled alone in the wilderness took dangerous risks. That had worried her.

She'd also been concerned about him finding enough food, since he was hunting for whatever he could get.

She thought the men worked well together and were considerate of each other's well-being. They took another couple of breaks for Ted. Mike woofed at him, and she figured he was giving him a hard time about taking so many breaks. Or maybe he was offering to switch places.

Ted shook his head.

But then Mike pulled at the backpack.

"We'll be there in another couple of hours," Ted said. "I could hike all day with a pack on my back. I'm fine. You just want to show off to the doc."

Mike woofed. Aidan smiled, and so did Holly. She suspected he meant showing off in front of her, not in front of Aidan. The guys were funny.

They headed out again, and she thought they'd make it to the cabin without incident until they saw elk running their way. That's when she saw a pack of wolves hunting them. Had to be wild gray wolves.

Holly and her party were in the direct path of the

stampeding elk. Everyone stood for a second watching the direction the elk were headed, as if they thought they'd suddenly veer off, but they weren't changing course, and she and the others scattered, racing out of harm's way.

Chapter 12

AIDAN BARKED A WARNING, TRYING TO SCARE THE ELK INTO stampeding in a different direction. Ted dropped his bundle and ran through the snow toward the trees for protection. The rest of the wolves scattered, though Holly was trying to protect Nick. Greg had headed in a different direction. Mike was trying to cover Ted's retreating backside since he was the slowest, sinking deeper into the snow in the snow boots. The wolves were lighter, their weight spread out more, and they stayed on top of the snow better.

His adrenaline pumping hard, Aidan stood firm, attempting to deter the rampaging elk, hoping he and the others didn't get into a confrontation with the wild wolves. Heart racing, he continued to bark.

The elk turned at the last minute, scattering snow in their wake, so close they sprayed him with it. The wild wolves were too busy hunting to bother with the scattering wolf pack. Relieved the wild wolf pack and their prey were headed away from them, Aidan heard a startled yelp and a bark. He spun around. Greg was way off to his right, stopping in his tracks to see what the matter was, Mike off to his left, running to see who was in trouble, and Ted was still headed for the trees. There was no sign of Nick or Holly.

His heart in his throat, Aidan raced through the snow in the direction they had taken, following their tracks and their scents when he saw a warning depression in the snow and slowed his approach. Ted turned around and moved back toward Aidan. Aidan barked at him to be careful. If what he feared had happened to Nick and Holly, he didn't want anyone else to risk falling into a crevasse. He prayed that hadn't occurred, but then his worst fears were realized when he heard Holly howl from what sounded like the center of the earth—directly ahead of him.

He howled to let her know he was nearly there. But he needed to dress and use a rope to help get them out. He'd have to climb down into the crevasse while the others held on to the rope. They'd have to shift, dress, and help Nick and Holly climb out. That was, if neither was injured.

Aidan lay down on his belly and inched forward to the edge of the hole they'd fallen through, sending a shower of snow down below. They must have fallen thirty feet or so. He woofed, trying to reassure them. Nick was sitting on a narrow ice ledge with Holly, the two of them looking up at him, ears perked.

"I'm getting Nick's climbing equipment from his pack, and I'm taking the same path that I just went on," Ted said, sounding a little winded as he hurried through the snow to reach Aidan. He was being careful too in case the snowbridge—an arc across the crevasse—stretched out to where he had already walked and he had just been lucky that it hadn't caved in on him.

Aidan woofed at him in acknowledgment.

Mike had returned to where Ted had dropped the camping equipment and was trying to drag the backpack with his teeth, but it was too heavy and sank into the snow too much.

"I'll get it, Mike," Ted said. "Did both Holly and Nick fall in?"

Aidan woofed an affirmative. He saw Greg running back to join them, but Aidan barked at him to take it slow and watch for crevasses. They couldn't afford another dangerous accident on their hands if Greg should fall through the snow and ice.

Aidan looked back down at Nick and Holly, surveying the long way down and the darkness below them that appeared to be a bottomless pit. He was damn glad they'd landed on the ice bridge and that it was holding their weight. From here, he couldn't tell if either of them was injured. Both were panting, looking straight up at him, willing him to come rescue them.

He heard Greg getting closer and woofed at him to stop where he was. He felt like they were on a minefield. One false step and the snow would give way to their deaths if they weren't as lucky as Holly and Nick.

Then he heard Ted and Mike coming up from behind him, and he turned to watch them, still on his belly, concerned that even where he was lying could be just a thin shelf of snow.

Ted must have assumed the same thing, because he set the pack down in the snow and quickly began unpacking it. He soon had spread all Nick's clothes out. Aidan inched back from the crevasse and then got up and ran over to the pack. He shifted, which caused his muscles to warm while he was exchanging his wolf body for his human form. The cold quickly slammed into him as he started jerking on clothes. Greg was inching toward Aidan, so Aidan quickly said, "I need you to be a lookout in case we have any other trouble—that wolf pack or elk, grizzlies, anything. We'll be concentrating on getting your sister and Nick out. You have to watch for other trouble."

Greg woofed, sounding eager to be the guard wolf.

Mike was waiting for his mission.

"Mike, I need you to shift and dress. I'll see if either Holly or Nick is injured. I'll take a bundle of clothes so they can shift and dress, and we'll bring them up that way. If either are injured, we may have to take the injured one up as a wolf."

"Okay," Ted said, getting a rope and an ice ax ready. Then he began bundling enough clothes for both Holly and Nick. "He only has one more pair of boots."

"They're too big for Holly. She can wear socks and shift, as long as she hasn't been injured. And he'll need the parka." Aidan pulled a pair of ice cleats over the boots.

Ted took off the other parka. "For Holly."

Aidan pulled the parka on so he'd warm it up while he climbed down to reach them. He took the bundle of clothing and shoved it into a lightweight hiking backpack, then added laser ice screws, an ice ax, and two ice picks, then pulled the backpack on. After securing the only helmet Nick had on his head, Aidan turned on the lantern. Holding on to the rope and carrying the ice ax and one of the ice picks, he moved low toward the edge of the crevasse while Ted and Mike held the other end of the rope farther away from the opening.

"Coming," Aidan called to Holly and Nick.

Holly woofed at him. He worried about Nick because he'd been quiet the whole time.

Aidan had nearly reached the edge when half a foot of snow collapsed in front of him. His heart thundering in his ears, he stopped dead in his tracks. *Now* he was at the edge. He remained still, not wanting to send another avalanche of snow on top of them.

He peered down at them. They were both covered in snow, but they didn't dare shake it off. Their double coat of fur would keep the snow from melting onto their skin and chilling them.

"I'm coming down."

Ted moved cautiously toward where Aidan was, and then Aidan moved around to climb into the crevasse, noting that as soon as he was using the cleats and ice ax and pick to descend, he could see he'd been lying on a shelf about a foot thick that went back toward Ted about three feet. "Snowbridge a foot thick, three feet in your direction, Ted."

"Gotcha. Watch yourself. You know Rafe would fire us if he knew you went down into the crevasse and we stayed up here."

"I'm counting on you and Mike helping to pull everyone up." Aidan continued to work his way down to them slowly, digging the ice ax in. The snow and ice gave way, and he slid a few feet, his heart taking a dive.

"You okay?" Ted asked, worried.

"Yeah. Be down to them in a few."

"Good. It's starting to snow."

Great.

Aidan's breath came out in a frosty mist as he continued making his way down. Seeing the deep, never-ending chasm on either side of their ledge, he felt his blood turn to ice. He was afraid one misstep by either of them while they attempted to shift and dress could mean their demise.

"If we have to, we can call for a helicopter rescue," Ted said.

"Not while any of us are wolves, we can't." Aidan looked down: another fifteen feet or so to go. He wasn't sure he could stand on the ledge with them, or if Holly or Nick would have the strength to climb up, even with the aid of the rope. Had she ever climbed an ice mountain before?

Nick had the gear, so he probably knew how to climb, but could he? Aidan noticed the way Nick was holding his front paw. He was clearly hurt.

Aidan moved carefully down a few more feet, shaking more snow loose. He was sweating despite the cold. When he finally reached them, they tried to make room for him. Snow fell from their wolf coats and showered down into the dark abyss.

He didn't want them to move an inch, yet there was barely any room for him too, and the extra weight on the shelf concerned him. He tried to cling partly to the snow wall behind him and began to remove the pack, holding on to the ice pick stuck in the ice at the same time. Everything was a struggle. He kept worrying he'd lose the pack and then somehow he'd have to carry them up using the rope. He couldn't think like that. Only positive thoughts.

Holly shifted. He hadn't wanted her to shift yet. But she took up less space in her human form, and she could help him with the pack. She took hold of it and set it at her feet, then began pulling out clothes to wear. "Are you injured?" Aidan asked Nick.

He nodded.

"Holly?"

Holly yanked on one of Nick's long sweaters. "I'm fine, scrapes and bruises, but otherwise okay."

"Good." Aidan managed to carefully maneuver onto the ice ledge, the cleats keeping him from slipping, but Holly would be in socks, the cold hard on her feet.

He reached her, pulled her into his arms, and gave her a kiss. "God, you scared the hell out of me. Both of you." He pulled off the parka, then helped her into it. "I need you to go up first. Can you climb?"

"I watched you come down."

Which meant the only training she had was his one demonstration. He couldn't risk her going up by herself. It would be too dangerous. "Okay, Nick, can you climb up with an injured wrist?" Aidan asked.

He nodded.

"I'll help you get dressed." Aidan had wanted Holly to get on her way so he'd have more room to help Nick. He was worried one of them would bump into one of the others and they'd all fall off the ledge, not to mention he wasn't sure how sturdy it was with all their weight on it.

"I read about this scientist who fell seventy feet into a crevasse. He was alone, big mistake. He'd broken his arm and several ribs," Aidan said, wanting to share a survival story with them to assure them they weren't as bad off and could do this.

Nick shifted, and Aidan examined his wrist. It looked swollen and slightly discolored. He began to help him dress.

"Is this an inspirational story, Doc?" Nick shivered, his heart thumping wildly.

Aidan smiled. "Yeah. He managed to get out. If some nerdy scientist can do it, Santa Claus, who normally climbs into and out of chimneys, should be able to, right?"

Nick gave him a wry smile. "I just need a little magic."

"What happened to the scientist?" Holly sat down and pulled on a pair of sweats. And then the socks.

"Not only did he have a broken arm, right arm too, but also a dislocated shoulder and several bad cuts and bruises from hitting all that ice on the way down. Did I mention he went solo? There was no one to rescue him. No one to know he was even in dire straits. The only way he was going to get out of there was on his own. But he did have enough presence of mind to call for help."

"He was alone," Holly reminded him.

"Yep, but he had service and Facebook messaged his friends, calling for help. Amazing, isn't it? He knew no one would find him in the crevasse in time, so he had to make the climb out. He thought about that other guy who had to cut off his arm to free himself when he fell into a crevasse and was wedged between rocks."

"Don't mention it," Holly said.

"Yeah, made me think of that too. It took him five hours of climbing with the ice ax, but despite all his injuries, he managed to make it out."

"All on his own. I hear ya, Doc. And I suppose you still want my blood after all this."

Aidan helped Nick on with his boots and cleats. "Yeah, I sure as hell do. In return, you'll have the best steak dinner you've ever had the good fortune to enjoy."

Nick smiled. "You're all right, you know?"

"Thanks. You are too. Let's get out of here so we can have that meal." Aidan gave him the helmet and helped him with the chin strap. "You're right-handed, correct?"

"Yeah. This should be a piece of cake. I've been doing this sort of thing for years."

"Falling down crevasses?"

Nick laughed and shook his head. "Not the falling into them, just the mountain climbing." He took hold of the rope. "Coming up!"

Aidan held the rope below him as Nick made the climb using the ice ax and ice pick, though he was having trouble using the ice pick in his left hand. Still, he worked through the pain to get where he needed to go.

"I can do what he's doing," Holly said with assurance.

"You could, if you had boots and cleats." Aidan didn't think she'd have the upper body strength to pull herself up and out of the crevasse. It was tough going for a strong male. Nick would have trouble pulling himself over the shelf when he got to that point. Any guy would. But being older and having a sprained or broken wrist, he would have a harder time. Aidan hoped Ted could help pull him out.

"I can do it. There's a lot of snow. I can dig my sock-covered feet into the snow and get some purchase. As long as I do what Nick is doing, making sure the ax is secure before I pull myself up farther, I can do it." Holly was so adamant that Aidan wished he could say yes.

"We can't risk it." He wasn't about to let her try. One false move and she could fall to her death.

She folded her arms. "Then what? Don't tell me you're going to try to carry me out of here."

"As soon as Nick is over the top, yes." He pulled her close while he held the rope so he could share his body heat with her as they watched Nick climbing. He had made it about ten feet, and the going was slow. He had to keep pausing to catch his breath. Aidan hoped he hadn't injured his ribs or anything else. "You're doing great, Nick. You're getting close."

Nick looked up. "Yeah." He was nearly out of breath when he said the word.

"You'll make it. Just keep going, keep resting, and then keep going."

"You're going to make it, Nick. It's me that has to be carried out of here like a sack of potatoes." Holly wrapped her arm around Aidan's waist and held him tight.

She was shivering, and he wished they had something more for her to wear on her feet. They had to be cold. Maybe she should have stayed in her wolf coat until he was ready to climb up. "You know we're going to have to start dating."

She gave him a half-frozen smile. "You don't count this as one? Didn't you say you wanted to do wildly exciting things?"

He kissed her cold nose. "This wasn't exactly what I had in mind."

"When we get out of here, I'm going to be so much more careful when running over the snowfields and watch out for pitfalls like this. Until it happens to you, you really don't realize how dangerous the area can be."

"I know. I was so busy watching the elk and wolves. After they turned and ran in a different direction, I'd seen Ted and Greg running. When the two of you had disappeared, I was certain my worst nightmare had come true."

Holly snuggled closer to him. "Believe me, it was mine too."

"You know we're going to have to get serious about this business"—Aidan squeezed her arm—"between us."

She looked up at him. "You mean we might have to get together when you're not rescuing me, Nick, or Joey?"

Aidan kissed her forehead. "That's *just* what I mean."

"Keep going," Ted said to Nick.

They both looked up to watch Nick's progress again.

"I'm going," Nick said, breathing out. He slipped and dug his ice ax into the ice, stopping his fall.

Aidan held his breath, tightening his hold on the rope, Holly clinging to him as they both continued to observe Nick's progress.

"A...little...setback." Nick tried again and slowly made his way up a few more feet.

"You're halfway there," Ted said.

"*Over* halfway there," Aidan corrected him. Nick wasn't, but Aidan wanted to encourage him.

"Yeah, that's what I meant to say," Ted said.

"Right," Nick grunted as though he knew better, but at least he wasn't looking down, just in the direction he needed to head. Forward was what was important, not where he'd been.

The light in the opening as the snow fell through was a welcoming beacon: freedom to the outside world. Aidan didn't even want to think about how far a body could fall into the crevasse, or how, if someone fell into a narrower opening, they could get stuck. He was glad they had his bodyguards here to help. If it hadn't been for them being here, he wasn't sure both Nick and Holly would have made it out safely.

"How are you doing, Holly?"

"My feet are freezing, but the parka is keeping me warm. You guys have to be cold without parkas."

"I'm fine. Can you stand on my boots, so you can keep your sock-covered feet off the ice?"

"I could, but I'm afraid we wouldn't be as stable with me standing on your feet. I wouldn't have the right balance either."

"I'll warm your feet when we get back to the cabin."

"Oh really."

"Yeah, that's a promise."

"Hmm, well, come to think of it, I might be cold in a few other places."

He smiled. "I'll be sure to warm those other places up too."

"Why, Dr. Aidan Denali, you're a real charmer."

"Not anything like my brother, and in fact, I'm sure no one believes I have a romantic bone in my body. It all has to do with meeting the right she-wolf."

"I have to agree with you there. I mean, for me. I'm not into hugging guys I don't know unless…" She shrugged.

"They're me."

She laughed.

He was glad he could make her laugh in a time of crisis. She got his mind off their dire situation too.

She shivered again. "Maybe I should have left my wolf coat on until Nick made his way out of here."

"I was thinking the same thing. Did you want to—"

"No. I'm not undressing and shifting. This ledge is too narrow to move around much."

"Nearly to the top, Nick!" Ted said.

He only had about ten feet to go, having made better progress nearer the top. But the remaining part of the snowbridge was going to be a son of a bitch to navigate, first underneath and then over the lip and pulling himself up. Ted would help, but Nick wouldn't have anything but air below him, no way to use his feet to climb up at that point. And if the part that he clung to broke off?

Nobody could talk Nick through it though. It was just something he had to work out for himself as he made his way to that point, feeling whether there were any solid holds to keep him safe. Neither Ted nor Aidan and Holly could tell from where they were.

Nick's age worked against him. If he tried to use his ice ax on the snowbridge and it gave way, he could be in real trouble. He kept at it, trying to find more solidly packed snow or ice, but every strike brought down more snow and chunks of ice.

Aidan wanted to ask him how his wrist was doing, but he knew it had to be killing him the way he kept stopping and squeezing his left hand into a fist.

Ted was knocking some of the soft, loose snow off the top of the snowbridge so he could reach for Nick when he started the climb underneath the bridge.

The snow showered down from the light above to the dark below.

It took forever for Nick to climb the ten feet, but when he reached the underside of the bridge, he really needed that reserve strength to make it. Aidan wasn't sure *he* could make it while carrying Holly.

Ted pushed more snow off the top, while Nick moved under the bridge, his feet tight against the wall of ice, the cleats holding. He reached over and above the bridge with the ice ax, trying to dig in. The ax plowed through the soft snow and slid back to him, bringing another snow shower with it. He tried again. This time,

the ax caught, but when he tried to use it to hold his
weight, it slipped out again. Ted couldn't reach him yet.

Nick tried again, slamming the ax at the top of the
snowbridge, finally getting some purchase and trying his
weight on it. The ax held. But he wasn't out of danger
yet. He tried to dig in with the ice pick, but the way he
hit the top of the bridge, it didn't look like he'd used
enough driving force to make it secure enough. He
started to pull himself up to the point where he could
reach his left hand up and over the bridge, but Aidan
was afraid he couldn't support himself with an injured
wrist. Then Ted had hold of Nick's arm and was pulling him over the lip. Aidan and Holly were practically
holding their breaths.

And then the nightmare renewed.

The ice cracked underneath the snowbridge with the
men's weight.

Immediately, Aidan held Holly closer to the ice wall,
fearing the ice could hit them and injure them badly,
praying Nick would be pulled to safety before the bridge
gave way and that Ted wouldn't be pulled into the crevasse if Nick fell.

As soon as Nick scrambled out of the crevasse with
Ted pulling him hard, the rest of the ice bridge fell with
a grating sound, hitting the wall of the crevasse and
bouncing off. Aidan pulled Holly down against the shelf
and covered her body with his, holding her and the rope
tight, praying the falling debris didn't kill them outright,
knock them off the ledge, or break it loose.

A chunk of ice slammed into the ledge and broke it
off. Holly screamed, he gasped, and they fell.

Chapter 13

HOLLY WAS FREEZING, SCARED TO DEATH NICK WOULDN'T make it. When he did and sent the snowbridge careering in her and Aidan's direction, she was afraid this was going to be the end of them. They fell onto a shelf covered in snow, and Aidan jammed the spare ice pick into the wall next to them, holding tight to her before they slid any farther into the abyss. They were safe enough for the moment, their hearts drumming hard.

She looked up, her eyes misty with tears as the snow fluttered down around them. She was thankful she'd still been in her human form. She wouldn't have made it as a wolf.

"Are you all right?" Aidan asked.

"Yeah, I'm okay. You? You took the brunt of the snowbridge when it fell."

"Yeah, some bruises, but they'll be gone before you know it. Besides, most of the ice hit the shelf we were on, which caused it to break. Mostly just snow hit me. Thankfully, you grabbed the backpack, which had the ice pick and ice screws we need. If it hadn't been for you, we would be in a worse situation." Aidan took her gloved hand and placed it on the ice pick. "Hold on to that. I'm going to use an ice screw to tie us to the wall, but it wouldn't have helped with that last fall."

"I'm glad you weren't hurt badly. I hoped the

backpack would come in handy. You had hold of me and the rope. I had to do something."

"You were protecting Nick when you were running from the elk."

"I should have been more careful. When he started to slip in, I grabbed for the rough of his neck with my teeth, and he pulled me in with him. It was just a natural reaction for me, but it was foolish. Now, I endanger both of us by being down here, and my action didn't help Nick either."

"Yeah, but you meant to save him, and that's all that matters. No one else was close enough to have made a difference."

She glanced up at the opening. It was wider now that the ice bridge had torn away. "Oh good. We can make it up that way easier now."

Aidan stopped twisting the ice screw into the wall and looked up. "Hell yeah. I was worried about trying to make it over the snowbridge from underneath it."

"With carrying me, you mean. You would have made it on your own. No problem at all."

"Hey, you all right down there?" Ted hollered down to them.

"Yeah, Ted. We fell…maybe another ten feet by the looks of it. But we're staying put for the moment, and we're okay," Aidan shouted up to him. "Is Nick all right?"

"Yeah, he's a trouper. Damn sorry for what happened."

"You and Nick got rid of the obstacle in our path, so good job, you two."

Holly admired Aidan for turning the near disaster into praise. She knew Nick and Ted had to feel awful about it, but she wouldn't have thought to say what Aidan did.

"Hell, Doc." Ted didn't say anything for a moment, sounding a bit choked up. "Yeah, that was the plan. Glad it worked."

"It's just a solid ice-and-snow wall now," Aidan said. "We can go straight up it. Much less dangerous."

Not that any of this was a piece of cake. Aidan carrying her out on his back? Holly had to admit she was afraid he wouldn't have the strength. Not unless he was an Olympic weight lifter. She was also afraid that if he slipped and fell, she could lose her grip on him and fall. She wasn't sure the three men could hold them with the rope.

She finally glanced down at the section of snow they were sitting on, sort of. "Terra firma, for now." At least it seemed solid enough, covered in snow but sloping dangerously down into the abyss. If they slid any farther, she couldn't tell where they'd end up. Another shelf? Or would it be the end of them the next time?

"We're lowering the ice ax, cleats, and helmet to you," Ted yelled. "Nick's making a harness for Holly, in case carrying her doesn't seem like it's going to work. Nick said there were a few ledges where he could rest a bit. You probably noticed them when Nick was climbing up here."

"Yeah, good show. We've got the other ice pick, and if we need them, the ice screws, so we'll use them too."

"Okay."

Holly knew poor Nick had to hurt when he was trying to use his left hand to make a harness for her, but she also knew Ted and Mike would be busy holding on to the rope to ensure they didn't lose her and Aidan.

They waited for Ted and Mike to lower the equipment using another rope.

"Hell, I was complaining to myself that Nick had way too much camping equipment with him, but I'm damn glad he had all this stuff," Ted said.

"You and me both," Aidan said.

"I never thought I'd be using it to get myself out of real trouble," Nick said.

The rope tied to the ice ax and harness slid down the ice wall, and Aidan grabbed it. Holly was holding on to his belt with one hand, the ice pick with the other, not trusting he wouldn't just slide off their "safe" spot, even though he'd attached the rope to the ice screw secured to the wall.

"Are you ready to do this?" Aidan asked her, crouching beside her, the ax driven into the wall, the cleats on the boots, and the helmet secured to his head. He was preparing to put the harness on her.

"Yeah." She wasn't really. But she had to be brave like Nick. She might not have the upper body strength of the men, but she was damned determined to do this. Before their last fall, she had been feeling a lot more confident.

Aidan stood, helping her to stand, and she was shivering from the cold and nervousness, when it wasn't like her to be nervous about much of anything. This was the ultimate test of a person's fortitude.

He helped her climb into the harness, then attached it to the rope and himself. "I don't trust it to be secure enough to have them pull you up by it, but it'll give us a little more security while I climb. Let's get out of here before Nick changes his mind about giving me some of his blood."

"Even after all this, you're still thinking about your research?" she teased.

"Yeah, it takes my mind off this."

"You two okay down there?" Ted asked.

"Yeah, we're coming." Aidan turned his back to Holly. "I want you to climb on my back and hang on tight. I'll climb a couple of feet to that point right there. And we'll keep inching our way up that way. If you feel like you can't hold on, let me know right away. I'll try to find another safe spot to stop. Don't wait until you're desperate. We'll take as long as we need to make the climb safely." He twisted the ice screw until he'd freed it and stuck it in his pocket.

"Okay. We can do this. Only I wish you'd let me try on my own."

"Later, we can go practice climbing. Not here. I won't risk losing you. Climb on. We need to get out of here and on our way."

As soon as she was settled on his back, he began to climb. Under any circumstance, it would be a job, but carrying her, it was ten times worse. Using the ice ax, he struck the ice wall and yanked—and the ax held. Holly realized she was holding her breath, and he hadn't even begun the climb.

Aidan dug the toe of his boot into the snow piled above him against the ice wall and took a tentative step up, then swung his arm up with the ice pick and jammed it into the ice wall a foot away from the other and up higher. And that's how he began the climb, holding tight to the ice pick, freeing the ax, climbing higher using the cleats on the boots, and slamming the ice ax higher. Then he was freeing the ice pick and beginning again until they reached the first of the ledges he felt was safe enough for both of them to sit on.

"Are you sure the harness won't work for me?"

He slid his arm around her shoulders and held her close, then kissed her cheek. "If it was a regulated harness made just for that purpose, sure. But not a make-shift one. Don't you trust that I can make it up the rest of the way with you?" He was asking in a serious way, not joking with her.

"It's a long way up there still."

"We'll keep going. So far, I've got this. And as long as you feel safe enough, we'll keep doing it this way."

"All right." She let it be his decision when he was ready to move again. She was afraid it would be dark before they made it to the top and worried that without being able to see the lay of the land, they'd get themselves into more trouble.

"If we don't make it out by the time it's dark," he said as if he'd read her mind, "we'll head for the trees. It will be a longer way around, but no crevasses there."

"Good idea. Hopefully, it won't take us that long." She regretted saying that as soon as the words left her mouth. "Forget I said that. We'll take it slow and easy."

He chuckled. "Come on. Let's take it one step at a time."

When they stopped the next time, they were still about two feet below where they'd been on the ice shelf initially.

"We're making good progress," he said, holding her tight again on the next ledge.

She rested against him, trying not to show how anxious she was and trying to get warmer.

"I think we're going to need two steaks apiece after this. I hope we bought enough for everyone. Ready to go?"

"Yeah. Did you hear my stomach rumbling?"

He chuckled. "I thought it was mine."

She wondered how he could hear it over her drumming heartbeat. She climbed on his back, and he began again. She didn't talk to him while he was climbing, not wanting to distract him. Everyone was quiet from up above too. She looked up. Ted was watching them, holding on to the rope, waiting for them to make the next move.

Aidan paused on another small ledge. "Would it be too early to seriously ask you to date me?" Aidan carefully rose and helped her up.

"I think we've already had a first couple of dates, at least as wolves. So no, it's not too early. In fact, I think all these adventures have gotten us further along than most wolves who are courting."

He smiled. "I was thinking more like dinners out or candlelight dinners in. A movie. Dance hall. Something a little less—"

"Adventurous? I like adventurous. Um, maybe not quite this much of a high adventure, but you know what I mean. In my work, I don't do much that's all that exciting."

"This has got to top the list."

"For you too?"

"Even for me. Ready?"

"Yeah." She was this time. He was being ultra-careful. She knew he had to be tired, his arms wearied beyond measure, but he was still pushing himself to get them to safety. Nearer the top, Nick had made it look easier. She was hoping it would be that way for them too.

They had climbed about two feet when Mike called out, "Hey, where's Greg?"

"If he went to get help, he'll be in so much trouble," Nick said.

"He's just worried about Holly and Aidan," Ted said.

What a mess that would be. She could just see him racing back to the cabins and causing all kinds of havoc. Her family would be horrified. Ronald and Jared and his other men would be ready to string the lot of them up after they rescued her.

She prayed they'd be out of the crevasse before anyone arrived.

A few minutes later, Mike said, "Forget it. He was just taking a leak."

Aidan managed a chuckle. He sounded as relieved as she was. She had no intention of telling her family how serious this had been. Yes, she'd have to tell them she and Nick had fallen into the crevasse, but not any of the details. Greg hadn't actually seen them. At least she hadn't thought he had. She hoped he stayed far away from the crevasse.

At the next rest spot, Aidan held her tight and closed his eyes. She couldn't, afraid he'd fall asleep and roll off the narrow shelf they were resting against. At least they were only about twenty feet from the top now.

Ted peered down at them. "You're halfway here."

Without opening his eyes, Aidan said, "Over halfway there."

She chuckled. "Glass half-full kind of guy, eh?"

"Over halfway full. Yeah." He glanced over the edge and looked down. "Besides, we are over halfway there."

She looked down but couldn't tell. "If you say so."

"I do." He took a longer break, because they were "over" halfway there. Then they began the climb again.

"How long is this going to take?" Greg asked. "I mean, what if one of you guys went down to carry my sister up? Aidan's got to be worn out. I know if I had to carry her, I'd have died twenty feet earlier."

"There's no place for anyone else to climb down to another ledge. Where we were standing broke off. It's gone. Everything else is either a one-man shelf or two," Nick said. "Aidan will get her up here. She may have to doctor him when he reaches the top, but he'll make it."

Holly loved Nick. He was always good with people, which made it so tragic that Ronald had banished him. Greg was a top-notch brother too, though his comment about how carrying her would kill him before he even got started on the climb? She'd have to remember to get him back for that.

She clung tighter to Aidan. She would give him a good muscle rubdown when they reached the cabin.

Aidan paused, clinging to the ice with the pick and ax, cleats dug in. "Are you okay?"

"Yes."

"Okay, worried you…were losing…your grip. Glad…to know…you just wanted…to hug me…tighter."

She chuckled. "Yes, that's what I wanted. After all these dates we're having."

He chuckled. "Good progress."

Dating?

"Dating," he clarified.

She smiled against his back.

They stopped again after ten feet to rest, and she looked up at the last ten feet they had to navigate. "Nick moved pretty fast up that last section. Are you sure you can't just drag me up by the ropes the last of the way after you climb to the top?"

"No. You're right. Nick did well the last few feet. We'll do this together. We're almost there."

She didn't think Aidan would make it up that section as easily as Nick did, not while carrying her. But she was thankful the snowbridge was gone. She was sure Aidan would never have made it up there with her.

"Hey, they've got to be dehydrated," Nick said. "Send them a couple bottles of this water."

Within a few minutes, Ted had lowered the water to them.

"Thanks, guys," Aidan said.

Holly untied the water bottles from the rope while Aidan kept hold of her and the ax dug into the wall. Then they sat down together to snuggle and drink the water. Once they were done, they started the last leg of their journey. Footholds were available going up, but there wasn't a shelf to rest on. Not any large enough for both of them anyway. Nick had rested against the wall several times while he was climbing up to the snowbridge. And then he'd had an awful time trying to navigate that. Holly had been so afraid he'd fall that she hadn't considered the bridge could break loose.

"You're almost there," Ted said. "Just another couple of feet."

Aidan had to keep taking breaks against the wall. He was exhausted. They were so close. She wished she could help, but all she could do was cling tight to him.

"Okay, another foot, Doc. You've nearly got it," Ted encouraged him.

Aidan moved up to the next foothold, and then the next, and finally, he used the ice ax to dig into the top of the crevasse.

Suddenly, Mike was on his belly, reaching out to grab Aidan. Or maybe her. Ted was on the other side, letting

Aidan get his footing. Trying to pull both of them up at one time would most likely be a disaster. He had to get a little higher.

The next thing she knew, they were pulling him over the edge, or at least Ted and Greg were. Nick and Mike were grabbing for her, knowing she couldn't hold on to Aidan as they pulled him up.

"We gotcha," Mike said. "Let go of Aidan. We're not going to lose you."

Praying they really did have her, she released her hold on Aidan—and swung free and slammed her body against the ice wall.

"We've gotcha. You're a lightweight." Mike quickly pulled her over the edge with Nick's help.

"Yeah, but don't tell Aidan that. He probably believes I weigh a ton." She was lying on her back on the snow, looking up at everyone, except for Aidan.

He was still lying on his belly, his head turned toward her, smiling.

"I don't know about this dating bit. You're supposed to tell me you barely noticed my weight," she said to Aidan.

"He would be lying," Greg said, sitting next to her.

"Are you okay, Doc?" Mike asked Aidan.

"Of course he's okay," Ted said sternly, though Holly suspected Ted was having some fun, relieved they were all safe. "How can he win the doc over if he says she wore him out?"

Everyone laughed.

"Should we run as wolves?" Mike asked. "Not Nick. His wrist is sprained."

"I don't have boots. I'll have to shift," Holly said.

Ted was already setting up the tent for her so she

could undress and shift inside, out of the icy wind. She quickly entered the tent and sat down to jerk off the socks frozen to her feet.

To her surprise, Aidan entered the tent and sat in front of her and took her cold feet in his hands and rubbed them. "Man, do they burn," she said.

"They'll feel better once you shift." He helped her out of the parka, sweater, and sweatpants. She gave him a hug and a kiss. He held her tight and kissed her back. But she shivered.

"Are you running as a wolf? Or are your arms too tired?" she asked.

"I'm running with you as a wolf." He began stripping out of Nick's clothes, and she helped him. Then they both shifted, and he followed her out of the tent.

Greg had stripped and shifted outside the tent and woofed at them. Ted and Mike packed up the tent.

"I guess I won't shift, and I'll help Ted carry all of Nick's equipment." Mike glanced back at Nick.

She knew Mike wanted to be on hand if Nick had trouble making it back but probably didn't want to say that out loud.

"When we get to the cabin, I've got some sweats you can wear, Greg," Mike added.

Greg woofed.

They all headed for the tree line, moving slowly, looking for any depressions in the snow, being careful they didn't run across any more crevasses.

"You should've had a helmet cam," Ted said. "You might have won an award for a video featuring the most interesting, dangerous, real-life adventure."

"No, he shouldn't have," Mike said. "You know

we'll get into trouble if Rafe learns we let the doc go down there on his own instead of one of us going."

"Yeah, but Aidan could have proved to the doc what a hero he is," Ted said.

Greg woofed in agreement.

"Thanks for coming to get me at my camp," Nick said. "That could have been me down there all alone, and no one would have found me. As a human or a wolf, I wouldn't have had any way to climb out."

"Well, this was one to write home about," Ted said.

Chapter 14

IT TOOK THEM MUCH LONGER TO REACH THE CABIN GOING this way, but it would be safer. Holly knew Ronald and Jared would give her a hard time when she and Greg got home. She hadn't wanted to tell Ronald she was going to stay with Aidan and his family for Christmas, but she needed to, in case someone had a medical emergency. They'd have to see a regular doctor until she returned home.

She was always on call and never left the area for something that wasn't work-related or pack-related. She was excited about taking a vacation that was strictly that. And without being on call for anyone's maladies. Even if someone in Aidan's family was injured or got sick, Aidan would be there to help.

Then they got a glimpse of Aidan's cabin through the Douglas firs. Greg looked back at Holly as if he couldn't believe the size of the cabin.

Mike stopped and stripped out of his clothes. "I'll run ahead and open up the house." He shifted and raced ahead to the cabin, and Greg took off after him as if he was racing the wolf. Mike barked at him and sped off even faster, sending snow flying. Greg was on his heels, trying to best the wolf. Mike wasn't going to slow down for him and allow the teen to beat him. He'd probably never hear the end of it from Ted. Greg gave it his all and bounded up the steps to the deck right after Mike.

Mike dove through the wolf door, but respectful of being just a guest, Greg waited on the deck, his tail wagging as he watched the rest of them making their way there.

Holly could have run to join him, but she was being mindful of how Nick had to be feeling, being the eldest of the bunch. Aidan was sticking by her side. Nick was keeping pace with Ted as if they had been friends all along, and she really appreciated the guys.

Then Mike opened the door, already dressed, and headed out to help take the rest of the burden off Ted. Greg waited for them inside the cabin. Ted and Mike carried the equipment the rest of the way while Ted talked to him about what else they'd prepare with the steaks.

Holly was thinking Aidan had gotten a real bargain when the men became his bodyguards. Once Aidan found a cure and had helped correct the situation with the other wolves, would he no longer need the men's services?

That would be a shame. He'd probably miss their company too.

As soon as Ted and Mike reached the door, Mike said, "Come on in. We'll have lunch prepared before you know it. I set out some of my sweats for Greg. They're on the sofa. You can use the bathroom to change in."

Greg grabbed the sweats with his wolf teeth and headed for the bathroom. Holly ran up the stairs to her bedroom where she'd left her borrowed sweats, feeling right at home here already. She loved this place.

Mike told Nick he had four bedrooms to choose from and headed up the stairs with all Nick's belongings. "We can wash your clothes too. You can borrow some of mine if you'd like."

"Thanks, I'd like that. I've been washing them in the

streams, but some good soap and water will be great. Mind if I take a hot shower first?"

"Bathroom is just down to your right. Spare tooth-brushes, toothpaste, soap and shampoo, and towels are in the cabinet. Enjoy."

"Thanks. I can't...can't thank you all enough."

"Hey, we're happy to help out any wolf who needs it. No problem at all," Mike said. "As soon as Aidan learned about you, he made it his mission to find you. We all did."

Holly dressed, and by the time she left the bedroom, she heard Nick running the shower in the bathroom down the hall. She was so glad Aidan had taken him in for now, that Nick had wanted to go with them, and that they had all safely navigated the crevasse.

She saw Mike coming out of the room where he'd left Nick's gear, his arms wrapped around a load of clothes as he walked toward the stairs. "I'm so glad Nick came with us."

"Me too," Holly said.

Ted had left the rest of the gear in the bedroom, and she assumed he'd helped Mike gather Nick's clothes to wash. "I think the notion he could have a steak tipped the scale in our favor."

She laughed. "I'm glad you had some. Enough for me too? My stomach was grumbling the whole way back."

"I heard. Yeah. We have enough food for several days," Mike said.

Aidan came out of his bedroom and joined them. "I promised I'd warm your feet, Holly. How are they feel-ing? Still burning?"

"They're fine now. After shifting into the wolf, they

warmed up right away. I want to massage your muscles after all that climbing you did while carrying me on your back."

"I'd say they're fine, but then you wouldn't have any reason to give me a massage."

She chuckled. "I would anyway."

When they reached the landing at the bottom of the stairs, Ted said, "I'm going to start a load of wash."

"Won't it affect the shower?" she asked.

"Nah, the cabin has two water heaters."

"Okay, good." She didn't want anything to disturb Nick's hot shower.

Someone had put on "Carol of the Bells," her favorite Christmas song. Christmas spice was scenting the air, and it smelled heavenly.

In the kitchen, Mike was showing Greg how to prepare julienne potatoes. She was thinking Greg needed to stay with the guys for a little while and learn how to cook. She and her mother and sister had tried to teach him, but since her dad only grilled out back in the summer, she suspected Greg thought that's all men were supposed to do. He looked eager to learn from a couple of tough and brawny wolves.

"I can't wait to tell Mom and Dad what happened to you and Nick," Greg said.

"You can't," Holly said, thinking what a disaster that would be.

"Are you kidding? You're all cut up. Do you think Mom and Dad aren't going to ask you what happened?" Greg asked.

"All right, but you can't go into all the gory details."

"I'll just tell them how you were kissing the doctor

down there, and then they'll know you weren't in any real danger."

"You weren't supposed to be near that edge."

Greg laughed. "I wasn't. Not until the end when I helped pull you up. You really were down there kissing him?"

Letting her breath out, she shook her head. She'd let the cat out of the bag on that one.

"I'll call them in a bit." She took hold of Aidan's hand and moved him into the living room. "Lie down, and I'll give you a massage. It's the least I can do."

"Are you sure about your feet?" He lay down on his stomach, and she kneeled next to him and began to knead his shoulders.

"Yes, but you can give them your personal medical inspection after I finish here."

"Gladly."

He groaned in a satisfied way as she used her fingers and thumbs to help work out the tension in his shoulders. "I've got to keep you around."

She chuckled. "Free back rubs during breaks in research?"

"Only if I can reciprocate. It can be tense work, you know."

She could imagine not ever getting back to work if he gave her back rubs. She'd just want to take a nap. She began working on his lower back and his sides, and he chuckled a little.

She smiled. "A little ticklish?"

"A little."

She worked on him for a good twenty minutes, loving the feel of his hard muscles and warm body.

Then he finally said, "Your turn before the guys tell us lunch is ready."

Nick came downstairs dressed in borrowed sweats and moved into the dining room to give them some privacy, though since the living room was open to the kitchen and dining room, they didn't have a lot of that.

Then Holly switched places with Aidan. "You're liable to put me to sleep after all the exercise and the ordeal we went through today."

"I'll wake you for lunch," he assured her.

When he began to massage her back, she felt both relaxed and sexy. She loved the way he was touching her, massaging her shoulders, back, neck, and sides. He tickled her, getting her back.

He was massaging all the tension from her body, and she was in heaven. She felt so boneless—as if she could just melt into the soft couch and fall asleep—but she wanted to soak up the feeling of his every touch. His massage was perfection, and she swore he was doing everything he could to apply for the position of her mate.

She was ready to take this to *his* bedroom.

"Hate to disturb the two of you, but lunch is nearly ready," Nick said.

She moaned. As much as she was starving, she could have had Aidan's hands on her for hours. "Thanks, Aidan. That felt fantastic."

"Yeah, I know how you feel. You did a wonderful job on me too." He helped her up from the couch, pulled her into a hug, and kissed her.

"Not that I'd want to go through that ordeal again, but having the massage definitely made me feel better. I'd better call Mom and Dad quickly to let them know we found Nick. I should have done it right away, but we sort of got distracted."

"In a good way." He pulled his phone out of his pocket and handed it to her.

"How many times have you had to kill anyone as a bodyguard?" Greg asked Ted and Mike in the kitchen.

"As a bodyguard, none. But I've had a lot of weapons and martial arts training. And we were both in the military. We saw some fighting. Since Ted and I were hired, no one has tried to kidnap Aidan. Which is a good thing."

"What do you do all the time then?"

"Guard duty. Just because nothing has happened since we began working for him doesn't mean something couldn't. Once an attempt had been made to kidnap him, his brother hired us. Rafe has bodyguards, too, because he's so wealthy. He worries about someone grabbing Toby, his son, more than anything. Or his mate, Jade," Mike said.

Before Holly got hold of her mother, Greg called out, as if she couldn't hear him if his voice was at regular volume, "Be sure to tell them everything that happened."

"I will, but it will be an abbreviated version." She didn't want to overly worry her folks, but it was a good idea to mention that no one should go to that part of the wilderness because of the danger. She sat down on the sofa, and Aidan brought her bottled water.

"Thanks," she said to him. Then she called her mom. "Hey, it's me. We're back at Aidan's house. Greg's with me, and Nick too." She got misty-eyed all of a sudden. She was so glad Nick had come with them and hoped he would find a pack he'd love. But she couldn't help still feeling shaken from them falling into the crevasse, despite Aidan's delightful massage. As soon as she closed her eyes, she saw herself on the ledge with Nick, and Aidan making his way down to them, so afraid he would fall before he reached them.

"Is he okay? Nick?" her mom asked.

"Yes, he just finished a *long*, hot shower. Both Mike and Ted, Aidan's bodyguards, are showing Greg how to cook."

"Ohmigod, that's unbelievable."

"I know. A Christmas miracle, right?"

"I heard that," Greg said from the kitchen. "Tell her about the crevasse!"

Her mom started talking at about the same time that Greg yelled out about the crevasse, so Holly didn't think she'd heard him. "Tell Dr. Denali he can keep him there for another few days, if Greg wants to learn to cook under his men's tutelage."

Holly sighed. "We're going to be eating in a few minutes. But…before Greg takes the phone away from me, I want to warn you not to go up to the northern route to the peak. We got into some trouble with a crevasse."

"You fell in." Greg spoke loud enough that Holly was sure her mother would have heard him this time.

"Ohmigod, are you all right?"

"Yes, Mom. We're all right. Nick and I both fell in. He sprained his wrist. I just have a few scratches. Any trouble back at the resort?"

"You got out all right by yourselves?" her mom asked, sounding hopeful it was just a short drop.

"Uh, no. Aidan had to come down to help us out." Holly knew her brother would tell their parents if she didn't.

"Wait, let me put this on speaker so your dad can hear."

Holly had figured this would happen. If she'd been in their place, she would have wanted to know all the details. She normally wasn't one to keep her family in the dark about anything going on in her life. Not that much was usually going on. Even so, she gave them an abbreviated version.

"Did Greg witness this?" her dad asked.

She assumed he would ask Greg what he'd seen to get his version.

"He was staying back away from the snowbridge, which was a good thing."

"It collapsed," her dad guessed.

"Uh, yeah." She hadn't meant to tell them about that. "We fell a few more feet."

"Ten," Greg piped up.

"Ten. But we managed to get out okay, and Nick was out by that time."

"You and Aidan fell another ten feet?" her mom asked, sounding shocked.

"The ice shelf we were on broke when the ice from the bridge slammed into it. Aidan protected me though, and all that matters is that we made it out okay. Right?"

"Yes, yes, of course. Ohmigod, yes," her mom said.

"Did you tell them about the kissing part?" Greg asked.

She gave her brother a look to cool it. He laughed, and she knew he'd tell them later. "Did Ronald or Jared give you any trouble about Greg and me being gone?"

"Yeah, I didn't want to mention it because I assumed you were so pleased to have found Nick and convinced him to come with you. I didn't want to spoil the news. And then…" Her mother choked up.

"Mom, are you okay?"

"We could have lost you."

"We're fine. We were in good hands. Everyone helped us out." She would never tell her parents how dangerous it really had been. She was glad they hadn't had a helmet cam to record it. As for Ronald, she had a sinking feeling he knew what was going on with her and Greg, that they had been running with Aidan and his men while looking for Nick. "Was it Jared? Or Ronald?"

"Both were looking for you. I said you left early to search for Nick. Greg was supposed to go with you, but he slept late and had a later start. Jared said he saw Greg leave but not you."

"Great. Well, after we eat, we'll be home. Before then, I want to visit with Nick. He's giving his blood, so I want to see what Aidan thinks of it."

"Nick has to be shaky after what happened to the two of you. Let us know how he's doing, and we'll tell everyone else. What do you want us to say about where he's going? Everyone will want to know."

"For now, Aidan's taking him to the pack in Montana. You know, where Everett and his family ended up."

"Everett Johnston? Oh, that's good. He'll already know someone. And Everett and his family are good people." Her mother paused. "You don't want me to mention that Aidan's taking him, do you?"

"Yeah, I do. Our people need to know there are other decent wolves out there."

"I think they know that about him and his men already. The word has spread about how he rescued

Joey. When we return home, Ronald is making another pack member play Santa for the kids to avoid having anyone else go out to see one at a mall. Nobody is happy about it, especially not the new Santa. He has the right look, which is why Ronald chose him, but he and his mate never had children, so he sounds more like the Grinch right now."

"Then someone should toss Ronald and his brother out on their ears."

"Hear, hear," Nick said.

Aidan was wrapping Nick's injured wrist with an Ace bandage.

"Greg and I'll be home in another couple of hours," Holly told her mom.

"Are you sure you want to come home? Sounds like you are having a nice visit with Nick and with Aidan too. You're not getting any younger, you know."

Truthfully? No, she didn't want to go home. But she felt she owed it to her family so Ronald and Jared wouldn't hassle them any further. "Yes, I want to come home."

"I'll stay," Greg said, glancing at Aidan to see if it was all right.

"What would your mother think?" Aidan asked.

"Greg wants to stay," Holly told her mother.

"I told you, if they'll teach him to cook, they're welcome to keep him there as long as it takes."

Holly laughed. But would that be an imposition to Aidan and his men? She didn't want them feeling like they had to offer just to please her.

"Ted and Mike are Aidan's bodyguards," Holly said.

"It's okay by me," Mike said, "if the doc is all right with it."

"We can always use another hand in the kitchen to help with supper tonight," Ted said.

"Yes!" Greg said, full of enthusiasm. "You can teach me to guard too."

"We have plenty of room here," Aidan said. "Greg won't be any trouble at all. Are you sure *you* want to return to your family's cabin, Holly?"

"I have to. But maybe I can return to your place later."

"Sooner," Aidan said.

"We'll see." She couldn't assure Aidan of anything, not until she knew how Ronald was going to react. Then she told her mom, "I'll call you back before I leave here so you'll have an idea when I'll arrive there."

"Have a good time until then," her mom said. "But you know, we'll be fine, and you don't have to return here to protect us."

"Thanks, but if Ronald gives you too much grief, I'll come home sooner."

"All right, dear."

When they ended the call, Holly said to Nick as he sat at the table, a toasty fire warming the room, "I'm so sorry about how Ronald treated you."

"I know, but it wasn't your fault. You and over half the pack spoke out against his actions, but unless someone replaces him, things will never change."

"If we could find someone to take over, who in the pack would make a better leader?" she asked.

Nick shook his head. "Who would make for a better leader for the rest of the pack? I don't know. A new leader would be a godsend. For me? Being in Seattle and around the pack reminds me too much of my beloved Millicent. I don't know if I'll feel at home with any of the other packs, but I'm willing to give it a try."

"Good. I'm glad. I couldn't be happier for you."

"Truthfully, I needed the time to deal with my mate's death. Not that being banished from the pack helped matters. I appreciated everyone's assistance. Ronald's an ass."

"I agree." Holly wished she could go with Aidan to see where Nick would end up, if he did indeed find a pack that would work for him. But she figured he might live with one for a while, and then another, just to find the place where he wanted to live permanently. "You'll let me know where you end up and how you're doing, right?"

Nick smiled at her. "Sure thing, Doc."

"Food's ready," Greg said, carrying the plates to the table.

Ted and Mike brought in the dishes of steaks, potatoes, and grilled asparagus and set them on the table. Greg carried in a plate of store-bought, peppermint-decorated brownies.

Then they all sat down to eat lunch.

"This is damn good," Nick said, cutting up several more bites of the rib eye steak. "You can't know how much I've craved having a steak like this. All I've had is fish and more fish." He caught Aidan's eye. "Right after we eat, I'll give you a sample of my blood, if you think it'll help you in any way."

"Thanks," Aidan said. "I appreciate it. Who knows? You might be the key to all of it. Holly's blood cells aren't aging any faster, so it will be interesting to see if yours are the same way. She says everyone else in the pack is like this. But Everett Johnston and his mother and sister showed the changes in their cells."

"I'll do whatever I can to help. Do you think Ronald's pack will be affected eventually?" Nick asked.

"That's what I keep telling Ronald, that it's possible it could happen to us too. Then what would he do? I have every intention of working on this with Aidan and helping him to solve the mystery, if he can and if he wants me to," Holly said.

"Yeah, I'm ready to add you to the team, full partners even."

Everyone stopped eating to see what Holly said to that. She felt her cheeks flush with heat. Was he asking what she thought he was asking? Or was it just a work commitment?

She needed a change of pace. The problem with wolves—which was good, really—was that they didn't get sick that much or need her for medical emergencies very often. No one was even having babies anytime soon. Joey and his siblings were the youngest kids in the pack.

"But I'm sure she'll need time to think about it," Aidan said.

"I'll do it." She didn't need to think about it. This was an opportunity of a lifetime.

Greg's jaw was gaping. Nick was smiling and nodding. Ted and Mike chuckled.

"You're leaving the pack?" Greg looked like he was ready to leave with her.

"I'll return to finish up whatever business I have with my practice and see if I can get blood samples from everyone first, but yeah. I've wanted to do this since Aidan made us aware there was a problem."

"Do you want to examine Nick's blood cells on the microscope before you return to your cabin?" Aidan asked.

"Yeah, I sure do." She wondered how her parents would view her leaving the pack to join Aidan in his research. Then she remembered her mother's comment that Aidan might not want anything more to do with her after the project was done.

A more pressing concern reared its ugly head. What if she and Aidan wanted to mate, and she didn't age as fast as him? What if it took decades to find a cure?

Chapter 15

"AFTER ALL THE EXCITEMENT WE HAD EARLIER TODAY, I don't think we can do an encore for tonight," Mike said, moving the dirty dishes to the kitchen.

"The meal and company were great," Nick said. "I was glad to get my mind off the crevasse incident."

"You've been climbing for a while?" Aidan asked.

"Yeah. Looked like you have been too."

"Yeah. For the fun of it. I try to get in a couple of climbs a year. More if the other guys want to go."

"I'd be ready," Ted said.

"Me too," Mike said.

"It's a deal," Aidan said, wondering if Holly would be interested in something like that. Something easy, though, until she could decide if she liked it or not.

"I haven't done any mountain climbing except as a wolf, but I'd love to do it." Greg quickly helped to pick up more of the dishes, as though he thought that if the tough bodyguards could do kitchen cleanup duty, he could too.

Aidan figured that was something Holly didn't see every day. She looked both amused and impressed.

"If I'm going to fall into crevasses, I need to have the training to know how to make it out of them on my own. I'd be willing to try it. I'm sure we'll have nightmares tonight about the accident," Holly said.

"Doc can do something about that." Ted carried the

tub of butter and empty serving dishes into the kitchen. "If you stay the night."

Smiling, she glanced at Aidan.

"Hell yeah. If you stay the night, I'll chase your nightmares away. If you don't stay here, just give me a call, and I'll be right over."

She laughed and motioned to Greg, who was washing dishes. "My kid brother is here."

"Hey, I'm almost an adult. Don't mind me."

She gave her brother a get-real look. "Right. And everything we say or do, you'll repeat to Mom and Dad."

"About the mountain climbing? I'd take you on some easier rock-climbing adventures and see how you like it. And I'm serious about you staying the night," Aidan said, wishing she would. Not only because of the ordeal they'd all been through today, but because he wanted to spend more time with her.

"Believe me, if I wasn't worried about Ronald pestering my family, I would."

"Do you want to get this business of taking a sample of my blood over with before I change my mind?" Nick stood up from the table.

"Yeah, let's do it." Aidan wanted to get it done, mostly because he still couldn't believe Holly's blood wasn't aging faster. He kept thinking it was an anomaly or she had some immunity to the change. "Coming?" he asked Holly.

"Yes, I sure am. We're partners in this, right?" She said it in a joking way, not like she really believed they'd be full partners.

He helped her up from her chair. "Absolutely. I can't wait to see your take on the research." Then he motioned to Ted, Mike, and Greg, who were all busy cleaning up the kitchen. "Carry on."

Ted saluted him with a clean spatula.

"What do you think the problem is with the blood issue?" Nick asked.

Aidan told him he suspected it had something to do with their DNA.

"I missed out because I was no longer part of the pack."

"We'll catch you up. Some of the other packs have doctors who take blood samples and send them to me. The ones that don't, I visit monthly to take samples."

The three of them went into the lab, and Nick sat down to give his blood.

"Are the two of you going to hook up?" Nick asked.

Holly glanced at Aidan, a blush creeping over her face.

Aidan couldn't help smiling. "That's all part of the plan."

Holly hadn't expected Nick to make the comment, or for Aidan to say he was working on hooking up with her. "Yeah, sure. We're going to spend Christmas together, meet the rest of the family..." Holly said, then quickly added, "Of course, I'm joking. Not about going to his family's place for Christmas..." Ugh, she was rambling.

She rarely got nervous, but wolves did look at other wolves as prospective mates and could quickly dismiss the notion or give it a second or third thought. Just as humans did when they were considering if a guy or gal would possibly be a good match for the long term.

She didn't want to admit how many times she had thought they might make a great team in and out of work. She certainly was attracted to him, and he seemed to be to her. That Aidan had risked his neck to come for her and Nick—and didn't wait for either Ted or Mike to do it—said volumes.

Aidan laughed. "It's definitely something I want to explore more. I think we'd make a great team—professionally and *otherwise*."

"I knew it. The moment I saw the two of you standing shoulder to shoulder up on the cliff, you looked like mate material to me. In fact, I was certain you had left the pack and mated the male wolf. And then the doc had to rescue you and me from the crevasse. Not his men, but the doc." Nick rolled down his sleeve. "I was really hoping you were coming down to speak with me that night. But I realized it was a long way down. Traversing that section in the dark without breaking your necks would have taken a couple of hours, and I suspected that if the doc hadn't hooked up with another pack, she needed to get back to her own or she would have created a lot of worry. After what happened to us in broad daylight, it was a good thing you waited."

"I'll say," Holly said.

"I was damn glad to see you with other wolves though. I knew Ronald wouldn't have opened the pack to others, so that's why I really thought you were with them now," Nick added. "When Greg came looking for me, I couldn't have been more pleased. After he ran into my camp, he went into my tent to shift, wrapped himself in my sleeping bag, and came out to talk to me. He said he was supposed to meet with you, but he smelled my scent and detoured in case he could find me. He said he had to rush off because he was already running late. I didn't have a chance to say anything but 'be careful,' and then he said he'd be right back, shifted, and loped off as a wolf. I'm damn glad he didn't run into the trouble we all did later."

"I am too. Where we usually go, it's not that dangerous," Holly said.

"Right, because of the families that are with you," Nick said. "I did worry about Greg because that old grizzly was hanging around and might give him problems. The next thing I knew, all of you showed up at the camp. Warmed my heart to see you. It was getting damn cold living out there all the time, with the winter really setting in. I can't tell you how glad I am that you came for me."

"I tried finding you several times," Holly said, giving him a scornful look.

"I didn't see you, but I'm not surprised you were looking for me. I really wasn't ready to deal with anyone from the pack. Not unless you'd come to say Ronald was gone, but I knew he wasn't. I've been to the cabins when the pack was there, learned the bastard was still in charge, and disappeared."

"I caught your scent a couple of times. I went looking for you at various times. But I could never find you. You were much too wily. When you let us see you last night, I suspected you were ready to visit with us." Holly was glad for that.

"You know why?" Nick asked as he watched Aidan look at his blood under a microscope.

"Aidan and his men were with us."

"Correct. I had hoped you had come to your senses and mated a wolf from another pack, that the other men were part of the pack, and they had taken your family in. Which was why Greg was with you."

"I'm ready to make a change in my life too. I can't live with Ronald's rules any longer." She joined Aidan at the microscope, and he left the chair so she could examine Nick's blood cells. "What do you think about his cells, Aidan?" Holly asked. "You're the expert."

"How old are you, Nick?" Aidan asked.

"Sixty-nine."

"I'd say that they haven't changed. If I consider his wolf age and what I've seen in cells for a wolf that old, I'd say these appear right for our original longer longevity."

"That's good news, Doc," Nick said.

Holly took a deep breath and let it out. Without being able to check his blood, she'd been worried about Nick. "You're certain?" she asked Aidan.

"Yeah, I am. I've taken samples of blood from so many wolves now, I can pretty well pinpoint the changes. But I'm still surprised that neither of you are changing." Aidan switched to another page on his monitor and showed her two blood samples. One of Nick's blood cells with the original longevity, and another blood cell sample that had faster aging from one of the older wolves in the Montana pack. "Now, of course, everything has to do with genetics, lifestyle, and so on. But I would guess there's a good chance his cells aren't aging that fast." Aidan paused. "Why would Everett's and his family's be different, if this has anything to do with your pack?"

"Maybe because they weren't from our pack originally?" Nick asked.

"Right, they weren't. And everyone else has always

been with the pack. What if we have some kind of immunity to the change?" Holly asked.

"Possible. Do you have any pack members who aren't royals?"

"No, everyone has had *lupus garou* roots for generations, so our strictly human gene pool is low." Holly found the topic of their longevity changing so drastically both intriguing and worrisome.

"Yeah, but you're from one of the oldest lines that we can tell," Nick said.

Aidan raised his brows, waiting for Holly to tell him more.

"Yeah, so is yours." She said to Aidan, "You know how some wolves like to brag that they are closer to the original *lupus garou*—the one who was the beginning of our kind? Dad always argued Nick's line wasn't as old as ours."

"And I know mine is," Nick said. "According to our oral history, we have roots that date back to the First Viking Age in 795 when the Vikings were raiding the Gaelic Irish coasts. Even though a lot of records for the period don't exist, we live so long that generations continued to repeat the oral history. According to my great-granddad and my granddad, we came from one of the early Vikings who landed on those shores. Could have been even earlier."

"Mine were in Iona, Scotland, when the Vikings attacked the monastery there." She raised a brow at Nick.

"Your families were from enemy camps." Aidan sounded fascinated.

"Back then, but we also settled in Scotland and Ireland," Holly said.

"You're not related, are you?"

Nick shook his head. "No one in my family would ever admit to that. Not back then."

"But it's possible," Holly said, smiling at him.

"I would think that those whose families have been wolves for more centuries would age faster. What about the rest of your pack?" Aidan asked.

"Royals, but none that approach both our families' history, at least that they know of. Some families didn't share the oral history of their roots, just like some humans do and others don't," Nick said.

Aidan was frowning now. "I've ruled out diet or environment, since everyone eats different foods and their locations are so varied. But maybe the environment in Seattle has played a role in your DNA."

"Oh, don't tell Ronald that, or he'll be afraid all the wolves the world over will go there." Holly was serious.

Nick laughed. "That would be a good one on him."

Not really. She was sure Ronald would take drastic measures. She wanted to get home to test out her pack's blood again and see if Aidan could tell any difference between theirs and the others he'd been testing that maybe she hadn't seen. She could compare the samples to earlier ones she'd taken to see if there was any significant change.

"What are you going to try next?" Holly asked.

"With this revelation about your longevity, I want to do a blood transfusion, if you're okay with giving a pint of blood, Holly."

"You think my blood cells could change yours to what they were before? Are you sure?" Holly asked.

"It can't hurt to try. We're the same blood type, and it might be a stretch, but you know how it goes when scientists are searching for a cure."

"Yeah, they come up with cures by mistake."

He smiled at her. "But it's only if you want to give blood."

"Do you want to take a sample of my blood?" Greg asked, coming into the lab.

"Our parents would have to approve," Holly said. "And really, the changes in our longevity don't normally occur until you're around eighteen."

"I'm nearly that. What if *my* blood could be a clue to help you solve this?" Greg reached his hand out to Aidan. "I'll call Mom."

Aidan pulled his phone out of his pocket and handed it to him.

Greg punched in a number. "Mom, I want to give Dr. Denali a sample of my blood. Is it okay with you and Dad? Uh, okay… Thanks." Greg handed the phone to Aidan. "You can tell Dad so he knows I'm not making it up."

"This is Aidan Denali… Yes, it's perfectly safe for him to give a blood sample. Also, he wants to stay the night. I think he caught sight of the hot tub." Aidan smiled at Greg.

"Hot damn!" Greg said, his eyes alight with excitement.

Holly wouldn't mind a dip in it too. She was rethinking going home tonight! It was lots more interesting here.

"He'll be fine with us, as long as his being here doesn't cause you any trouble." Aidan looked at Holly.

"She says she's going home, but convince her she needs to return soon after. She's invaluable to my research... Uh, yeah, hang on." He handed the phone to Holly. "Your mom wants to talk to you."

"You don't have to come back here. In fact, your dad and I are thinking of heading home early."

"Aww, no, Mom. Unless you just want to. Or is it because Jared and Ronald are giving you a hard time? Or you think..." She hesitated as Nick, Aidan, and Greg listened in. She was going to say they were messing up her love life if she returned to the cabin. Her face felt hot all over again.

When she didn't finish her sentence, her mom said, "You know how we are about leaving the store in someone else's hands for too long. Your dad just wants to go home. We've had a great time running as wolves in the wilderness, but we're ready to return now. You know how your dad is. He's such a workaholic, and you know what a micromanager he is. It kills him to relax."

That was true. Sometimes, he even stayed at the shop longer while they came out here to have fun, and he would join them later. And he returned home early. "What about Marianne?"

"She's staying with the Dewitt family to help with Joey and the other kids. You don't have to return any-time soon if Greg's not coming home tonight."

"Let me ask Greg what he wants to do." Holly told Greg their parents wanted to return home tomorrow. "What do you want to do?"

"Stay here with them." Greg motioned to Mike and Ted, who were standing in the doorway now.

"I was thinking we'd take Nick to one of the packs' homes tomorrow and see how he likes it," Aidan said.

"Tomorrow would be fine with me to check on the pack, if it works for your schedule," Nick said. "Tonight, I want to sleep in a nice, soft bed. And that hot tub sounds inviting. Another home-cooked meal appeals too."

"Okay, Aidan is taking Nick to visit with another pack tomorrow. Greg will go home with you if he doesn't want to stay with another family at the cabins for a while longer. But he'll stay here for the night," Holly said.

"What about you?" Greg asked Holly. "Are you going with Dr. Denali?"

"She's going with me." Aidan looked pleased about the arrangement, though he watched her to see if she'd agree.

She closed her parted lips. "I'll go with Aidan to see how the other pack suits Nick. Besides, I'm working with him now." This was going to be a Christmas to remember.

"Wait, you're working with him as in long distance, right?" her mom asked.

"I really hadn't discussed the arrangements with Aidan yet."

"Tell her I have a lab set up at my place, and you're free to stay with me. Plenty of room, if you don't mind Ted and Mike watching over us."

"Aidan's offered for me to stay at his place."

"Ohmigod, Holly. It's about time."

Holly couldn't help but roll her eyes. "I want to test your blood and Dad's before you leave in the morning. Is that all right?"

"Why? Is there an issue?" her mom asked, sounding concerned.

"No. I just want to let Aidan take a look. He's the expert. I want to share our blood tests that I did last month too. I hate to say it, but I need to test everyone's in the pack again, even though I said I'd wait until next month. I want to see if he can confirm whether my observations are correct or not."

Greg sat down in the chair and rolled up his sleeve. "Take my blood, Dr. Aidan. I'll go back with Mom and Dad tomorrow. But I want to know about my blood cells too."

"Did you hear that, Mom? I'll stay the night and bring Greg back tomorrow, and you can leave. He'll go with you. And if he hasn't already told you, he's the one who found Nick."

"No, he didn't. We're so proud of him. Tell Greg we'll have a special something for him when we arrive home."

"I will. Thanks, Mom. See you in the morning." Holly couldn't believe how relieved she was not to be returning to their cabin. She was eager to try out the hot tub with Aidan. She hoped it would be just the two of them though.

As soon as Greg gave his blood, he pulled down his sleeve, got up, and hovered over Aidan's shoulder as he examined the blood.

"Looks like any normal seventeen-year-old's blood cells," Aidan said. "There shouldn't be any sign of any change in aging."

"Great. Okay, I'm ready for the hot tub." Greg's grin couldn't have grown any bigger.

"I'll put out a spare pair of swim trunks for you," Mike said, coming into the room.

"Mom and Dad have something special to give you when you go home...for finding Nick," Holly said.

"Cool!" Then Greg looked at Nick. "But I would have done it anyway. Who wouldn't have wanted to find Santa Claus for Christmas?"

"The rest of your pack," Nick grumbled.

"Ronald, his brother, and some of his henchmen who do whatever he says. Everyone else is afraid to go against them, so it's not the rest of the pack," Holly corrected Nick. She wanted him to be straight on that fact. "Go, enjoy your hot tub time, Greg."

"I'm going with you." Nick's eyes were suddenly alight with excitement. "You haven't told me what you want for Christmas, Greg."

As if he wasn't too old to play the game, Greg didn't hesitate to tell him. "A bright-red Lamborghini."

Aidan smiled. "I wouldn't mind one of those either."

Nick laughed. "That's why I was only Santa for the little kids, way before their toys wiped out Mom and Dad's bank account."

Greg and Nick left the lab, and Mike folded his arms. "Okay, so about this blood transfusion..."

"I have to try it. It would be like any other kind of blood transfusion, receiving blood intravenously, except that I'd be watching to see if Holly's blood would alter mine, giving me an immunity to the cell-aging issue, or not."

"She's my blood type if she's the same as yours. Ted's too, because Rafe wanted to make sure we could give you blood if you ever needed it after a fight, though he would never have guessed what you might need to do with our blood—when it comes to your research," Mike said. "You can experiment on me. If something happened to you, we'd both be fired."

"It's just a regular transfusion," Aidan assured him.

"Then it would be safe for me."

"Then you wouldn't be able to protect me for a while. At least, you'd need to take it easy, not any real roughhousing."

"As if I'm ever called on to protect you. Ted can handle things for a little bit if something unexpected happens."

"Yeah, I can, unless you want to give me the transfusion instead," Ted said.

"Mike offered first. But it's up to you guys," Aidan said.

"I'll do it first. If this doesn't work like Doc hopes, you can do it next time," Mike said.

"Okay, sounds good."

Holly sat down on the chair to give more blood first. Once she'd given a pint, Aidan finally agreed and motioned for Mike to take a seat. "This might not be enough blood to make a difference, and it may take a good long while to see a result, if there is any change at all, but we'll try it with the small amount of blood she gave."

"Do you need more?" she asked, willing to give Aidan what he needed.

"No. Later, we could do more, if nothing much happens with this. Our blood builds up faster than humans, so instead of waiting eight weeks, it's only about three to four for us. But even so, you'd have to wait."

Ted motioned to the doorway. "I'm going to do some guarding."

"Okay, alert us if you see any trouble," Aidan said.

She was certain he meant if someone from her pack showed up.

From the other side of the house, they heard Greg shouting, "This is sooo cool!"

Aidan and Holly laughed.

Mike smiled. "I knew that would be a hit."

"You're really going with me when we take Nick to see the first of the packs I had in mind?" Aidan asked Holly as he began to prep Mike.

"Yeah. I want to see how well he's received."

Mike winked at her. She felt her cheeks heat. Yeah, all right, so she wanted to go with Aidan to be with him, but she didn't want to say so.

"I'm hoping this gives me superpowers," Mike said.

"If it changes your cells so they age more slowly again, you *will* have superpowers." Aidan started the transfer. "If this works, we'll need more blood from your pack, depending on if everyone is aging the same as you and Nick. Your brother's blood doesn't count," he said to Holly.

"I can't guarantee that anyone else will offer, but I will," Holly said.

"Do you think it will work?" Mike asked.

"A red blood cell has no nucleus or DNA. However, transfused blood has white blood cells that do contain a significant amount of DNA. Even when white cells are filtered out, the transfusion can still contain a high number of white cells."

Mike smiled at Holly. "She looks like she's got a lot

of good DNA." Then he frowned at Aidan. "How long would the DNA stay in my bloodstream?"

"According to studies, donor DNA can last up to seven days in a patient. In women, a year and a half in some cases when the recipient has lost a lot of blood and received more of a transfusion. Now, this is minuscule compared to the patient's actual DNA. However, with our healing genetics, it's possible our body will accept the change and it won't be lost and could even change our DNA so that we have our longevity back. It might 'see' it as an improvement and change it."

"If my DNA replaces yours, you could be me," Holly said, smiling.

"I'd rather *have* you than *be* you. No offense, Doc." Mike grinned. "What if it works, but we have to have transfusions periodically to keep our cells from returning to their current state?"

"Then we won't have found the right solution, and we'll still be working at it. I'll check your blood before you go home to your family for the holidays, Mike. You'll need to keep in touch with me if you begin feeling any different. I doubt you'll notice anything has changed. If this works, it could be a giant step for wolf-kind."

"I'll let you know if I begin to feel strange."

"Good. Thanks for being my test wolf. And thanks, Holly, for donating your blood and helping me with this."

"This is the part where you kiss the girl," Mike said, "but I'll vamoose first."

Holly noted Aidan appeared to be thinking along that line, and as soon as Mike was done, she was all for letting Aidan thank her...properly. But she needed to discuss her concerns first. "I have another idea too. I want to test my pack members' blood again to see if anyone is exhibiting signs of faster aging. I told them I wouldn't test them again for another month, so they'll wonder what's up. But I don't want to hold off on giving them the news if I see a big change."

"Do you want to go to your place in Seattle after we drop off Nick, if he likes the first pack we take him to visit?"

Aidan really did want to make this a team effort. She hadn't wrapped her head around the idea that she'd be leaving her pack and family behind.

"Will you come with me to my clinic in Seattle?" Though if Ronald got wind of it, he wouldn't like it.

"Yeah. I want to see the results too, and using your last quarter's results, we can compare them."

"What about those who have been more newly turned in the other packs? If having more pure *lupus garou* roots is keeping us from changing, wouldn't the ones who are newly turned have cells that age more like a human's longevity?"

"They do. They haven't had the increased longevity, so it's hard for them to imagine how different their lives could be. The real concern is for royals mated to newly turned wolves, if wolves who have purer *lupus garou* DNA are not being affected by this change in their longevity. It's hard to believe that no other wolves have a similar background to yours or Nick's. At least that I've met."

"In the case of the newly turned wolves, they would age, and their royal mates wouldn't." She hoped for the best. That somehow her blood would change Mike's in a way that would reverse or slow down the aging issue, that her own people's blood hadn't changed, and they could all share their blood with others, if it made a difference and reversed the trend. "Thank you for helping me find Nick and wanting to find a pack that will be his forever home. And saving us. Watching you come down to rescue us was like watching a trained Army Ranger."

She wrapped her arms around Aidan's neck and kissed his lips. She didn't know if this was pushing things a bit too far too fast, but she was totally fascinated with the wolf, and she'd never felt like that about any other wolf. She attributed it to their line of work. Their need to help others. And just how sexy he was.

Oh, and the way his body always reacted when they got close. How could that not excite her own?

Chapter 16

AIDAN KISSED HOLLY BACK, FULLY GIVING IN TO THE moment. She pressed her soft, curvy body against his, and he was already becoming aroused. He couldn't help it when he was close to her like this. She licked his mouth in a sensuous way, parting her lips, offering him entrance. He ran his hands through her silky hair and plunged his tongue into her mouth, caressing her tongue.

Their hearts beat in sync as she rubbed her body against his, such an instinctive reaction to another wolf, wanting to leave her scent on him as he left his scent on her. Her pheromones were kicking his into warp speed, sending a blaze of red-hot desire coursing through his blood.

She pulled her mouth away from his and licked her lips, which made him want to kiss her all over again. She wasn't pulling that sweet body away from him though, indicating she wasn't through where they were concerned. Or maybe she was ready to melt into the floor, and she needed his support to steady her. She was one passionate she-wolf.

"Hot damn, you're going to be one helluva partner."

She laughed. "Do you think we'll get any work done?"

"I think I'll be taking more breaks from my research than I ever have."

"I'd agree with that."

They heard someone coming, and Holly pulled away before Aidan wanted to let her go.

Mike poked his head in. "I'm going to walk around the place. Ted's out there doing a perimeter search too."

"Okay, just take it easy. I don't want you passing out in the snow. For our kind, you need to rest between twelve and twenty-four hours. Seriously. Which was why I said you couldn't be doing guard duty for a while, and why I should have been the guinea pig this time around."

"Hell, Doc, why didn't you say so in the first place? Then you could have let Holly pamper you, being that she's a doctor too. She probably needs some pampering too." Mike laughed. "Just taking a walk. If anything happens that means a fight, I'll let you know, and you can take care of it." Before he left, he added, "Course, then Rafe will fire me…"

"If your blood turns out to have a miraculous change, all in the name of science, Rafe will understand."

"I know you'll put in a good word for me." Mike left the lab.

Holly was frowning. "He shouldn't be out there, serving on guard duty."

"He's been in a lot worse scrapes than getting an extra blood transfusion when he's perfectly healthy and managed to do fine. I only said that about the time frame because I don't want him to really overexert himself. Besides, being a guard is his job, and I swear he'll generate more blood faster if he's doing what he feels he must. Do you think anything I have to say will change his mind? Rafe pays their salaries, so they listen to him."

Holly sighed. "As long as we don't have to haul his body back into the house later so he can recuperate."

"I agree. Do you want to see the rest of my charts and records on the tests I've been doing?" Aidan asked.

"Yeah, sure." She sat down at his desk, and he set up the laptop so she could access his files.

"Do you want something to drink?" he asked.

"Hot tea?"

"I'll bring up a selection of tea bags for you to choose from. Be right back."

Aidan headed to the kitchen, unable to shake free of the concern he had as soon as Holly told Ronald she was leaving. He didn't like that she'd have to face Ronald or Jared in the morning when she and Greg returned to their cabin. He suspected they'd be angry with her for being with Aidan all day and then overnight. They would smell his scent on her, so she couldn't hide the fact that she'd been with him. He assumed they would be just as irritated that Greg had been with them. Aidan was also very interested in her pack's blood samples, but since Ronald hadn't agreed to Aidan getting involved, he was certain there would be trouble.

He wanted to accompany her and tear into Ronald himself, or Jared if either of the men gave her a hard time, but he suspected she wouldn't want him to be with them and maybe cause more of an issue.

He was glad Nick was taking him up on checking out the Montana pack and hoped they would be perfect for him, but he was just as glad that Holly had agreed to go with him. He hoped she would be agreeable to joining him in the hot tub later.

Aidan fixed himself a hot cup of coffee and hot water for her tea and carried them to the lab.

"I'm glad you're going with me. I think Nick will feel better about it too," Aidan said, setting the tray down next to the computer so she could pick out the tea she wanted.

"You doing this for him is so nice. He really deserves to find a home with a pack," Holly said.

"He does. I can't imagine what it was like for him to be kicked out for no good reason."

"It was a rotten thing to do."

Aidan took a seat next to her after she'd made her tea and was looking over his research again. "I have to say I'm worried about you and Greg returning tomorrow to your cabin. I want to go with you." Aidan knew it had to be Holly's choice, but he wanted to be there as her backup if either she or Greg had any trouble. His research and caring for wounded or sick wolves was what he was meant to do. But he'd been involved in any number of wolf altercations over the many years they'd lived, so he had no qualms about tearing into trouble-some wolves.

Eliminating a pack leader wouldn't automatically mean the pack would do well on their own though. They'd need another leader, and Aidan was certain Jared would jump at the chance to lead the pack and also fight him. Though his bodyguards would be in the middle of the conflict too.

"No, I'll be fine. If you and your bodyguards show up, there'll be a fight for sure, and Ronald and the others won't just scuffle with you to prove something and send you on your way. Others who don't like Ronald's actions concerning Nick will side with their leader, showing their pack commitment. You know how that goes."

"Yeah, I do. But I don't want the bastard to bully you."

"I've never had someone stick up for me like that."

"Any decent wolf should. What about telling him

you're leaving the pack?" That was what he was really concerned about. How they would react.

"I'll be up front with him, but I'm not going to burn my bridges."

"You mean if you and I don't work out?" They were going to work out. Just like he was sure he was going to find a cure. Someday.

"I've had relationships *not* work out. If we solve the issue of the longevity, we might not have anything further to base our relationship on." She raised a brow.

He only smiled at her. Okay, sure, it was smart of her to leave her options open, but he had every intention of showing her that she really had only one option worth considering. But staying with him could mean she'd be mating a wolf who aged faster and died long before she did. She might feel that was too much of a risk to take. Which meant he'd have to work a lot harder to find a cure.

She was the perfect incentive.

⌇⌇⌇

Before they had supper that night, "Let There Be Peace on Earth" and other Christmas music was playing. Even though they hadn't intended on staying here for the holidays, hadn't even planned to be here for them, the guys were making an effort to add a little Christmas cheer for their unexpected guests, and Aidan really appreciated it.

Ted and Mike were speaking in private in the kitchen, but Aidan overheard a little of the conversation while he, Holly, her brother, and Nick were piecing together a thousand-piece wildlife puzzle on the coffee table in the living room. Everyone who visited the cabin tried putting the puzzle together for a time. They usually did so many outdoor activities that this was an evening pastime when they wanted to wind down, drink beers, sit before the fire, and have something more to do while having a conversation.

Ted and Mike were saying something about making spaghetti for Nick, Greg, and themselves, because they didn't have enough for all six of them. Aidan knew better. They always overbought food supplies when they picked up groceries, as if they were cooking for a whole army of wolves for a month, and they'd take the more perishable, uneaten food with them when they left. They'd have plenty of meals. They planned to serve a special dish of veal marsala over egg noodles and wine for the docs. They sounded like they had taken on the role of matchmakers too. Maybe they believed Aidan needed help in the romance department. With Holly, he didn't need any encouragement or assistance, though he could use more privacy.

He eyed the puzzle but then looked again at Holly as she pushed another piece into place. She'd placed twice the number that he had. He and Rafe and the others who came here with them hadn't finished a lot of the puzzle, maybe a hundred pieces since they'd bought it a few months ago, and hadn't been up here but once since then. With the progress she was making, she'd have it done in short order. He was trying his darnedest to find another piece that would fit next to some of the border, since that was completed.

She watched him for a minute and pointed to a puzzle piece that was lying among the ones he'd spread out. "Can you hand me the blue one that has a couple of orange leaves floating on the water?"

There were lots of blue ones. And lots of fall leaves. Any of which could be the one she was looking for. He looked at the spot she wanted to add it to, but he couldn't see any that might work there.

She smiled at him and leaned over him, brushing her body against his in a sexy way when she could have easily avoided touching him. He took advantage of the opportunity to wrap his arms around her and kiss her cheek. "Have you put this puzzle together before?"

"No." She reached for the puzzle piece. "This one. See how that part of the leaf fits in there with the partial leaf on that part?" She pointed out the parts of the small puzzle piece, but he still couldn't see that it would work.

He also realized that even if she had put the puzzle together before, the puzzle had too many pieces for her to be able to know where they would all go again. She'd eyed the picture of the finished puzzle on the box cover for a long time before she had begun doing her part.

He was still trying to find a puzzle piece while she placed three more. If he was in a race and not doing this just for fun, he would have felt outdistanced in a hurry. He studied her for a minute more, watching her place another piece, and frowned. "Do you have eidetic memory?" It was rare to find an adult who still had it.

"Some think so. I can see a visual of something, like the puzzle box cover, and remember where everything goes for a short time. When I see the pieces, I can recall the bordering ones they connect with. But not long term. If we did this for a couple of hours, I would have to look at the cover again."

"That's a heck of a lot better than I can remember. We've got to do this as teams when we go to the chalet, just for kicks."

She laughed. "You mean you and I would team up against Rafe and Jade? That would be cheating. Now, if Jade and I took you guys on—"

"You'd have an unfair advantage."

She laughed again.

Greg shook his head. "I'm still looking for my first piece, and she's already filled in fifteen."

"That's a remarkable gift," Nick said.

"Some children have it, but unless it's nurtured, the ability is lost. I guess I just was interested in recalling visuals I'd seen, and it helped to keep that ability alive."

"I wish I'd done that. Not long enough attention span for me though," Greg said.

Ted came in. "We're going to split up into groups for dinner tonight. We'll eat first, and then we'll run with Greg, while Nick is going to turn in early, and the docs can have dinner then."

Aidan realized this was a bigger conspiracy than he'd imagined.

"Mike has to take it easy," Aidan reminded him.

Mike smiled. "Of course. I'll walk. The others can run."

"We don't have enough spaghetti for the six of us, so we'll slap something else together for you two later." Ted shrugged as if it was a no-brainer. "We figured you could spend some more time talking about your research when we go running."

Mike gave Ted an annoyed look that said talking about research wasn't supposed to be on the agenda, and he was afraid that's just what *would* happen, given the suggestion.

The "slapped-together" meal that Aidan had over-heard them planning warranted five stars, if this was as good as the meal they'd prepared before.

"Ted and I like to get some extra exercise in when-ever we can. Isn't that right, Ted?" Mike asked, as if he had to further explain why the bodyguards weren't staying to protect them.

Aidan knew they'd be outside, watching the cabin, not running all over, but he still didn't want Mike to overdo it.

"We sure do. That way, if we have any bodyguard missions, we're in shape for them," Ted said, returning to the kitchen.

"I can use the exercise too," Greg said.

"Not me," Nick said. "I've had my year's worth of cold weather and exercise in the couple of months I've been out there. I need to give my old bones a rest, and going out in the snow right now doesn't appeal."

Aidan worried Nick might feel the same way about joining the pack in Montana if he didn't like the cold weather.

Nick added, "I mean, living in it, day in, day out. Having a nice toasty fire and a hot cup of coffee in a warm house? That's a different story."

Aidan was glad to hear it because he thought that since Nick already knew a family in the Montana pack, he might fit right in.

Mike brought everyone mugs of spiced cappuccino, with whipped-cream Christmas trees decorating the tops, and then returned to the kitchen with Greg to help

Ted make the spaghetti. Aidan smiled at the little white Christmas trees. "You're a class act, guys."

"You mean the whipped-cream Christmas trees? You don't want to know how mine turned out. One of you has more whipped cream in your drink because I had to stir it into the cappuccino. The second try came out just as messed up," Ted said. "Mike graciously offered to see if he could do better before someone had ten times the whipped cream in their mug."

They all laughed.

Holly sipped hers. "This is delicious."

Everyone else agreed.

"Thanks," Mike said. "I'm the drink maker back home for Christmas."

Ted filled a pot with water. "Ha! You could have told me that before I made such a mess of the whipped cream."

"It was more fun watching you making the one, staring at it, getting rid of it, and trying again. You have to keep after it before you get it down pat."

The lighthearted banter continued back and forth between them as Holly said to Nick, "I'm so sorry about Ronald banishing you. Once we learned what he'd done, we tried to reason with him, but he threatened to banish everyone who objected. You know how much his henchmen like their positions in the pack, so we couldn't all rally together to get rid of Ronald and his brother. They could also have hurt a lot of the pack members' businesses, and that's all they really have."

Nick sipped from his cappuccino. "I don't blame you, Doc. Some of the ones running the pack, yeah. If I were a younger wolf, I would take them all on and lead the pack again. But that's for someone else to do now."

"We'd take care of 'em, if we didn't have a job to do," Ted said from the kitchen. "All three of us—Doc, Mike, and me."

Nick raised a brow at Aidan. "I would think you were more of a healer than a fighter."

"Oh, he's fought in plenty of wolf skirmishes, and he's all for righting a wrong," Mike said. "You should have seen the wolf fight he was involved in recently when Jade's brother tried to steal her son away."

Though what they said was true, Aidan figured Mike and Ted were saying so to show he could be a fighter, not just a science geek. He wished they hadn't mentioned it. What if she liked science geeks and wasn't into a macho warrior wolf?

"Yeah, and he loves kids. That time, he rescued Toby in the Pacific Ocean too, when his brother was trying to rescue his mate," Ted said.

"Okay, enough, guys." Aidan didn't want them to overdo it, and he wasn't ever in the limelight. That was Rafe's job. Rafe had to keep up appearances. Aidan was just his twin brother, the doctor working in his lab all the time, and he preferred it that way.

"He's also way too modest," Ted said.

Holly laughed. "It's good to know he's not just another pretty face." She smiled and winked at Aidan.

Aidan chuckled.

Thankfully, Ted announced the spaghetti was ready and the others could eat. "We'll fix your meal as soon as we eat."

"No hurry." Aidan knew they would wolf down their food so they could prepare his and Holly's meal next, and they wouldn't have to wait too long. Aidan tried to figure out another piece of the puzzle. And found one! "Were you born around Christmastime?" He didn't really believe she had been, but it was a conversation starter since her name was Holly.

She rolled her eyes. "Yes. In about three days. My parents thought Holly was the perfect name for me because I was born so close to Christmas."

He smiled. "I like it. It suits you."

"You should tell him what your name really means," Greg said. "She looked it up when we were teasing her about being named after a shrub."

"Oh?" Aidan said.

"Lover of nature. Self-sufficient. Strong-willed, courageous, and bold. See? I would have climbed out of the crevasse, given the chance."

"You needed boots and cleats," Aidan reminded her.

"I agree," Nick said. "It was hard enough for me to make it *with* them."

"But you had a sprained wrist," she told Nick.

"You still would have needed boots and cleats," he said. She sighed.

"Tell them the rest," Greg said.

"What? About my name? Well, I attract success and wealth. I don't know when, but someday, I guess."

"And you want to make a difference in the world. That's why Ronald really irked her. When she heard about your research, she wanted to help," Greg said.

She placed another piece to the puzzle. "And you and Dad didn't want me to."

"I've changed my mind. I mean, what if you're right? I want to have the longevity that the rest of the wolves have." Greg took another bite of spaghetti.

"We'll have to celebrate your birthday, Holly." Aidan was eager to do so.

She laughed. "Usually, it's lumped in with Christmas. Oh sure, this present is for Christmas, and this one is for my birthday, but…"

"Yeah, she has a raw deal." Greg chowed down on a piece of toasted garlic bread. "You should have your own special day. Marianne and I always tell you that you should have your birthday in May along with us."

"I know, but May just doesn't seem right."

Aidan wondered what he could get her on such short notice for her birthday. Their kind didn't wear jewelry because of the issue with shifting. He didn't have time to order something online, and if he took her shopping, it wouldn't be a surprise. Then he had an idea. Before they went to see the Montana pack, he'd ask if they could pick up a birthday cake and a couple of presents for her from him. He was certain Lori Cunningham wouldn't mind at all. But he didn't want to involve Lori and Paul's pack in the actual party. It would be something he could share with Holly and maybe Ted and Mike and Nick too.

"Hey, I've got to make a couple of calls to let Lori and Paul Cunningham, the leaders of the Montana pack, know we're coming so they can make arrangements for everyone to stay there for a day or so," Aidan said.

"Okay. You do that, and I'll finish the puzzle before you return."

He looked down at the puzzle. "Another 850 pieces? I'll take a bet on that."

She laughed and continued to find pieces.

She might not be able to do it in the time he was

making a call, but he was certain she'd have a lot more done when he returned than he would have. He went upstairs to his bedroom, wanting to make this private. He hoped they didn't think he was worried that the Cunningham pack wouldn't take Nick in, despite Everett saying they would. And he hoped Holly didn't suspect he was making her birthday arrangements. He wanted it to be a fun surprise.

When Lori answered the phone, Aidan said, "Hi, this is Aidan Denali. Everett said he cleared it with you to bring Nick Cornwall to stay with you and check out the pack."

"You found him? Oh, that's wonderful," Lori immediately said. "Absolutely. We understand the duress he must have been under, and he'll be well loved and welcome here. Everett has told us all about him. And we're excited about the prospect of having our own Santa, if he would like to be ours. The rumor got out that a widowed male could be joining us, and the widowed she-wolves are all a-twitter. We've told them to be cool about it because he may still be feeling bad about his mate. But you know how that goes. The ladies are eager to make him feel better."

Aidan chuckled. "As long as you all can intervene if they get to be a bit much for him. He's looking forward to meeting with you." Aidan paused. "I have a small favor to ask, if it wouldn't be too much trouble."

"More blood tests? I thought Christine sent the blood work last month."

"Uh, no. Actually, it's about the Seattle pack's doctor who's coming with us. She'll be working with me on the research, so you might be hearing from either of us regarding this. The good news is that she and her younger brother are aging the same as we were when we had the original longevity. We're hoping for a break-through. Don't tell the rest of your pack though. Just Paul and whoever you trust with the information. I don't want to get anyone's hopes up just yet. It could still take years to find a cure."

"Ohmigod, that's such good news. We'll keep it under wraps. But I'm so thrilled."

"Me too. Now, Holly has a birthday in three days, but I don't have any time to arrange it. I thought maybe you could pick up a cake and a couple of presents. I'll pay for them. It'll just be private, maybe Nick, Dr. Holly Gray, and my bodyguards. I don't want to embarrass her or anything. I'm sending you an email showing a couple of things she might like. That's about it."

"Sure thing."

"Her family always celebrates her birthday on Christmas, so I wanted to make it special, separate from the holiday. She'll be spending Christmas with my family and me."

"Absolutely. I'll take care of it personally. We'll have a place for you to stay. Everyone's eager to see you again, so expect a welcoming party."

"Much appreciated."

"*You're* much appreciated for tirelessly working on this research that can change our lives for the better."

"I sure hope we can come through for everyone."

"I hope so too. I shouldn't ask, but is Doctor Holly becoming a permanent wolf in your life?"

"I sure hope so."

Lori laughed. "All right. When will we see you?"

"I'll keep you posted, but hopefully by tomorrow afternoon or evening."

"Okay, I'll get right on it. Take care. We'll see you soon."

"Thanks for everything, Lori. Looking forward to seeing you again." Then Aidan searched for a few things he'd like to give Holly for her birthday. Well, and for Christmas, but he'd have to figure a way to get those, maybe when they reached the chalet. Then again, he could call Jade. She'd have a field day at learning he was bringing a she-wolf to the chalet.

He called Jade next to give her a heads-up. "Hey, Jade, I'll be bringing my research partner with me to the chalet."

"Oh my, sure. Is he going to be working with you at your place on a permanent basis? I can't believe you've found someone who can help you with this."

"She. And I hope so. She's said yes to working with me at my place."

Jade didn't say anything for a couple of heartbeats, mulling that news over, he suspected. "Oh wow, Aidan, I'm thrilled."

"It doesn't mean a mating, but since she's coming for Christmas, do you think you can pick up a couple of things for me to give to her? I won't be out of her sight, so it's going to be hard for me to shop for her, and I won't be able to order anything online at this late date."

"Absolutely. Just send me your list. And if you think of anything we could get her, I'll shop for that too."

"Okay, thanks."

"Rafe will be shocked and pleased. Also, did you find Nick?"

"Yes, he's doing fine. We're taking him to see the Montana pack tomorrow. Sorry I didn't tell you we'd located him already."

"No problem, and I'm so glad to hear it. Where did you meet her? Wait, is she the doctor you met at the mall when you saved the little boy from being kidnapped?"

"Uh, yeah."

"From the Seattle pack?"

"Yes."

"Oh wow, okay. What does her pack say about her leaving?"

"They don't know yet, but we'll deal with it tomorrow."

"If you need Rafe's men's muscle, you tell us. Don't you go trying to take on a whole pack by yourself, Aidan. I know you. You're as stubborn as your brother when you want to get something done."

"I'll call if we think we'll have trouble. After we drop off Nick at the Montana pack, we'll have to go to Holly's office and clear things out, so it might be a few more days until we head to the chalet, but we'll let you know."

"You're actually going to Seattle?"

"Yes, and don't tell Rafe we need an army of men to deal with this. We'll be fine unless I call, all right?"

She let out her breath in exasperation. "All right, but I'm not keeping it a secret. I'm so excited for you. I'll let you go. Toby's getting into his swimsuit, and I need to watch him."

"All right. Give him a hug for me."

"I will. He'll be excited to meet her too. Don't be surprised if he thinks she's your mate."

"I won't. He's young. Talk to you later, Jade."

"See you soon."

They ended the call, and Aidan was afraid his brother would still send an army to Seattle to watch his and Holly's backs when they went to her clinic. He could see Ronald believing they were going to try to take over his pack. The thing of it was, they could. Easily. But if there wasn't anyone strong enough to put in charge of the pack, they'd have to leave one of their own men, and he doubted that would go over big with the pack or the man who got stuck with the job.

Aidan went downstairs, but Holly wasn't in the living room putting the puzzle together any longer. He immediately glanced in the direction of the kitchen.

Ted and Mike had already cleared their dishes and started preparing the next meal.

"She's gone to make a call," Nick said. "She's in the sunroom."

"Okay, thanks." Aidan guessed she needed to check on her parents.

"Man, you guys eat fast," Greg said.

"Comes with the job." Ted rinsed the dishes. "Sometimes, we'd have to catch a meal when we could. That was before we began to work for Aidan. Well, most of the time. Tonight is an exception."

"Do you think they're on to us yet?" Greg asked.

Aidan chuckled, assuming Greg meant the business of matchmaking. "Probably."

Greg smiled at him. "I told them we couldn't get away with this without you realizing something was up, 'cause you're too smart for that." He took another bite of his spaghetti. "Okay, I'm done." He carried his plate into the kitchen, then began washing his dishes.

Aidan suspected Greg wasn't always that helpful in the kitchen, but he was trying to prove something to the guys. He was a likable kid.

Holly reentered the living room, joining Aidan, and whispered in his ear, "If my parents could see him now, they'd send him with you just so the guys would be a good influence on him."

Her whispered breath tickled his ear, and he smiled at her. He was glad the guys were trying to give them some alone time.

Chapter 17

TWENTY MINUTES LATER, MIKE SET THE PLATES OF VEAL marsala—veal covered in a mushroom-and-wine sauce and Parmesan cheese—on the table, along with egg noodles. "Dinner is served." He brought in chocolate cheesecake while Ted poured glasses of red wine.

Nick finished his spaghetti, and Greg hurried to take his plate.

"Now that's what the women like," Aidan said. "A man who helps in the kitchen."

"Do you help in the kitchen?" Greg asked.

"Sure, when Ted and Mike let me. They usually tell me they have it covered and to go do my research before we all fade into oblivion. Before they came to work for me—"

"You were skipping meals, they said."

"True, but the meals I made were good, and I cleaned up after myself." Aidan didn't want Holly to think he was a slouch at cooking or cleaning up. He did have a maid, but sometimes he liked to do the dishes to give himself time to think about what else he could try with his research.

"Thanks, guys." Holly joined Aidan at the dining-room table. "This looks delicious."

"I have to agree," Aidan told them. "Just perfect."

Ted slapped Greg on the back. "Come on. Let's go before their food gets cold."

"Heading upstairs to bed," Nick said. "Just don't let there be any crazy and wild parties going on when you all get home. Night all."

Holly smiled at him. "Night, Nick. Pleasant dreams."

Nick snorted. "If I don't hear the wind whipping the tree branches and snow, I probably won't be able to sleep."

"I know the feeling when I've been camping out too long. Night," Aidan said. "We'll see you in the morning."

"See you then." Nick disappeared up the stairs.

Ted, Mike, and Greg were already rushing out the wolf door as wolves.

"They're not running too far away, are they?" Holly sounded worried they might get into trouble, especially when her brother was with them.

"Nope. Their job is guarding me, so they'll just be... guarding. They'll hang around the area. Hope Greg knows that and doesn't get bored too easily."

"He's a good kid. He loves being one of the men. He's used to being around two sisters and his mom, so this has been good for him. Dad is so busy with the shop that he's worn out when he comes home. I hope Mike doesn't overdo it after having that blood transfusion." She took a sip of her wine.

"You either, after giving blood."

"What will you do if you find a cure for our people and no longer need bodyguards?"

"I wouldn't be able to enjoy their culinary expertise. They're always trying something new out on me, and I swear they've never made a bad dish. Except for the time they burned a pan of tilapia. Each one thought the other was watching it."

She smiled. "That's easy to do when there are too many chefs in the kitchen."

"I have the same problem when it's just me in the kitchen. But that has to do with me going back to look at my lab work and forgetting about the meal I'm cooking."

She laughed.

"I suspect Rafe will want me to continue to have bodyguards because of my wealth."

After finishing their meal, Aidan said, "The hot tub is free tonight. At least for now."

"What if the guys want to use it after they come back in from their 'run' to work on all those muscles?"

"They'll have to wait. Besides, they'll be disappointed if they find they've left us alone together and we didn't use the time wisely. Do you want to soak in the hot tub?"

"Greensleeves" was playing inside and out, so they'd have relaxing holiday music to listen to while in the hot tub. Nothing could have been more perfect for a romantic interlude.

Holly looked out the window at the bank of white snow and firs providing a backdrop for the tub, which was surrounded by snow, the deck warmed and wet. Golden lights illuminated the deck and snow. A light shone inside the tub, highlighting the blue water, and the whole area was covered in a fine, misty snow fog. "It is beautiful. And enticing. Definitely beckoning me to slip into the hot water and enjoy it."

Aidan was thinking it couldn't have been prettier or more romantic than this. "I'm ready when you are."

She tugged at the sleeve of her sweatshirt. "No bathing suit. No bra or panties to substitute for a bathing suit."

He smiled at her, but he was afraid he gave her a much-too-wolfish look, because she promptly laughed and blushed. "You can wear a pair of my boxer briefs and a T-shirt if you'd like, although the steam is rising from the hot water in the tub and mixing with the cold air. I'll barely be able to see you as it is. Or you me."

She smiled. "Right."

"We shifted in my bedroom before, so it's just the same old thing." Not really, because sitting in the hot tub with the beautiful she-wolf while they were naked was bound to heat things up, unlike earlier when they were just stripping to shift. Though, even then, he couldn't help but take a long, interested look while she took in all of him in the same interested way. "Besides, we're both doctors."

"Uh, yeah, so we'll see each other in a strictly impersonal way." She gave him a once-over, but he swore she was recalling when she was looking at him earlier.

"Right." He finished his wine.

"Ted and Mike should hire out as chefs," she said. "I enjoyed every delectable bite."

"They love to use their muscles to deal with trouble. Since they came to work with me, I haven't had that kind of trouble. It's nice knowing they're not bored."

They carried their dishes into the kitchen. Holly started to clean the plates, but Aidan took her hand and led her out of the kitchen. "They'll clean up. If we don't get into the hot tub soon, they'll be back and might even want to use it. The question is, how will we dress for the occasion?"

"Draped in mist." She was half smiling, impish but sexy too.

He loved the way she thought. "I'll grab some bath-robes from the bathroom for hot tub guests." He walked into the room, which had a private toilet, shower, and sink. Long, white robes were hanging on hooks, and they were nicely warmed. He grabbed one of them and carried it out of the bathroom to where Holly was waiting for him. "For you, my dear."

"What about for you?"

"I'll be in the water so fast, you won't even see me, but when we get out, you can have a new warmed robe. I'll grab one for me too then."

"Okay." She began stripping out of his sweats and set them on a bench in the room off the deck. Then she slipped on the robe. "Very impersonal." She boldly watched him remove his clothes as she belted the robe.

He was partially aroused in the warm room. He couldn't help it. Watching her undress while he was stripping out of his clothes—not to mention having her observing him—was making him hot.

She smiled at him and then walked out onto the warmed deck. He quickly joined her and held her arm so she wouldn't slip. Though he said he was going to jump right in, as soon as she untied the robe, he helped her out of it, and she hurried into the hot tub. He set the robe on a bench and made his way into the tub in a macho way, not hurrying like she'd done, trying to get in before she froze to death.

"This feels sooo good." She smiled at him when he navigated across the hot tub to sit close to her but not touching, waiting for her to give permission. She reached for his hand and pulled him close.

He wrapped his arm around her, loving the warm,

silky feel of her and the water. "I have to admit, this is the first time I've enjoyed the hot tub with a woman."

"Not with just any woman. A doctor too, who is interested in your research. Aren't you worried I might try to steal the cure from you if you discover something that could help us? Especially if my pack is beginning to have issues too?"

"I would gladly give the cure to you and your people. Anything you wanted. Aren't you afraid that if you are the one to discover the cure, I might want to claim it as my own?"

"You wouldn't dare."

He laughed, and then he leaned down and kissed her, her head tilted up to maximize the pressure of his mouth on hers.

He loved how she responded, her hand sliding up his waist, her other hand caressing his thigh, and he was instantly aroused. He was trying to concentrate on the kiss, but her hand was so dangerously close to his erection that he was having a difficult time thinking as the blood rushed south.

She brushed her hand against his erection with a whisper of a touch. So much for this being anything but very personal. Not that he was complaining.

He pressed his tongue between her parted lips, and she sucked on it with zeal. He groaned. Where had she been all his life? Here, in Washington, and he'd been in California, not that far away. But too far away to make this a deeper and more meaningful relationship, because seeing her daily would be tantamount.

He moved his mouth to her neck and began pressing kisses on her soft skin. She shivered, and he was afraid she was getting cold, but she ran her hand over his chest, brushing her fingers over his nipples, her free hand cupping his head as he continued to lick and kiss her skin. "God, you're beautiful," he whispered against her throat.

"You're one hot...wolf," she said, pressing her mouth against his forehead and kissing him.

Every time she touched him, it sent a surge of adrenaline coursing through his blood and ratcheted up the desire to take this further.

He ran his hand over the back of her neck, her long hair floating on top of the steamy water, making it appear that she was a blond mermaid. She shivered. He pulled his mouth away from her breastbone. "Are you getting chilled?"

She smiled, though her eyes were misty with lust. "This is the first time I've ever been in a hot tub. I think I could live in one for half the day. This feels so good with the cold breeze brushing my face and tugging at my hair while the rest of me is buried in hot water. Between the hot water and you, I'm toasty warm."

"Maybe we can get a little warmer."

"Whatever the doctor suggests."

"As long as the doctor is of the same opinion." He pulled her onto his lap and kissed her mouth more.

"Oh, believe me, she is. This is just what the doctor ordered." She wrapped her arms around his neck and pulled him deeper into the tub so they were submerged to their necks to stay warm. She kissed him again, snuggling on his lap, and he began thinking of moving this inside.

But he didn't want to stop. They couldn't go too

far, as in having consummated sex, or they'd be mated wolves, but he wanted to share the same space with her tonight. In bed.

She let him up for air and smiled. "Do you think we would have ever gotten together if it hadn't been for Joey and us meeting you at the mall?"

"Yeah. I would have called you once Everett told me you would be looking for Nick at the same time we were in the area so we could do it together. I would have worried about you going it alone, even though I wasn't sure you'd want to run with wolves outside your pack. One way or another, I was planning to talk with you, professional to professional, as someone who was interested in locating your pack member."

"And you were hopeful I didn't share Ronald's viewpoint concerning meeting with other wolves."

"Yeah. I had no idea your longevity wasn't an issue for you. That was a real shock. It could change everything." He ran his hand over her arm in a gentle caress.

"Ronald's an idiot to believe it couldn't change for us too."

"I hope not. I'm hoping you're the cure."

She smiled, and then they kissed again. With her sitting on his lap, her thigh bumping against his steel-hard erection, he was dying to get some relief. He could imagine her underneath him in his bed and pumping into her as they kissed each other with abandon.

He was mindful of the time they'd been in the hot tub though. Fifteen to thirty minutes was all they should allow for, but as cold as it was, a shorter time was better. It had been fifteen minutes, and as much as he hated to give this up, her sweet, soft, naked body pressed against his as she sat on his lap in the hot water, they needed to. Not only because they could become light-headed, but especially since she'd given blood.

"Are you ready to get out? I think the only way the guys are going to be able to come home is if they think we've returned to the cabin and gone to bed. Not to mention, we've probably stayed in as long as we safely can."

"Yeah, this has been so nice. I'm feeling a little sleepy, probably from the heat and giving blood."

"We've got a hot tub at the chalet in Colorado too. We can enjoy it there."

"Then I'll give this one up for now."

"Let me get a fresh, warm robe for you. Stay in the hot water, and I'll be right back."

"Thank you." She slid off his lap and he kissed her cheek, then climbed out of the tub and grabbed the cold robe off the bench. He used it to dry himself off as he moved quickly to the door and entered the room. After grabbing a warmed robe and wrapping it around himself, he carried another out to her.

He was hoping she'd agree to sleeping in his bed with him tonight. Where she was concerned, he was ready to move this along.

As soon as she climbed out of the tub, he helped her into the warm robe, tied the tie for her, and lifted her into his arms to carry her inside. To his bedroom.

He told himself he was carrying her because he was afraid she was too light-headed and he didn't want her collapsing, but he would have done it for her anyway. They'd had a wild day with all the running they'd done to reach Nick, falling down a crevasse and climbing back out of it, and then making it the rest of the way through the snow to his cabin, and her giving blood. She had to be exhausted.

But he couldn't help worrying that tomorrow there would be real trouble with Ronald and Jared when they learned she was leaving the pack.

Chapter 18

HOLLY LOVED HOW ROMANTIC AIDAN WAS. BY THE WAY Ted and Mike had orchestrated things so she and Aidan would have an ideal evening alone, she'd thought that Aidan wasn't truly a romantic at heart. But he proved he was all on his own. "Ted and Mike didn't mention this side of you when they were extolling all your other virtues."

"They've never seen me with a woman I'm damn interested in before. They've only been with me for two months."

"They act like they've known you forever."

"Yeah, we make a great team. We all get along well. I didn't expect their matchmaking efforts though." He carried her to the stairs.

"I don't believe you needed their help, though it was nice they took my brother with them so we could have some time alone. And having our special dinner was lovely too." She wrapped her arms around his neck. "I *can* walk." But she liked the way he was pampering her. And she wasn't sure, as light-headed as she was feeling, that she could make it all the way upstairs, except at a much slower pace.

"I'm keeping you warm. Shoot, I forgot to grab my clothes and the sweats you were wearing from the bathhouse." Then he shook his head. "That's okay. I've got more."

As soon as he reached the landing, he walked down the hall. Since her bedroom was next to his, she wondered if he was waiting for her to tell him which bedroom she wanted to go to. What did *he* want to do? She suspected he wanted her to stay with him.

She couldn't wait for him to reach the rooms before she commented. "The suspense is killing me."

"I want you in my room, in bed, with me," he said quite honestly.

"Okay, just making sure. That works for me."

He chuckled. "Good, because I hate to have to beg. Though I would have. I wouldn't sleep a wink all night, thinking about you catching z's next door when you could have been snuggling with me."

"I wouldn't want you to lose sleep over me."

"Excellent." He carried her into his bedroom and shut the door. Then he set her down on the floor. They both disrobed. "Any preference to which side you like to sleep on?"

"Left side of the bed. You know the old adage: Waking up on the wrong side of the bed? Well, researchers have said that people who sleep on the left side of the bed are more optimistic and get more accomplished during the day than those who sleep on the right side."

"Really. That works for me too then."

She climbed into bed, and he got into bed on the right side but scooted over until he was on her side of the bed and pulled her into his arms. "I sleep on the left too."

She chuckled.

They heard someone heading up the stairs. Then someone followed him.

"It worked," Greg said, his voice hushed.

"What?" Ted asked.

"They're in Aidan's bedroom. I wonder how Mom and Dad are going to feel about that."

"Glad. Go to sleep, or we'll make you pull guard duty."

Greg sighed. "Night."

"Night."

Then it was quiet. Holly was wrapped blissfully in Aidan's arms, her back to him as he stroked her arm and pressed a kiss against her hair. He sighed. "I hope some of tonight made up for the horrors of the crevasse earlier today and you don't have nightmares about it."

"But you promised you'd chase them away."

"I will."

"I had a lovely time. And if I ever fall in a crevasse again, I'll want you to rescue me. Being with you gave me hope and encouragement. You were truly heroic, and I appreciate you and everything you've done—including helping me look for Nick." But tomorrow was back to reality and dealing with Ronald and his issues.

"I've enjoyed every minute with you, and your brother too. And I want to say that I hope this is only the beginning for us."

"Hmm, I'm hoping for the same." But she was also hoping she didn't cause huge problems for her family. Then she turned toward Aidan and began to kiss him. She'd wanted a real wolf in her life forever. But finding one outside the pack wasn't easy. And finding one in the pack wasn't about to happen. Aidan made her heart sing, and she wanted to finish what they'd started in the hot tub, no restrictions on how long they had to fool around this time.

She turned her face up to kiss him, her hand stroking

his waist and hip, his mouth closing in on hers. His large hand glided over her hair in a soft caress and then moved to cup a breast, kneading, his thumb rubbing over the sensitive tip, making the nipple stretch out for more, the erotic touch filling her with burning need. Her inner feminine muscles clenched, and she leaned into his touch, wanting more, wanting him inside her, wanting to climax. *Now*.

Their hearts were beating erratically, their pheromones going to town as he licked and kissed her mouth and she licked and kissed his back. She ran her hand over his buttocks, feeling the hard muscle tighten. She captured his tongue with her mouth and sucked. He smiled and speared her hair with his fingers before reaching down to spread her legs, gently pushing her onto her back.

Lustful hunger burned in his gaze as he kissed her mouth again, his fingers working magic on her clit, her nether region dewy with anticipation. Their musky scents mixed together as a powerful aphrodisiac to their enhanced wolf sense of smell.

She wanted him inside her in the worst way, to fulfill the ache that had begun the day she'd first met him, the way she'd felt his hard muscles pressed against her, felt his arousal burgeoning, smelled his sexy wolf scent— yeah. She'd wanted him that first time. And then in the hot tub...

She felt like a nymphomaniac with him, when she'd never felt that way toward any male, wolf or otherwise. She'd thought there'd been something wrong with her. But she just hadn't met the right wolf.

She reached down to stroke his hard cock, but he

began coaxing a climax out of her, rubbing faster, harder, as if he couldn't allow her to distract him before she came. And she loved him for it, loved the way his fingers so expertly pushed her and drew her into mind-shattering bliss as the climax hit. She quickly took charge of him, stroking him from the base to the tip of his cock, while he kissed her mouth, tonguing her, and finally let go with a wolfish groan.

They kissed again, hugging each other tightly and enjoying the intimacy between two wolves in the after-math. She was hoping he was the one for her. And was really glad they had a bathroom in the master bedroom, so they could shower together.

Aidan hadn't been sure Holly would want to go that far with him this early on, but he was certain that's where they'd been headed all along. They couldn't disguise the way their bodies were reacting to other and, in particu-lar, how their pheromones told them what they wanted to know. There was no mistaking they were hotly into each other.

He was glad she had decided to be with him and work with him, but he hoped she'd want a mating with him before too long. She was just too irresistible. They showered, changed the sheets, and settled down to sleep while he tucked her in his embrace, physically showing how much he wanted her to be his, permanently.

Even though he'd been thinking of Holly, the hot tub and what they'd started there, now that he'd put his other head to rest for a bit, he could concentrate on the longevity issue. His scientific brain took over once again with mysteries and puzzles colliding and demanding to be solved. Though if they started kissing again, all bets were off.

Knowing that her blood and Nick's hadn't changed was a real game changer. He'd been so stuck on trying to come up with other theories. Now that he had a moment to relax, knowing Nick was safe and well on his way to finding a home with a wolf pack, Aidan was back to pondering over the situation.

He began thinking about the wolf fights Holly said her pack had had in the early days. That made him wonder what had happened to the other wolves. Where were the packs living? He couldn't shut down his brain when it came to wanting to locate other wolves, any of whom might be the key to their dilemma.

He suspected Holly wouldn't be happy about dealing with them, but she wouldn't have to. He'd take care of it, if he could locate them.

He began stroking her arm, not as a prelude to sex, but he didn't want to just start talking and wake her if she'd gone to sleep. She sighed and snuggled closer to him. "Either you didn't get enough, or you're worrying over something."

"Thinking."

"Ah. If I had to venture a guess, it's about my blood." She wasn't sleeping soundly, and he suspected she was lying awake thinking too. Maybe not about what he was, but he was glad he hadn't woken her.

"Yeah, I was just wondering about the wolf packs that attacked yours with the notion of trying to take over. Where did they end up? Do you know?"

"You want to test their blood too?" She didn't sound

annoyed with him about wanting to find them, more like she wasn't surprised. "Nick or my parents would know more about them than I would. I was only a baby when the last pack of wolves tried to take over. The others tried to take over before I was born. I'm sure it's still a sore subject with many of the wolves who fought them and suffered."

"I completely understand."

"You're right in wanting to learn about any other wolves out there whose blood might hold a clue. There's got to be a reason our DNA isn't changing. All I know is the wolves that fought our pack were all males. In each of the cases, they were looking for an established pack that had several females. I think they believed they could overpower us because they had so many males who were of a strong fighting age. But our females fought them too. And some died in the wolf wars. My parents were only courting the first time we were attacked. My mom fought alongside my dad as if they were already mated wolves. After our pack killed off the attacking wolves, my mom and dad mated."

"So that was the deciding factor for them. I don't blame them." Aidan wouldn't want Holly in the middle of a war like that, but he knew if some wolves had tried to take over, he would have done anything he could to protect her and not waited on a mating afterward either.

"Mom's parents were adamant she wait longer. But you know when someone special captures your interest and there's no letting go of him, so there's no sense in putting it off. In any event, they killed some of ours. I don't know what happened to theirs."

"That was before you were born. When you were a baby?"

She sighed. "Okay, I told you Ronald was against having anything to do with other packs because of the issues we'd had in the past. There's more to the story than that. His father actually befriended and mated their mother. He was a leader of another pack and got friendly with ours, learning our strengths and weaknesses, and then attempted to take over. Not just fighting with the pack leader—who, at the time, was Nick—but his men fought all of our men who were capable of fighting to get rid of the stronger males, including my dad. A wolf pack defending their own— their mates and children—can be stronger than a bunch of aggressive, bachelor males. Ronald and Jared's father was killed in the battle, but I don't know about the rest of the wolves."

"Hell, no wonder your people don't like outsider wolves."

"Just Ronald, Jared, and a few of the ones in charge. They all lost someone in those battles, and I think Ronald and Jared are trying to prove they won't let it happen again, probably feeling as though everyone half-way blames them because their mother mated one of the wolves. Though, as far as I can tell, this information wasn't passed on to younger generations. Nick finally told me about it because I had to know why they were so against having other wolves join the pack."

"Okay, it makes sense."

"But you're not going to sleep. Because you're going to keep thinking about those other wolves. And what happened to them. And if you can sample their blood.

But you're not going to call my parents or wake up Nick to satisfy your need to know."

He smiled and kissed her head.

She snuggled against him. "Good. Because I wouldn't want to think you were obsessed with your work or anything."

"I'll just think of us making love, and that will obliterate any other thoughts I might have."

She chuckled. "Good. And if you need any further inspiration, just let me know."

"With an invitation like that, how can I say no?" He wanted Holly to get a good night's sleep.

But, if she initiated anything further, he was going to take full advantage of her generosity.

Chapter 19

AFTER MAKING LOVE AGAIN WITHOUT CONSUMMATING their relationship, Holly had finally fallen fast asleep. Yet something woke her. She wasn't sure what had disturbed her. She lay in Aidan's arms, and he was sound asleep. She was glad he'd finally given in and quit thinking about the wolves that had attacked her pack.

Now, she couldn't sleep. Giving blood and spending time in the hot tub had made her thirsty. She got up, pulled on the robe, and cinched it, then went downstairs to get a glass of water.

She peeked out the kitchen window and saw the security lights on outside. In the foggy snow, a gray wolf was skulking around the trees. *Shit!* It was Jared. Were Ronald and more of his minions out there?

Hoping to circumvent a wolf fight, she set the glass of water on the counter, tore off the robe, and tossed it over the back of a dining chair. She quickly shifted into her wolf, the heat filling her cells as the shift took over, and raced for the wolf door. Thankfully, the door wasn't locked when she pushed at it with her nose, probably so the guys could switch places on guard duty without any trouble. She barged outside and ran into the snow, the full moon glowing on the snowy night.

She heard movement and saw Jared in the brush, sneaking nearer to where Mike was prowling the snowbank in his wolf form.

Furious with Jared, she veered off to tackle him, knowing she wouldn't be very successful because of his much larger size, but he wouldn't be expecting it. Or at least she thought he wouldn't. As soon as she charged him, he turned and snapped his jaws at her. She wasn't used to fighting wolves for real, so his reaction startled her. But she had gone too far and couldn't back down now. She wasn't going to let him attack Mike if she could stop him. Hopefully, Jared would back off when he realized she wasn't going to put up with his actions. He had no business being here.

From a distance, Mike growled and snarled. She didn't want either man hurting the other, but she knew if she turned and headed inside, Jared wouldn't stop trying to fight Mike. Not when Jared was the pack leader's brother and second-in-command. He had to prove to Mike and the others that they needed to keep their paws off her and everyone else in the pack.

She snapped back at Jared, lunging and biting at him. He dodged back, and she assumed he didn't want to hurt her. How would that look to the pack? She was their doctor, and if he injured her, it might turn pack members who'd been on the fence about her helping Dr. Denali against him.

She continued to bite at Jared, and he finally ignored her and charged at Mike, who raced to reach them. Her heart about gave out as the two wolves clashed. Then she saw two more wolves running full out to join them. One was Ted; the other, Aidan. She bit at Jared to get him to quit as Mike and Jared stood on their rear legs, their front legs resting on the other wolf's shoulders as they danced around, teeth exposed, biting, trying to get the best of each other.

As soon as Aidan and Ted drew close, they snapped and bit at the big gray. Jared was tenacious, not wanting to show defeat in front of the other wolves and not wanting to show he'd back down. Holly tried to separate the wolves, still believing Jared wouldn't want to harm her and she could get him to stop. But Jared turned on her so quickly that she couldn't jump away in time, and he sank his teeth viciously into her shoulder. She yelped, then growled. She didn't know if he'd bitten her on purpose or by accident, but she tore into him, furious. Damn his male wolf pride.

Probably feeling guilty that he'd bitten her, he didn't fight her back, and she backed off. But Aidan moved in to fight the wolf. She barked at Jared to go home. He was bleeding, and so was she. Once Aidan clashed with him, he was too. And so was Mike. What a mess.

She had so hoped this would be a simple mission, but now she was certain Ronald would declare war on Aidan and his pack. She was torn between returning home and taking care of Jared's injuries and trying to smooth things over with Ronald, just for her family's sake, and staying with Aidan. But once she'd made the decision to leave the cabin and work with Aidan, she had made her choice.

Her brother came out of the cabin in his wolf coat, and then Nick emerged too. They caught Jared's attention, and he stopped to stare at them, as if he couldn't believe they were both here in the enemy's camp too.

All the wolves waited to see what Jared would decide to do.

Because they didn't just kill him, she assumed they were trying to keep the peace and not have an all-out war with her pack. Aidan was standing so stiffly that she knew he was ready to tear into the wolf again, waiting for any slight move on Jared's part that indicated aggression. Jared switched his growly attention from Aidan to her. This was it. She could turn and head back to her parents' cabin and Jared would go with her, or she could stay with Aidan and his men.

She looked at Jared's growly expression and was reminded of how much he'd been like that lately. She needed a break from the pack. Maybe permanently, if things went well with Aidan. Right then and there, she decided she was staying. She and Aidan stood a good chance of being mated wolves and solving the problem with the others.

Letting Jared know where she stood on the issue, she headed toward the cabin. She felt bad for her family, and she felt bad for her people. But she had known all along she would someday leave them to find a mate. She supposed she was like Nick, needing to have an offer of a pack or home before she could make the change.

Aidan turned and loped with her toward his place, while his men waited with Jared, making sure he would return home and not come after Aidan or her. She hoped Ronald wouldn't punish her family for this, but she'd get in touch with them right away to let them know what had happened. Aidan licked her cheek and considered her injured shoulder. He looked so growly that she wanted to reassure him she'd be fine. Though her shoulder was burning like the devil. She might not be able to handle falling into a crevasse very well, but she'd play-fought with wolves over the years, and though she was a smaller female, she could get some good bites in.

Greg joined them and drew close, nuzzling her cheek with concern and affection. She licked his face, knowing he had wanted to take on the big gray too, but Nick had been standing on the porch with him, making sure Greg didn't move in that direction. She loved Nick for it.

She wanted to witness what would happen next, to see if Jared left, but she didn't want him to know she was anxious about it. It would be a disaster if they killed Jared, but she figured he'd run off to their resort and tell the pack what had happened. His version anyway. Knowing him, he'd say he was trying to locate her, worried about her, when he came upon the cabin and Mike attacked him without provocation.

She ran through the wolf door first, Aidan and Nick waiting on the deck to ensure Mike and Ted had more backup if they needed it.

Greg went inside with her and raced up the stairs after her. He went to the guest room he was staying in. She headed to Aidan's bedroom and shifted, turned on a light, then grabbed a towel from his master bath. She wrapped it around herself, not wanting to put on one of the pool robes and get blood on it. Her shoulder was bleeding and throbbing, which just made her madder at Jared.

"Hey, Sis," Greg called out from near Aidan's bedroom.

"Coming." She left the bathroom, but he walked into the bedroom, passing her, and entered the bathroom.

"We're in trouble now." Greg rummaged around in the bathroom and emerged with a first aid kit in hand. "Why don't you take a seat, and I'll fix that. You probably want to take care of the doctor next and Mike too. I can't believe Jared bit you. Then again, I couldn't believe you bit him."

"I was trying to make him go away and not fight Mike. To let him know I was here of my own free will and he wasn't wanted. He was getting ready to attack Mike, and Mike hadn't seen him yet." She sat on a chair in the sitting area of the bedroom.

Greg crouched down to wash her bite wound. "You should have known he would bite you back. It was a stupid thing to do. He's aggressive enough, and he was angry you were here. I would've bitten Jared myself, but Nick growled at me to stay put."

"Good thing too." She sucked in her breath as Greg applied antiseptic to the wound.

"Sorry. Don't you think we'll be in trouble?"

"Yeah. If we were with a normal pack, we wouldn't be. It's not our fault our leader is such an isolationist. If he wants to be that way, fine. We shouldn't be forced into it too. We didn't bring Aidan and his men into the resort to be among our people. We went to see them. And that should be fine."

"Except that Jared thinks you belong to him." Greg put some salve on the wound and then began to bandage it.

"He was the one who called it quits, just because I said I wanted to see Aidan. We really didn't see eye to eye on a lot of issues, and there was never any spark between us."

"Not like you have with Aidan, right? Ronald was pushing that business with you and Jared, thinking if you mated his brother, you'd never leave us."

"Believe me, it would never have happened."

A wolf pounded up the stairs and quickly ran into the room. *Aidan.* His eyes hard and his mouth grim, he shifted and stalked over to check out her bite mark. Greg quickly removed the bandages to let him see. "You did a good job, Greg." Aidan's voice was growly, hard with steel, angry.

"Did he leave?" Holly prayed Jared had come to his senses and gone back to their cabins. She hadn't heard any more fighting, so she figured he must have left. She still felt she needed to return to take care of his injuries, as much as she was fuming with him for coming here. She was still the pack doctor.

"Yeah. Took him a while. He kept staring at the bedroom window where he assumed you were. He must have seen you moving around up here. Then he paced for a time." Aidan said to Greg, "You can put the bandage on Holly again. You did a fine job."

Greg beamed at the compliment. Aidan was good with kids of all ages, it seemed.

"Maybe you've found your calling," Holly said to her brother.

"Being a doctor?"

She expected him to say no way, but instead, he glanced at Aidan as if getting his opinion on the matter.

"Packs can always use their own doctors." Aidan pulled on a pair of boxer briefs.

"Yeah, well, maybe I could. Uh, I'll let you take care of the doctor, Sis. I'll check on Mike."

"Thanks," Aidan said. "There's another first aid kit downstairs in the bathroom."

"On it." Greg hurried out of the room.

"Let me take care of you." She checked Aidan over and tugged gently at his boxer briefs.

He helped pull them off and then stood still while she went over all his bite marks with antiseptic, then covered

them with salve **and bandaged** them. "I'm so sorry." She
knew Jared was only picking a fight with Mike because
she was here. Seeing Greg and Nick had probably put him
in a worse mood. She couldn't help but feel responsible.

"You had nothing to do with this. I really had hoped it
wouldn't come to this. I suspected it might, if they were
keeping as close an eye on you as you had indicated. I
hope you're not regretting your decision to come see
me. I feel responsible for you, and for your family, if
anything should happen to any of you."

She snorted. "This is all Jared's fault. Not yours."
She finished bandaging Aidan and then was torn about
leaving. She worried Ronald would gather a bunch of
his men and attack Aidan and his men. If she returned
to the cabins, she might be able to calm Ronald down.

"I wasn't going to return to the cabins tonight, but I
believe I need to."

Aidan rubbed her bare arms with a gentle caress. "I
was afraid you'd say that. If you go, we'll have to take
you. You're not going alone. I really don't want you to
return there tonight."

"I don't want Ronald to gather his men and attack you
here in the middle of the night. And they're likely to do
that after Jared tells him whatever he wants them to hear.
He's liable to say he was searching for us, worried because
Greg and I hadn't returned to the cabin, and followed our
scent trail here. Then Mike attacked him without provocation. Then the rest of you ganged up on him. I know
how he manipulates the truth to suit his own agenda."

"All right. Then we leave now."

"What? Just pack up and drive off? You mean, we'd
head out to Montana? In the middle of the night?"

"We can drive to the private airport near here and take Nick to Montana, or we could head down to California, stay at my place until everyone gets some sleep, and then head out later that day for Montana."

"What about my family?" Holly had to get word to them right away. She couldn't believe she was even considering just taking off. She didn't want to leave her family in a bind either.

"We can pick them up first." Aidan crossed the floor to his bedside table and handed her his phone, looking serious about taking care of them too, no matter the danger to him and his men. "Call them and see what they want to do. We can drive there and pick them up. Or they can slip out to meet us on the road near there. They have their own vehicle and didn't ride with some-one else, I take it."

"Yeah, they have a Suburban. I'm afraid they're not going to want to leave Seattle permanently. They'd have to sell off their business. I imagine Ronald would make it difficult for them to return."

"They know him better than we do. It's entirely up to them. If they want our help, they've got it." Aidan tugged on his jeans, shirt, socks, and boots. He pulled her in for a hug and kiss. "I'm going to check on Mike. I'll be right back."

She kissed him back, telling him this was where she wanted to be. With him. Now and in the future. She decided to let it be her parents' call.

She called her dad, but he wasn't picking up his phone, and she got voice mail. She tried her mom; same thing. "Come on, come on, wake up and answer your phones."

Chapter 20

HOLLY KEPT TRYING TO GET HOLD OF HER PARENTS, THEN called her sister, who slept harder than her parents, so she didn't believe she'd reach her.

Aidan returned to the bedroom, and as she called each of her family members again and got no answer, she shook her head. "They must be asleep, though I thought Dad would at least hear his cell phone ringing."

"Unless Jared has reached them already and taken their phones away so you couldn't contact them," Aidan said.

"I don't think Jared would have made it to the cabins this soon. Not when he was injured and hanging around here for a time." At least she was really hoping he was still making his way back and didn't howl a warning. Then again, she suspected her parents would have heard the howl if nothing else.

"Then we wing it. We try to get there before Jared does and slip them out. If we run into Jared or Ronald, we'll tell them we want to speak to your family and see what they want to do. Maybe we can deal with this man to man instead of as wolves. Though I don't trust Ronald or his brother to be honorable. Not after what Jared pulled here tonight."

"I agree."

"And if they don't want to go with us? What do you want to do?" Aidan asked.

"Go with you." She decided that's where this was headed, no sense in prolonging the situation any longer. Then Aidan's phone rang, and Holly was so relieved when she said to Aidan, "It's Mom." She took a deep breath. "Mom, trouble is headed your way."

"What's wrong?"

"Can you pack up and leave? Don't even pack up. Just leave."

"What's going on?"

Holly could hear her father moving around in the background, opening drawers.

"Jared attacked Mike, one of Aidan's bodyguards. Aidan and Jared got into it, and Jared even bit me when I tried to break them up."

"Ohmigod. Are all of you all right?"

"Yeah. Jared's on his way back there, but he's wearing some bite marks, and you can imagine what he's going to tell Ronald. I want you and Dad and Marianne to leave. Now."

"We'll let you know if we make it out okay."

"Hurry. As soon as Jared reaches Ronald, all hell will break loose."

"Okay, got to go."

Holly couldn't believe the turn of events. But they had another issue. What if her people's blood cells were changing too? What if by causing this trouble for herself and becoming friends with Aidan and his men, she wouldn't be able to test her pack members to learn if they needed help too?

She decided she wouldn't worry about it for now. She would try to reach some of the pack members when she could and see if they wanted to be tested behind

Ronald's back. She did feel bad about her parents' business, their home and hers, and the pack members who would no longer have a wolf doctor to care for them.

Searching in Aidan's drawers, she found another pair of sweats, navy blue this time, and pulled them on.

She'd been so thrilled about working with Aidan, initially thinking she would be keeping in touch long distance after the holidays. She'd never expected this to happen. That she'd want Aidan like he wanted her.

She hoped her parents and her sister would leave the cabin and make their escape before Ronald stopped them. She couldn't help worrying he might catch up to them and try to use them to force her to return.

As soon as she was dressed, she hurried downstairs to see what was going on. Ted was rushing to pack the car. Greg and Nick were helping him, though Greg was told to just bring down the bags, not take them out to the car in his sock-covered feet in the snow. And Aidan had warned Nick not to use his sprained wrist. Aidan was finishing bandaging Mike, who had a comforter on his lap.

"I'm so sorry, Mike." Holly squeezed his uninjured shoulder.

"I'm finally getting paid for what I was hired to do. No problem." Mike smiled at her. "I've got to run up and dress."

She still felt bad. "What can I do?" she asked Aidan.

"Help me to pack." Aidan tore up the stairs, and she followed him.

Aidan quickly threw his clothes from his chest of drawers into a bag, while Holly grabbed the clothes in the closet.

"What's going on with your family?"

"They're getting ready to leave."

"Tell them to meet us at the private airport near here. We can fly them out to Seattle or anywhere they want to go until they decide what they want to do long-term, just to keep them safe until Ronald and his brother cool down."

"There's a private airport out near us. We don't live in Seattle. We needed a place to run. We could go there first, drive out to our houses, and at least pick up some of our stuff. I told them not to pack, just go."

"I imagine Ronald will be suspicious when he hears their vehicle leaving the resort." Aidan headed down the stairs with bags in hand.

Carrying his laptop and another bag, Holly descended the stairs after him. "He will be, but their cabin is at the end of the row. He's at the opposite end. They're closer to the entrance. They'll have a head start."

"Good. Keep my phone. They've got my number and can let you know if they make it out okay, right?"

"Yes. I'm sure Ronald will think they're heading to Seattle if he hears them leave. If they go to the airport, he'll be clueless. We could even have a chance to pack a few things at our homes."

"Right, and I can have some of our men pick up their vehicles and deliver them wherever they want. To my place or somewhere else, their choice." He paused at the front door where more bags were stacked.

"I can't believe Jared did this." She ran her hand over Aidan's arm.

"He must have followed your trail here. He looked surprised to see Nick, though if he had followed your trail, he should have known Nick and Greg were here too. I'm sure that pissed him off even more."

"He might have realized Greg and I ran with you last night too, when we pretended it was just the two of us. I'm sure he was furious."

Nick shook his head. "Serves him right."

She agreed. If Jared and his brother had been decent, she wouldn't have needed to look for Nick, and as long as Aidan and his men weren't doing anything illegal or causing trouble for their pack, Ronald and Jared should have been at least civil to them. Especially after they rescued Joey!

They packed up the car, and Aidan swept Holly off her feet so she wouldn't have to walk in the snow since she was only wearing a pair of socks, no snow boots. Greg ran lickety-split to the car, not about to have anyone carry him. That was just for girls. Greg sat in the far back seat with Nick.

"That's one way to get the adrenaline pumping," Nick said as everyone buckled their seat belts, "but Jared sure ticks me off. I was enjoying the comfort of that nice bed."

"We'll have you on the plane soon, and you can make the chairs recline like a bed," Aidan said.

"It still won't be like a real bed."

Holly was sitting on pins and needles, concerned about the rest of her family as Aidan wrapped his arm around her and pulled her close. She called her mom.

"We're on our way," her mom said before Holly could tell them to go to the airport.

"Go to the private airport near there."

"Eddie, turn around. We need to head to the private airport… Yes, yes, surely they know what they're doing."

"Aidan's got a plane waiting, and he can fly us to the

airport near our house. We'll have a head start and can pick up some things from our homes."

"We won't have any transportation from the airport," her mother said.

Mike was on his phone calling someone. "Okay, bring two cars. There will be..." He turned to Holly. "How many are we transporting to the Grays' homes in Seattle?"

"All of us." Then Holly said to her mom, "Mike's getting us transportation so we can grab stuff from our homes. We'll return to the airport and take a flight out." She looked at Aidan to confirm, putting the phone on speaker.

"Yes, or if they want, they can take one of the vehicles with their things and go to my house in the Klamath Mountains. They can just stay there until we figure out what to do next."

"What did you want to do, Mom? Drive all the way to California, or fly down there?"

"Fly. If Aidan can get us another vehicle to use while we're down there—"

"Chauffeured even, if they'd like," Aidan said.

"Cool," Greg said in the back. He and Nick had taken pillows and blankets with them, and he sounded half-asleep.

"Okay, Mom?"

"Yes, so far so good. Jared didn't howl his distress. It bought us a little time. No one's come after us, but if they did, they'd probably head the wrong way. There wouldn't be any reason for us to go in this direction, which would be out of our way."

"Okay, good. Is Dad okay with this?"

"We were all asleep. I don't think this is the time to talk about how we're feeling."

"Okay, I'll ask later. Just let me know if you run into any trouble. We'll probably be behind you soon, the way Ted is tearing down the road."

Ted nodded. "You better believe it. If we get stopped, at least we can keep Ronald and the others from delaying your parents and sister."

"Great," Nick said. "I can see me ending up back in the wilderness again."

"That's not happening," Aidan said.

"I'll let you go for now," Holly said. "Oh, wait, I think I see your taillights. Apply your brakes."

The car's brake lights flashed.

"Good, it's just us closing in on you."

"That's good news. Your dad was driving like a maniac. You can slow down, dear. It's just your daughter, Greg, and their friends." She said to Holly, "We'll talk soon."

"Okay, love you." Holly ended the call with her mother.

"I don't know how you could live under that controlling SOB," Nick said. "I put up with it because Millicent wanted to stay with the pack. After she died, I didn't know where to go."

"I understand," Holly said. "It's been difficult, more so of late. It's important to help our kind, whether the wolves are part of our pack or not. I've always had issues with Ronald, but I put up with him so I could provide medical care for our pack. One time, he didn't want me to take care of a sick family passing through Seattle. I ignored him and assisted them anyway.

"The mother had pneumonia, and the rest of the

family was sick with the flu. Once they were on the road to recovery, Ronald lectured me big time. I was never to disobey him and go behind his back. I told him if he wanted me to stay with the pack and continue to provide medical assistance, he would have to allow me to assist any sick or injured wolf who came through our territory. Naturally, he didn't like that.

"After that, I never saw anyone else who needed my attention who wasn't part of our pack. It could be that no one else ever needed my assistance, or they didn't know a wolf doctor lived in the Seattle area."

"Or Ronald made sure to steer them out of Seattle so you would never know about it," Aidan said.

"Yes, my thought too. His policy of excluding any fresh blood is one of my greatest concerns."

"You'd think people would leave the pack."

"Some do. Some love the Seattle area and have always lived there, so they don't want to leave. You can't live there unless you're a member of the pack. Some feel loyal to the group as a whole and don't want to leave friends and family behind. Others hate change too much. Finding another pack that suits them... Well, you know the old saying 'The grass is greener on the other side of the fence'? Some were afraid they'd end up in another pack that was just as restrictive or even worse. And finding one that would accept new wolves could be an issue too.

"No one is strong enough to fight the leader and his brother and the four enforcers we have in the pack. That means six aggressive males to fight to have any change. After other packs tried to take us over without success, those who might have thought they had an inkling of a chance don't even try. And no one has shown any interest in being a leader. Then again, without a chance to become the leader, no one has expressed any interest in taking over. Anyone who hinted at it would probably be a dead wolf."

"Sounds as though you need some leadership changes," Aidan said.

"Are you applying for the job, Doc?" Mike asked, leaning back in his seat.

Aidan smiled. "No."

Holly considered that Aidan could be their pack leader. He had fought Jared well. He was caring and protective. Not that he had any interest in doing anything else but his research, yet she kept thinking how great it would be to have another doctor in the pack. Leading it. Allowing them to grow and have a say. Bringing Nick back into the pack—if he could be convinced to return.

"That could work," she said, smiling at Aidan. "You could encourage others to join. Allow me to treat any wolf who came into the area. Convince Nick to return to the pack."

Aidan and his men laughed.

"You'd have to take a mate too." Ted winked.

"I'd help remove the bad leadership," Mike said.

"Not without me, you wouldn't," Ted said.

"You guys are already looking for a new job?" Aidan sounded amused.

"We're in the business of protecting people, and if Holly's pack needs a protector or two, I'd certainly be willing to do it," Ted said.

"You're supposed to be protecting me, which means I'd have to lead the group," Aidan said.

"Seriously?" Mike asked.

"Hell yeah. Maybe someone would step up to the plate to lead the pack. But with more democratic rules," Aidan said.

"There are six of them," Holly warned. "And you're supposed to be helping Nick get to Montana."

"Yeah," Nick said.

"And my family to your house," Holly added.

"If his house has a hot tub, I'm all for hanging out there," Greg said.

"I thought you were asleep."

"No, the conversation is too interesting."

"I have a hot tub and a heated swimming pool."

"Even better," Greg said.

"All right, we go ahead with this plan, then after Christmas, we can see about helping your pack make a change in leadership, if they want it." Aidan kissed her head. "We can see if anyone else my brother usually hires for missions like this would be willing to assist. Ousting Ronald and his men will only work if the pack agrees to have new leaders. What if the majority want the leadership to stand as it is? What if someone else takes over, and everyone's as unhappy as before? If they're unhappy now, that is."

"You're right, of course." Holly settled back against her seat. "Some secretly speak out against Ronald and his men, but others are quiet. I don't know if the vast majority would welcome change or not. I would. My family would, especially now, I believe. I'm not one hundred percent sure about the rest of the pack. You know how some can bad-mouth a situation, but when you tell them to put up or shut up, they melt into the background."

"That's all too true."

"What are we going to do, Doc?" Mike asked.

"We'll go to my place first, unless the Grays want to stop in Seattle and gather some more belongings. Sorry, Nick."

"I can deal with it. Anything is better than being out in the cold and snow for another night. I kept thinking I'd get used to it, but I was getting tired of it awfully quick."

"I'm glad you're good with being with us." Aidan said to Mike, "Then after that, we'll take Nick to Montana. I'll let the Cunningham pack know we'll be arriving later in the day."

When they reached the private airport, they saw a plane's engines running, and Holly was relieved.

"Okay, that's it. Let's go," Aidan said.

They drove up to the hangar, and everyone piled out of the two cars. Holly hurried to hug her parents and her sister, tears in her eyes. "I'm so sorry about all of this."

"Why? Jared's the ass." Nick carried some of his camping gear onto the plane.

Greg had his arms full of stuff, but he paused to get a hug from his parents and sister. "We've got to hurry."

"Yes." Her mom sighed and began carrying bags to the plane. Holly was surprised they'd packed up that quickly.

Dressed in a white shirt and epaulets that looked like an airliner uniform, a dark-haired, dark-eyed pilot welcomed them. "I'm Cesar Alvarez, your pilot, and eager to get you to where you need to be."

"Thanks, Cesar. He's been flying for us for years," Aidan said.

Everyone else thanked him too.

The guys helped with Holly's family's stuff and got the rest of the gear on board. Then everyone climbed into the craft, found seats, and buckled themselves in. "We grabbed your things too," her mom said.

"Oh, good," Greg said.

"Thanks, Mom, Dad, Marianne."

"Mr. and Mrs. Gray, did you want to stop off at your place near Seattle and get some more of your things?" Aidan asked.

"Please call us Margaret and Eddie. Can we do that? Would we have enough time?"

"We should be able to," Aidan said. "Ronald or his men would take at least an hour and a half to drive there. Maybe longer. They might go to my cabin first to take care of us and be even longer."

"Yes, then let's do that." Her mom relaxed a little, but everyone looked worn out.

Holly told Cesar which airport to fly to and he taxied until they were airborne and on their way.

"We need to drop by my house," Holly said. "I need to grab my computer, more clothes, and other essentials."

"And our Christmas presents," Greg said. "Can't forget those. Unless you think we're going to return here before Christmas."

"I doubt it," Margaret said.

"I have another idea. We could have your vehicles driven to my place now. They'll get there in a couple of days. The drivers can load up whatever you want to take, once you decide what that is. I still prefer you riding in the plane," Aidan said.

They all agreed.

"Here we are," Cesar said thirty minutes later as they approached the private airport near their homes.

As soon as they landed, one of Rafe's drivers met them there.

"Cesar, take a break for a while, and we'll see you in a bit," Aidan said. Nick had crashed on one of the reclining seats on the plane. "He can stay here with you."

Everyone climbed into the stretch limousine, and Greg and Marianne were sliding on the long seats. "Wow, a party bus. Too cool," Greg said.

They rode the short distance to Holly's parents' home, and Mike and Ted stayed to help them pack. The chauffeur, who also served as a bodyguard, went with Aidan and Holly to her home, which was about half a mile away.

"Are we going to have enough drivers to take my car and my mom's car too?"

"Yeah, the drivers will be arriving soon." Aidan went inside Holly's place and looked at all the Christmas decorations. A seven-foot tree decorated in red poinsettias, red and gold balls, and red-and-green-plaid bows, the scent of Christmas cinnamon spice, and a large collection of Santas sitting on top of her bookshelves and fireplace mantel made her home warm and inviting for Christmas. Aidan was visualizing where she could put them in his house, if they became mated wolves. He'd never had any interest in decorating for the holidays. Until now. She would definitely make his house a home.

Holly stopped to see what he was looking at. "That part's kind of sad. But I wasn't going to be here for Christmas anyway." She sighed, then went into her office and began gathering her computer. Aidan hurried to carry it for her.

"I'll get this. Just tell us what you want us to grab, and then you can pack whatever else you need."

"All right. Just all that and the files in the top drawer. I'll be right back." She'd gotten a call and, worried that the others were in trouble, had pulled out Aidan's phone and nearly dropped it. She returned to her office. "Ronald's calling."

Aidan took the phone. She wanted to hear what was being said, but more than that, she wanted to change into her own clothes and pack her things so they could be out of the area as soon as possible. So she left to let Aidan handle it.

Chapter 21

"This is Dr. Denali. What can I do for you, Ronald?" Aidan asked the pack leader on his cell, glad Holly and her family were safe with him now. Holly had chosen sides, and Aidan hoped the wolf leader and his brother would be man enough to give her a break, but he was afraid—if their history was any indication—they'd be hardheaded about this.

"Where are they? The Grays? They had no reason to run off in the middle of the night. What did you tell them? That I'd make them pay for what you did to my brother?"

"Jared came to my cabin and attacked one of my men. If we did that at your place, you'd have every right to defend yourself." Aidan wasn't about to explain the Grays' actions or concerns with Ronald.

"You've taken the woman who's to be his mate," Ronald growled.

"Not according to either of them. Apparently, that's only your idea."

"Like hell it is. What about the rest of the family?"

"They left?" Aidan smiled.

"You know they did. I want them returned at once."

"Maybe you didn't know this, but as a pack leader, you can't dictate your people's lives. You can ask them to keep in touch with you, but you're running a dictatorship. It's up to them to decide what they want to do. Leave, stay, or return home."

Ronald hung up on him.

"How'd it go?" Holly rolled two bags out of her bedroom. She had changed out of his sweats and socks and was wearing a pair of her own jeans—formfitting, sexy—a sweater, a parka, and high-heeled boots that accentuated her long, shapely legs.

He was glad she was able to dress in her own clothes again, though she'd made his sweats look damn sexy. "He wants all of you returned at once."

"Forget it. Don't tell my folks what Ronald said. I don't want them changing their minds, and I'd be afraid Ronald would try to use them to get at me. Unless Jared and Ronald are no longer in charge, I'm not going back to stay. I care about my people, but I can't live under the pack leader's rules any longer."

Aidan got another call. "It's your dad." They hauled the rest of the stuff out to Holly's car. "Yes, sir. Is everything going all right over there?"

"Yes, we're ready to go." Eddie sounded anxious.

"Okay, we're coming to get you."

A car pulled up, and a male passenger got out. He was another of Rafe's men, Harvey Walton. "I'm supposed to drive the car to your place, right, Dr. Denali?" He was another former elite service member, this one an Army Ranger. Though it seemed someone with that kind of training shouldn't just being delivering a car somewhere, these guys were all buddies of theirs: hard-charging, ready for any emergency or mission no matter how big or small. Rafe paid them top dollar no matter what the situation entailed.

"Holly, this is Harvey Walton. Not only will he make sure your car and belongings arrive at my home safe and sound, but he will protect them with his life on the way there. This is Dr. Holly Gray, and the car is hers."

"The honor's all mine," Harvey said.

She smiled and shook his hand. "Thanks."

"My pleasure." Harvey winked.

"Her parents and sister and brother will be at the house when you arrive. I'll see you later."

"Right, Doc. Doc." Harvey took the key Holly offered to her car and got in to drive off.

Holly had a couple of bags of clothes, her computer, and files she was taking with her. Afterward, they drove to her parents' place and loaded everyone and the belongings they would need for a couple of days. The rest of their belongings would arrive after that, and since they would be staying at Aidan's place, they didn't need to take as much with them as Holly did. Like Holly, Greg had dressed in his own clothes. He didn't trust the driver with their Christmas presents though. Not that he would steal anything, but Greg was afraid when the guy had to sleep, someone might break into the car.

"We have safe houses we stay at." Harvey looked stern, annoyed Greg would even insinuate he couldn't keep their stuff safe, but Aidan knew he was just pulling the teen's leg.

Greg looked at the large plastic bags of gift-wrapped presents and back up at Harvey. "You promise you'll protect them?"

"With my life."

Aidan smiled, but the truth was, Harvey would. No one stole anything from him without paying for it.

"All right." Greg helped the driver load the presents

in the car, though there was barely enough spare room to do so.

It was a good thing too, because they didn't have room on the plane for anything more.

"Oh, Holly, I totally forgot. Marianne grabbed your phone and gave it to me for safekeeping. Jared called a dozen times or so. I didn't answer it and put it on mute." Margaret pulled the phone out of her purse and handed it to Holly.

"Thanks, Mom. Has Ronald tried to get ahold of you?"

"We all have our phones turned off, but yes, each of us has received calls from him."

Greg pulled his phone out of his pocket. "Even me."

"Text messages?"

"Yes, just saying he needs to talk to us. And asking what the hell is going on," their dad said. "We shut them all off in case he could be tracking us."

"Okay, good, though I think they can be tracked with the right equipment unless you pull the battery out, and you can't with these phones," Holly said. "He wouldn't be able to catch up to us anyway, and I doubt he'd want to at this point. Not once we're out of his territory."

Once they arrived at the airport and were loading up the plane, Aidan got another call. Expecting it to be Ronald again, he was surprised to see it was Rafe. He was certain Ted or Mike—or any of the guys who'd come to help them on this adventure—had apprised Rafe of the situation.

"I knew you'd get yourself in a bind if you went anywhere near where the Seattle pack was staying," Rafe said.

"Yeah, well, I've got another doctor on my team

now, and we're going to solve this longevity issue one way or another. If Jade hasn't talked to you yet about it, I'm bringing Holly with me for Christmas."

"This sounds serious."

"It is. Here's the kicker. Her pack's blood cells show they haven't been having the issues that the rest of us are."

"You're kidding. What the hell is going on?"

"Not sure, but when we checked Nick's blood, it was the same as Holly's. I've tested Holly, and her aging process appears to be as slow as it should be. I want to test her parents—with their permission, of course—to see if there is any change for them. What's interesting to note is their *lupus garou* family roots date back to 795. What if they haven't changed because their genes are more stable or able to fight off this change?"

"Sounds like you've finally got a possible lead. That's great."

"Mike will probably tell you I gave him some of Holly's blood. I was going to try it on me first, but he wouldn't let me."

"I hope you know what you're doing."

"It's just like a regular blood transfusion. Did the guys tell you our schedule?" Aidan assumed they would have.

"Your place, then to the Bigfork, Montana, pack to deliver Nick, and then to the chalet?"

"Correct. As long as Nick likes the pack well enough and wants to stay for a while. If not, I'll take him wherever else he'd like to go."

Nick opened his eyes and interjected, "I'll stay with

the Montana pack through the holidays at least. That way, you can see your brother and continue working on your research."

"Okay, did you hear that? Nick says he'll stay with the Montana pack through the holidays."

"Good. I won't mention it to Toby yet, until we know you're on your way."

"Sounds good."

They ended the call, and Holly's parents said, "Yes, we'll give you a sample of our blood."

"Mine too," Marianne said, "and I hate giving blood, but for this, I will."

"We give permission if she wants to," her mom said. Her dad concurred.

"Okay, at the house, I'll take your blood samples and examine them. Marianne is probably too young to show anything different, but I'll check it just in case." Aidan sure hoped Holly's blood would prove to be a life-changer for them. If it made a difference, he hoped it would be long-term and not something that had to be added to the bloodstream periodically.

———

They finally arrived at the airport closest to where Aidan lived while the sun was beginning to rise. Another driver with a limousine picked them up. Everyone was wolf tired.

Their driver dropped by a coffee shop for coffee, doughnuts, and hot chocolates. All the grumbly wolves perked up and were feeling better right away. Though most were planning to take a nap later.

Then they drove the rest of the way to Aidan's home,

which was situated on a hill with a fantastic view of a lake and surrounded by pines, firs, and hemlocks.

"Beautiful," Holly said, loving the setting as much as the house.

"It's so sparsely populated out here that you can run as wolves to your heart's content. No real wild wolves out here, just black bears, red and gray foxes, cougars, bobcats, lynxes, to name a few."

"This is like paradise," Margaret said, "always living in the wilderness."

"And you live here all by yourself?" Holly couldn't imagine living alone here for months at a time. With a mate, sure. But before that? He must have been a recluse.

"Ted and Mike live with me. But yeah, I used to live here all by myself. I was busy with my research. But I was flying to various pack locations to get blood samples and would spend some time getting to know the pack members. Now, some of them send their blood samples to me monthly. In the beginning, I met with each of the packs to personally talk to the leaders and their people. I can't imagine living alone now. And I'm glad I don't have to."

"I know what you mean," Nick said. "I thought I could get used to living alone, but I couldn't. I didn't know where other packs were, and I didn't want to live just among humans. You can't know how much this means to me, being with my own kind again."

"We're thrilled to see you again too," Margaret said. "I'm glad Aidan is taking you to a pack where I hope you can be at home. We'd love to visit you when you're all settled."

"I'm all for that."

Margaret said, "We hope we're not going to be too much of an imposition for you, Aidan."

"Not at all. Even if I was there, it wouldn't be a problem. The house would have been empty for the next three weeks, so I'm glad you're staying here. And I have plenty of rooms here, so feel free to take whichever room appeals, and you're free to stay as long as you like."

They hauled their stuff into the expansive living room. The room was centered on a massive stone fireplace, with a large, carved oak coffee table, a sculpted rug, and seating for a dozen people. Bookshelves covered one wall, with floor-to-ceiling windows on another.

"It looks like you could throw big parties here," Holly remarked.

"For wolves only," Aidan said. "Rafe has parties for humans and a few wolves at his place because of his business dealings. Mine are strictly for wolf friends and family. I have enough bedrooms for overflow guests when we have them. Seven bedrooms, five bathrooms, and the master bedroom and bath. It's a nice wolf retreat."

"I hope I can return and enjoy the company and place a little longer someday," Nick said.

Aidan nodded. "Absolutely. If you ever need a ride from where you're living, we can send the jet."

"Even better."

Holly couldn't believe it as she looked at the high vaulted ceilings and all the ornately carved wood cornices and tried to envision the house decorated for Christmas. She'd thought the cabin would have been fun for Christmas. This place was even better.

The dining area and kitchen were open to the living

area, making the house feel even bigger. Double fridges, ovens, huge granite counters—perfect for a chef or two. She could see why Ted and Mike would like to prepare meals here.

"You're going to leave Ted or Mike here to cook meals, right?" Greg asked. "I'll help."

"They've got to guard—" her dad began to say, just as she opened her mouth to say the same thing.

"Fine by me," Aidan said. "We're just going to Montana and then to Rafe's place, so there's no need for you to go with us. And then you can go home to your families once you've taught Greg all you know."

They laughed.

"My regular maid comes in daily when I'm in residence, and I have another bodyguard who will be here, and a woman who can cook too," Aidan said.

"We'll have to check in with Rafe," Ted said.

Aidan shook his head, though he didn't look like he really minded.

Everyone checked out each of the bedrooms to decide which room they would stay in. Her parents picked one of the rooms that had a view of the lake. Both Greg and Marianne took rooms that overlooked the pool.

Holly had to peek at the master bedroom. When she walked into it, she was impressed. It was like a corner apartment with a view of the pool from one window and the lake from another. The king-size bed sat against one wall, a fireplace opposite it with sofas and a coffee table. High vaulted ceilings added to the enormous size of the room. Just beautiful. And way too big for just one person.

Aidan joined her, running his hands up her back in a light caress. "Well, what do you think?"

"Do you sleep alone?"

He chuckled. "Always."

"Then I think you need some company in that big bed."

"We've got a date when we return."

"Agreed." She headed for the bathroom. Her jaw dropped when she saw the beautiful, apricot-colored tile, the chandeliers casting sparkling lights on the arched ceiling, and… She stared at the long shower with three showerheads! One had a long, winding handheld showerhead. "Okay, now, you shower alone, right?"

He laughed and folded his arms. "Yes, and the shower has so many showerheads for the resale value. You know Rafe is in the real estate business. All our places are built with resale in mind."

"Okay, just checking."

She eyed the large tub, big enough for two, and the window behind it with a view of the lake. She checked out the closet and found it stretched way, way up so it had racks and shelves four racks high.

"You could fit a whole family's wardrobe and more in here," she said. "Just wow."

He'd only used the bottom two poles for his clothes. A built-in ladder was used to reach the upper clothing poles and shelves.

"You can put your clothes on the lower poles, and I can move mine up to the next level."

She stared up at the upper poles and shelves. "I'd have to do a lot of shopping to fill all this up."

He laughed.

"I'm not moving in with you permanently." She didn't want him to feel she thought this was her home now.

"Temporarily then?"

"Yes. Until we can get somewhere with your research and we can deal with Ronald."

"Or, I can get you to agree we're perfect for each other."

She smiled. "You might get tired of stumbling over me in this place."

"I doubt it. I'm sure that I'd find even more of a reason for you to stay."

She sighed. "We'll see." She wasn't jumping into a wolf mating and then regretting it for the rest of their mated lives—since wolves didn't believe in divorce. "We'd better go find Nick and take him to Montana before they wonder what happened to us."

Aidan drew her to the window that overlooked the pool, and she saw her brother, sister, and parents looking at the pool. She laughed. "I guess we're on our own then."

Aidan got a call on his cell phone as they left the bedroom and headed into the living room where Nick was lying down on a couch, sound asleep again. Poor old wolf. "Rafe," Aidan whispered to Holly.

She assumed it was about the guys going with them. If she were Rafe, she'd say the bodyguards would have to go with Aidan.

He answered the phone. "Just a sec." He took her hand and moved her out on the deck that overlooked the lake. "Yeah, Rafe?" He put the phone on speaker.

"Ted and Mike go with you. I'll send a couple of other men to watch over the place. Your cook and housekeeper can do the rest. I want to make sure both you and Holly and her family are protected, just in case Ronald has any notion to cause trouble for them."

"All right."

"Thanks, Rafe," Holly said.

"Holly?" Rafe asked.

"Yeah, and thanks for letting me come to see you for Christmas."

Rafe laughed. "Don't be surprised if Toby calls you his aunt. He calls all the guys who work for me uncle, and he doesn't have an aunt yet."

She smiled at Aidan. "Okay, thanks for the heads-up. And that's fine with me."

"Jade would like to talk to you too, Holly. She can call you."

Holly gave him her phone number, thinking it was nice that Jade wanted to talk with her personally before she visited.

"We're leaving as soon as I can wake Nick," Aidan said. "I'll let Ted and Mike know about the bodyguard status. Talk later."

After they ended the call, Aidan took Holly into his arms and kissed her. "The whole family is ready for me to be a mated wolf. They think I can't look after myself out here."

"They think you need more than just work to do."

"Well, that too. You sure could change my mind about work anytime."

She laughed. She could imagine neither of them getting *any* work done.

"Let's get your parents' and sister's blood samples before we go."

"I'll go find them." Holly found them sitting around the pool. "Hey, unless you've changed your mind, can Aidan check your blood before you go swimming?"

"Yeah, sure," her mom said.

After he took samples of their blood, he checked the cells over. "They all look good. No changes."

Everyone let out a sigh of relief, but Marianne was the first out the door of the lab room. "Going to swim. Last one in is a slowpoke wolf."

Holly said goodbye to her parents, and to her sister and brother, who were already in the pool. "You ought to come in," Greg said.

"Water's great," Marianne said.

"Later! Have fun." Holly told them about the setup with the bodyguards and then said goodbye.

Her mom and dad hurried out in swimsuits and both jumped into the water, amusing Holly. She swore for the first time in her life, her dad really didn't care about returning to the business.

"We'd give you another hug, but then you'd be all wet," her mom said.

"Save it for later. Love ya! And Merry Christmas! I'll open my presents when I return."

Then she left the pool area to find a new bodyguard crew arriving. Rafe, or his administrative assistant, sure was fast. She guessed with the kind of wealth he possessed, he could get things done with a snap of his fingers. That must be nice. She also assumed he had a lot of headaches in his line of work.

Aidan was waking Nick. "Sorry, Nick. We would have tried carrying you out of here so you could sleep, but..."

"I'm fine. I'll sleep on the plane and be wide awake when we arrive in Montana."

"How's your wrist?"

"Good. Don't even notice any sprain at all."

"Good." Aidan unwrapped it and checked him out

anyway, and Nick shook his head, indicating he wasn't feeling any pain. "All right. Let's go."

Then Holly got a call, and Aidan glanced in her direction, looking concerned, probably figuring it was Jared or Ronald.

"Just Jade."

Aidan looked relieved, and as Holly said hello to Jade, they headed out to the car.

"I wanted to know if there's anything special you'd like to eat while you're here," Jade said.

"If you have chocolate on hand, I'm good to go."

Aidan smiled at Holly as they got into the car with his bodyguards and Nick.

"Now, I don't want you to feel in any way that I mean for you to get us any Christmas gifts, but you and I could run into town and have a ladies' day out if you'd like, see all the Christmas decorations, have lunch at a Victorian tearoom, and shop, or window-shop."

"I'd love that." Holly had wondered how she was going to be able to get away to shop for everyone for Christmas. This would truly be special.

"Great. The guys can entertain Toby, and we'll entertain ourselves. I can't wait to meet you."

"Same here." Holly really hoped she liked Jade and Rafe—in the event they became family.

Chapter 22

ON THE PLANE RIDE TO MONTANA, THEY ALL SLEPT, EVEN Ted and Mike. They wanted to be well rested by the time they arrived at Bigfork. Holly hoped Paul and Lori's pack didn't overwhelm Nick at first, but then again, maybe he needed to be shown that other wolves would love to have him in their pack. She kept thinking Ronald should be embarrassed that other packs would see him for what he was. He thought he was better than them, his blood purer, far superior.

She expected just a small welcoming committee at the airport, not the crowd of wolves waiting near the private hangar. Half a dozen kids were holding up a sign welcoming Santa Claus, and another twenty or so adult wolves were smiling and cheered to see them.

Nick was smiling, all misty-eyed. He did look like a thinned-down version of Old Saint Nick, even without the red suit.

Holly's eyes watered at the sight of the lovely welcome he was receiving. She ran her hand over his back and whispered, "See, they love you already."

He chuckled, and she knew he was thinking it was because they saw him as Santa Claus, but who wouldn't want to take in a widowed wolf who was as kindhearted as he was?

His gaze switched from the kids to the adults and

locked onto a group of older women, none of them accompanied by mates. He smiled.

They were all wearing cheerful expressions, dressed to impress, looking as though it was killing them not to move forward and personally welcome him. Holly knew then he was going to feel right at home here.

"You may need our protection," Ted said softly to Nick.

He laughed, a belly laugh, just like Old Saint Nick.

If the women didn't fight over him too much, Holly thought he was going to be the life of the party. Not that he wouldn't think about his beloved mate, but maybe he could make another widowed wolf happy and they'd be content in their remaining years.

Holly half expected the women to spirit him away, but the pack leaders waited for him to crouch down and greet the kids with hugs first—which brought tears to the adults' eyes—and then they escorted him to an SUV. If Ronald's name hadn't been mud with this pack before this, it was now. They could see the kind of person Nick was, not some old ogre who created havoc for a pack.

Paul's SEAL buddy and diver friend and his diver mate, Allan and Debbie, joined them, along with Aidan, Holly, Nick, and Aidan's bodyguards.

Paul pulled out of the parking area to take them to Lori and his cabin on the lake. "We've opened a pack-size clubhouse and lodge that has bedrooms, kitchen, living area, bathrooms, and a deck with a view of the lake. It's right next door to our cabin, just through the woods. If you'd prefer staying with one of the other families instead, everyone is eager to say they were lucky to have you stay with them. Either way would be fine with us."

Lori handed Nick a list of the widowed ladies who were eager to open their homes to him. "All the widowed women but one have put their names on the list, Nick, if you'd care to stay with one of them until you decide what you would like to do permanently."

"Thank you, and I understand," Nick said.

"All the families are also eager to have you spend the time with them. Bachelor males too. Or you can stay with us. Or at the lodge."

"Or with us," Allan said. "We have a place on the mountain, no view of the lake, but beautiful views of the forests and mountains."

"I'm overwhelmed."

Not much overwhelmed Nick, but Holly could tell he was really touched because his voice was rough with emotion.

"Understandably. We have a friendly pack, and everyone is willing to help everyone. Or, if you feel you're not up to it and want to stay at the lodge, you're welcome to. It's entirely up to you," Lori said.

"We'd like to stay at the lodge," Aidan said, "since my bodyguards go wherever I end up. And Holly's not leaving my side either." He smiled down at her.

She squeezed his hand. "I teamed up with him to work on the longevity issue."

"Good show," Paul said. "Two heads should be better than one. Have you learned anything more?"

Aidan explained about the Gray family's blood and Nick's too.

"That sounds like something could come of it," Lori said.

"I sure hope so," Mike said, "since I'm the docs'

first test subject. I'd love to feel I've had a positive part in this."

They talked about what Aidan would do next if he found that Mike's cells were not aging as they would normally for the next several months.

Nick suddenly asked, "Can I call the little lady who didn't want me to stay with her?"

Holly was surprised he'd want to stay with someone who hadn't offered her home to him, but he was always into lost causes, giving special attention to children who held back and weren't practically fighting to reach him. Not that this woman was a lost cause, but Holly suspected that her reluctance had intrigued him.

"It isn't that she didn't want you to stay with her," Lori clarified. "Just that she was afraid if her name was added to the list, you wouldn't choose to stay with her." She gave Victoria Snow's phone number to him. "She's an Arctic wolf."

"Arctic wolf." Nick immediately got on his phone, and Holly was proud of him. "Hi, this is Nick Cornwall. I was wondering if you could put me up for a few days, if it wouldn't be too much trouble. I don't snore, and as long as I can get some milk and cookies, I'm easy to live with."

Holly chuckled. He sounded just like their good old Santa.

Nick laughed. "Okay. As long as it's not too much trouble," he repeated. "I don't want to put you out none… All right. Don't worry about getting ready for me. I'm easy. Really…" He smiled. "Okay, then we'll be over…" He looked at Lori to confirm a time.

"We can make a detour to her place. It'll take us about half an hour. More time if she needs more."

"Half an hour unless you need more time." Nick sighed. "We'll see you then. And don't put yourself out for me. I insist. See you soon." He pocketed his phone.

Everyone was silent as they drove to Victoria's home.

Then Lori said, "Thank you. She's really a sweet woman, rather shy, but she loves to bake, so she'll have a plate of hot cookies ready for you in a jiff."

Nick laughed and rubbed his stomach. "I like to keep in shape, so it just means extra runs, but if she'd like to get out and run with me, that works for me."

Holly was praying they'd find kinship and mutual interests.

They pulled up into the driveway of a one-story, gingerbread-trimmed Victorian house with a white picket fence and a wraparound porch. A light-pink house trimmed in white fretwork. Maybe that's why Victoria had been reluctant to offer her house for his stay, afraid Nick would feel it was too feminine for his tastes. Scalloped shingles; louvered, shuttered windows; arched openings to the deck; cornices; three window dormers in the roof; steep turrets; and all with lacy trim work welcomed guests to visit. Sparkly lights trimmed the inside of each window and all along the roofline, the pillars, and the railings on the steps leading to the brick front walk.

Fresh snow covered the yard, gingerbread Victorian birdhouses hung from a tree out front, and lighted candy canes lined the walkway. A golden candle glowed at each of the windows. Smoke curled from the chimney, making anyone feel welcome, Holly thought.

She didn't know about Nick, but she loved the house. He didn't comment. She knew him well enough to know he wouldn't say anything negative about the place. He was too kindhearted for that. Not that he didn't have his growly moments. When it came to Ronald and the way he led the pack, Nick had no reservations about making his feelings known.

A woman opened the door, her white hair all pulled up into a bun on the top of her head and a white lace-trimmed apron covering her blue dress as she dried off her hands on a red towel. She looked a little anxious but smiled when everyone began piling out of the car.

"Victoria, this is Nick, and, Nick, this is Victoria," Lori said.

"The pleasure is all mine," Nick said and took Victoria's hand in his and kissed it, looking into her eyes the whole time as if he was already smitten.

Holly had seen him treat his wife in a loving way all the years before her death. It looked as though he was dealing with his grief well enough now. One thing she hadn't considered, since both were widowed, was that Nick and Victoria had something in common to share and could talk to each other about how they felt about losing their beloved mates.

"I was afraid you wouldn't like to stay here because…" Victoria's cheeks pinkened. "Well…" She motioned to her house.

"It's charming. I wouldn't have felt quite at home anywhere else. I hate to drag all my stuff into your house though."

"No, no, the house is all yours. I have four bed-rooms you can choose from. I mean, I have five bed-rooms." She blushed terribly again. "But four you can choose from."

He laughed. "I'm sure one of them will be perfect."

Everyone began hauling his stuff inside the house, and Holly smelled sugar cookies.

"Boy, do I smell something good," Nick said.

"Lori and Paul planned a pack gathering and a feast tonight at the clubhouse. I baked some sugar cookies just for you. I mean, for everyone. For your welcoming party." Blushing further, she led him into the kitchen.

"Which bedroom do you want to use?" Ted asked.

"He can have the one near the end of the hall. It's the largest."

"You can just put the camping gear in the…garage?" Nick waited for Victoria to say where it could go.

"Yes, there's room in the storage area of the garage. Would anyone else like milk and cookies?" she asked.

"No, we're going to the lodge to get settled in," Aidan said. "But thanks."

"Thanks for bringing me here," Nick said, shaking the guys' hands, then giving Holly and Lori hugs. Then he sat down to eat his cookies and drink his milk.

"We'll see you at the lodge tonight," Lori said. "Don't you two forget."

Nick winked at her.

This time, Lori blushed.

They left the house and climbed into the car, and Lori said, "Ohmigod, he's a real charmer."

Holly was delighted to see that everyone loved him. He truly was lovable. "Believe me, I haven't seen him that cheerful in months. It appears this could be a good move for him."

"He's adorable," Lori said. "I'm sure we'll love him to pieces. I can't believe Victoria moved him to the bedroom next to hers. She's been widowed for five years. If there's a mating and wedding, will you all return for it?"

"You bet," Aidan said, tugging Holly under his arm as if he was claiming her before any wolves in Lori and Paul's pack got any ideas. He got another call and pulled out his phone. *Ronald.* "Yeah, Ronald?" He put it on speaker so Holly could hear what Ronald had to say.

"What are the Grays going to do about their shop? They need to return there to take care of it. Their friends can't watch it forever."

"Some changes need to be made in your leadership."

Ronald ignored his comment, and Aidan was surprised he didn't act angry. Maybe he thought he'd better back down, attitude-wise, if he was going to get his pack members back. It had to have been a blow to his ego when they left without him having the chance to banish them. And Holly was a valuable asset he couldn't afford to lose. "From what I understand, you're resettling Nick, so that can't be an issue."

"We need to do some blood testing of your people to learn if there are changes in your blood now or in the future," Aidan said.

"Holly already does that for us."

"That's good. But I need to see the results and compare them to see if she's missed anything."

There was a long pause. "You have plenty of test subjects. You don't need to use my people for your research."

"Neither the Grays' nor Nick's blood have changed. It's possible no one in the rest of the pack will have an issue. But what if they do?"

"Holly will take care of it."

"If she doesn't return?"

"You can't hold her hostage. She needs to be here for our people."

Aidan patted her shoulder. "Maybe she has other plans."

"I do," Holly said. "I'm working with Dr. Denali on a cure. I want everyone in the pack who agrees to give blood samples to do so, then we can see if there are any changes. It's up to you. Do you want to be the bearer of bad news if our people's blood begins to change? If they could have learned this early on but didn't because you wouldn't cooperate?"

"You can do that from here and still take care of our people. You have an obligation to them and to my brother. Hell, you took off when he could have used some doctoring after Aidan and his bodyguard injured him."

"It was his fault for entering Aidan's territory and starting the fight. Mike wouldn't have initiated it. Jared had planned a sneak attack on Mike. He had no call to attack him."

"My job is to guard, not to serve on the offensive," Mike said from the back seat.

She left out the part about her attacking Jared before he reached Mike. She wondered if Jared had told his brother what her part in all of that had been. She suspected not.

"I don't have any obligation to your brother. In case you don't recall, once he learned I wanted to speak with Dr. Denali, Jared said he wouldn't consider mating me. Not that I was considering mating him either. Not only that, but after Jared bit *me*, I needed medical attention."

Prolonged silence. "I said you can take the blood samples from our people from here and stay here." Another significant pause. "Hell, all right. You can share the results with Dr. Denali, but that's it."

"I'm staying with the Denalis for Christmas. After that? We'll see. There'd have to be a lot of changes in pack leadership. Open friendships with other packs. If wolves from other packs need medical attention when they're in the area, I can take care of them. Outsider wolves can join our pack, and our people can freely come and go as they please. And, we welcome wolves into our territory when they show up, instead of muscle telling them to leave our territory pronto." That was only if things didn't work out between her and Aidan.

"How about we kick everyone out of the pack who agrees with you? For starters?" Ronald asked, obviously being his usual bristly self.

"We'll take in whoever you want to banish," Aidan said. "We'll make sure they have jobs and homes. So do your worst." Aidan hung up on him.

Holly frowned at Aidan, surprised he'd end the call without allowing her to have a final word.

"He's the kind of pack leader that's so hard-nosed, you have to be hard-nosed right back. There's no negotiating with him. Maybe he'll change his mind, but at this point, I doubt it. Anyone who sides with you and your family is the enemy."

"You don't think we should go back and try to pacify him, just to get his cooperation so I can get my people's blood samples?"

"Hell no," Aidan said, and Paul and Allan said nearly the same thing. "He might mind his p's and q's with you because you're valuable to the pack, but anyone else? He'll make them toe the line. And that includes your family. He might say he'll allow some of the things you want, but when you're back there?"

"He'll renege."

"There's a good chance he will. He's in charge, and he won't like that you, or anyone else, is dictating to him on how to rule the pack."

"I agree," Lori said. "I wouldn't trust him or his brother. What if his brother believes you should mate him when you go back?"

"She's got too much invested in me," Aidan said.

Holly chuckled. "You are so sure of yourself, aren't you?" She got another call a few minutes later and figured it was Ronald calling her back to give her an ultimatum—to have the final word. Instead, it was Jared calling. Now what? "Yeah, Jared?"

"I apologize for biting you, all right? Hell, you bit me first! In the heat of the conflict, battle lines blurred, and I lashed out. I didn't mean to bite you."

Yeah, he did. He was angry she'd bitten him. He could have stopped himself before he bit her. He only regretted it after she told his brother what he'd done, most likely.

"If I'd been thinking right, I would have only snapped at you."

"Apology accepted. I'm surprised you're apologizing though." She suspected his brother made him.

"So, no hard feelings and you'll return to the pack, right?"

Yep, Ronald must have figured Jared's actions had made her decide she'd had enough. "That's what the apology is all about? I have other plans, Jared. My decision to leave the pack has been long in coming."

"You'll regret it."

"Thanks for the warning." She hung up on him this time.

"Bad news?"

"I'll regret leaving the pack, Jared said, hoping an apology for biting me would change my mind, but he wasn't sincere in the least. I'm sure his brother made him apologize."

Aidan had already gotten his hackles up. "If they think they're going to do anything to make you regret leaving the pack, they'd better think again. They don't want an all-out war."

Chapter 23

WHEN THEY ARRIVED AT THE CLUBHOUSE AND LODGE, A delightful surprise was waiting for them. A two-tiered birthday cake decorated with lollipops, candy canes, a snowman, Santa, and a wolf sitting on top—perfect for a birthday so close to Christmas—was sitting on the kitchen island counter. A *Happy Birthday, Holly!!!* banner hung overhead. Four presents in colorful boxes sat next to the cake.

Holly just stared at the gifts and cake for a second, wondering how in the world they had known it was her birthday.

Lori quickly said, "Happy Birthday, Holly, courtesy of Aidan. We're going to get out of your way so you can have your birthday celebration. We've got all kinds of arrangements to make for the welcome celebration in a few hours. Go ahead and get settled in. We'll see you all soon." Lori and Debbie gave Holly hugs, and so did Paul and Allan afterward.

After they left, Holly gave Aidan a hug and a kiss.

"Happy birthday, Holly." He kissed her deeply in front of his bodyguards, and they cheered.

She couldn't believe Aidan had arranged to have this done before they got here. Then she remembered the call he'd made in private. She'd been afraid he was worried the Cunninghams wouldn't agree to take Nick in. Now she knew that wasn't all Aidan had been calling about. She thought the world of him for arranging to celebrate her birthday early, rather than in conjunction with Christmas.

She smiled at the question-mark candle. Ted found a lighter in a kitchen drawer and lit the candle for her.

"Make your wish," Mike said.

She wished with all her heart that she and Aidan would be the right wolves for each other, though everything he did for her made her love him more. She blew out the candle, then hugged and kissed Aidan again.

Everyone eagerly waited for her to open her presents, Aidan especially. No matter what he'd gotten for her, she would love the thought.

She removed the ribbon wrapped around the first box, opened the lid, and dug into the polka-dot green-and-red tissue paper. Folded neatly in the middle of the tissue paper was a shimmering blue swimsuit. She pulled it out to show everyone. She smiled at Aidan, and he smiled at the swimsuit. "It's beautiful. Thank you."

"If the size, or color, or style doesn't work for you, we can exchange it."

"It's just beautiful. I'm sure it'll fit." It reminded her of the sauna and not having a swimsuit, but being draped in mist had been perfect for that occasion.

"For the swimming pool, any season. And the chalet has a swimming pool and a hot tub."

She smiled. "I can't wait to wear it." She figured no going naked around his family. When she was alone with him, all bets were off.

She set it aside and opened the next box. It was a bigger box, but whatever was in it was smaller. She kept digging in the box until she found a house key decorated with a gray wolf surrounded by pine tree branches.

"To my house," Aidan said.

Ted and Mike chuckled.

She laughed. "How did you get one made in time?"

"I asked Jade. They have a copy of my house key. She sent it overnight to Lori."

"Wow, Aidan, this is the nicest real birthday I've ever had." She suspected he wouldn't have gotten her a key that fancy unless he was thinking she'd stay with him permanently.

She eagerly opened the next box, and this one had her *really* smiling. "A thirty-two-thousand-piece puzzle of a sunset in paradise. Ohmigod, Aidan!"

"That one will take you a little longer, but I figure the guys and I can help you out."

"It must mean you have a table we can use to put it together."

"Yeah, in the den."

"I can't wait to get started on it." She opened the last present and found a soft, white cashmere sweater. She hugged it to her body. "This is so soft and fluffy. I love it."

"It's warm enough for Colorado and dressy enough for Christmas. Most of all, I'll love hugging you in it."

"It's beautiful." She wrapped her arms around Aidan and kissed him. "Thank you for celebrating my birthday early, rather than on Christmas Day."

"You're so welcome. You should always have a special birthday for your special day."

Ted and Mike headed into the kitchen, scrounging for food for lunch so they could share the birthday cake afterward.

"We expect a fashion show while we make some sandwiches," Mike said.

"Yeah, the swimsuit first," Ted agreed.

She laughed. "We need to pick out a bedroom first." She grabbed her gifts.

The clubhouse was decorated with a rustic country Christmas look. A fireplace sported an ornate wrought-iron fire screen in front of warm flames wavering around the logs. A Christmas tree stood in one corner of the expansive clubhouse against one of the maple panel walls. White Christmas lights and rustic wooden, felt, and metal stars covered the nine-foot tree in the high-ceilinged room.

Large hand-braided rugs covered the wood floors, and Christmas quilts hung on two of the walls. Candles were burning, the smell of Christmas pine filling the air.

Holly smiled at the decorations. All the crafts looked like pack members had made them with love.

Even the deck was decorated in lights and red bows.

"We're sharing a room, right?" she asked Aidan as he grabbed their bags.

"We'll take rooms back that away," Ted said, motioning to the north side of the lodge.

Aidan and Holly headed to a bedroom farther away from the ones his men selected.

"Unless you don't want to," Aidan said, but he didn't sound serious.

"The guys worked so hard to try to match us up, I don't want to disappoint them."

Aidan smiled down at her. "Just what I was thinking." He set the bags down on the wooden floor in the last bedroom. The room had a private deck that overlooked the lake, and paintings of the lake at different seasons decorated all the walls. What caught her attention most was that even the guest room was decorated with a country Christmas theme. Wooden Christmas trees hung on one of the walls, a Christmas patchwork quilt in greens and reds covered the bed, a red ruffled skirt and red and green decorative pillows finishing the ensemble. This room had a private bath, and Holly was glad for that.

"I've been thinking." She walked over to the window and looked at the clouds filling the sky and the sun beginning to sink beyond the mountains, the oranges and yellows rippling across the lake in ribbons of color.

"Sounds ominous." He moved behind her and wrapped his arms around her waist, brushing kisses across the top of her head.

"I need the pack members' blood samples. I won't get them if I don't return home."

"Do you think Ronald will force you to stay and mate Jared if you return home?"

"He can't do either." She pulled Aidan's arms tighter around her. "I could forward the results to you as we talked about before, and you could analyze them and see what you think. You could compare them to the old samples I have."

"No," Aidan said softly against her hair in a way that said he wasn't telling her what to do.

She sighed and turned around in his arms to look up at him. "We need those samples. You know we do. If we're the only ones who haven't changed, we need to figure out why and if that can make a difference for the rest of our kind."

"We do, yes. But you're not returning—"

She opened her mouth to object.

"By yourself, I was going to say. I'm going with you."

"What if Ronald doesn't agree?"

Ignoring her question, Aidan added, "And I'm bringing my two bodyguards for protection. Just in case."

"Okay, back it up. I said, what if Ronald doesn't agree to you showing up with or without your fierce warriors?"

"I can't force you to stay with me, but I don't want you to go. Not by yourself. Ultimately, it's up to you."

"We need the blood samples. They may reveal no change whatsoever, and if they don't, we'll figure it out from there. I had some files at home, but I need to get the rest of the notes I have on the computer at my clinic. And if I'm going to stay with you, I need to get more of my things."

"I completely understand. Would it be too soon to express my undying love for you? To convince you we should mate and continue to work together?"

She smiled at him but then frowned. "If we were to mate, you would expect me to stay with you and not return to the pack to get any of my files?" She had to know the truth. Would he back her in this or want to keep her from returning, worried about her safety.

He let out his breath in a frustrated way. "I won't deny I was hopeful you would stay with me, but I understand why you would be reluctant."

She pulled him in for a kiss, sliding her tongue into his mouth and against his tongue in a mating dance. "I'm not reluctant to stay with you. In fact, you'd have a damn hard time getting rid of me. I've got a key to your place now, you know."

"And the key to my heart already." He kissed her as if this was only the beginning, that she had already said yes to a mating, his hand moving under her sweater and blouse and massaging her breast.

"I'm definitely swimming in your pool in that swimsuit," she said, moaning out the words as he continued to stroke her breast. "Maybe soaking in the hot tub with you too. Swimming in the ocean? The lake?" She pulled her mouth away from kissing his ear. "Okay, look, I'll return home, get the blood samples, and share them with you, but I think it would be better if you stayed away, less antagonistic to Ronald."

He rubbed her arms and she knew from the look of lust in his eyes that he wanted her as a man wanted a woman, but she also knew he was having a hard time letting her do this job on her own.

"Aidan, I've got to do this."

"Call him and tell him I'm coming with you. See what he says."

"If he agrees, it's settled. You'll accompany me. If he doesn't?"

"Then you can do what you have to do, and I'll be calling you every minute of the day to make sure you're okay. And don't be surprised if I bring Rafe's Rangers to take care of Ronald and his minions if you have any trouble with him or his hired henchman."

"I'll be okay." She pulled away from him and brought out her phone. "We agree on this, whichever way it goes, right?"

"Yeah. Not willingly, if it doesn't go my way though. Any male who lets his prospective mate go into a dangerous situation without protecting her—"

She smiled at him. "I'm not heading into danger." She called Ronald. "I'm returning to take blood samples of everyone. Aidan and his men are coming with me."

"You'll come alone, and I'll agree to your working here and sharing your results with Dr. Denali."

She put her phone on mute so she could talk to Aidan without Ronald hearing her. "He won't go along with you coming."

Aidan growled. "Bastard."

"I agree he is. Can you accept this?" she asked Aidan.

"I want you to get it done as quickly as you can for as many of your pack members as you can. Share your findings with me as soon as possible, and I'll begin looking them over to see if there are any changes."

"He already said I could work with you long distance. As soon as I get the members' permissions, I'll share the earlier information with you."

"We could rendezvous outside Seattle to see each other if this drags on too long."

"You mean like at a cheap motel?"

He laughed, and she was glad to hear the sound of his laughter when he was being so growly about this.

"I hope to get this done in a couple of days."

His expression lightened.

"What did you think? That this would take weeks, months to do? No way. I'm quick and efficient. As long as Ronald doesn't put roadblocks in my way, I'll be done in a couple of days. A week at the most, but I don't plan to stay that long."

"You're returning to me? For good?"

"Any man who is so desperate to offer his undying love, rescues me from crevasses without hesitation,

and celebrates my birthday on a separate day from
Christmas? Yes, Aidan. I will return. To you. For good."

"Then we have some unfinished business before I
take you back to Seattle."

"A mating?"

"Hell yeah. Between the time you return home and
I get you back, I don't want some other wolf to think
you're available."

She laughed. She knew Aidan was the one for her
from the way he was attempting to help all of wolf-kind
and how he'd helped a lonely old wolf in the wilderness.
She couldn't imagine a better, kinder, sexier wolf to be
her mate. "Uh, yeah, let me finish this call to Ronald,
and I'll talk to my parents next." She unmuted her
phone. "Ronald? Okay, I'll be there."

She smiled at Aidan, letting him know he'd said all
the right things, which was why she was taking him with
her, despite what Ronald wanted.

"Soon. Let everyone in the pack know I'll need blood
samples from them, and I'll be sharing the results with
Aidan, with their permission. He will be coming with
me. I'll call my receptionist to schedule appointments
right away. I'll be returning first thing in the morning."
She raised her brows at Aidan, hoping that was all right
with him.

Smiling at her, he nodded, looking like one happy
wolf.

"Hell, you're mated? What about your family?"
Ronald asked.

"I'll call them right after I get off the phone with you
and see what they want to do." She hoped they'd stay
in the area with her and Aidan and never return to the

Seattle pack. Not only to prove that Ronald no longer had any say in their lives, but so they'd continue to be close like they were now.

And that had her missing them for Christmas already.

Chapter 24

AIDAN COULDN'T HAVE BEEN MORE THRILLED THAT HOLLY wanted to be his mate, but he still had a bad feeling about her returning home. He'd wanted to give her time to get to know him better. He already knew he wanted her in his life permanently. Wolves did so instinctively.

But he hadn't wanted her leaving him without him mating her first. He was glad she'd agreed and changed her mind about him going with her, telling Ronald she was bringing him. The smile she'd given Aidan was so wicked that he wanted to tackle her to the bed and have his way with her right then and there, forgetting that she was still on the phone with Ronald.

Aidan suspected Ronald would cause delaying tactics so she'd be stuck longer in Seattle. As pack leader, he could do whatever he wanted. But he couldn't change that Aidan and Holly were going to be mated wolves.

"Mom, Dad, here's what I'm going to do, and you can do whatever you like. I'm going home to get blood samples from our people tomorrow, but I'm not staying there for long. If I can't do it in a week or less, that's it. I'll be putting my house up for sale. As for you all, you can remain at Aidan's place or return home; it's up to you. Just so you know, we're tying the wolf knot." She smiled at Aidan. "Yes, he's thrilled I said yes… Yes, I'm taking him with me. I'm so glad you're so happy for me. Believe me, I am too. We have to go. Talk to you later when you've had a chance to discuss it." She paused. "Um, let me ask." She covered the mouthpiece. "Can you help them to start over in your area so they can be close to the kids…when we have them?"

Aidan smiled. "Hell yeah. Tell them we'll put up the money and everything. We have plenty of room. They can build a home on the forty acres."

"He said yes! You can build a home on the forty acres so you'll be close by and can help with the kids…when we have some. Marianne and Greg too. We have to get down to business. Call later… Um, sure, I'll let you talk to Aidan." She handed the phone to him, but as soon as he had the phone to his ear, Holly began unfastening Aidan's belt. Clearly, she'd meant it when she said they had to get down to business.

"Thanks for helping us out, Aidan," Eddie said. "You won't regret it."

"I know I won't, and I'm glad to help out. Choose any spot where you want to build your home, decide the kind of house you want, and we'll get it done. Rafe and I always have money in a slush fund to use in case of"—Aidan paused when Holly slid his zipper down and began to tug his jeans down—"an emergency."

"Thanks, Aidan. We'll talk later. Kids are saying they want a pool. I don't think anything else matters."

Aidan laughed. "I don't blame them. We'll iron out all the details later. Welcome to our loosely knit pack where every man, woman, and child can think for themselves."

"That sounds really good. Talk later."

They ended the call, and Aidan began to pull Holly's sweater off in a hurry because she'd already pulled his jeans down to the floor, and he hadn't even removed his boots yet. Vixen.

She pushed him against the bed, and with his jeans around his ankles, he couldn't stop the backward fall. He wanted to grab her in his arms and roll her underneath him, pinning her there and kissing her. But he needed to remove his boots and pants before he could go much further. She tackled his boots, removing one and then the other. Then she pulled off his socks. He kicked off his pants. Once she reached for his boxer briefs, he grabbed her and pulled her into his arms like he'd wanted to and rolled her underneath him. She smiled up at him, looking like a beautiful blushing bride. Which made him think if she wanted to, they could have a simple wedding. Though he suspected if Jade and Rafe got involved, which no doubt they would, there would be nothing simple about it.

He'd planted his knees on either side of her thighs, pinning her down, and began kissing her and unbuttoning her blouse, one button, two kisses. The minx reached between his legs and began caressing his cock. He gave up on the kisses and began tugging at her buttons until he could pull off her blouse. Hell, she was going to have him coming in his boxer briefs before he could even pull off her pants.

She chuckled, and he smiled.

He got off her and pulled off her boots and socks, then moved to unbuckle her belt, unbutton and then unzip her jeans. After yanking off her jeans, he slid his hands over her thighs, his thumbs stroking up the center of her. She shivered in anticipation, and her red lace panties were already moist. Her pheromones and her musky scent announced she was so ready for him.

He licked her panties, pressing between her feminine folds, and she arched her back. "Ohmigod, Aidan. Do that again, and I will come."

He smiled at her. "That's what I'm working toward." He licked a trail up her flat belly, tickling her navel before moving to her breasts. He studied the design of her red lace bra and realized it had a front clasp. He quickly unfastened it and pulled it away from her breasts.

He rubbed his fresh stubble gently against her naked nipples, and they instantly peaked into pale-pink nubs. He sucked on one, caressing the other with his hand, rubbing his cock against her legs. The friction and her lusty scent, her exquisite moans, and the way her body was reacting to his touch sent a wicked, hot fire roaring through his blood.

Her hands slipped to his waistband, and she tried to tug his boxer briefs down. Her warm fingers on his flesh scorched him, and he quickly dispensed with his briefs, his cock springing free to touch her wet panties. He pulled the panties off and began stroking her in earnest, kissing her around the neck and throat, spreading her legs. She was exquisite, the perfect mate for him, and he couldn't have been more relieved that she'd agreed to mate him.

She ran her hands through his hair, and he loved the way her fingernails gingerly scraped his scalp. He was stroking her, and she was digging her heels into the bed right before she cried out. He kissed her mouth and said, "I need to be inside you."

He wanted her permission because this was forever. No going back. No changing their minds.

"I want you inside me now." She tugged at his hips, her eyes burning with desire.

"Good." He thanked God she hadn't changed her mind. He drove in, taking her with him. Rocking inside her, pulling his cock slowly out, and thrusting in again. Stroking inside her, he felt the ripples of her climax, at the same time enjoying the smell of her sex. He was ready to burst, but he wouldn't let go, not until she began clutching his hips and arching her back. He sensed when she was ready to come before she even came.

He'd never experienced anything as erotic or fulfilling as he did when having sex with her.

He came, realizing at once they hadn't used protection, but then again, that was part of who they were too. Bringing new little *lupus garous* into the world. He would be happy to be a daddy to her babies.

"Holy...wolf. Aidan...you...you rock my world."

He smiled and kissed her slowly and deeply. "You are the only one for me. I love you with all my heart."

She wrapped her arms around his body as he pressed kisses to her cheeks and mouth. "I love you too." She sighed. "I guess they're expecting us for lunch."

He chuckled. "Yeah. What I wouldn't do for a nice long wolf nap with my mate."

"Me too. We might as well get dressed and give them the news."

"Something tells me they might already know."

<hr/>

After they'd quickly showered and dressed, they left the bedroom. She was wearing the new sweater Aidan had bought her. She adored it and adored him. He was one fantastic lover.

They joined the guys for lunch, and Aidan happily announced, "We're mated."

"Hallelujah. I didn't think we could go into the matchmaking business without at least one success story," Mike said.

"As if we had anything to do with it," Ted said, and they both saluted Holly and Aidan with creamy eggnog. "But I'm damn glad they tied the knot. Wedding in the plans?"

Holly looked at Aidan, wondering if he'd considered a wedding or not. Their kind didn't need one. They sometimes had a wedding to celebrate the mating with others and to have a marriage certificate for financial reasons.

"I'm all for it if Holly wants to have one."

"I guess a small one. I know my mom and sister would love to be involved."

"And Jade and Rafe for certain," Aidan said. "I guess I need to tell Rafe too."

"Maybe we could have a wedding after the New Year, to have something to celebrate every year after New Year's so it's not too much stuff at the same time. My birthday, Christmas, New Year's, then our anniversary."

"Maybe the end of January to give everyone time to prepare for it."

"But if it's small…"

"I suspect by the time Rafe gets involved, it'll be a big event. All wolves, just so you know."

She smiled. "I can handle it."

"You will look like a fairy princess walking down the aisle," Aidan said.

"And my Prince Charming wolf will be there waiting for me."

They sat down to eat finished their grilled chicken sandwiches, though Aidan noticed Mike and Ted must have stopped preparing them until they heard them getting ready to leave the bedroom, because the sandwiches were hot off the grill. Then they enjoyed slices of birthday cake. Aidan was glad it was nice and sweet, because he had a real sweet tooth and so did Holly.

"Love the sweater on you," Mike said, finishing off his piece of cake. "Any chance we can see the bathing suit modeled?"

She smiled and squeezed Aidan's hand. "Next time I swim in it and you're around guarding, sure."

Aidan smiled at his men, raising his brow, letting them know they were stepping into *his* territory.

Ted laughed. "You get guard duty on the perimeter that day, Mike. I'll watch the house, specifically to protect the she-wolf in the pool. Though I'm sure her mate will be there protecting her too."

"We'll have to toss a coin for that assignment," Mike said.

Holly smiled at them, and Aidan imagined they would do it too.

Following lunch, they had time before the celebration, and they opted for a wolf run in the woods for a couple of hours. They asked if Lori and Paul wanted to go with them because it was their property. They were happy to and were at the lodge within a few minutes dressed in their wolf coats.

Aidan's men had shifted too, but Holly and Aidan had gotten distracted when they went to the bedroom to shift and dress. That was the problem when they got naked now. They didn't have anything holding them back…well, except they had people waiting to run with them.

———

"You know how much I want to tell them to go running without us?" Aidan said, holding her hips, pressing her tight against his groin.

She welcomed his burgeoning arousal and slid her hands down his tight ass. "Yeah, I can tell, and if it wouldn't be rude, and if your bodyguards wouldn't hang around anyway, I'd have my wicked way with you." She sighed, kissed him long and deep, then pulled away, hating to do so. "We'll have to make sure we return before the celebration begins."

Reluctantly, they both shifted, and she raced out of the room ahead of Aidan. Thankfully, everyone had gone outside to give them some privacy.

Grizzlies roamed in the area, other wolves too. It was good to run in a pack. A wild wolf pack or a grizzly bear would be no match for them. Also, it was nice to have the leaders show them where to go since they didn't know the area. Paul and Lori led the way, running through the snow ahead of them while Aidan and Holly ran in the middle and Ted and Mike followed as the bodyguard detail.

After about an hour of exploring the area, Holly tackled Aidan out of fun. He wasn't expecting it at all, which was why she did it. She felt so full of life here with Aidan, her mate; the crisp, cold mountain air; the new scents; and a new place. Mostly, she just loved having fun with a male who would be her forever mate. He was already her hero.

He fell into a snowbank and she tackled him, biting and nipping, and he stayed on his back, playing with her, nipping back, showing how much he loved her and could have just as much wolf fun back.

This was what she loved. Not just the sex between them, but the wolf moments too. They were just as important. And she loved the way he was, one minute letting her be in charge and then the next jumping up and tackling her. God, how she wanted to return to the lodge and make love to him. He finally let her up, and they shook off the excess snow clinging to their fur.

That's when they noticed Mike and Ted looking the other way for trouble and to give them some privacy, waiting for them to run again, and Paul and Lori watching them, smiling, knowing what it was like to be newly mated wolves.

Holly woofed with glee, and they all ran off again. They finally reached a rocky area where they saw white-haired mountain goats clinging to rocks. She was glad they hadn't needed to climb anything like that as wolves. Which made her think of the crevasse, glad there weren't any around here. It might be fun learning to rock climb with Aidan as humans.

After about an hour and a half of seeing the sights, and even catching a glimpse of a grizzly and her cubs, they began the long run back to the lodge. This had been so much fun, and she loved that they'd been able to see the area before they returned to Seattle tomorrow. She was glad her parents were staying near them and not returning to stay with the pack in Seattle. She couldn't be any happier. She didn't think Ronald could ruin anything for her now.

Yet she knew it wouldn't be a happy return to her home when she went there to pack up her stuff, sell her house, and remove her personal items from the clinic. The pack had purchased the clinic for her to work out of, so it was still theirs. Which was fine with her. Maybe they'd find a doctor again. At least they still had a nurse.

When they reached the lodge, Holly wasn't sure she could make love to Aidan. Not until after she had a nap. After Paul and Lori woofed at them and headed for their cabin and Ted and Mike sat outside, she changed her mind.

She wanted Aidan in the worst way. Now. Naps were overrated.

Aidan loped with Holly to the bedroom, glad everyone was giving them some privacy, in the guise of guarding the place. He was hoping she wanted to make love to him before the party, which put the pressure on them too, because he was certain everyone would be chomping at the bit to come over and set up for it. Maybe Lori and Paul would let everyone know they had to wait for the newly mated wolves to get on with a little more business before they celebrated Nick's coming to stay with the pack.

Holly entered the room first and Aidan followed, shutting the door with his shoulder. She shifted and was mouthwateringly naked before she climbed into bed. He shifted and hurried over to the bed and joined her. One nice thing about running as wolves—once they shifted, they were ready for lovemaking, with no time wasted removing clothes.

He slipped on top of her and began kissing her mouth, his fingers combing through her silky hair. "You are so beautiful and all mine."

"You are too." She reached up and threaded her fingers through his hair. "Just beautiful." And then she pulled him down for more kissing, her hand sweeping down his side and over his ass, then squeezing. "Hard… all…over."

"And you're generously soft where it counts." He molded his hands around her breasts and gently squeezed. "Delectably soft." And then he took her nipple in his mouth and teased it with his tongue. "And tasty. Love the way you taste, like peaches and cream."

She smiled at him. "You're all hunky spice, my favorite."

He began kissing her again, loving the feel of her soft lips against his, pressuring, searing, welcoming. Her lips parted, and he plunged his tongue right in, loving the way she poked and prodded his, the way she curled hers around his. Her hands were busy too, stroking his waist and his ass, pulling him harder against her as she spread her legs.

Her pheromones teased his, her sweet, sexy scent begging for satisfaction, arousing his overwhelming need to have her, to complete this.

He began stroking her clit, inserting a finger into her moistness, pulling it out and teasing her clit again with his wet fingers. She was arching and moaning, her fingers clinging to his waist, her head sinking into the pillow as she concentrated on what he was doing to her and how he was making her feel.

He loved seeing her response and knowing he was doing it to her. His cock was ready for the plunge. But he kept up the pressure, bringing her to the end before he took his turn. She cried out his name, and he was glad his men were outside. Though with their sensitive hearing, they might have heard her anyway, not that they wouldn't have known what they were doing.

"I have to learn to be quieter," she whispered.

"No way in hell," Aidan said, and she laughed.

Then Holly was kissing him again, loving him for being who he was. She suspected she was going to be the end of his workaholic ways. She realized they hadn't used a condom the first time, and he didn't seem to want to use one this time either. Which was fine with her. They didn't have the health issues that humans could have, and it was time for her to have babies.

He kissed her other breast, licking and sucking on the nipple, his hand caressing her belly. She wrapped her leg around the back of his and caressed his leg with the sole of her foot. His darkened eyes were hot with desire, and she tugged at his hip for him to join her. He kissed her mouth again and centered himself between her legs, penetrating her with his cock and plunging it deep.

He resettled her legs over his shoulders, and she smiled. He was going for maximum penetration, and she loved it. He was all hers.

He rocked into her and she tightened her hold on him, her inner muscles clenching him. His muscles were taut, his face tight with concentration, but then he gave her a wicked smile. It reminded her of the wicked smiles he'd shared with her before they were even mated wolves. She gave him one back.

He turned a little, angling into her deeper, and she came with the unexpected twist and thrust, gasping out, "Holy shit."

Growling, he released inside her, bathing her in his hot seed, and continued to pump until he finished with a satisfied wolfish groan. "You are so good for me," he said, rolling onto his back and pulling her into his arms.

"You won't mind the breaks from work to get in some exercise?"

"Taking breaks won't be an issue. Ever. In fact, if we have a breakthrough, I can't think of a better way to celebrate."

She laughed. "As much as I'd love to cuddle with you, I guess we should dress and let everyone know they can set up for the party any time."

They kissed and hugged, then took a quick shower and dressed. Aidan's cell phone rang, and he grabbed it off the bedside table and smiled. "Your dad."

She finished dressing while he put the call on speaker.

"Yeah, it's Aidan. Is everything all right?"

"We picked out the house plans, but you let us know if it's too extravagant. We'll use the proceeds from our home—"

"And mine," Holly interjected, then pulled on her boots. "I won't need the money to purchase a new place."

"You can use the funds for whatever you need, including new furnishings and to start up your new business. We'll provide the house, whatever the plan."

"You can change your mind anytime," Eddie said. "I'm emailing you the blueprint."

Aidan opened the email and smiled. "Looks like the kind of style Rafe would approve of. I'll send this over to him, with your permission, and I'll send you a copy of the survey done on the property. You can pick out a spot to build. Rafe will get with one of his builders to start planning construction."

"Thanks, Aidan, and Holly," Eddie said. He paused, then said, "Okay, got the survey. We'll check over the land to figure out where we want to situate the house. Everyone wants a view of the lake like you have, but we want to be far enough away that we aren't intruding."

"You won't be intruding. I was surprised to see you agreed on a place so fast."

"When we decide something, we're on it. Just like Holly with you, it seems."

Aidan smiled at Holly and handed the phone to her so he could get dressed. She looked over the plans. "Wow, that's beautiful. If Ronald knew about the upgrade in residences we've had, he'd be jealous."

"We ought to send him a picture when it's done," Greg said in the background.

"No," Holly said. "No sense in aggravating the pack leader." She didn't trust that Greg was just joking. "Is everything going all right?"

"I think Marianne and Greg turned into part-time fish," their mother said. "Forget being wolves. They're only out of the water to eat a little supper, then in again."

"I'm glad they're having fun. I have to let everyone know they can use the lodge to set up for the welcome celebration for Nick, but Holly can visit with you further." Aidan leaned down and kissed her, then headed out of the room and closed the door.

"Is he gone?" her dad asked.

"Yeah, Dad."

"Did you do it?"

Holly chuckled. "Yes, we're mated wolves."

Her mother sighed with relief. "We began to worry he would be afraid he'd age more quickly than you and would want to find a cure first."

"No. It gives us all the more reason to find a cure as soon as we can, but we weren't letting anything stop us."

"Okay, good. We have a question for you, but we want you to be perfectly honest with us."

"I always am."

"Right, but this time, you might worry about hurting our feelings," her mom said.

Holly wondered what was wrong now.

"Aidan secretly called us and asked if we'd like to join you all at the chalet for Christmas, because we're a close-knit family and family should be together at Christmastime."

Holly quickly brushed away the tears filling her eyes and spilling down her cheeks. She couldn't believe Aidan had offered. She adored her wolf. "That would be so wonderful. He must have cleared it with his brother and his mate."

"Are you sure? We thought you might want to get away from us for once in your life during Christmas."

"I can't think of anything nicer than you being there. I was already missing you. We'll have a lovely time."

"Okay, then should we keep it a secret from Aidan? And pretend it's a big surprise for you?" her mother asked.

"I would never be able to pull it off. Thanks so much for asking though. We'll have lots of fun. And

Marianne and Greg can help babysit Toby. I hear he can be a handful."

"Okay, we'll let Rafe know we're all coming. And you can tell Aidan. He's a real keeper, honey," her mom said.

"He is. I couldn't be happier." She heard people entering the lodge. "Oh, sounds like they're starting to set up for the party. I'm going to see if I can help." And give Aidan a big hug and kiss for being such a wonderful mate.

"Okay, have fun. Then you're going to do what?"

"Return to the clinic in the morning. Hopefully to see patients. In any event, I'll pack up my house and put it up for sale. Though because Rafe is into real estate, I'm hoping he can handle it."

"He said he would. And our place too, and the business."

"Okay, good. When are you returning home?"

"Soon. The cars and presents won't get here until tomorrow, and we've given Rafe everything he needed to put our house on the market, but Rafe said he'd have us flown out there with bodyguards accompanying us."

"Okay, good. Talk later."

"Have a good time. We're glad you and Aidan mated, and we're here!"

"It's the best thing for all of us. Oh, hey, before I let you go, I meant to ask you: Do you know what happened to the three wolf packs that attacked ours?"

"I don't think any of those wolves survived. Ask Nick. He'd know for sure."

"Thanks, Mom. I will." Well, that settled that. If Nick confirmed the wolves all died, she and Aidan wouldn't have any other wolf packs to check out that they knew of.

They ended the call, and Holly headed for the bedroom door. As she left the room, she saw Aidan helping to pull covers off platters of food. Ted and Mike were busy making hot spiced wine for everyone. She still couldn't believe Aidan had been so considerate as to ask her family to join them for Christmas. There were really no words for how she felt about him and his generosity.

She headed straight for him, tears in her eyes and a big smile on her face. He looked quizzically at her and crossed the floor to join her. She swore everyone stopped what they were doing to see what was going to happen next. Newly mated wolves and children were prized by everyone in a pack.

She reached Aidan and pulled him into her arms, kissing him long and deep without any reservation. "Have I told you how much I love you?" she said to him.

He was smiling down at her, holding her tightly. "You have, but I suspect this is for something new."

"Thank you for inviting my family for Christmas."

"It was supposed to be a surprise," he said, but he was smiling.

"They wanted to make sure we weren't doing anything wildly exciting."

"Oh, we'll have our wildly exciting moments, even when they're there."

She smiled. "Good. My expectations are sky-high."

Chapter 25

IT WASN'T LONG BEFORE PEOPLE FROM THE PACK BEGAN arriving and setting up food and drinks at long tables for the welcoming party at the lodge, though Holly kept worrying about tomorrow and facing Ronald. Aidan was helping to set out the food, but when he caught her eye, he came over and pulled her gently into his arms and kissed her. "Don't worry about tomorrow. We'll deal with whatever we have to. Tonight, just enjoy the celebration. This is so good for Nick. Tomorrow will be another day."

She smiled up at Aidan and hugged him. "How did you know I was worried about it?"

"You were wearing a worried frown as big as the crevasse we fell into. Seriously, we'll get through this one way or another tomorrow."

"You haven't called your brother for tactical support, have you?" She could see what a disaster that could be.

"No, but he knows that's where we're headed. Don't be surprised if he sends some guys in rescue mode and they're a stone's throw from where we'll be."

She smiled and kissed Aidan. "I can't promise I won't worry, but I'll try."

"Okay, good show. I want you to have fun tonight. You deserve it as much as Nick does."

"It's beautiful, don't you think? I think Nick will be so honored."

"He will be. I don't think we could have picked a better pack for him to belong to, though I kept wondering about him with one of the Highland packs and them convincing him to wear a kilt."

She chuckled.

The pack had decorated even more than before with welcome signs and balloons. Lights sparkled off the roof of the clubhouse, all over the deck, and inside, where the food sat on the tables dressed in red tablecloths. The pack Christmas tree, stretching ten feet high to the cathedral ceilings, was lit, and everything looked so festive. Holly knew Nick would be so happy to be with this pack during the holidays and beyond.

The guests dressed in everything from Christmas sweaters and more casual apparel to cocktail dresses and suits and ties. Former Seattle pack members Everett and his sister, Tara, and their mother visited with Nick and Holly while Aidan slipped away to grab drinks for everyone. She was as glad to see Everett and his family as they were to see her.

"So, how's our old pack leader? A pain in the butt as usual?" Everett asked.

"Yes, Ronald's just as much of a jerk as always," Holly said. "I'm returning to get the blood samples from the pack, and then Aidan and I are leaving for his place to work on the cure."

"Permanently?" Nick asked, a small smile curving his lips.

"Yes," Aidan said, returning with a tray of drinks. "If she hasn't told you, we're old mated wolves now."

"Speak for yourself." Holly kissed his cheek.

"We didn't want to mention it when this party is

for you, but I'm sure the word will get out anyway," Aidan said.

"Nonsense. There's nothing more important than matings and babies," Nick said.

"Congratulations," Everett and his family said, raising their glasses in salute.

Without further ado, Nick gave his best *ho-ho-ho* to get everyone's attention, and that sure did it. Everyone smiled at him. He didn't need to wear a Santa suit to sound and look like the real deal. With everyone listening, he announced Holly and Aidan's mating. "There's nothing more magical at any time of year than when a couple declares their love for each other. They have a special place in my heart because they brought me here to be with you at the most joyous time of year. I give you Drs. Holly Gray and Aidan Denali."

Everyone cheered them.

Holly smiled at everyone, thanking them and Nick. She couldn't believe he'd silenced the partygoers to celebrate her and Aidan's union. Then again, she could. She was so hopeful he'd be happy with the pack, and from all appearances, he was thrilled. It might not be long-term, but at least for now, he was really having fun. He needed to be with a pack.

"Nick, I need to ask you before I forget and you leave tonight... Did any of the wolf packs who fought ours have any survivors?" Holly asked.

"Not a one. They were all male, all wanting to take over, no matter who they hurt. Ending their miserable lives was the only way to handle such deceit."

"Okay, so no one else is left who could have their blood tested," Aidan said.

"Afraid not. We couldn't have them return to retaliate."

"I understand completely," Aidan said.

A few minutes after Nick announced Holly and Aidan's mating, several of Lori and Paul's pack members came over to congratulate them personally and offer sage words of advice.

Six widowed ladies began catering to Nick, and he looked like he was having the time of his life. Holly was so happy for him. And for herself and Aidan. She noticed Victoria, the woman he was staying with, busy talking to others, as if she wasn't laying claim to Nick. Maybe Victoria and Nick had decided it was best if he got to know as many single women as he could and not just set his sights on the first woman he was staying with. Or maybe he really didn't like her pink-and-white house.

Holly didn't think he was that shallow though. Then she noticed he kept glancing around the room when other women were talking to him, and every time, his gaze settled on Victoria. He seemed satisfied to see where she was and resumed listening to the other women. Holly smiled. Looked like Santa might have found Mrs. Claus after all, but he was playing it low-key for now.

Aidan filled a plate with goodies for Holly while she was talking to Lori: spicy meatballs, chicken wings, cheese squares, bacon-and-cream-stuffed mushrooms, and asparagus wrapped in phyllo dough.

"What would you like, Lori?"

Lori eyed Holly's plate. "Same as Holly's having. Thanks, Aidan."

"Be right back." Aidan returned to the kitchen.

"He's a dream. From the first time we met him, we fell in love with him," Lori said.

"Aidan rescued one of our pack members' little boys at the mall from an attempted kidnapper. That's how I met him. That was only the beginning."

Aidan returned with two plates, one for Lori and one for himself. "What did I miss?"

"Holly was telling us you rescued one of her pack members from a would-be kidnapper," Lori said, lifting a meatball off her plate.

Aidan leaned down and kissed Holly's cheek. "She probably didn't get to the part about how she saved my life when I was bleeding all over the place."

Holly chuckled. "He'd suffered a head wound. The woman clobbered him with her purse, which contained a gun. She was in big trouble. Aidan would have lived without my help."

"That was just the start though," Aidan said.

"I'm glad the two of you didn't wait. Paul took forever to realize his place was with me and leading the pack. It was always meant to be. It just took him a long, long time to get with the program."

Paul smiled at her and winked. Holly suspected he'd overheard Lori, and she'd said it just loud enough for him to hear. She smiled back at him.

Holly could tell they were still fairly newly mated wolves.

Paul joined them with a plate of food piled high.

Lori frowned at him. "Did you leave anything for anyone else?"

Paul laughed. "You know how the ladies are. They said I needed all that extra energy for helping you lead the pack. If anyone wants some of the extras off my plate, you're welcome to them, or else I'll have to run ten miles tonight to work all this off."

Holly took some of his asparagus, Aidan grabbed a couple of meatballs, and Lori took all of his chicken wings. She smiled at him. "Thanks, honey."

Smiling, he just shook his head. "I may have to get a refill on the chicken wings."

"Dessert, anyone?" Aidan took orders and headed into the kitchen to get plates filled with sweet treats.

Lori eyed Paul as if to say he should be doing that for her. "Hey, if I wasn't still eating all this food, I would have gotten the desserts."

Holly laughed. What a difference they were from Ronald and his brother. Nick would fit in perfectly.

After the festivities ended, everyone went home for the night, except for Victoria, who was trying to help Ted and Mike clean up the kitchen, and Nick, since he'd ridden over with her. Victoria had already motioned for Nick to leave the kitchen when he'd tried to help her, saying, "You're the guest of honor. We'll clean up here."

He joined Holly and Aidan in the living area, and Holly privately asked Nick, "What do you think? Do you think you might want to stay with the pack for good?"

"Are you kidding?" Nick glanced at the kitchen where Victoria was playfully arguing with Ted about helping with the dishes and he was playfully keeping her from them. "Yeah. If the way I've been treated so far is any indication, I think this is just where I belong."

"You let us know if you want to check out any other packs," Aidan said. "Truthfully, I think you'd have a hard time leaving." He pointedly looked at Victoria, laughing at something Mike said.

"You planned it like this, didn't you?" Nick said.

"I did know about all the widowed women in the pack. But Everett and his family were also part of the Seattle pack, they knew you, and they wanted to see you again," Aidan said.

Nick smiled at Victoria.

"A possibility?" Holly asked.

He just chuckled. "Lots of kids in the pack. If I find the right woman for me, she'll have to be a good Mrs. Claus. And one who could put up with all my failings."

"I'd bet there'd be one or more willing to take on the job. We want to wish you the best of luck," Holly said. "You deserve it."

"Well, if you won't let me help, I guess I'll say good night and take Nick home with me," Victoria said to Ted and Mike.

"Night," Nick said. "I'll visit you one of these days to see how you are getting along. Get a little swimming in that pool."

"Sounds like a good deal," Aidan said, shaking his hand.

Nick gave Holly a hug, and then he and Victoria left the lodge.

"Thanks for telling me to take my mind off the issue of tomorrow. I didn't give it any thought," Holly told Aidan.

He was glad for it. "I'll keep your mind off it for the rest of the night."

She chuckled, then took hold of his hand and pulled him toward the bedroom. "You can start right now. Night, guys."

"Night, Doc. Doc. See you in the morning," Ted said.

"Paul and Lori are taking us to the airport first thing," Mike said. "Night."

"Thanks, Ted, Mike. You're always a great help."
Aidan ushered Holly back to the bedroom because
he meant what he'd promised. He wasn't going to let
Holly think of anything but how much pleasure he could
give her.

Tomorrow would be another story.

Chapter 26

EARLY THE NEXT MORNING, AIDAN TOLD TED AND MIKE the plan. "We'll return to Seattle, and you can stay at Eddie and Margaret's home while Holly and I go to the clinic. Eddie and Margaret have decided to return home to pack up their personal belongings and ready their home to show."

"Afterward, you'll be staying at Holly's home," Mike said, a brow raised.

"Her house is only half a mile from her parents'. If we have trouble, you'll be over in a flash. We'll call in and let you know how it's going until then."

Ted shook his head. "Guarding a body means being closer to the body than that."

"Ronald didn't even agree to Aidan being in the area. He wasn't going to decide that when Aidan is my mate. So you aren't supposed to be there either," Holly said.

"All right, but we'll have to tell Rafe," Mike said.

"You see what I have to put up with?" Aidan asked as they boarded the plane, leaving in plenty of time to be in Seattle for Holly's first scheduled appointments.

She chuckled. "Yeah, they want to keep you safe."

"Or Rafe will fire us," Ted reminded them.

When they arrived at the private airport near Holly's home, her father met them with his car, but he wasn't alone. By the time they'd flown to the airport, Rafe had sent five hulking men to Eddie's house, and they'd driven in two more cars to the airport.

"Here's the plan," Aidan told them. "You'll stay with Eddie while Holly and I go to the clinic and take the blood samples."

"Boss said we're to be with you at all times," Chet said.

"Rafe is my new brother-in-law, so I'm all for keeping peace in the family. You can come with us to the clinic. Ronald will possibly have a conniption, but he'll see it for what it is. You're there doing your job protecting Aidan," Holly said.

"And you," Aidan said.

"I need to return to the house. We're still getting it ready to show to prospective buyers. Whoever wants to stay with us can," Eddie said.

"We'll call when we're on our way over there, and we'll help you do whatever you need in getting it ready to sell," Ted said.

Eddie's grin couldn't have stretched any further. "Now that's what I like to hear!"

Then they piled into the two cars while Eddie drove home.

"I was going to say the guys could wait in the doctor's lounge. That might be a tight squeeze," Holly said.

"Would it cause too much trouble if a couple of us sat in the waiting area?" Ted asked.

"No. My pack mates will smell you're there anyway. You can't hide from them. If they see a couple of you, maybe reading magazines, they won't feel as intimidated. Not that all would anyway. Only the betas in the pack might."

When they arrived at her clinic early, the guys carried

a stack of boxes to pack her stuff while she unlocked the door. Inside, she found the clinic just like it was before she'd left to go to Glacier Peak Wilderness. She couldn't believe how everything had changed for her since then. A pack vacation had turned into a wolf mating and her helping to find the cure for other wolves. And finding a home for Nick. She had halfway expected Ronald to have had the clinic ransacked, angry with her for leaving the pack and mating another wolf outside the pack. Then again, it was their clinic. He wouldn't want to trash it. Maybe he was playing it cool in case she changed her mind and wanted to stay with the pack, if they'd allow Aidan to join it.

She felt a little sad that she was leaving. She'd spent so many years working here. Yet she felt good about the change too. Not to mention having her hot wolf mate made all the difference in the world. She'd miss her pack members, but certainly not Ronald and his ruthless minions.

She turned on the Christmas tree lights. Lollipops and candy canes decorated the tree and were treats for adults and children to enjoy after they visited her at the office.

"'Rumpelstiltskin' is my log-in, if you want to go in my office and see my notes on the computer." She changed her sign in the window from *Closed* to *Open*.

"Sure, I'll do that. Rumpelstiltskin, eh?"

"Yeah, one of my childhood favorites. I'll call my receptionist and nurse. Usually, they're here before me. They must have been confused about me returning today."

The men stacked the boxes in her office, and then the other bodyguards went into her break room while Ted and Mike sat in the waiting room, one reading a magazine, the other texting on his phone. Mike said, "Just letting Rafe know we're here, and so far, everything's good."

"Okay," Aidan said from the office. "I hope that it's just a matter of your nurse and receptionist being confused about the time when they should have reported, Holly. If it isn't, we'll do what we can here, and if you want, we can hang around longer to see if your pack members will show up tomorrow or the next day. Even if Ronald has sabotaged your business by telling everyone to stay away, maybe a few will change their minds. We can stay at your place in the meantime. We still have plenty of time before we're off to see Rafe and his family. I'm sure you want to pack what you can at your house too."

"Thanks tons," Holly said and wrapped her arms around her mate in a hug. She felt bad her pack members weren't here, but she still hoped some of them would show up sooner than later.

She called her nurse first. Holly hadn't wanted to let on in front of Aidan how disappointed she was, but she was afraid he could tell. When Sally answered her call, Holly said, "Hi, Sally. I'm taking care of any of the pack members' health issues and checking blood before I leave the pack for good. Are you coming in?"

"Oh, I'm sorry, Dr. Gray. I have my day all planned out and can't make it in."

"No problem. No one has arrived anyway, and if they do, I can manage by myself. Well, Dr. Denali is here too. He can help if I need any."

"Won't Ronald be upset about him being here?" Sally sounded both shocked and worried.

"Aidan and I were mated. If Ronald doesn't want me

taking care of the pack's medical needs before I go, then I'm sorry. I'm here for them for the time being. If you change your mind, I'll be here for a couple of days, more if I need to be."

"Okay, I've...I've got to run."

Sally ended the call, and Holly couldn't help but notice that Sally hadn't even congratulated her on the mating.

"Any trouble?" Aidan asked from the doorway to her office.

"She has 'other stuff' planned today. I suspect that has to do with Ronald pressuring her not to come in. That's okay. I can handle it." She motioned to the empty waiting area.

Aidan pulled her into his arms and gave her a sound hug and kiss. "I'd say if we don't have any patients soon, we could head over to your place and check out your bed. But if anyone shows up..."

"Yeah." She kissed him back. "I would do it in a heartbeat if I had a crystal ball and knew for sure if anyone was going to drop by or not."

"I assume Ronald doesn't want us to draw anyone's blood either," Aidan said.

"Right. If no one's sick or injured enough to need my aid, they'd stay away. I'll call my receptionist and see if she has an excuse for not showing up. At least they could have called and told me they weren't coming in, just as a common courtesy. It's not like either of them." She'd call Harper next, but she expected more of the same.

She wondered if anyone had even called her patients to schedule them to come in. That was next on her list to do.

—✦—

Aidan felt bad for Holly, but he figured if her people didn't have longevity issues, they were in the clear. At least for now. If Holly's blood worked for the rest of the wolves, then they really wouldn't need anything from her former pack or vice versa.

He found her files on the blood samples and considered the ages of the wolves and how that compared to what they should be.

"This is Holly Gray. I'm at the clinic. Are you coming in today? Looks like it'll be light traffic-wise, so no problem if you can't. If you can, just let me know. You've got my number."

"Answering machine?" Aidan called out.

"Yeah. I'll start calling my pack members and ask if they want to get tested again before I leave or need me to check on anything else that's bothering them. Sally can do it after I've left, but she wouldn't know what's she's looking for, and I doubt Ronald would want her to send the samples to us when I'm no longer with the pack." Holly sat on a chair in the office, sounding so upbeat. He was proud of her. "Are you seeing anything?"

"Yeah. Three of the ten I've checked are aging faster, more like the other packs."

"Ohmigod, which three?" Holly jumped up from her chair and checked the charts he was referring to.

"Rock Rockledge, one of Ronald's enforcers; Sally, your nurse; and Trudy, Joey's mom. I checked Ronald and Jared first, just to see if they might have issues, but they don't. I figured if they did, they might change their minds about having us work with them."

"Are you sure?" She was leaning over his shoulder now, and he pulled her onto his lap so they could look at the figures together.

"Yeah, I am. I'll keep looking at the rest of your people's blood work. I'm taking notes. You can share with whoever you want."

"With individual patients, sure. Not with Ronald or his brother. They're on their own. Let them worry."

Aidan smiled at her.

She let out her breath. "I'll just say we won't check their blood without their permission. I wouldn't put it past him to try to keep us here against our will just to find the cure for him, if he thought his blood had issues."

"True. Hopefully, we'll find a solution for everyone else. Now that I'm seeing problems with some of your people, I have to wonder why some are fine and others are not."

"I agree." Her phone rang, and Holly answered it. "Yeah, Mom?" She listened for a moment, then she smiled. "Oh, Mom, that's good news." She said to Aidan, "Mom and Dad got an offer on their house, and they're accepting it. They're a wolf family who needed a bigger place and more room to run. The people who always work at their business when things get hectic or Mom and Dad need a break bought their store."

"That's great news!" Aidan was relieved everything was falling into place as far as her family resettling near them.

"Mom, Aidan's here with me. Nobody showed up at the clinic. No, not even Sally or Harper... Yeah, I know. Ronald got to them. We'll be here for a little while. But Aidan found a problem." She explained to her mother about some of the pack members' blood aging faster while others weren't. "Yeah, I know…but I'm not telling Ronald or his brother theirs are fine. Aidan has gone through ten patients' records so far, and three of the ten have issues. We'll try to figure out the common denominator once he goes through the rest of the pack members' records. Congratulations on the house. I'm calling patients just in case no one's gotten the word I'm here." She smiled at Aidan. "Yes, love you too, Mom, and you bet I'll give Aidan a hug for you. And for me too."

She called another number and said, "Hello, Trudy? This is Holly Gray. You were scheduled first thing to come in for me to check your blood work." She frowned. "You can't make it? Okay, well, did Ronald tell everyone not to come in to see me? If that's the case, there's no sense in me sitting at the clinic for no reason."

"Trudy's blood is also aging faster," Aidan reminded Holly.

"Right." Holly looked at the sample on the monitor, as if she needed to see it again. "No, I'm talking to Dr. Denali. He's my consulting physician, and he's found issues with the blood sample I took from you last month… Yes, your cells are aging faster… Of course he wouldn't lie… Listen, you're not the only one. There are two others in the pack who have this issue that we know of for now. I can't say who, because it's a privacy issue. If they want, they can share with the other pack members."

"Trudy's mate is fine," Aidan said. "If no one's coming in, do you want to pack up some things and go? We can examine these at home. In the meantime, we'll get your household goods packed up and get your place ready to sell."

"Trudy, I'm sorry. If it's any consolation, all the other wolf packs are experiencing the same issue… Your mate? He'll have to call me to learn about his work-up. We've got to go. Talk later." She ended the call with Trudy, retrieved her boxes, and began taping them up in the office. "I'm ready to pack everything up, but go ahead and check the rest of the patient records in case anyone shows up after Trudy learns she's got issues. If Ronald learns of it, then I bet you anything he'll be the first one over here to have his blood retested."

"All right."

"I understand why everyone's afraid to go against Ronald's ruling, but it's still annoying. You saved her son."

"Well, if her husband learns he's going to live a lot longer than her, she might stand up for herself." Which was the same problem Aidan faced with Holly.

Holly's cell phone rang, and Aidan paused to see who was calling. He suspected Trudy was calling back.

"Uh, Micky, well… Dr. Denali hasn't gotten to your file yet." She glanced at Aidan.

He shook his head. "Let me check." He pulled up Micky's file on Holly's computer and checked the blood work. "He's good."

"Your blood is fine." Holly took a deep breath. "Tell your mate to call me, and Dr. Denali will pull up her file next." She hung up and said to Aidan, "Cynthia." Then her phone rang again. "Oh, hello, Cynthia. Aidan's checking it now. Yes, Dr. Denali… He's now my mate."

"Hers is good," Aidan said.

"Your blood work looks fine… No, I don't know if it

will change later. That's why we need to keep checking, and we need to keep looking for the cure. When I took a sample of your blood, you were fine." She looked over at Aidan. "Okay, good. See you soon." She smiled. "Bye." She set her boxes aside. "Looks like we're in business. At least we have one patient coming in. Probably her mate too."

Chapter 27

WITHIN HALF AN HOUR, TWENTY PEOPLE WERE IN THE waiting room, ready to get their blood drawn, while Trudy and her mate were first in line. Trudy was teary-eyed, and Clifford was consoling her. "They'll find a cure before long."

Aidan realized no one was parked in front of the clinic, or he would have heard them drive up. It was more than strange, but he assumed they were trying to avoid Ronald learning about their visit to the doctor's office when he'd probably told everyone to stay away. They would have, if it hadn't been for the findings Aidan had made.

"Aren't you worried that Ronald will show up and tear into Dr. Denali for being here?" Trudy asked.

"Aidan and I are mates, and we're working together on this."

"Oh heavens, yes, you mentioned it. I've just been so upset over you leaving and Ronald being angry about it. Congratulations. You deserve a good man, and I'm happy for the both of you. We had word that you took Nick to Montana, and he's joining Everett and his family in the pack."

"Yes, he's very happy, and I think he might even find another mate, given time. Lots of widowed ladies out there. I'm just so glad he's found a home with a decent pack. They have really good leaders."

"That's wonderful. I'm sorry I canceled on you. Ronald told everyone in the pack we were forbidden to see you. He's angry your whole family left. I think he's afraid others may follow in your footsteps. And he's not about to change. He doesn't like losing control. All anyone needed to see was someone taking a stand. You and your family did, and no one could believe it. Then again, when you found your mate, you couldn't very well return here with him to stay for good. When Jared hears it, he'll be furious." Trudy smiled.

"Too bad. It never had to be this way." Holly finished the blood tests for Clifford and Trudy and gave them to Aidan to review. Then she took the next couple in while Trudy and her mate sat with Aidan in Holly's office, waiting to see what he had to say, and he explained what was going on. Then Ted offered to make them some coffee, and Trudy and Clifford left the office to help him.

"No one's supposed to tell Ronald we're here. No one's telling him what you've found. It would serve him right if his body is aging faster for all the grief he's given all of us, and all the bad-mouthing he's done about Dr. Denali after he saved Joey, for heaven's sake," another of her female patients told Holly.

Aidan was glad they were keeping quiet about it, though he suspected word would get out soon enough. Someone was bound to spill the beans.

Though Aidan was in another room, between the door being open to both rooms and their enhanced wolf hearing, he heard everything that was going on. He just hoped Ronald stayed out of their business until after they were ready to leave.

After her patients left, Holly joined Aidan in the office and wanted to look over the lists he'd made. "I'd say half of your pack is affected. What we need to know is how many have really ancient genealogy," Aidan said.

She looked over the names. "Most of those who aren't affected by the change have ancient genealogy. They're proud of the fact. I don't know about these five. Some don't really talk about family history. They may not know it as well as others. Most shared their oral history over generations. This one—Rock, on the changes list—has always said his ancestors have ancient wolf genealogy."

"It looks as though there could be a correlation, at least for most of your people. I need to see how far back royals go in other packs and if any have similar ancient histories. If they do, that throws out the supposition that ancient family history could be affecting longevity. How well do you know Rock?" Aidan said.

"Hmm. Well, since it hasn't mattered in the past if someone is fudging a bit on their family history, it's possible his family roots don't go back that far."

"You mean he's been lying," Aidan said.

"Possibly. As an alpha male and a pack enforcer for Ronald, he's not going to want to admit it. The other possibility is that his family has always told that story, and the more recent family members have been sharing the made-up tale, believing it to be true."

"We need to know the truth. We can check with the other packs about their roots and compare them," Aidan said.

"If this is the reason, then none of the other packs have ancient *lupus garou* roots?" Holly said.

"That's what it looks like. Though I thought my

family dated back at least that far, unless those tales were fabricated."

Ted and Mike were fixing coffee for everyone and adding peppermint candy canes for those who wanted them. Trudy and her husband returned to the office with their cups of coffee.

"Thank you, Dr. Denali," Trudy said. "It's not the best news, but I'm glad Clifford is fine. Once you leave, then what happens to us?"

"If Sally can take the blood tests, she can send the samples to us. We can monitor them."

"Thank you." Trudy said goodbye to Holly and Dr. Denali. "We'll keep in touch, no matter what Ronald wants."

Holly smiled. "Good. He can't deal with all of you if you stick together."

Then Clifford and Trudy left the clinic, but they turned right back around and ducked inside. "It's him! Ronald is heading for your parking lot entrance."

"Okay, we have a choice. We can stand together and tell him the truth, that some of his pack members have issues with their longevity now. Or you can all hide in my office. But I won't guarantee he won't check in there."

Clifford snorted and folded his arms. "I'm not hiding."

"Me either," Trudy said.

Suddenly, Sally burst into the clinic. "Ohmigod, Trudy told me what happened to her. Ronald's just parking his truck. I nearly hit his vehicle with my car, trying to get in here to warn you first. I'm sure he's livid about it."

Everyone turned when Ronald opened the door to the clinic. He stared at all the pack members there, his glare spearing Holly next. Aidan joined her, not about to let her deal with Ronald on her own.

"I want everyone to leave," Ronald said, spying Aidan's men all at once. "Now."

"I've got work to do. I won't be staying long. I've tested maybe seven patients' blood. If you want me to test yours, I'll take care of it for you. I know you have a lot of work to do."

"You're no longer a member of this pack," Ronald said.

"Some of our blood is aging faster," Trudy said, angry. "You want to deny our people a cure if Drs. Gray and Denali can discover one? What if they do and they don't give it to us because you are against having anything to do with wolves from other packs? Our son could have been taken from the mall, and we might not ever have seen him again! It was due to Dr. Denali and his men's efforts that he was saved. Let them do their work and help us too."

"Who says our blood is aging faster?" Ronald asked.

"Aidan has been studying this for over a year. He's the expert. If anyone knows what to look for, he does," Holly said. "If you want to know if your blood has aged faster, just let me check."

Ronald gave her a disdainful chuckle. "Now you're doctoring the records, and then you can get what you wanted all along?"

"As if I would want to stress anyone out by telling them their longevity has shortened considerably for our kind."

"Has yours?"

"No," Holly said.

"Mine has," Trudy said. "Clifford's hasn't. Do you know what that means for us? It means we won't grow old together. I'll die way before he does."

Another truck pulled up, and a few minutes later, Jared stormed into the clinic. "What the hell? Ronald tells you all to mind your own business, and you're all here?"

"Not everyone's here," Holly said. "No one would have come if we hadn't given Trudy the information she deserves to know. There are more than that who are aging faster. Aidan is reviewing the records and making a list of who has longevity issues. He's only halfway through the records. I wanted to do blood tests before I leave to verify we haven't made any mistakes."

Holly noticed Sally had sneaked a couple into the lab to take blood.

"Let me see that list," Ronald said.

"Right this way." Aidan led him into the office.

"I can't believe you're leaving your pack behind," Jared said to Holly, irritated.

"I've mated Aidan. I can't bring him into the pack. I'm part of his now."

"I don't have any problems," Ronald said in the office, looking at the list that included the wolves who weren't aging faster.

"We need to have a pack gathering and learn what's different about those who are aging faster and those who aren't," Aidan said.

"Like hell we do," Ronald said. "You might have discovered a problem with the blood for some. But you're not taking over the pack."

"Nope, have no intention of doing so and no interest. But I do want to solve the longevity issue."

Jared headed into the office to see if he had any difficulties and took a relieved breath when he found he didn't.

"It could take us decades to learn the truth, or even longer. If we can pin down why some are fine and others are not, we might be able to find a cure, or even learn if you and your brother and the others who are okay might continue to be that way."

"Holly and her family are in the clear," Jared said.

Holly smiled and ushered the next couple in while the other couple thanked her and left.

"I don't see any correlation between the two lists," Ronald said.

"Nick told us his and Holly's family have really old *lupus garou* roots," Aidan said, hoping to learn more about Ronald and Jared's family roots.

Ronald snorted. "Good luck with that. Not all of us know our family history."

"Because your father was from another pack and tried to take over this one," Aidan said.

Ronald's face turned red, and he stalked over to the door and slammed it shut. "Where the hell did you get that idea?"

As soon as the door slammed closed, it opened again, and four bodyguards rushed into the office, Ted and Mike at the forefront.

Looking ill at ease, Ronald stepped back away from the men.

"We're fine here," Aidan said to his men. "You can stay, if you like, and we can close the door if Ronald wants some privacy."

"Close the damn door," Ronald growled.

Ted closed the door.

"All right. I take it you don't know anything about your father's parentage."

"My mother's *lupus garou* genes went as far back as Nick's and Holly's families'," Ronald said.

"What about the others on the list who haven't changed?" Aidan asked.

"Clifford's line is old. Trudy's isn't. I've overheard them teasing each other about it. Some of the ones on the 'safe' list aren't as old as us. Some that have been affected are."

Aidan frowned at the news. He hadn't wanted to hear that. Though he had wondered, because he'd made a cross-reference to *lupus garou* roots to see if it could have been that with other wolf packs, but he hadn't been able to make the correlation.

"It can't be your environment, not with some changing," Aidan said. "Unless some have more resistance to change. I still don't think that's it."

Holly entered the office and shut the door. "What's going on?"

"You need to stay here and take care of this," Ronald said.

"We'll stay as long as it takes to do the blood work, and then we're leaving. I'll keep in touch with Sally, and if we have to, we can return once a month to check on everyone." Ronald wasn't going to push Holly or her family around any longer. "I came in to tell you we could check your blood before you leave."

"Ronald doesn't believe the longevity has anything to do with the older *lupus garou* roots, based on some of your pack members' blood tests," Aidan said. "There's definitely something going on with your pack. We still need to talk to everyone to see what we can learn."

"We should include Nick," Holly said. "He's like those of us who haven't changed. Maybe he'll have some insight."

Ronald stared at the two lists for what seemed like forever, as if weighing how much trouble he would be in with the pack if he didn't agree to help with this. "I'll call a meeting for an hour from now at my place, but none of your goons can come."

"No," Holly said, surprising Aidan and everyone there. "If we're going to figure this out, they'll be there too. They have just as much at stake here as any of us do. And they're Aidan's protection."

"We'll meet in an hour then." Ronald headed for the door, and Ted opened it for him, being the nice guy that he was.

Jared said to Holly, "I was serious about being sorry for biting you."

"All right, apology accepted."

Then Jared headed out after his brother. Rock was still hanging around, and he poked his head in, his black hair windblown, his black brows furrowed. "If you need my help with this, just ask. Gotta go, but Doc's got my number." He hurried out after Jared and Ronald.

"I'll be back in a few minutes after I help take the rest of the blood samples," Holly said.

"Okay, honey. I'm still going through the records. Have you got earlier records for all the wolves?"

"You mean before I was even a doctor for the pack?"

"Yeah. Maybe it has something to do with your blood."

"They're not online. They're in files boxed in a warehouse of records."

"We would need only those of your current members, not the ones who have died, to see if there's anything that would help clear up the mystery."

"We can do that. I'll be right back." Holly hurried out to take Ronald and his brother's blood samples, glad Ronald was finally working with them, though she could just imagine the revolt he'd have on his hands if he stuck to his guns and didn't want to help now that some of his people were affected.

Clifford asked Holly as she left her office, "What can we do to help?"

She took him and his mate into one of her exam rooms to speak to them privately. "Aidan had the notion to try a blood transfusion to see if my blood would help to change the person receiving the blood."

"Would it?"

"We don't know, but he wanted to test out his theory. Our healing genetics may see the transfused blood as alien, or it might recognize the blood is better than the patient's and replicate it. That's what we're hoping, but it's just experimental. He doesn't want to test it on anyone else until he knows if it will make a difference or not."

"I want to have Clifford's blood tested on me," Trudy said.

"You don't have the same blood type. But yours is the same as mine. I just gave blood for his bodyguard. We have to wait. We don't know if it will have any bad effects or if it will even work. You're not aging as fast as a human. Don't worry. We'll get it worked out. I'm sure of it."

"Can I give blood in the event you can use it?" Clifford asked.

"Yes. We can store it for forty days. Longer, if we freeze it. Up to ten years, actually. But our blood replaces cells within two to three weeks."

Ronald came out of the room with Sally, who was giving Aidan Ronald's blood to test. Then she returned to take Jared's. The high-and-mighty pack leader was finally agreeable to having Sally work with him instead of Holly. Good, because he was going to have to get used to it.

"I'll get you set up to donate your blood, Clifford." Holly did that, and once he was done, she put the blood in the fridge for storage.

She ended up having ten more people with the longer longevity donate blood. Things were going much better than she'd ever expected.

Then Ronald stalked out of the clinic, not saying anything to anyone, his expression stormy. "Jared, contact everyone in the pack. We have a meeting in forty-five minutes, no exceptions."

Holly smiled and joined Aidan, and he promptly left her chair and gave her a hug.

He kissed her forehead. "Are we done here?"

"We sure are. The last of them left a few minutes ago. We have some more coming in tomorrow who couldn't get away today. They're unhappy about this issue, of course, but they're glad you and I are working on it."

"There's no change in the ones who seem to have an immunity," Aidan said.

"I asked some of our members to get the stored pack records for those now in the pack, and for Nick, of course. But we have to go to that meeting first."

Chapter 28

THEY HEADED OVER TO RONALD'S HOUSE, AND THOUGH Holly's family considered not coming to the meeting since they were no longer pack members and they didn't want to see Ronald and Jared, they came to show their support for the rest of the pack.

Holly set up a computer so Nick could be there too.

"I'm opening the floor to Drs. Denali and Gray to explain why they wanted to meet with all of you," Ronald said. "Seems Holly was right in worrying that some of us could have the same issues as others in the rest of the wolf packs that Aidan has located. To that end, we will fully cooperate with the doctors so they can do their research and find a cure."

"We're going to go through all the old records to see if anything stands out for us," Aidan said. "But we have a few more people to take blood from. We'll be doing that tomorrow."

"Tonight," Ronald interjected. "That should have been taken care of already."

Holly couldn't believe Ronald's change of heart. "We're still trying to determine the reason some are changing and others are not. It may have to do with the last wolf war."

They didn't receive any more answers to their questions during the meeting. Afterward, Holly and Aidan and his men returned to the clinic to take the rest of the blood samples. They compared them and found two more who had the changing longevity. She'd hoped they wouldn't find anyone else with the condition.

When they went to her place that night, she was exhausted, but not so much so that she couldn't enjoy loving her wolf mate. "You were wonderful with Ronald and Jared."

"Believe me, I wanted to do more than accommodate them. But we'll be leaving, and everyone else has to deal with them. I wanted to try to keep the peace as much as possible."

"Thank you."

Ted and Mike were in the kitchen making shrimp pasta and poinsettia mimosas—made of triple sec, cranberry juice, maraschino cherry juice, and topped with tangerine spirals—for dinner when someone rang the doorbell.

"Expecting anyone?" Aidan asked, going with her to the front door.

"No. Not unless someone was concerned about their blood work. I'm sure if anyone was, they'd call first."

Ted and Mike both quickly joined them in body-guard mode.

When they reached the door, she peeked out the peephole and took a deep breath. "Ronald and Rock."

She opened the door and folded her arms, not inviting them in. "We're just starting our dinner. What's so urgent that you couldn't have called like you usually do?"

"I want to speak with Denali," Ronald said.

Now *that* surprised her.

Ronald said to Aidan, "We want you to join our

pack. You've mated our doctor, and you're working on an important cause, which will make you a valuable pack member."

She closed her gaping mouth. She couldn't believe Ronald would come around like this. Then again, he had a stake in this now. Maybe he thought he could benefit from it financially. Or maybe he was worried Aidan wouldn't provide him with a cure.

"Thanks, but no thanks. I have a pack of my own that Holly and her family are now part of." Aidan put his arm around her but then looked down at her as if he remembered that she had a say in this.

She smiled up at him and frowned at Ronald. "I told you all along that we might be affected by this change, but you wouldn't believe it. Hopefully, we'll find the cure, and we *will* share it with everyone."

"As long as you don't give Holly and her family any more grief over leaving the pack. And if we need Sally to send us blood samples each month to try to help find a solution, you'll agree she can do it. Your pack members freely gave us permission to use their blood to try to figure this out," Aidan said.

"We still plan to go over the health records that could be pertinent to the case tomorrow. Maybe we'll learn something from that," Holly said.

Ronald let out his breath in annoyance. "All right. Have it your way, but you keep me informed."

As soon as he and Rock left, Ted and Mike served the food. Holly and Aidan joined them at the table.

Holly took a sip of her poinsettia mimosa and then a bite of her pasta. "Ohmigod, you guys can't ever leave us."

They chuckled.

"Everything they fix is great," Aidan agreed.

"Except for the burned tilapia that one time," Ted said. "Mike was supposed to be watching the fish."

"Ha," Mike said. "I was baking the broccoli-and-cheese side dish. You were supposed to be watching the fish."

She just laughed, enjoying their company.

Once they had eaten and the guys said they'd clean up, Aidan wrapped his arm around her shoulders and escorted her to their bedroom. He shut the door and pulled her into his arms and lowered his head to kiss her, his fingers combing through her hair, their tongues tangling as she yanked his shirt out of his jeans.

"Wait." He released her, yet she didn't want to stop touching him, feeling his touch on her, until she saw he was yanking aside her comforter. Then he smiled to see the red sheets and pillowcases. "Hot."

"For Christmas."

"And hot." He hurried to remove her sweater and smiled at her red lace bra, his gaze turning dark and interested. "Really hot."

"For Christmas." Smiling at him, she ran her hands up his shirt and tweaked his nipples with a light touch. *He* was really hot—and making her blood sizzle already. His touch and his rough voice made her panties wet.

He molded his hands to her lace-covered breasts and brushed his lips across hers. His breath was warm and mimosa sweet. She closed her eyes and gave in to the feel of his hands sliding her bra down, freeing her breasts from the lace. Leaning down, he licked her nipples and she clung to his shoulders, ready to collapse on the bed, losing herself in the feel of his hot, wet tongue circling each nipple. She groaned. She swore he could practically make her come just by doing that.

He paused to tackle her belt and jeans, but when he pulled them down her hips, he had to stop and remove her boots. He scooped her up—and she nearly squealed at the unexpected action—then set her on the bed and slid off her boots, socks, and jeans. "Red lace panties. Hot."

She chuckled. "For—"

"Me."

She laughed.

He made short work of his own clothes, all except his boxer briefs, and she admired his cock as it stretched at the black fabric to be free. She wanted to pull his briefs down to free his cock, but he moved her farther onto the bed and nudged her legs apart to center himself on her.

His stiff cock rubbed against her mound as he moved his body against hers, his mouth pressing kisses over her exposed breasts and nipples. She arched against him, encouraging and loving the friction between them. Their pulses were racing, the pheromones heady, the adrenaline rushing through their blood.

He kissed her belly and moved to nuzzle her mound with his cheek, and she wanted the rest of their clothes off now! She ran her fingers through his hair, arching her back to bump his cheek, and he moved off her to slide her panties down, then unsnapped her bra.

Before she could sit up to pull off his boxer briefs, he was yanking them down and tossing them to the floor, his cock springing free. "Now that's hot," she said, eyeing his impressive erection.

He smiled wickedly at her and rejoined her on the bed, his eyes hungry with need.

"God, how I love you." She ran her hands through his hair, and he began kissing her mouth again, his groin resting against her naked thigh.

He moved his hand down her breast, sweeping lower until he found her clit and began to stroke. "Wet, hot, mine," he whispered with a ragged breath against her cheek.

She was ready for him, on the verge of climax when she tugged at him to join her. She wanted to come when he was inside her. He obliged, sliding into her, then building a thrusting rhythm that had her teetering on the edge. She dug her fingers into his shoulders, moaning, nearing the top, ready to splinter when she felt the end slam into her. But he didn't quit, deepening his penetration, thrusting until his explosive, wet heat filled her.

He groaned with satisfied release and held her tightly for some time, his cock still inside her, stirring.

"Damn, Aidan," she said.

He smiled at her. "Hot, huh?"

"God, yes." And she wrapped her arms around him. She wasn't letting go until he was ready for her again.

"If you can hold on…"

"I'm holding."

It didn't take long for him to begin kissing her again. She loved her hot wolf.

"Love you, Holly," he whispered against her ear, his cock lengthening, growing.

"Love you right back, Aidan." She anchored her heels against the backs of his thighs and encouraged the building rush to sweep them away again.

Now she knew what other mated wolves had. Two

people who were different, similar, sharing an unbreak-
able bond that would last their lifetimes, and being there
for each other, not just like family and pack members,
but sharing an intimacy that only mated wolves could.

———∿∿∿———

Early the next morning, Holly was all set to head into
the clinic to look through the old records, but Aidan,
still waking up after their last bout of lovemaking, had
another idea. He was sure Mike and Ted would think
they'd never leave the bedroom this morning.

"Why don't we get a few things done at the same
time," Aidan said. "We can look over the records in the
comfort of your living room while the guys help pack.
That way, they're with us, but doing something useful.
You can direct them about what you want to have them
pack and what you're leaving behind."

"All right. Sounds like a winning idea."

They got a call from Jared a little after that. "Ronald
told me to call and see if you could use my help in going
through the records."

Aidan agreed.

"Yeah, sure," Holly said.

"Okay, I'm supervising moving the files, but several
other pack members want to help," Jared said.

"Sounds good. Bring them to my house." This was
the way it should have been all along, the pack members
helping each other and working with other wolves.

When they finally arrived with the records and had
spread them all over the long dining room table, Holly
began organizing those with changes and those without.

"I wish the doctor who had kept these records was

still alive. I can barely read his hen scratches," Holly said, looking at one of the records.

"Is his nurse still around?"

"Yes, actually. She probably would be able to read them better than anyone." Holly called Anita and asked her to join them at her home.

Anita Wellington soon came, her blue-gray eyes assessing them, her step slow but steady as Ted assisted her to the table. "Oh my," she said, looking at the first of the records, her eyes filling with tears. "I do miss that man."

"I never knew him," Holly said.

"He was a good man, would help anyone at any time, and had an absolute weakness for apple pie. Okay, tell me what we're looking for."

Sally arrived at the house to help them too, because she knew a lot of the medical abbreviations.

"Anything that makes those with the change in their longevity different from those who have stayed the same," Holly said.

Aidan had a messy pile of records in front of him, and Holly wanted to straighten them out for him. She couldn't see how he'd learn anything that way. On the other hand, if that was his process and it worked for him, she would leave him alone. She was busy looking through her own neat stacks of records, having separated them out into different categories. She'd put Jared to work with the other men packing her clothes, food, and household items. If they couldn't find anything after they had gone through all the records, she was ready to drop this stuff off at her new home and go visit Jade, Rafe, and Toby.

"I've got records for some of the earliest years that

we had records for," Anita said. "What are we looking for exactly?"

Aidan sat back on his chair and studied her for a moment. "Anything that could affect DNA."

"We're looking at blood tests to see when those in the pack changed?" Anita asked.

"Blood transfusions," Holly said. "What about blood transfusions?"

"Yes, look for those. Or, hell, bite wounds," Aidan said.

"From fights with other packs?" Sally asked.

Jared walked in with an empty box and asked, "Paintings go too?"

"The wolf paintings. Everything else can stay with the house," Holly said, but she saw Aidan staring at Jared, his brows raised. "What?"

"Check all the records for the time when Jared's father fought the pack. All the bite wounds where the patient was treated but lived. We need to know which had bite wounds, and if any of them have the decreased longevity."

"You're thinking Jared's father had something to do with this?" Holly asked.

"Maybe not, but think of it this way. A lot of blood was spilled, Jared's and Ronald's blood hasn't changed, but they weren't even born yet. They had half their father's blood. Now, this is only speculation, but what if their father's pack was one of the oldest? What if the dad's people were the key, only they were wiped out in the fight?"

Everyone was searching through the files, looking for the ones relevant to that time.

Jared just stared at Aidan. "Even though he tried to take over the pack and killed off several of our people, he might have saved all wolf-kind in the end, if what you're thinking is true."

"Yeah. Only he hadn't known it. None of us knew this was coming," Aidan said.

"Then some of the pack who are still living received some of the blood during the fight," Holly said. "Both my mother and father were in the fight."

They found the files for all the pack members still living who had been alive during the last wolf fight and sorted them into four piles—some of each going to Sally, Anita, Holly, and Aidan.

"August 20 is when the wolf fight occurred," Anita said. "Look for that day and a couple of days following that. If anyone was badly injured, they would have been treated that day, but the ones who didn't need any treatment might not be recorded. You know how some men are when they don't want to look like a sissy wolf, even if they have a wound deep enough to require some attention."

"I've got Nick's records. He'd been the pack leader, so he'd led the attacks and was chewed up pretty badly. Says he had thirty-four stitches for eight severe bite wounds, a broken leg set, and bed rest for a week, though the doctor said after two days, he was up and checking on the rest of his pack," Holly said. Nick put the current pack leaders to shame. She noticed Jared was listening. She hoped he could see what a difference one man could make. Nick had saved their pack from Jared's own father and then was put out to pasture when his mate died.

"Here's another one," Anita said. "Geoffrey, an accountant for the pack, had received twenty-two stitches for claw marks and bites. He came down with a fever two days later but then recovered."

"And he has the longer life-span. I'm thinking that Clifford wouldn't have been born back then, just like Holly, Jared, and others," Aidan said. "They more than likely received the genetics from their parents."

"Which means we'll have to look through any of the deceased members who are the biological parents of those who haven't been changed." Holly pulled out her phone to have Trudy pull more files.

"I'll take care of it," Jared said. "Be back in a little bit."

Aidan gave him a list of the pack members' names.

Holly was hoping to God they'd finally find the clue they needed.

Half an hour later, Jared returned with a stack of files, but this time, Ronald was with him. "He said he thought you had a breakthrough on this case," Ronald said.

"We're not sure," Aidan said.

"Holly, I checked your mom and dad's records, but neither of them showed they had any treatment," Sally said.

"I'll call them." Holly immediately got on her phone and reached her mom. "Mom, I'm going to put this on speaker because we're going over the older medical records to see if we've found the reason why some wolves haven't changed."

"Oh my, that's good news. Okay, dear. Go ahead."

"When the third wolf war occurred, you and dad were involved in the fighting, right?"

"Yes. Every able-bodied wolf was."

"Were you and dad wounded?"

"Both of us were. As much fighting as went on, we all were chewed on, just as much as we clawed and bit the aggressor wolves back."

"You didn't see the doctor to treat your wounds."

"No. He was concentrating on those who needed a lot of care. We licked our wounds, went to bed, and healed on our own. A day later, the doc asked if anyone else needed their bites tended to, but we were on the mend, so we didn't bother seeing him."

"Then others could have done the same thing."

"Many did. Only the badly injured needed his care. Everyone else took care of their own wounds. You think that fight had something to do with it?"

"Possibly. Maybe Jared and Ronald's dad had an immunity to the change in his system, and he shared that with Jared and Ronald. Then anyone he bit, possibly Nick and others, received the immunity. Maybe others in his pack also had it, and that's why so many were affected. But not all, if they didn't fight because they were too young or infirm. Did Clifford's parents fight in the battle before he was born?"

"Yes. His dad nearly died. He was the first to go down, and we thought he wouldn't make it. But he survived and lived to a ripe old age."

"Okay, thanks, Mom. Got to go. I'll let you know what else we find."

By midnight, they had narrowed the list down to only two men and a woman with the longer longevity that they hadn't found a reason for.

"We're going to need everyone who lived during the

war and is still alive try to recall anything they can—"
Aidan said, but Anita cleared her throat.

"Judith was just a baby at the time, but her dad fought
in the war."

Holly wondered how that explained anything regarding Judith.

"When Judith was fifteen, she was horsing around
with some other kids at night, ran into the corner of an
old wagon, and gashed her head. Her father gave blood
to her. She was at the clinic for five days."

"If the other two cases have similar results, we might
have our solution," Aidan said, smiling.

Holly thought he looked like he was the happiest wolf
on earth. She was too.

To think they could have eliminated the pack that
saved them all in the end was sobering.

"Okay, we need to look for any time after that when
they received blood from anyone who might have the
immunity up until today's date." Holly was ecstatic.
If they were right, that meant blood transfusions from
immune wolves could be used to make other wolves
immune. Or bites even. Jared had bitten Mike and
Aidan. He might have passed on his immunity to them.

"We're going to make some lunch for everyone," Ted
said. "Taking sandwich orders."

"I'll help," Jared said.

She couldn't believe he was turning around. Maybe
the Seattle pack would become the kind of pack it should
be. Like others that were more welcoming. Sure, wary to
an extent, but not threatening if other *lupus garous* had
to go to Seattle for human business.

"I've got the records for Phil. If we can divide up the

dates of the records between two of us, the other two can divide up Mixon's records," Holly said, joining Aidan.

Sally and Anita split up the records and started hunting.

Ted and Mike made ham, roast beef, and turkey sandwiches and brought them over to the table. Everyone grabbed what they wanted and took a break in the living room.

"If what you think could be true, I'm willing to donate my blood," Ronald said before he took a bite of a ham sandwich.

"Me too," Jared said.

"Once we've proven those who have the old longevity were changed by blood, we need to verify that those whose longevity has changed didn't receive blood from anyone whose blood hasn't changed," Aidan cautioned. "It's still a small sample compared to the whole of the wolf population we know of, but I believe if we find both to be true, we can assume this will work. At least in theory. And we can test it out on a small group of volunteers. Mike is already carrying Holly's blood."

Holly wanted to tell Roland *See what a little cooperation can do?* But she refrained from commenting. Ronald was smart enough to see the consequences of working together with them.

"She didn't give you her blood?" Jared asked Aidan, sounding surprised.

Mike spoke up. "It's my job to protect Aidan, in case anything goes wrong with this."

Then Jared frowned. "When we fought, I could have given you and Aidan some of my blood."

"Yep." Aidan finished off his chicken sandwich and went back to work.

Holly finished her ham sandwich and rejoined Aidan to search Phil's records some more.

Sally and Anita returned to their records for Mixon, and after another hour, Sally said, "Yes! Okay, he got into a wolf fight over the woman he took as his mate some years after the wolf fight. He'd been too young to participate in that. The wolf he'd had the conflict with was—"

"Me." Ronald sounded annoyed over it. "I should have known she'd go with him."

"They'd been courting for some time already," Anita said. "Now we just need to figure out Phil's situation."

"We need to learn if any of the wolves who have changed had blood transfusions or fights with other wolves that could have given them a mix of blood. If they did and their blood is still changing, we could be wrong about this," Aidan said.

"We'll get on that," Sally said, sorting through the files.

"So far, I don't see anything in the medical records on Phil that indicates he went to see the doc about any issues." Then Holly frowned. "Wait, not in the old records. About a year ago, his boy bit him while he was a wolf pup and broke the skin. Phil came in just in case he needed a tetanus shot. We've already determined his mate probably received the immunity from her parents who had fought in the battle. When Phil and his mate had the boy, he had his mother's immunity."

"All right, then everyone who hasn't changed has been verified to have received blood from someone whose blood hasn't changed." Aidan sounded pleased but reserved too. Finding one person who didn't fit with the scenario could still blow their whole theory out of the water.

They had dinner later that night after clearing four of the fifteen people whose blood had changed, though if they were like some of the others, they might not have seen the doctor, but taken care of injuries on their own.

"That's good enough for me," Ronald said. "I want everyone who has an immunity to the change to give blood to those in our pack who don't." He got up from the sofa and headed for the door.

"We have to see if there's a chance any of these people did receive blood and it didn't help," Aidan said. "If that's the case, it might not help anyone else. We need to do this right."

"You know what? We need to just call each of the people. Ask them if they recall being bitten by anyone on the list who's been cleared," Holly said. "We haven't found any blood transfusions that were given to these four. I think it might be faster to just call them. We'll have to anyway afterward if we can't find anything in the records."

Jared was talking privately with his brother in a corner of the living room, and Holly wondered what was up. Especially since both of them glanced her way and then looked away just as quickly.

"Offer less," Ronald told Jared.

"How much less?"

Ronald said something, but she couldn't overhear him this time.

"I think Jared's interested in buying your house. Don't let him steal it from you," Aidan whispered to her.

"I'd let Rafe handle it, but there would be harder

feelings that way. I'd much rather a wolf from the pack buy it."

"I'll buy it," Sally said. "We could use the room, and the family that bought your parents' place are good friends of ours. Our kids play with each other all the time. They'd love it out here in the country."

Holly smiled. She'd much rather sell it to her nurse than Jared. "At my asking price?"

"Yes."

"We have a deal then. I'll let Rafe know that it has sold." Holly got on her phone to Rafe and said, "Good news. My nurse is buying my home. We're all set. Thanks for selling my mom and dad's home."

"Tell them to keep their money for setting up their new shop and any furnishings they want to pick up. I'll take care of building their new home."

"Thanks, Rafe."

"It's my Christmas present to you and your family. I'll get the paperwork drawn up for you and the new buyer."

Holly couldn't thank him enough, and they ended the call as Jared headed her way. "I'll offer twenty thousand less than the asking price on your home, which is a damn good deal."

"I just bought it for the full price. It's totally worth it for the land and forests surrounding her place and her parents'. Sorry." Sally smiled, not sounding sorry in the least, and then went back to work pulling a file. She got on her phone to call the patient.

Jared just stared at her like he couldn't believe it. Holly was proud of Sally for offering and then sticking to her guns on it.

Holly called the next patient while Anita was already

talking to hers. "Are you sure you never got into a wolf fight, even in playing, with any of the wolves who don't have blood issues?" Anita asked. "No blood transfusions either? Yes, I know I have your records, but if you didn't come in for any treatment... Yes, we're trying to determine if a bite from an unaffected wolf would change those who... Yes, a blood exchange."

Holly figured Anita was talking to Idabel, their sun lover. She would never let anyone finish a statement without making another comment.

"Okay, you're sure? Yes, I mean, no, I'm not doubting your memory. Thanks. Yes, that could be good news." Anita ended the call and put the file into a new stack for those they were relatively sure had never received blood from an unaffected wolf.

Sally placed hers on top of Anita's. "Two, no blood transfers, right?"

"Yes. As far as she knew." Anita called the next person on the list.

"Are you certain?" Aidan asked the patient he was speaking with. "Just sparring with the wolves who are changing? Best buddies. And you were too young when the last wolf war started. Gotcha. No blood transfusions. All right. Yes, we might have found the cure. We'll let you know."

"Need anything to drink?" Ted asked.

"Coffee," both Aidan and Holly said. She didn't think they were going to get through all these records. Not before midnight anyway. And she wanted to make love to Aidan again.

Holly was talking to one of the men, but he was having a hard time remembering some details. He'd been much older when the wolf war had occurred. "You weren't bitten by any of the other wolf pack?"

"Yeah, I was."

"You didn't go in to be stitched up."

"No, healed up in a few days."

"But the attacking wolf was from the other wolf pack, and he broke the skin."

"Um, no."

"You said the wolf bit you."

"Yeah, but he was one of ours."

"One of ours bit you? During the war? Which wolf?"

"White. He and I were tearing into the same wolf, but the wolf twisted free and White accidentally bit me."

"White died some years ago."

"Yeah, we'd been friends forever."

"You didn't get any of the attacking wolf's blood in an open wound of your own?"

"Nick finished the wolf off. How would I know if a drop of blood mixed with mine?"

"Okay, and no other wolf confrontations later with any on the list who haven't been affected?"

"Oh, I had a few friendly confrontations later on, but I can't remember which resulted in breaking the skin and which were on the list. Sorry, Doc."

"No problem. We live long lives. It's hard to remember so many details over the many years we live."

When they ended the call, she set his file in another pile. But by the time it was one in the morning—luckily, no matter what the time was, everyone wanted this resolved—they had set the files all in one pile, except for Gadson's. "He couldn't remember who all he tackled in fun when he had some scrapes."

"I'd say the odds are that this could work." Aidan helped Holly up from the table. "That's about all we can do for tonight."

Ted helped Anita to stand. "Do you want me to take you home?"

"Jared drove me."

"I'll take her back." Jared cast Sally an annoyed look, then he said, "Do you want me to take the clinic records back to storage?"

"Yeah, that would be great. Thanks," Holly said.

Jared gathered the files and escorted Anita out to his vehicle.

"What's next on the agenda?" Ronald asked.

"Now we wait to see if there's any change in Mike's DNA."

"For how long?"

"We'll check his blood work monthly and see if there's any change. That's all we can do for now. There's a possibility it won't change his DNA, or that it could only be temporary. We really have to give this more time."

"If our wolves who received blood transfers developed the immunity, then I don't see why it wouldn't work with the rest of our people," Ronald said.

"It could. We don't know how long it took though."

"All right." Ronald was irritated he didn't have all the right answers right this moment. "You're leaving then?"

Aidan deferred to Holly. "Yes, to spend Christmas with Rafe and his family. I'll have a mover here, picking up the rest of my stuff. My parents are already doing that at their home. We'll be leaving tomorrow."

Aidan wrapped his arm around her shoulders and

kissed her cheek. He seemed pleased to hear she was ready to leave.

Holly said to Sally, "Rafe is getting the paperwork drawn up on the house."

"Okay, good. Let me know if I need to do anything more with this other matter," Sally said.

"We will."

Then they hugged, and Aidan gave her a hug before she left.

Ronald said, "Keep me updated." Then he left the house.

Ted and Mike were cleaning up all the dishes. "Nice thanks from their pack leader for all your hard work," Mike said.

"Typical Ronald style," Holly said.

"Well, I'm headed to bed if you folks don't need me for the rest of the night," Ted said.

"Night, Ted, Mike. Thanks for all your assistance," Aidan said. "Glad we didn't need you for a wolf fight."

"Unless one of the unaffected wolves bit me," Ted said.

Aidan chuckled.

Then they all went to bed.

As soon as Aidan and Holly had stripped off each other's clothes, she got a call. "What now?" She checked the ID and saw it was Sally. "Yeah, Sally?" She was hoping she hadn't changed her mind about the house or that Jared had changed it for her.

"We might have a problem. I didn't want to call Ronald about it, and I'll take care of it, but just so you know, Clifford bit Trudy to try to transfer the blood over that way."

"But he has to be bleeding too."

"Yeah, he cut his arm and rubbed his blood on her wound."

"They're not the same blood type." Holly let out her breath. "Okay, that's something we didn't check. Blood types, to see if the mixing of blood had to be with the same blood type. We won't know what the wolves' types were in the other wolf pack, but we should be able to check the ones we know of within the pack."

"Tomorrow, first thing?" Sally asked.

"Yeah, only make it a little later in the morning."

Sally laughed. "I understand. Night, Doc. See you tomorrow."

"Problem?" Aidan asked, climbing into bed with Holly.

"Yeah, expect a rash of wolves biting one another."

Aidan shook his head. "We'd better handle this differently with the rest of the packs when the time comes. For now, this is all I want to handle." He leaned down to kiss her breasts, and she combed her fingers through his hair, ready to enjoy their mated bliss.

Chapter 29

EARLY THE NEXT MORNING, AIDAN AND HOLLY DISCOVERED it didn't matter what blood type the wolves had in the cases where the wolves seemed to develop an immunity. Having done all they could there, Mike and Ted were flown by the other private jet to their family's homes while Aidan and Holly stopped in at Aidan's home to pick up more clothes for the trip. Then they left for Colorado to spend Christmas with Rafe's family.

When they arrived at the chalet, Rafe greeted Holly and Aidan. Rafe looked similar to Holly's mate, except he was about an inch taller and his brown eyes and hair were lighter than Aidan's.

"Jade just put Toby down for a nap. He'd been playing with Marianne and Greg because he was excited to see you, and they were trying to keep him occupied before you got here. They finally wore him out," Rafe said.

Aidan laughed.

"He'll be up in about an hour. We have five separate suites, each with their own private bathroom and sitting area, and four more bedrooms that share two more bathrooms. One of the rooms is Aidan's and yours," Rafe said to Holly, and she was delighted to be here and welcomed to the family.

In the common area, a great living area was situated around a fireplace, and a live, seven-foot-tall Christmas balsam fir sat in a corner of the room, decorated to the hilt in red, gold, blue, and green.

They smelled steaks grilling in the kitchen and heard Ted and Mike talking to each other about which special drinks they were going to make.

Holly looked at Aidan, but he seemed just as surprised to learn they were here.

Rafe smiled. "Mike and Ted said they had a new mission. They diverted the plane to come here once they learned their parents are taking a Caribbean cruise together. They thought Mike and Ted were going to have to work with Aidan over the Christmas holiday, since neither had told them otherwise. Mike and Ted said they had to teach Greg more about cooking anyway. Though Marianne is in the kitchen learning some more too."

"That's good news. Where are Mom and Dad?" Holly smelled their scent in the living area. She knew they were here and would have come with Marianne and Greg.

"They went for a run in the woods. They should be back soon."

"This is truly beautiful. Thanks for inviting my whole family here," Holly said.

"All of you are family now. And we're glad to have you. It just makes Christmas all the merrier. Jade's delighted too."

"And we're a pack. You might not have bargained for it, but you're now officially in charge of a pack. You and Jade," Aidan said, glad his brother and Jade took on the role. He'd prefer solving the mysteries of the universe with Holly.

Jade joined them, her blond hair pulled back in a

chignon. She had beautiful dark-brown eyes and was genuinely smiling when she welcomed Holly and Aidan. "We're glad you're both here, and that your family is also here for the holidays. And Aidan's bodyguards too. They earn their pay in cooking meals. Since your mother and sister are here, I figured we'd have our special shopping excursion together tomorrow. The guys will figure out something to keep them occupied in the meantime."

"I can't wait," Holly said. "Hey, Aidan, do you want to stretch our legs, and we'll look for Mom and Dad?"

"Yeah, let's do that." They'd had a long couple of days without any real wolf downtime. He was ready to play with his wolf mate.

Holly and Aidan ran as wolves to track down her parents and finally found them sitting on a boulder, watching a bear and her cubs at a lake a long way off.

They quickly greeted them, and Aidan was glad he'd invited her family to be with them for the holidays. They didn't stay out for long, because he was certain Toby would wake and be upset he'd missed Aidan and Holly when they went on the wolf run. They were starting to head back to the chalet when they heard Jade and Rafe howl.

Aidan howled back to let them know they were on their way, but Rafe, Jade, and Toby met them halfway. Toby tackled Aidan, but once they had a tussle in the snow, he looked shyly at the other wolves as if he hadn't realized they were even there. Recognizing Holly's parents, Toby ran over to greet them, and they licked him.

Holly lay down on the snow to be more his size, and he inched over to see her. She smiled, and he moved a little closer. She leaned down and licked his cheek, and he looked back at Aidan to see if it was all right to greet her.

He nodded.

Toby snuggled up to her, rubbing his body against her. She was now officially part of *his* pack.

They spent the next few days enjoying the pool and the hot tub, making snowmen, and playing as wolves. One of the highlights for Holly was going out with the ladies for the tea party. And at night, Aidan and she slipped off to make love in their room at the chalet. It was finally Christmas Eve, and after a wild afternoon of building snow forts and having snow fights, they settled in to have Christmas Eve dinner with a fire crackling in the fireplace, all the Christmas lights sparkling, and Christmas music playing in the background. The aroma of the Christmas Eve dinner—tenderloin roast, mashed potatoes, gravy, broccoli, fresh-baked bread Holly's mother had made, and a fruitcake Jade had made—filled the air.

No packages were under the tree, but that was because Toby was young, and they wanted to keep the spirit of Santa Claus alive for him a little while longer. He was a cute kid, all blond curls, reminding Holly of herself and her brother and sister when they were little, except that they had blue eyes when Toby had dark-brown eyes like his mother.

What surprised them more was the doorbell ringing right before they sat down to eat.

"Who could that be?" Rafe asked, winking at Jade. "Be right back."

Everyone waited to see who would be coming for dinner now.

Nick and Victoria, or Santa and Mrs. Claus, entered the house, surprising and pleasing everyone.

Nick was dressed in an old-world Santa costume—a long, red velvet coat and red pants, black boots, and all the white fur trimmings. Victoria looked too much like Mrs. Claus to be anything but in her red velvet Victorian gown trimmed in white fur along the hem and sleeves, with a matching bolero velvet jacket that was fur-trimmed along the collar, down the front edges, and all the way around the back.

Toby's eyes were wide with excitement, but he didn't budge from where he was standing with his mom.

"Come say hi to Santa," Rafe said to Toby.

Toby looked up at his mom to get her okay. She smiled down at him. "Go ahead, Toby. Remember, we made cookies for Santa. Mrs. Santa came too, just for you."

"And Marianne and Greg," Toby said.

Jade chuckled. "Yes, for them too. Santa and Mrs. Santa Claus are going to eat dinner with us."

"Then we have to get on our way," Nick said. "Busy night of the year, you know."

Toby ran across the room to give Santa a hug, and Nick lifted him off his feet and gave him a big hug. "This is the reason I needed to be with a pack." Then Nick looked down at Victoria and smiled, holding Toby on his hip and wrapping his arm around Victoria. "And this is the reason."

She blushed beautifully.

Aidan couldn't have been happier for them. Then they all sat down to eat. Aidan had so many things planned for Holly to do in the next couple of weeks. For now, this was all just family fun. Though he knew the family would like to do things with them too.

After dinner, Santa read Toby bedtime stories and then said, "Now, all good little girls and boys have to go to bed and then I can unpack my sleigh."

Toby looked at Marianne and Greg as if that meant them too.

Greg laughed. "Yeah, sure. Come on, Toby. I'll read you some more stories, but then we've got to go to sleep, and then Santa can give us some presents. As long as we've been good."

Marianne took Toby's hand. "Me too." Then they headed down the hall to Toby's room.

The adults all had coffee and fruitcake in front of the fire.

"I have to tell you, nothing's the same since Nick came to stay with us," Victoria said very seriously.

Nick smiled at her. "You can say that again."

She blushed again.

"We couldn't have been more surprised or thrilled that you came for Christmas Eve," Aidan said.

"I wouldn't have missed it for the world. As soon as you left, I called Rafe to see if I could make arrangements to come," Nick said.

"I couldn't have been more thrilled to hear he and Victoria would make this night even more special," Rafe said, and Jade agreed.

"We do have a bit of a problem with the pack though. Everyone has asked for samples of my blood. Somehow, the word got out that wolves were biting wolves in the Seattle pack. Paul and Lori laid down the law and said if anyone bit me on purpose, they would be banished from the pack," Nick said.

Aidan laughed and shook his head. "Keep your doors and windows locked at night."

"I'll protect him," Victoria said.

"Yeah, she's got one helluva shotgun she keeps in case of trouble. Not that she's had any need to use it. But she knows how."

"You bet," Victoria said.

"And if you haven't guessed, we're mated wolves," Nick said.

"Congratulations, you two," Holly said and gave them both a hug.

"We're not getting any younger," Victoria said. "And we were ready. Both of us."

"I'm happy for you," Aidan said.

Everyone else chorused the congrats, and then Greg and Marianne joined them. "He won't go to sleep until his uncle Aidan reads him a story. He wants his aunt Holly there too, for real," Marianne said. "I didn't think I'd ever have to pretend I still believed in Santa Claus."

"Me either," Greg said.

"Just wait until you're mated and have little tykes," Holly said.

"But wait on getting mated," their dad said.

Everyone laughed.

"We have to find new wolves to meet," Marianne said, "like some more our age."

"That can be arranged anytime," Rafe said.

Aidan and Holly went to Toby's room, which was decorated in dinosaurs and a jungle—age-appropriate, not scary.

Toby smiled and patted the bed, then handed Aidan *The Night Before Christmas*. After that, Holly read *The Polar Express*, and then he wanted her to read *Little Wolf's First Howling*. Then Toby was asleep. They both kissed him and then quietly left the room.

Aidan wrapped his arm around Holly, thinking how much he'd love to have his own kids. "Let's bring out the presents."

Everyone began bringing out presents and setting them under the tree. Ted and Mike went outside to grab the ones in the limo that had brought Nick and Victoria here. After eggnog cocktails and more cookies, Nick and Victoria said their goodbyes, and the limo took them back to the airport to ride in Rafe and Aidan's jet, Nick's version of a sleigh and reindeer, to return to Montana.

"Ohmigod, that was wonderful. I hope Nick's former pack leader is regretting his decision to oust Nick from the pack. He's worse than an idiot," Jade said. "Nick and Victoria are adorable."

"We all agree with you there," Aidan said.

"And the poor guy they've roped into serving as Santa is not a jolly old elf in the least. He has the white beard and hair, but that's about all." Holly took Aidan's hand. "Ready for bed?"

Aidan grinned at her. She quickly blushed.

Jade and Rafe rose from one of the couches. "If Toby gets up early, we'll keep him occupied for a while, and then our guests can sleep in a bit."

"We'll do the same with Greg and Marianne," Margaret said.

They both rolled their eyes at her.

"We might get up early, but we'll play with Toby until everyone's up," Marianne said.

"Not me. I'm sleeping in," Greg said.

Aidan would play it by ear. He and Holly needed some time to sleep, because he knew what they were going to do once they hit the sack.

Christmas Day was a joyous affair as everyone sat with mugs of hot chocolate and whipped cream in front of the tree while Greg and Marianne played Santas and delivered everyone's gifts. Ted and Mike had gifts too, some sent by their parents to Rafe and Aidan's chalet, some that Aidan had bought for them that he'd sent to their parents, thinking they'd be there with them. Everyone else had gone shopping for them too, so they'd feel part of the pack.

It was total chaos with Christmas songs playing in the background, a fire in the fireplace, all the Christmas lights sparkling on the tree, and wrapping paper being torn off the packages and flying everywhere. Being the organized guy he was, Ted soon began bagging the paper for the recyclable trash. He couldn't take the mess any longer. Aidan was glad for it too, because he was feeling the same way.

Rafe and Jade's gifts to everyone were long-distance skis, including a little pair for Toby, even though Rafe had said his gift to Holly's parents was the house.

"I know what we're doing after breakfast," Marianne said.

Aidan had ordered everyone bikes with fat tires for bicycling in the snow, all wearing bows on the back deck.

"Well, maybe *that's* what we can do after breakfast," Marianne said.

Aidan also had bought Holly indoor and outdoor rock-wall climbing clothes and gear. "I know a wolf family who has their own indoor rock-wall climbing facility that we can visit, and you can practice to see if you'd like to do that."

"Yes! No falling down crevasses and having to be carried out," Holly said, giving Aidan a kiss. They were sure going to get their exercise, but also have lots of new experiences.

"Wildly exciting enough for you yet?" Aidan asked.

She laughed and hugged him tight. "Since I've met you, it's been nothing but." She really was looking forward to spending some quiet time with Aidan. Maybe everyone would go skiing without them, and they could take a nap.

When he unwrapped one of her presents to him, Aidan eyed the ice skates with a devilish smile. "You'll have to hang on to me to keep me upright."

"I will, but I know you'll get the hang of it before long."

"Now that will be wildly exciting for me." Then he opened a set of books on herbs. "Now I'll be able to really get into these."

"Me too."

Nick had given fancy steak gift packages to all the adults, camping equipment for Greg and Marianne, and a little tent and sleeping bag for Toby. Victoria had baked fudge for everyone.

Toby was playing with the Lincoln Logs while Marianne and Greg helped him build a fort. Holly was glad one of Aidan's gifts seemed to be a big hit with the tyke, and her brother and sister were having fun with them too.

Holly's mom and dad joined them, and her dad cleared his throat.

Marianne and Greg looked up at him.

"About that 'special' present for you for going to Nick's aid," his dad said.

Greg shook his head. "I did it for him, not for a reward."

"Yeah, we know, and we're so proud of you. We've discussed the business about you going back east to a college and decided we'll send you."

Greg's mouth dropped open. "Um, I agreed I'd help Ted and Mike guard Aidan and Holly when I had free time. I decided I'd go to the college closer to home."

"Ha! It all has to do with the swimming pool we're going to have," Marianne said, continuing to help Toby build a fort.

"And I need to watch out for Marianne too," Greg said, straightening his shoulders.

"Oh brother," Marianne said, but Holly knew she was relieved her brother was going to the same college as her.

"So thanks, Mom, Dad. I appreciate the offer," Greg said.

Holly was just as proud of her parents for conceding and making the offer as she was of Greg for staying in the area. She believed he liked his new pack too much to leave now.

Ted and Mike had finished opening their presents and were in the kitchen cooking breakfast. Aidan took Holly back to the bedroom while everyone else was busy cleaning up and enjoying their gifts.

He slipped his hand under the bed, pulled out a box, and frowned. "That isn't it."

"That's mine for you."

He laughed. "Great minds." He reached under the bed again, pulled out another box, and handed it to her.

She removed the bow, then the paper, and found a beautiful red lace nightie, a red swimsuit, and a white toweling robe with her initials monogrammed on it.

"For bed, the beach, and the hot tub or pool."

She laughed. "I love them. They're beautiful, and I can't wait to wear them. Now open yours."

He pulled out a pair of red boxer briefs, a robe with his initials monogrammed on it, a pair of reflective sunglasses, and blue-and-aqua board shorts to match her blue swimsuit. She hadn't expected him to get her another. And a matching pair of blue sweatshirts with the saying *Wolves That Howl Together Stay Together*.

"These are great. I love you, Holly. I can't imagine having a better Christmas present than having you for my mate."

"Ditto, love of mine. Do you think anyone will notice we've disappeared for a while?"

"Yeah, everyone will. We're wolves. They'll understand." With that, Aidan began undressing her, quickly removing her sweater.

Christmas music and conversations faded into the background.

"Wait." She snagged her red nightie. "I'll be right back." She was certain she wouldn't be wearing it for long, but she wanted to try it on and show off her Christmas present anyway.

The lace was soft and stretchy, and after she stripped

off all her clothes in the bathroom, she pulled the see-through lace nightie over her head and down her body. It was wickedly sexy as she stared at it in the mirror, her nipples already poking against the fun fabric.

She swept her hair off her shoulders and left the bathroom. Aidan was smiling appreciatively, arms folded across his naked chest, and he was wearing the blue board shorts she'd gotten for him.

She loved them on him, showing off the beginning of an erection and his nicely muscled legs, abdomen, and arms. "Really nice." She joined him, pushing him onto the bed and straddling him. She pulled on his drawstring to untie it.

"Really, really hot." He ran his hands up her bare thighs, his hot gaze focused on her nipples.

"*You* make me hot." Already her pulse was racing as his cock bulged under the fabric, and she pulled his board shorts down, freeing him. She ran her hand over his erection and purred. "For me?"

He groaned. "Always." And then he caught hold of her arms and pulled her forward so he could kiss her. As soon as he did, he slid her nightie up and ran his hands over her ass, kissing her mouth, licking, tonguing her.

She rubbed her breasts against his chest, her bottom still in the air as he moved his hand between her legs and began to stroke. She'd never felt as wickedly sexy as she did when he was touching her. She was ready for him, for this, the most perfect ending to opening presents on Christmas Day, the best for last.

She fought dropping down on top of him, his strokes making her lose all awareness of anything but their sexy scents and his touch. She moaned and pressed against his hand, wanting more, needing to finish. His free hand reached up to massage a breast through the lace, the fabric creating friction against her already sensitive nipples. She couldn't hold on any longer and cried out. He quickly covered her mouth with his, but too late. Her cheeks felt like they were aflame as he took hold of her shoulders and pushed her back this time.

Aidan was kissing her, not pausing, the momentum building, his aching, hard arousal needing release inside her. Now.

He spread her feminine lips, pushing his erection home, and began to thrust. He figured the lace nightie he gave her would be off in a jiffy, but she was just too beautiful wearing it and sexier than hell. He lifted it higher so he could kiss and lick her breasts, the red fabric resting above them.

He slowed his thrusts, concentrating on licking and sucking a nipple, her fingers caressing his hair. Her touches made him mad with need. He began to deepen his thrusts, faster, pulling nearly out and pushing in. Ripples of her pleasure caressed his cock and he came, loving her and all that being with her meant to him.

"God, you're the only one for me." He waited a few minutes, then pulled out of her, left the bed, and pulled her into his arms.

Glowing and looking perfectly satiated, she wrapped her arms around his neck and smiled up at him. "This was the best Christmas ever."

"And many more to come. Love you, honey. You made my Christmas complete." He carried her into the bathroom to run a hot bath and slipped the red nightie over her head.

"Love you right back, Aidan."

Christmas would never be the same, just as it would never be the same for his brother and his mate. Aidan couldn't have been any more pleased. If only they could deal with the longevity issue and get that behind them.

───◆───

After breakfast, they all went skiing, and after lunch, Aidan and Holly tried out ice skating. He was right. He had no sense of balance on skates, but he was having a ball learning. "I needed to learn how to do this when I was younger."

"Nonsense, you'll be a professional ice skater before you know it." She held his hand while he skated, wobbly, before falling and pulling her down with him.

He hugged her tight and kissed her as she lay on top of him. "Remember, you have to get up after you fall down and keep trying."

"I'm finding this much more interesting."

She laughed and kissed him back.

After he tried for another hour, he said, "Want to go snow biking with the others?"

"Sure, and a wolf run tonight. We're sure to run off all the food we've been eating over the holidays."

They returned to get the rest of them to snow bike. Rafe pulled Toby in a sled behind his bike while the rest of them tried out their new bikes.

Once they returned, they had a delicious Christmas feast of turkey and ham and all the trimmings. Everyone was helping to put away the leftovers, the kids playing with some of Toby's toys by the Christmas tree, when Holly got a call.

Aidan glanced at her and noticed she was frowning.

"What's wrong?" Aidan asked, joining her.

"Ronald said we've caused all kinds of trouble for their pack. Three wolves from another pack attacked their people, hoping to get some of their blood to improve their own."

Rafe said, "We'll send men to help out."

"I'm going back. They don't have a doctor now. Sally's falling to pieces."

"We'll both return."

"Us too," Ted said.

"Yeah, you know it," Mike said.

"Can we do anything?" Eddie asked.

"No, you just stay here, and we'll be back as soon as we can," Holly said.

Rafe was already getting hold of his men to send a team to protect the pack.

"Told you it would be like *The Walking Dead*," Greg said. "Those who feel there's a cure out there will do anything to get it."

"We're not even sure it will make a difference, but we have to protect the pack. Nick too," Aidan said.

"I'll send some men to the Montana pack too," Rafe said.

"All right, let's go." Aidan paused to give Toby a hug and kiss. He was having so much fun with his new friends and toys that he didn't appear to mind that Aidan was going away for a while.

Holly gave him a hug and kiss too, and then they all packed bags.

They were ushered to the private airport where the plane and pilot were waiting for them.

"Surprised you'd be returning so soon," Cesar said. "Sorry to hear there's trouble."

"Hopefully, we'll get reinforcements in place to protect the pack until we can learn if what we've found is truly the cure." Aidan carried his bags onto the plane, Holly following. Ted and Mike carried her bags and theirs.

"This is like a repeat of what happened before. Ronald and his enforcers are sure to react like they did previously, having nothing to do with other packs," Holly said.

"They'll have to allow Rafe's men to mingle with them to protect them."

"Yes, that's true."

"Another thought I had is that some of the pack members could disburse. Stay with the various wolf packs so we have a bigger group of people to protect them. The Silver Town wolf pack would ensure they stayed safe. The Highland wolves? No one would mess with them. Nick should be fairly safe with the Montana pack because of their SEAL wolves, but even so, Rafe wants to send him some personal bodyguards."

"I don't know if any of the pack members would want to join other packs, maybe worried that those packs might have people who would want the same thing. I'm certain Ronald wouldn't go along with it."

"Whatever is best for his people," Aidan said. "No matter how we do this, the people have to have some say in it. What pack do the wolves belong to who attacked your pack?"

"Some from the Nevada pack."

"Nevada pack?"

"I thought you'd heard of them. One of our pack

members left our pack and joined them. They must have learned of the potential breakthrough from him." Holly got another call. "Yeah, Sally?" She put it on speaker.

"All hell's broken loose. We're barricaded in Ronald's home, but it's not that secure. There are at least twenty wolves shattering the windows."

Breaking glass and screaming could be heard in the background.

"We're on our way. Hold tight, however you can. Rafe's sending men, and we're on our way," Holly said.

Aidan was on his phone updating Rafe.

"Tell them the first contingent should be there in twenty minutes. I'll call for more backup."

Aidan told them what Rafe had said. "We're on our way. We'll be there soon." Aidan squeezed Holly's hand, tears filling her eyes.

Then Sally screamed, and the phone went dead.

Chapter 30

HOLLY WAS TERRIFIED HER FORMER PACK COULD BE WIPED out, but then she remembered her family. As if Aidan suddenly thought of it too, he said, "Rafe didn't come with us because he'll be there with his bodyguards to protect your family. He'll call in reinforcements, in case anyone learns where your family is now."

Aidan got a call and put it on speaker. "Good, we'll be there in…"

"Another hour," Cesar said.

Holly gritted her teeth.

"An hour. Hold the fort until we get there."

"There are three of us on the ground now, five more with an ETA of twenty minutes, more after that."

"Okay, we'll let you do your job, Harvey."

"Out here."

Everyone was tense, wishing they were there already to help, but Holly knew the men on the ground would be doing much more than her own people could. She just prayed they wouldn't find a bloodbath when they arrived. Ronald's place was out in the country, and only other wolves lived in homes near him on a private road. Most likely, the police wouldn't be alerted to the trouble they were in, which was the way they wanted it.

As soon as they arrived, three men from Rafe's team met them at the private airport with an armored Humvee.

"What's the situation?" Aidan asked as two of the men off-loaded their bags into another vehicle.

"They broke into Ronald's house and took the pack members there hostage. I swear they're like a bunch of bloodthirsty vampires. Ronald told them you were coming, and they could take you in and you'd help sort out this mess," Harvey Walton said. He was special forces, hard charging, and a no-nonsense kind of guy.

"As a hostage?" Holly couldn't believe Ronald would actually stoop that low. Not after all Aidan had done for them so far. They didn't know for sure if this was going to work, and he could still be their only hope for a cure.

"That's fine," Aidan said.

"Like hell it is," Ted said.

"Yeah, like Ted said," Mike agreed.

"If it means freeing their people, I'll go along with it. Holly can treat the wounded, but only after the hostages are released. I want her protected at all times behind enemy lines. They're not going to kill me if they want a cure, and they can't take my blood, because, as far as we know, it hasn't changed."

"You received some of the unchanged blood, Doc?" Harvey asked.

"Yeah, while in a wolf fight with the leader's brother," Aidan said.

"Me too, though I had already received a pint from Holly," Mike said.

"You have the good blood," Harvey said to Holly.

"Yeah."

"Which means, damn it, she needs to be protected at all costs."

"Right, Doc."

They pulled up a couple of hundred yards from the house. Vehicles were parked all over the yard, all the way to the trees.

"Some of them are my pack's vehicles, but not all of them. The others must belong to the attacking wolves," Holly said.

"Patch me a line to the leader of these thugs," Aidan said.

Harvey called someone. "Both docs are here. Aidan wants to talk to the head butcher. Thanks." He turned to Aidan. "Call should be ringing through any second."

Aidan's cell rang, and he answered it. "I'm Dr. Aidan Denali. Who am I addressing?"

"Oats. Step out of the Humvee, and come to the porch."

"Release the women and children in good faith first." Aidan knew giving in to the guy's demands without asking for anything in return would make the guy warier. Besides, he hoped to get the women and children out of the line of fire in case this went south in a hurry.

"If I release them, you'll stay in the Humvee and won't do what I say."

"I'm a doctor who is looking for the cure for all our people in a civilized way. I don't want a bloodbath. Release the women and children. I'll come in and speak with you."

"We'll send out five."

"All…the…women…and…children. All."

"Ronald said you're a hard-nosed son of a bitch and wouldn't tell him which of them have the untainted blood."

Thank God for small miracles. "That's because I was afraid of just this kind of thing happening, even between their own people." And Aidan had been right. "I don't know you. I've been trying to reach all the packs that I can."

"We're a Nevada pack. One of the former Seattle pack members, Neil Booker, joined us over a decade ago. He still keeps in touch with a friend in the Seattle pack, guy by the name of Barry, who wanted to tell him the good news. Of course, we don't know if Neil has the good blood either."

"Maybe your blood is all right and could help others," Aidan said. "I can test it and see. Just let the women and children go, and I'll join you."

"Then you'll try to storm the place."

"Not when you could kill everyone in there. Which would be a big mistake, because some of them might have the blood we all need for a cure."

"I'll let half the women and children go."

Aidan hung up on him. "Tell me the situation," he said to Harvey.

"He's got twenty men, at least. A few are inside; others are at sniper locations. Anyone who comes out of that house will be a target."

"Who's taking out the snipers?"

"We only have a fix on three of them. Any one of the others could take out the innocents."

Aidan's phone rang.

"Don't hang up on me again," Oats said.

"Send out the women and children, and then I'll head in."

The front door opened, and this time, Oats ended the call.

Four women and six crying kids left the house.

"That's only a fraction of our women and children," Holly said. "Unless they're holed up somewhere else. But Sally called us, and she's not with the women."

Aidan called the leader again. "Where are the rest of the women and children?"

Two of Rafe's men pulled up in an armored vehicle and provided some cover for the women and children. The men rushed them inside, then drove farther away.

"We'll send out more once you come inside."

Aidan ended the call. "What's the intel from the women?"

Harvey was already on his phone, checking to see what the women had to say.

"Four men are inside. Sally was taking care of the injured, but she was wounded also. Ronald and another of his men were shot. Another man has a broken arm, and others have bad bite wounds."

"I need to get in there and treat them," Holly said.

"After we get control of the situation. You can check over the women and children for now." Aidan wasn't letting Holly near the house.

"I can go with you, Doc. I was an army medic, as well you know. I can pretend to be your assistant," Mike said.

"They'll know you're one of the team."

"Right, but I really do know how to take care of

injuries, and as long as they don't tie me up or knock me out, I can watch your back and help take care of the wounded."

"All right, but if he says no, you stay." Aidan called the leader back. "One of the men who assists me with my work is a former army medic. The women said there are several wounded men who need medical attention. I'm bringing Mike with me to treat the wounded. If you want our help, we need to keep Ronald's people alive." Aidan ended the call. "Imbecile."

"You didn't wait to hear if the asshole would go along with the plan," Ted said.

"He'll go along with it." Aidan hugged and kissed Holly. "Stay and take care of the women. They'll be traumatized. As soon as things are under control, I'll try to send the wounded men out, and you can take them to the clinic to finish patching them up. All right?"

She nodded, gave him a hug, and kissed him back. "Love you, Aidan." Tears filled her eyes, and they about undid him.

"I'll be safe. I love you, honey." Aidan got out of the Humvee with Mike, each with medical kits in hand, and headed for the front door, adrenaline charging through his blood.

As soon as they reached the porch, two men grabbed them and hauled them inside and checked them for weapons. Looking pale, Ronald was holding his bandaged side and seated on a brown leather couch. Two other men looked just as colorless.

Sally was lying on another leather couch, her eyes closed, head bandaged, blood seeping through. Her breathing was steady, and Aidan thought she might be playing possum. He sure as hell hoped so, but he was furious with the bastards who had orchestrated this.

"Doc," one of the men said, his hand over a bandage on a shoulder wound.

"Clifford."

"I'll take care of them," Mike said, then glanced at the blond-haired man wielding a semiautomatic rifle, "with the gray's permission."

"Granted. One false move and you're dead. We only need the doc." Oats turned his attention to Aidan. "Why don't you come into the dining room with me, and you can tell me all about your research."

Kids were crying in one of the rooms down the hall, and women were trying to console them. Aidan hated bullies. Finding new packs was something he usually delighted in, but when they were bad news like this? Eliminating them was the only solution. Any pack that would harm people for their own self-fulfillment didn't deserve to live among them.

Hell, for all Aidan knew, the Nevada pack might actually have the untainted blood, as they called it.

"First, you can tell me who in the pack has the good blood," Oats said.

"My records are back at the chalet in Colorado. Why didn't the former Seattle pack member get in touch with me to learn if his blood had issues or not?"

"His friend didn't tell him other wolf packs were at risk." Oats narrowed his eyes at one of his men. "What if your blood is untainted?" He turned to Aidan. "Is his?"

"I don't know. We only checked for current members of the pack." Aidan was trying to keep his tone civil and not growly like he felt.

"Check his blood."

"I'd have to check it at their local clinic. I don't have a blood-testing kit here."

"Tell your commandos to get it and bring it here. And anything else you need to figure it out."

"Let the rest of the women and children go, and the badly wounded. Both gunshot victims need to be in the clinic," Aidan said with authority. "Since Sally's unconscious, she does too."

"I won't let the women and children go. The three wounded victims can go. Wait, do they have good blood?"

"I told you I don't know." Aidan couldn't help sounding annoyed, which was part of the act. In truth, he was angry, ready to take these men down.

"You'd remember if the pack leader did."

"True. Ronald and Jared have tainted blood, which is why they finally let me work on this. You think I'm a son of a bitch? Ronald and his brother are ten times worse. Hell, you probably know that based on what your man must have told you."

"True. The three more critically wounded can go. Two of your men can carry them out, one at a time. No weapons."

"Can I call them?" Aidan about ground his teeth for having to placate the bastard at all.

"Yeah, unless you planned to send up smoke signals."

Good. Just the in they needed. Aidan called Ted. "I need you and Harvey to come take the severely wounded out... Ronald, Clifford, and Sally. In the meantime, have someone pick up the blood-testing kit and the microscope. Just the two of you will pick up the wounded, one at a time... Sorry about Christmas dinner. The three of

us will have to do that later. Women and children are in
a backroom. Kids are crying but otherwise sound okay
and will be right here until this is over with… Thanks,
Ted. See you in a few."

Then Aidan ended the call with Ted so they could
retrieve the injured. Aidan explained to Oats about how
only a few people had the untainted blood in the pack,
and he couldn't just do transfusions because blood types
had to be matched. And how he wasn't even sure that it
would work. "It'll take time to see if it makes a difference. Even if it does, we won't know for a while if it will
make a permanent difference."

"How come some are immune to this and the rest
aren't?"

"We still haven't determined that."

"They're here," one of Oats's men said.

Ted and Harvey came inside and carried Ronald
out first. They returned for Clifford after that and then
Sally. Both men were trying to pretend like they weren't
assessing the situation, but they were.

They were good men, and if anyone could help him
take control of the situation, they could.

"The two of them can bring in the medical equipment
you need."

Mike was taking care of the other men's injuries,
including Jared's, who was sitting in the living room
scowling. Rock was looking just as peeved, but the men
looked like they still had some fight in them. Which was
good. As soon as the blood-testing kit got here, all hell
was going to break loose.

Chapter 31

HOLLY WAS SEEING TO RONALD AT THE CLINIC NOW, concentrating on repairing any internal damage and stopping his bleeding. Sally was helping her, having pretended to be unconscious at Ronald's house, and for that, Holly was grateful.

"That man of yours is planning something. He's not giving in to that Oats's demands, even if he sounded like he was going to."

"I know," Holly said, "and though I love him for it, I don't like that he'll chance getting himself killed."

"Aidan and the others have to stop them. These men are ruthless, and they're not going to let Aidan go until they see results. The only reason they didn't kill anyone yet is because they didn't know who had the good blood, and Ronald said Aidan wouldn't tell them."

"I thought Ronald was being a bastard as usual." Holly had been furious to learn of it.

"Not this time. He suspected Aidan could help the pack get out of this bind, if anyone could. Though he wouldn't say it to his face, he was coming around about meeting other wolves until this happened. Anyway, it might be years before Aidan and you find a real cure. They have to do something now."

"I agree. I was afraid Aidan was going to let them take him somewhere else to work on the cure, but it appears Oats doesn't want to part with your pack's blood supply, if it turns out that's the cure for the rest of us. If they haven't been tested, they don't even know if they have an issue with their blood."

"I heard him saying to one of his men that if it had to do with having roots that could be tied to the earliest *lupus garous*, that left him out. At least Aidan gave Rafe's men the information for a full-scale rescue attempt: the kids and moms are in the room on the right side of the house, and there are three men in the room with Aidan and the others. There's only one man with the kids and moms. The snipers are the ones we have to worry about. If Aidan and the others take out the leader and his men in the house, Rafe's men know where three of the snipers are. Maybe they'll locate the others before they can cause trouble."

"I wish all these men hadn't stayed here to protect us. They should be out there protecting Aidan and the others." Holly was sure no one would come looking for them here.

"You know if Oats's men had the chance to take you hostage and make Aidan do what they want, they would."

Holly knew Sally was right, but she kept feeling that every available man should be storming Ronald's house, killing the snipers, and setting Ronald's people free. She finished closing Ronald up. "I'm glad you're all right. But I still need to take an X-ray of your head."

"After we take care of Clifford."

One of the men watching out for them poked his head into the room. "The fight's going down now. Be ready for more wounded."

As soon as it arrived, Ted and Harvey carried the blood-testing equipment into the house—not the portable blood-testing kit, but the one they used in the office that weighed about sixty pounds—and the microscope, some notebooks, and the supplies to take the samples.

"Just set them on the dining room table," Aidan said, turning his gaze toward Oats.

As soon as their hands were free, Ted lunged for Oats and broke his neck while Jared tackled one of the men watching them in the living room. Aidan was damn glad Jared had realized they were taking out the men.

Harvey had a dagger out and threw it at the remaining man before he could say a word. The dagger struck him in the forehead, while Mike caught him before he could drop. "That's all we need, Ted, Harvey," Aidan said to his men, playing out the scenario. "You can leave now." Pretending to talk to the group's leader, he said, "Okay, Oats, I'll need to sample the blood of all the men who are here. One in the bedroom to the right? Okay."

Aidan headed down the hall with the blood-testing kit toward the bedroom while Ted and Harvey silently moved around him to wait on the other side of the door-jamb. Jared opened and closed the front door to simulate Ted and Harvey leaving the house. Thankfully, the bedroom where the women and children were being held was on the opposite side of the house. Whoever was in there guarding them wouldn't see that no one had exited the house.

Aidan rapped at the door. "I'm Dr. Aidan Denali, and Oats wants me to take your blood."

The guy opened the door. "Make it quick."

"We will."

Ted and Aidan tackled the man and broke his neck before he could react. Huddled in the corner were seven children, ranging approximately from age eight to fifteen, including Joey—who quickly gave Aidan a hug—and three women, one of them Joey's mother. "We've got to take care of the snipers outside. For the time being, everyone's staying here," Aidan said.

The women and children looked shell-shocked.

His phone in hand, Jared joined them. "Ronald's got a basement. No access except for the inner door."

"Good, take them down there. You and your men can protect them if we don't manage to take out all the snipers," Aidan said.

"Here's Oats's gun." Mike handed Jared the semiautomatic weapon.

"I never thought I'd be thanking any of you, but I am now. I texted Holly once you took out the last man. She's just finished surgery on Clifford. He and Ronald will recover. Sally had been pretending to be unconscious, though Holly said she was getting ready to run tests on her now. I told her you and the other men were safe."

"Thanks." Aidan pulled his phone out and called Holly, hoping she wasn't in the middle of taking X-rays on Sally.

"Hey, Aidan. Are you okay?"

"Yeah, Jared and some more of his men are going into the basement with the women and children to protect them."

"And you? What are you doing?"

He smiled, loving her concern. He'd fought in many battles over the years. He hadn't always been a doctor. "I'm staying in the house. We've got men trying to take

out the snipers. Others are staying here to help protect
those who are here. You know Ted and Mike. They're
not leaving my side."

"I'd prefer if you had a whole army there protecting—"

Glass from two windows at the clinic shattered.

"Holly!" Aidan yelled, his heart practically seizing.

———～～———

Holly had been checking Sally's X-rays when Aidan
called, Sally watching over her shoulder, and the results
looked good. When the windows at the front of the clinic
shattered, her heart leapt in her throat. She jumped up
from her chair and ran to the doorway, intending to protect Ronald and Clifford in the room they were staying
in to recover. Sally was fast on her heels. Two of Rafe's
men rushed to block them, and she knew this could be
bad. One of the men had gas masks and handed them to
the women.

"Do you know how to use them?"

"Yeah, thanks. What about Ronald and Clifford?"

"We've taken care of them. Others are protecting
them. They have gas masks too."

The men made sure the women seated the gas masks
properly and put on their own. "Get behind the desk and
stay there. They're trying to smoke us out."

Gunfire sounded. "They're using suppressors," one
of the men said.

The two men stayed in the room and gunfire was
returned, louder, not suppressed. Holly hugged Sally.
She wanted to turn into a wolf and help, but she'd be no
match against guns, and she couldn't wear a gas mask
as a wolf. The room had no windows, and she didn't

like that they had no way to escape if their protectors were killed. On the other hand, those making the assault wouldn't be able to come in any other way but that one doorway.

She told Aidan, "We're under assault. I'm wearing a gas mask. Weapons are being fired."

"I'm on my way."

Feeling panicked that he could be in the line of fire, she didn't want to hear that. "No, just stay there. Rafe's men will take care of these guys."

"I'm on my way," Aidan repeated. "I'll be there in fifteen minutes tops."

Which meant he'd already headed there, probably after the windows shattered, and he'd heard them.

"Don't get yourself killed!"

"I have no intention of it, but what kind of a mate would I be if I didn't come to rescue you?"

She knew no amount of arguing with him would keep him away. "Don't get shot. I don't have any more beds at the clinic."

"I just need *your* bed. Stay on the line, honey. I'll be there soon."

She was praying Rafe's men would take out their attackers, and by the time Aidan got there, he would only have to join her and give her a hug.

"When I said I was looking for a Christmas that was wildly exciting…"

One of Rafe's men near where she was hunkered down snickered.

"I deliver, right?" Aidan asked.

Holly laughed. She loved him with all her heart.

It didn't take long, and Aidan told her, "We're here."

"Be careful."

"No more weapon fire."

"Clinic is all clear," one of Rafe's men said.

"All clear outside," another said.

"Coming in," Aidan told her. "We're good. And I didn't even have to rescue you."

She was out of the room in a flash, heading for the recovery room. "Checking on Clifford and Ronald."

Sally was with her, and Rafe's men had opened the windows and had cleared the air, the cold wind whipping through the room. Both Holly and Sally pulled off their gas masks, then Holly removed the masks from her patients. Sally quickly shut the windows before the men caught pneumonia, and she and Holly covered them with more blankets.

Aidan rushed into the room, and Holly threw herself into his arms and kissed him long and hard. When she finally let him up for air, he smiled at her. "Hot damn, Doc, now that's what I call mate material."

She laughed, then she frowned. "What's the status of the rest of Oats's men?"

"Dead. Ronald's man, Barry, who had secretly visited the Nevada pack, confirmed they were all dead. He told us the Nevada pack has some older men, a couple of families. As long as they don't want to cause any trouble for anyone else, we'll check their blood and give them the news about their men. Everyone who needs looking after is coming to the clinic for us to check them out. The guys are blowing the rest of the smoke out of the clinic. We'll have our work cut out for us. For what it's worth, Jared thanked us for coming to their aid."

"He'd better," Sally said, "or he and his brother can be replaced."

Aidan frowned down at Holly. "We need to compare notes and see if you know about any other wolf packs I don't know about."

"I only know that one of our men had joined them years ago. I thought they were one of the packs you'd tested. Then there's the Montana pack that Everett and his people joined, and that there was a newly turned Arctic wolf pack living in Minnesota who used to live in the Seattle area."

"And here I wanted to learn about other packs." Aidan kissed her again.

⸺⸺

Three days after Holly and Aidan were assured that Clifford and Ronald were on the mend, and everyone else who had been injured had been taken care of, they returned to the chalet to spend the rest of the holidays with their new pack. From their own point of view, everyone who had been at the fight had to repeat what had happened to the gathered families. Teams of Rafe's men stayed behind to protect Ronald's pack in case they had any further trouble. And Nick and his mate had their own bodyguard force watching over them now.

Though it was hard not to worry about what would happen with the cure, for now, Holly and Aidan were in the business of fun-filled activities, including swimming alone in the pool in their new swimsuits, returning to their room in a rush to make love—the complication of swimming alone in the swimming pool together—and everything else they enjoyed doing during the Christmas holidays with friends and family.

Most of all, they loved that they had found each other and had mated, making this truly the best Christmas ever, with many more to come.

Epilogue

Six months later, Aidan and Holly rechecked Mike's blood and found what they'd wanted to learn. Holly's blood cells, and maybe a few of Jared's, had changed Mike's. His cells weren't aging as fast as they would have without the transfusion. It could still take some time to learn if this was temporary or if his blood would be changed permanently.

"Hell, that's good news," Mike said as Ted stood in the lab watching. "Can I give some of mine to Ted?"

"No. I think it's best if we use someone's that has always had the good blood," Aidan said.

"Let's check yours, Aidan," Holly said, elated. "If Jared and you fighting and exchanging small amounts of blood made a difference, we need to know."

"I was thinking the same thing. It would save your people from having to donate massive amounts of blood."

Holly took a blood sample from Aidan and looked at it under the microscope. "Holy cow. It worked!"

Aidan looked over her shoulder. "Then the wolves who transferred small amounts of blood in Ronald's pack should have changed theirs too, though I don't want wolves cutting themselves to transfer blood to the rest of them. We need to do this in a healthier way."

"One pint should be enough for a whole lot of wolves. I'll call Sally and tell her to take blood samples from everyone who was bitten or exchanged blood in some other way six months ago and send it to us so we can compare."

"Don't you think that could cause your people to begin wide transference of blood on their own?" Aidan asked.

"Uh, yeah. Can we use one of the jets?"

"Yeah. I'd say we should give Ronald a call, but let's just arrive unannounced and get this done right."

Mike motioned to Ted. "But Ted first, right?"

Holly and Aidan smiled. "Yeah, him first," Aidan said.

"I'll call Jade and tell her we have the cure, at least temporarily, if not permanently."

"Okay, sounds good. We'll need to fix them up next and then work from pack to pack. Ready for some pack hopping?"

"For this, yes! You're a genius, Aidan."

"We did it together. Sally and Anita helped too. And your pack. Ronald and Jared's father was the key. Who would have ever thought the most disagreeable pack—"

Holly raised her brows.

"—um, pack leaders could change the wolves back to the way they were."

"Sounds like a reason for a celebration. And we have one other."

"Oh?"

"Our first baby…or two…will be here in the winter."

Aidan's smile couldn't have been any bigger than it was now. He lifted her in his arms and twirled her around. "Hallelujah!"

"I love you, Aidan."

"I can't be any happier for us. I love you and the little ones right back."

Ted and Mike folded their arms, both frowning. "Do we get hazard pay?" Mike asked.

Aidan and Holly laughed. "You will make great uncles," Holly said.

"It's about time," Aidan said. "Just think of all the wild adventures you'll have, and with your improved blood, that will be for a very long time."

"See what our matchmaking got us into?" Ted asked Mike.

"Yep. We'll have to learn how to make baby food next."

Read on for a look at book 1 in
Terry Spear's new Heart of the Shifter series

You Had Me at Jaguar

Coming soon from Sourcebooks Casablanca

DRINKING A BEER AT THE SAN ANTONIO CLAWED AND Dangerous Kitty Cat Club, Howard Armstrong looked more relaxed than Valerie Chambers had ever seen him. Though she'd only seen him during vigorous training exercises. Howard was all hard muscle, nothing soft about him. He made her think of long, hot nights and impossible, sexy dreams.

Why was he here? She should have known she'd run into him again—they were working for the same jaguar police force.

She had been astonished to learn he had left the Enforcer branch to work with the JAG's new United Shifter Force (USF) unit. And a little disappointed. She'd thought she might see him again on the training course. She'd wondered if he'd gotten as much ribbing about her taking him down as she had.

"He let you so he could get up close and personal," some of the women she worked with had cracked. "Good move to take him down as if we were in the field and not in training," one of the guys had told her, impressed with her wiliness. "He must be getting soft," another male Enforcer had joked.

The Enforcer branch was a specialized jaguar policing force that eliminated jaguar shifters who were guilty of committing violent crimes against humans and shifters alike. The agents of the USF worked as a combined force of wolves and jaguars. Like many of the Enforcers, Howard was a loner. She couldn't understand why he had changed jobs to be a team player with a mix of shifter types.

Howard still worked out of the Houston office, as far as she knew. She'd wondered if he was working on a case in San Antonio. When she'd spied his vehicle here for so many days with no sign of him, she'd asked both her boss and Howard's if he was on a mission. They'd both denied it. She didn't think the USF agents went solo on missions. Was he really just on vacation?

Sipping a margarita at a table across the club, Val watched Howard snack on chips. Then a brunette joined him at his table—pretty, petite, wearing a short red dress and low red heels. Was the woman with him a jaguar or a wolf? Maybe a date?

When she'd seen Howard's black pickup truck with the distinct jaguar in a jungle painted on both sides, and smelled his scent around the vehicle, she figured he still owned it. Even so, she ran his license plate to make sure someone else hadn't bought it. She suspected Howard was after someone. But this was the first time she'd actually seen him or the woman, which meant he had to be undercover.

The jungle music made Val involuntarily tap her boot on the tile floor, and she had the greatest urge to get up and dance. The smell of sweet mixed drinks, beer, humans, jaguars, and a few wolves drifted to her. Palm trees in pots, vines stretching to the ceiling, and a skylight way above simulated a jungle scene like most jaguars loved. The summer sun was still high enough to spread sunlight through the windows and down through the living foliage. Since she couldn't get away to the jungle very often, she enjoyed going to one of these places to immerse herself in the jungle feel from time to time, more so when she wasn't on a mission. Here, it was air-conditioned, a light mist spraying the plants, water droplets collecting on the leaves. Dancers wearing leopard-print fabric were on elevated stages and the dance floor, and bright lights flashed across them, making it appear otherworldly.

She again glanced at the tables that were cast more in the dark, just in case Benny Canton had already arrived and she'd missed seeing him when she had walked through the place earlier searching for him. This was the kind of job she loved: eliminating rogue jaguars, the murdering kind. She hadn't heard of a case like this in a good long while—a jaguar who'd murdered his wife, just because she threatened to leave him. That was one of the differences between the wolf shifters and jaguars: the wolves mated for life; jaguars could divorce.

She'd considered that he might have gone across the border, because the shifters often did to play in the jungle as wild jaguars. And for a rogue, he would have extra incentive to leave the country.

She watched the door open—two single males arrived, neither of them her perp. Benny was known to frequent this club ever since he left his job as a construction worker after the murder. He had no family, and she hadn't found any other place he could have holed up. So she'd staked the place out for the past three days, watching for him or some of his friends, who proved to be just as elusive as he was. She'd had no luck.

But it was the only lead she had.

———

Taking another swig of his beer while the jungle beat raised the roof of the club, Howard tried his darnedest not to look in Valerie Chamber's direction. He would never reveal that he'd been attracted to her from the first time he'd seen her in advanced training as an Enforcer. He still couldn't believe his boss had asked him and gray wolf Jillian Greystoke to watch her back, surreptitiously. He'd much rather be up front about what he was doing when helping other agents.

As soon as he'd seen the striking redhead again, he was reminded of how she'd pinned him during training. She'd cast him the wickedest smile. With his back on the floor, her on top of him, he couldn't help smiling back at her. Of course, after her unorthodox move, the testers had made a new rule: no one was to move before the bell rang or they were afraid they'd have chaos. When they'd mentioned the new rules, Howard had glanced in Val's direction, and she'd given him a similar cat-who-ate-the-mouse look. He'd only smiled, thinking they might have a chance at dating.

The three branches—the Enforcers, JAG, and Guardians—all had a common mission: deal with jaguar shifters who posed a threat to humans and shifters alike. Though each handled different situations: Guardians provided more aid to injured jaguars; JAG went after the rogues, or humans who were dealing in jaguars, but the result depended on the situation—incarceration or death for the rogues. The Enforcers were sent to terminate murdering jaguars. Period. They didn't consider jail time for the offender. Howard and Jillian were with a special section of the JAG, the USF, taking care of both jaguars and wolves creating trouble or in trouble. They were the only two agents who had a break in cases. Since Howard was a former Enforcer, his boss felt he would be right for the job. The branches would work together when necessary, but usually, all agents involved would be well aware of the situation.

Jillian got another text, the fourth one in half an hour. She texted back.

Howard didn't have to guess who it was from. Jillian was mated to Vaughn, a gray SEAL wolf who was busy tracking down a murderous wolf, along with the two other jaguar team members of the USF. "Vaughn should have taken you with him."

"This guy that Val is trying to neutralize is supposed to be a lot less violent than the one our team is trying to track down. At least as far as the general population is concerned. Benny's wife was a different story."

"I still wish Martin had allowed us to tell Val we are here watching her back."

"The boss said she doesn't like working with anyone else. Since many Enforcers work alone, she'd think her boss felt she couldn't handle the case on her own. How well do you know her?" Jillian asked.

"I've been in training with her before. Never worked with her though. She's got some kick-ass moves, and I have to say she's extremely quick-witted."

Jillian smiled at him. "Did she ever get the best of you?"

He gave her a dark smile back. "Not that I'd ever admit to." He ordered another beer. "You know, her mother, Gladys, was the first female Enforcer we had in the branch, and she and her mate, Jasper, are still on the force."

"Wow. They don't want to leave all the excitement behind?"

"That's about it. They're both good people, wanting to right the wrong and deal with the bad guys. And Gladys wanted to prove to her dad, who was an Enforcer before that, that she could do as good a job as any man. She and her mate have one of the highest success rates for eliminating rogue jaguars. They make a great team. But there's got to be a time Enforcers need to retire, when they might not be as quick to react or strong as they had once been. Their boss just doesn't want to force retirement on them. Not while they've been so successful, despite being in their golden years."

"I think it's great. Better to die doing what you love than live to an old age, wishing you were still fighting the good fight."

He smiled at Jillian. "Easy for you to say. Your kind lives much longer lives than we do. What a deal."

"True. You know, Val's been watching you. And she's been watching the entrance. Do you think she's onto us?"

"I doubt it. What would the odds be that Martin would send two of his USF agents to protect an Enforcer in a simple take-down operation without her being informed?"

"Not likely. Do you want to dance?" Jillian grabbed Howard's hand before he could object.

"Hell, do you want this to get back to Vaughn? As a SEAL wolf, he'd kill me."

Jillian laughed. "He knows we're undercover, and this is just for fun." She dragged him to the dance floor. "You never dated Val?"

"No. I never dated anyone in the Enforcer branch. How do you know she's been watching me?" he asked as they danced to the loud music, the lights flashing. "Wait. It was when you went to the ladies' room. That's why you took so long to return. You were observing her."

"And others. And you."

"Me? I wasn't about to blow our cover. What if she had a meltdown because we're here to protect her?"

"You did good. You only looked her way five times and only when she was busy ordering a drink, telling a patron to bug off, and looking around at other people at the time. If you had caught her eye, though, then what?"

"I would have waved. She knows me. I know her. It would be foolish to pretend I didn't recognize her."

They continued to dance as the beat quickened, which Howard was glad for. He really didn't want Vaughn to get any ideas about him and Jillian.

"You ought to ask her to dance. You're no longer an Enforcer. Then she'll know we're not together in a boyfriend/girlfriend way. It might help our mission if it looks like we're just here to have fun."

"She's on a job."

"Right. But you aren't supposed to know that. You'd be her cover too, though she wouldn't realize it."

"All right. You just don't want it to get back to your mate that I only danced with you."

Jillian laughed.

He led her back to the table, but the next dance was a slow dance, and he wasn't going to ask Val then. Not that he didn't want to, but he hated being here under false pretenses. What if they got a little too hot and heavy on the dance floor, like he'd hope to, and then she learned he was only there on an assignment?

He sat down across from Jillian.

She smiled. "Coward."

"Next dance." But it was a slow one too. "Next fast dance," he clarified.

Then again, Val might wonder who Jillian was. A date? Even though that would work for a cover, he didn't want Val to think that. So much for really getting into this assignment. And here he was, always a professional when it came to his missions.

The next dance was fast-paced, so he rose from his chair and saw some guy trying to take a seat at Val's table. Howard headed over, though he told himself he wasn't in rescue mode. Not when he was sure she wouldn't appreciate it. So why was he making a beeline straight through the dancers, his gaze hard on the man at her table, and why was he walking so damn fast?

Maybe she wanted to be with the guy, but he suspected not from the way her brows furrowed, and she was motioning for him to get lost. She'd probably do the same with Howard.

The guy suddenly noticed Howard advancing. The guy had had too much to drink, smelled of whiskey, and was unsteady on his feet, finally planting a hand on the back of the chair next to Val as if to keep from falling down.

"Hey, Val," Howard said in greeting. "Is this guy hassling you?

The human glanced at her, then turned his attention to Howard.

Howard had dealt with enough ugly drunks to know the guy was trouble.

"What's it to you?" He tried to shove Howard, but Howard didn't budge and gave him his most growly look. Though he would have preferred to do so as a jaguar. That would have gotten the guy's attention. "Get. Lost. Now."

The drunk glowered at him. Howard made a move for him, his posture threatening, and the drunk quickly backed off, heading for another table.

Val folded her arms and focused on Howard, raising a brow as if to ask what *his* problem was.

He wasn't surprised. He knew she could have handled the drunk, but it still bothered him enough that he wanted to step in and protect her.

"Did you ditch your date already?" Val asked.

He didn't offer his hand in greeting or an explanation, instead asking, "Do you wanna dance?"

Val toyed with her glass. "I've heard you're a high guardian. Or noble watchman."

"You've totally lost me."

"Your name. Howard. Suits an Enforcer more than a Guardian." She frowned. "Why USF?"

He'd never looked up the meaning of his name.

He shrugged. "I guess I just got in with the right people, and I'm still up for terminating the bad guys when I need to." He wondered how she would know what his name meant, unless she'd been interested in him, even just a little bit. Maybe not so much now that he was no longer an Enforcer though.

She gave him a half smile, then motioned to Jillian. "Your date must be getting lonely." Then she eyed him with speculation. "Unless you're here on a mission." She glanced back at Jillian, considering her for some time. "I've never seen her before. Wolf? Jaguar? Human?"

"Wolf, mated." He still hadn't blown his cover, but he wanted her to know they were looking after her, whether she liked it or not.

Val raised both eyebrows this time.

"Her mate is a SEAL wolf. Jillian and I are on a job."

Val leaned her head back and smiled. "Okay. And you're undercover so you want to dance with me in case her mate gets upset with you for not dancing with anyone else." Then she frowned again. "You don't suspect me of anything, right?" she joked.

He shook his head. The only thing she was guilty of was being stubborn when it came to having a partner on a mission. At least, that's what his former boss, Sylvan, said about her when he briefed them on their mission.

To his surprise, she rose from her seat and moved toward the dance floor. "What's your case? Jaguar murdered wolf? Wolf murdered jaguar?"

So she didn't realize he was here because of her. He could understand what she thought they were looking for, because those were the kind of cases they normally handled. Still, he really didn't want to have to lie about this. Her attention switched from him to someone to their left. He turned to look, and sure enough, it was Benny, her target. Shaggy blond hair and blue eyes, wearing jeans and a muscle shirt, showing off a lot of bicep. Howard knew he'd been in construction, and he looked like he did some heavy lifting on the job.

"Problem?" Howard asked. She had to know he suspected the guy was *her* case.

"Have to take a rain check on the dance." She frowned, and Howard turned.

Benny was dancing with a blond woman who looked similar to his murdered wife.

The music changed to a slow dance.

"Can I help you with anything?" Howard asked Val.

"Still an Enforcer at heart?" She pulled Howard into her arms and began dancing with him. She didn't rub her body against him in a way that said she wanted more, but just to add a bit of realism, he thought.

He smiled, glanced over at Benny, and realized why Val was dancing with him. The perp and the blond were close by. "You'd better believe it."

"And Jillian?"

"Absolutely. And the truth is *you* are *our* mission."

Val patted him on the chest. "Good to know you're ready to come clean."

"You already knew?"

"I saw your truck parked near the club three days ago. It made me suspicious that you were here every night that I was, yet…weren't here. Once I called your plate number in to ensure you still owned it, I did consider the idea that you could be here on vacation. Or a case. But I wanted to learn the truth."

Howard figured out where this was going. She didn't seem to be upset about it, so that was good.

"I contacted my boss. I told him who you were and that you were USF. And he said he didn't know anything about the USF agents' cases. Except he would, if he and your boss were in collusion. I called your boss.

He gave me the same song and dance. Only it was *way* too similar. When my boss has something to hide, he says, 'Let me make it perfectly clear and in no uncertain terms...' When your boss does, he says—"

"'The truth of the matter is—'"

"Right. So they were in agreement. But I still didn't know what you were doing down here. Were you on some secret mission that had nothing to do with mine, and they didn't want to break your cover? Maybe, but then I thought it would be too much of a coincidence, particularly with the way our bosses responded to my inquiries. I didn't think they'd be so underhanded to have other agents take down my perp."

"We're not here to take over your case. We're strictly here to provide backup. Your boss was worried about this guy and about you."

She looked relieved, sighed, and pulled Howard closer. Benny was dancing farther away from them, and Howard fit her even more snugly against his body. He was taking protecting her to heart, wrapping his arms around her waist.

"You must already know the situation. Benny murdered his wife in cold blood for the insurance money and to stop her from divorcing him. He'd turned her six months earlier, so the consensus is that she wasn't dealing well with the changes. Maybe he felt he couldn't handle her like he thought he could. And living with her was getting out of control. For whatever reason, he murdered her, and he's going down."

Howard couldn't believe it. "Who all knew she was human to begin with?" No one had told them that bit of information.

"It wasn't something we knew until after he'd murdered her. You can't tell when someone's newly turned, unless they have the urge to shift and don't have any control over it. He must have kept her locked up so no one would know about her. Everyone who was a jaguar who knew him thought he had mated a jaguar. But when I began interviewing her friends and family, learned they were all human and she hadn't been adopted, we put two and two together. It all fit. She had frequented this club, then dropped out of her family's and friends' lives as soon as she met Benny and they were married. Everyone worried about her, thinking he was keeping her hostage, controlling her. But he couldn't let her out of his sight for fear she'd shift into a jaguar. At their home, claw marks were all over the place—doors, mainly. The arm of one of the chairs was crushed—a jaguar's bite could crush a tortoise's shell—so it looked like she had been one angry cat. Who could blame her, really."

"But it was her saliva on the crushed arm of the chair, not his?"

"Correct. You sure don't know much about the case, do you?"

"We're here strictly to be your protection."

"*Why* are you undercover?"

"According to your boss, you refuse to work with—"

"He's on the move."

Acknowledgments

Thanks so much to the lovely ladies, Dottie Jones and Donna Fournier, who help so much to keep me straight, no matter how little time they have to do it. You ladies are the best. And thanks to Deb Werksman, who believes in and continues to support my wolf and jaguar world after all these years, when no one else gave me a chance. Through her and visionary Dominique Raccah, our publisher and CEO, I've been able to share my world with my readers. Thank you! And thanks to my cover artists who create the most beautiful covers to give a face to my jaguars and wolves. And, of course, my readers, who cheer me on every step of the way!

About the Author

Bestselling and award-winning author Terry Spear has written over sixty paranormal romance novels and four medieval Highland historical romances. Her first were-wolf romance, *Heart of the Wolf*, was named a 2008 *Publishers Weekly*'s Best Book of the Year, and her subsequent titles have garnered high praise and hit the *USA Today* bestseller list. A retired officer of the U.S. Army Reserves, Terry lives in Spring, Texas, where she is working on her next wolf, jaguar, cougar, and bear shifter romances, continuing with her Highland medieval romances, and having fun with her young adult novels. When she's not writing, she's photographing everything that catches her eye, making teddy bears, and playing with her Havanese puppies and grandbaby. For more information, visit terryspear.com or follow her on Twitter @TerrySpear. She is also on Facebook at facebook.com/terry.spear and on Wordpress at Terry Spear's Shifters: terryspear.wordpress.com.

Follow Terry for new releases and book deals at bookbub.com/authors/terry-spear.

Also by Terry Spear

Heart of the Wolf
Heart of the Wolf
To Tempt the Wolf
Legend of the White Wolf
Seduced by the Wolf

Silver Town Wolf
Destiny of the Wolf
Wolf Fever
Dreaming of the Wolf
Silence of the Wolf
A Silver Wolf Christmas
Alpha Wolf Need Not Apply
Between a Wolf and a Hard Place
All's Fair in Love and Wolf

Highland Wolf
Heart of the Highland Wolf
A Howl for a Highlander
A Highland Werewolf Wedding
Hero of a Highland Wolf
A Highland Wolf Christmas

SEAL Wolf
A SEAL in Wolf's Clothing
A SEAL Wolf Christmas
SEAL Wolf Hunting
SEAL Wolf In Too Deep
SEAL Wolf Undercover

Heart of the Jaguar
Savage Hunger
Jaguar Fever
Jaguar Hunt
Jaguar Pride
A Very Jaguar Christmas

Billionaire Wolf
Billionaire in Wolf's Clothing
A Billionaire Wolf for Christmas

White Wolf
Dreaming of a White Wolf Christmas
Flight of the White Wolf